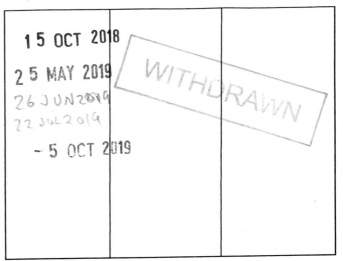

First published in Great Britain in 2011 by Comma Press
www.commapress.co.uk

A CIP catalogue record of this book is available from the British Library.

ISBN   1905583338
ISBN-13   978 1905583331

LOTTERY FUNDED

The publisher gratefully acknowledges assistance from Arts Council England, and
Literature Northwest, as well as the support of the Institute of Physics and the
Manchester Beacon for Public Engagement for their support in the commissioning
of seven of the stories included (specifically, those stories featuring physics
breakthroughs, or early career researchers as consultants).

IOP Institute of Physics

Set in Bembo 11/13 by David Eckersall
Printed in Great Britain by the MPG Books Group, Bodmin and King's Lynn

LITMUS

Short Stories from Modern Science

Edited by
Ra Page

For Farris & Kieren

Contents

Introduction

As a physics undergraduate in the early nineties I was once let into a 'secret' by an American tutor – a story he had been told by his own professor, who had in turn been present at the Manhattan Project. It told of a young physicist – a friend of my tutor's tutor – who, working in the lab one day, suddenly noticed a plutonium core getting dangerously close to a neutron source in its casing. As the story had it, the young physicist, realising that meltdown was imminent, forced his colleagues out of the room, broke through the gamma ray-proof glass shield, and with his bare hand, and no thought for his own safety, reached out and pushed the plutonium away. In a single stroke the entire Manhattan Project had been saved, whilst the physicist took two, slow, agonizing days to die.

The story seemed instantly believable. It had a paradoxical heroism to it that defied fabrication; a bittersweet irony that one man should have given so much for a greater and fundamentally questionable 'good'. It wasn't until nearly twenty years later that, talking to a historian of physics, I was finally disabused of this fallacy. There had in fact been two fatal accidents at Los Alamos, coincidentally with the same piece of plutonium (leading to it being christened the 'demon core'), and although versions of the heroic scientist story may have been circulated at the time (possibly for the sake of morale), all evidence points to them being simple accidents: the dropping or mishandling of material by physicists who then died of the exposure. No sacrifice, no heroism, just error. In hindsight, perhaps, I shouldn't have been taken in by the story; indeed I should have spotted it for the strain of science apocrypha it clearly was. Versions of the self-sacrificing scientist permeate popular culture – from comic book superhero Dr. Solar to Spock's demise in *Star Trek 2*. Indeed the innocent scientist exposed to radiation is a common 'origin story' for most earthbound superheroes (Dr. David Banner, Peter Parker, Dr. Manhattan, etc).

The apocrypha of science have a viral quality to them. They quickly supersede research papers and published biographies in the public imagination, replacing complex and nuanced historical fact with myth and exaggeration. In Christine Poulson's story, we're told how a nucleotide has the ability to search vast strands of DNA to pick out specific sequences that match it, and then, with the help of a certain enzyme, replicate those sequences. The public's imagination works in much the same way. It seems to travel along the vast sequence of historical events that lead to a scientific breakthrough, and pick out and replicate only those small bits that it agrees with: some ironic turn or moment of sudden drama. It replicates only that part of it, and discards the rest. The wider reality of the scientific process – its failed attempts, its methodologies, the long catalogue of experimentation – all of these get binned.

So what does our 'myth–nucleotide' look like? I would hazard that it has at least two, key components. The first is the widely-held conviction that science promises us watertight answers, definitive 'litmus tests' that eradicate all doubt, forever. We ask science a question, out pops an answer, and that's the end of it. The second building-block myth is simply an image – that of the isolated scientist having an iconic 'eureka moment', like Rodin's 'The Thinker', a light bulb suddenly pinging into existence above his head.

Both of these are fictions of course. Any historian of science will tell you (and James Sumner later in this book *does*) that eureka moments don't actually exist. Place the historical record under any scrutiny, or enter into the point-of-view of the scientist at the time, and very quickly this so-called eureka moment vanishes. In its place we find a significant event surrounded by countless other equally significant events, each of which helped make the breakthrough possible. Time, and more importantly teaching, distills this 'zoo' of ongoing experiments and discussions into a single, dramatic moment; giving science teachers an invaluable device for telescoping into the biography quickly, and grabbing some idealized, bite-sized science.

Likewise, any scientist will tell you there is no such thing as an absolute litmus test, in the sense of a definitive proof. The only proof that science possesses in its kitbag, as Karl Popper argued, is disproof. The only certainty, doubt.

But if these two concepts are so far from the reality of science, how do they get a purchase on it in the first place? The answer must have something to do, in part, with faith; our instinctive need for there to at least *be* answers to our questions, even if we personally don't know them. We all of us love a boffin. Partly to take the mickey out of, for his poor social skills, but partly, also, to put our minds at rest: to know that we have people working on the problem; that the problem is finite – a knowable unknown. To put it another way, knowledge and power are equivalent, so just as conspiracy theories assume that someone *must* be in control, the public's imagination seems to insist that someone *must* be in the know. We need the boffin.

But the answer must also have something to do with the fact that accounts of scientific discoveries fit rather neatly with the way we tell all stories. Indeed the 'discovery story' maps quite uncannily onto the structure of the classic short story. Both set up an initial tension (an unsolved problem), and then compound this tension with certain pressures (in the case of the scientist, academic rivalry, scientific failures, outside forces). Hence the first two acts: conflict; complication. The final resolution comes when an unexpected backstory – a new paradigm in fact – suddenly crashes into view, and we realize that much that has preceded has actually been misdirection (of either the reader of the scientist). The short story reader calls this an epiphany or a reveal; the science teacher would call it a eureka moment. In both cases what arrives casts everything that's gone before in a new light, a light that picks out details and anomalies in the preceding text which would otherwise have gone unnoticed. Indeed when a scientist, like Professor Rizzolatti, writes about his own discovery being down to a co-mixture of 'merit and luck' (in his afterword to Trevor Hoyle's story) he might, in another language, be talking about self-determination versus fate or *deus ex machina*.

But writers are not like scientists, however similar their stories may appear. Writers have motives, while scientists have methodologies. By the former, I mean simply the motive to engage, entertain, or elicit sympathy from a reader. Scientists have motives as well, of course, and can be corrupted like the worst of us (Thomas Kuhn taught us to keep a close eye on the subjective and socio-political drivers behind all scientific progress). But it is far easier to see how motives might manifest themselves in a writer's published output (a novel, for example) than in a scientist's (a peer-reviewed publication).

Fortunately some, more serious, authors have started to reach beyond the common mythologies of science and approach it as a discipline, *with* discipline. Writers such as Ian McEwan are distinguished by their willingness to immerse themselves in research and apply core scientific concepts to the shape or texture of their work. But even here we have to be careful. When does the borrowing of a scientific idea become a misuse of it? When does research (by a non-scientist) become appropriation? Writers often tell us that they don't know the point or shape of a novel until they're halfway through writing it (rather like scientists discovering, for example, an echo of the Big Bang when they were actually looking for something else). But is this always the case? Is it not more often the case that writers know exactly what they're looking for before they even set off?

INTRODUCTION

This anthology strives, in its own small way, to give science a better deal in its relationship with storytelling. The 17 authors gathered here have been commissioned to write discovery stories that genuinely engage with the science behind them and even, dare we say it, make science the *subject* of their stories. With specially appointed scientists and historians working as consultants, the authors have been steered away from well-worn clichés of science myth (Newton's apple, Crick and Watson's double helix, etc), and have been asked to tackle lesser-known breakthroughs. The authors range from literary novelists to writers of historical fiction, crime writers to poets, and through their diversity and sheer number it is hoped that no single literary motive or agenda will dominate.

The brief was always to write fiction, of course: liberties could be taken with biography, new characters invented, events simplified. Only the science had to be accurate. Some authors responded by sticking close to the historical record, telling their accounts from the scientist's-eye-view; for example Zoe Lambert's story of the discovery of fission, or Jane Rogers' account of Alan Turing's last theory. Others, like Michael Jecks, Maggie Gee and Kate Clanchy, chose to set their 'discovery stories' at one remove, behind the main plot of their stories but providing them with meaning. Two authors – Trevor Hoyle and Adam Marek – turned reality entirely on its head and transported well-documented historical facts into altogether separate universes. All of them, however, challenge the two base-myths – the eureka moment and the litmus test. Some foreground the intrinsically collective nature of scientific research – Tania Hershman's story, for example, is told in part from the perspective of an unknowing research 'participant'. Many stories smear out the single, isolated eureka moment into an ongoing to and fro of experimentation, dispute and rivalry across disciplinary, geographic or even political boundaries – as in the furtive correspondence between the exiled Lise Meitner and her former colleagues Otto Hahn and Fritz Strassmann in pre-war Berlin.

The stories also avoid the hagiography of so much science myth; the pioneers are never presented as heroes – nor, in the stories where so much ill came of their work – as villains. Instead we're presented with complex, beleaguered, unexaggerated, and imperfect human beings, who happen to be hard-working scientists. Luck is given as much credit as merit in the unfolding of many events. Indeed reading Professor Wearden's afterword to Annie Clarkson's story, it seems remarkable that an entire school of psychology, not to mention nearly a century's worth of politically-motivated torture, have been built on one man's response to a flash flood. In the final story – Sarah Hall's take on the discovery and ongoing treatment of Aids – we see the tortuously slow reality of science in all its tragic inadequacy. If only there *were* a lightning-bolt eureka moment in that particular story, the reader wishes.

In writing these stories, the authors – like the scientists they wrote about – worked under difficult conditions. Each author had an appointed consultant peering over their shoulder, like a prying supervisor or a meddling funder. In many cases the protagonists of the stories are still alive, and in the case of three authors the very scientists they were fictionalising gave them feedback (Denis Noble, Giacomo Rizzolatti and Kary Mullis – though the latter didn't write the afterword).

Inevitably some authors saw the project as a challenge to marry the physical world of science with the internal, philosophical or spiritual world of the story's protagonist. Thus old tensions aren't entirely absent – the 'non-overlapping magisteria' of religion and science (to use Stephen Jay Gould's phrase) are given due permission to overlap, quite harmoniously, for example, in Frank Cottrell Boyce's paean to the 'Keats of Astronomy', Jeremiah Horrocks. Less harmoniously elsewhere, like in Sean O'Brien's 'Swan, 1914'. There are even moments, in Michael Jecks' story and Professor Al-Khalili's afterword, where science steps up to do religion's job for it, offering its own non-spiritual consolation. But in all accounts, what the authors offer is something tangibly *more* than the science teacher's anecdote, and tangibly *less* (in a less-is-more way) than anything the biographies and history books have to offer.

Because, ultimately, science has to stick with story-telling. It cannot live without it, or even without myth-making. The task of a project like this is not to jettison myth or demolish popular constructs, but to keep them better informed. Science needs eureka moments and litmus tests, just as stories need turning points and plot facts. For the only way we can understand science, it seems, is through story. Anything else just doesn't compute.

RP

The Pitch

Frank Cottrell Boyce

WE OPEN WITH a heartbeat. The heartbeat of Jeremiah Horrox, aged 21. The troubled heartbeat of a weak and unreliable heart. The heartbeat of a man who is afraid of discovery. As he tiptoes through the house on this freezing November morning in 1639, carrying his own bedsheet. He ducks into the little room, the one that overlooks the orchard, and drapes the sheet over an easel, weighs it down with his books.

A heart that misses a beat.

Someone behind him. One of his charges – the little boy Abiezer. He stares at the sheet. 'Master Horrox,' he says, 'Are you working on't Sabbath?'

This is a Puritan household. The Stone family do not believe in worldly authority. Kings, bishops, priests – they are all rags of the Beast. They are banished. The house is a tiny utopia with Master Stone at its head. Jeremiah teaches the children and reads all the prayers. No one works on Sunday. Sundays are for savouring the Word of God. Nothing else. No work. No play. Not even church – church is too sociable and the walk there too distractingly lovely.

Jeremiah takes the boy now and rounds up the others and says a psalm. The eighth. *O Lord, Our Lord, how excellent is thy name in all the earth! Who has set thy glory above the Heavens!* While they savour the psalm he wonders – maybe this is work, maybe I am doing wrong. But he is also thinking – I need to set up the telescope.

He sends the children off to their father to ask for his blessing. There are eight children. Eight blessings. Each blessing going into some detail about the shortcomings of the child. That should give him time.

Heart pounding again, he tries to run discreetly. Back to the back room. He sets up the telescope he bought in Manchester. It cost him two shillings and sixpence. He earns forty shillings a year.

He uses his rule and his calculations to fix the position of the telescope. Surely anything that involves a ruler and bits of paper, that's got to be work. Really, he shouldn't be doing this.

But surely God wants him to see this.

He was at Cambridge when he came across Kepler. The idea that the planets revolve in harmonic chorus around the Sun. So beautiful. But the maths was wrong. He could see that right away. He was twenty. He had a patient fervour for truth. He made his own observations and calculations. In 1636 he predicted that Venus would transit the Sun on November 29th 1639. With a helioscope a man could see it. See the motion of the planets. Glimpse the clockwork of the solar system. He has waited years for this. Afraid his heart would give out before then. But he's alive. It is today.

But it's a Sabbath.

And he's trapped in his own dizzy orbit of duties. The bell. It's breakfast. He runs to the dining room and reads from Baxter's *Narrative of the Most Memorable Instances of Grace,* while the family eats.

He had stayed at Cambridge by working as a servant. He broke ice on water. He hauled wood to the students' rooms. Maybe it was there his heart grew weak.

At last breakfast is over. Back to the room.

No.

Master Stone would speak to him.

Can they walk apart. In the garden.

No. Yes, of course.

Master Stone opens his heart. He has doubts and anxieties. He is anxious that he is not one of the Elect, not one of the saved. The anxiety has brought him to despair. He thinks often of taking his own life.

Jeremiah thinks – it's clouding over. What if it clouds over. Venus will transit the Sun today and not again for one hundred and twenty one and a half years. All will be wasted if he doesn't see it.

What think you, Master Horrox?

It's clouding over...

What?

But there is a wind. That will blow the clouds away. I hope.

What?

Oh. Jeremiah realizes he has not been listening. He sees with a soft shock that Stone is weeping.

I see! says Stone... you are saying these doubts will pass if I am simply patient. They are a kind of trial. They are the weather of a man's spirit.

Yes. Exactly that, says Jeremiah, thinking – what time is Sunset? How long have I got?

Master Horrox, you have this day plucked me from the face of a dark, precipitous cliff. That you have.

No problem. (A quarter before four – that is the Sunset). I am right glad.

We must mark my deliverance and reassurance, Master Horrox. After we have eaten our midday meal. You must lead us all in prayers of thanksgiving. For an hour. Or two.

Two? No. One and a quarter. It must be done by three.

Three o'clock? You are very precise, Master Horrox.

I serve, says Jeremiah, a very precise God.

Over the beef, Stone tries to discourse with Jeremiah – a thing he never does – but Jeremiah cannot listen. He thinks – why are time and means forever denied me? And on a sudden sunlight slants through the window, making the pewter shine like silver. 'The Sun!' says Jeremiah. Here is the Sun!

It is a figure, says Master Stone, of my redemption.

And what if, thinks Jeremiah, what if the glass of my telescope is even now condensing the Sun's rays to a spot of heat and kindles a fire in the sheet? What if the house is burning down? That would be a judgement on him. On all of them.

He must go but no. Stone says, And now Jeremiah will lead us in an hour or more of prayer. Of thanks for my deliverance from a temptation.

The shadow of Jeremiah's goblet moves across the table like Death's finger.

Then he hears the clock... it strikes three.

And... Amen, says Jeremiah.

And he runs. Heartbeat again.

No smell of burning. So, good.

Into the room. He pulls the drapes, smothers the afternoon light, all light except that solar disk which the telescope has brought to the white sheet.

And there it is. Indenting already the solar limb. A spot. No bigger than a fly. A spot.

The shadow of the planet Venus.

He will sit here now until a quarter before four.

And for half of one hour he will watch something no one has seen before – a planet, Venus, transiting the great face of the Sun. The operation of God's clockwork.

And from the recollections of this half hour, he will correct the orbital elements. He will measure the size of Venus and its distance from the Earth. He will prove the eccentricity of its orbit and propose – what Newton will formulate many years later – the centrifugal and attractive forces that move the Sun and planets. Gravity. He will be the first to imagine gravity. Time and means will always be denied him – his frail heart and poverty will kill him in a year or two

– but before that he will radically remove Liverpool and all the planet from the still centre of things to the vertiginous, spinning edge.

All this will come from sitting on a Sabbath afternoon, watching this pinpoint shadow that has travelled a hundred million miles to move across a bed sheet in Much Hoole.

And he knows that he is not Sabbath breaking.

He is reading. Reading from a great, encompassing revelation, spelling out the unending syllables of light and time, describing the incalculably slow reliable heart beat of the solar system.

And as he reads he listens to his own, frail answering heart as it proclaims...

O Lord, our Lord, how excellent is thy name in all the earth! Who has set thy glory above the heavens! When I consider the work of your hands which you have ordained, what is man that you are mindful of him? Mortal man that you care for him? For you have crowned him with glory and honour.

Afterword:

1639: Jeremiah Horrocks and the Transit of Venus

Kathryn Harris

THE TRANSIT OF Venus was first predicted by Johannes Kepler. He studied the motion of the planets and predicted that Venus would cross the plane of the Sun. The transit itself is similar to a solar eclipse. The planet passes between the Earth and the Sun, casting a shadow. Despite the fact that Venus is four times bigger than the moon, the Moon is a lot closer and therefore blocks out more sunlight.

A transit of Venus is even rarer than a solar eclipse. The orbit of Venus is inclined relative to Earth's orbit so that most of the time when the orbits of Earth and Venus coincide, Venus will pass above or below the plane of the Sun on the sky. However, in a pattern of 243 years, the orbits are such that an eclipse occurs. Transit events follow a pattern where events are separated by 121.5 then 8 then 105.5 then 8 years, before starting again.

The first consequence of a transit observation like Horrocks' is that it enables us to accurately calculate the Earth's distance from the Sun (the Astronomical unit, AU). By parallax – a method which uses the time taken for the eclipsing body (Venus in this case) to pass across the Sun's surface, viewed from two points on the Earth separated by as much distance as possible – the exact distance to the Sun can be calculated by using simple trigonometry.

The first transit was observed in 1639 by Jeremiah Horrocks in Much Hoole near Preston as well as by his fellow 'North Country Astronomer' William Crabtree in Salford, Manchester (although the latter was hampered somewhat by intermittent cloud cover)[1]. With the clear-sky observation in Much Hoole, and Crabtree's corroboration, Horrocks was able to estimate the distance to the Sun as 0.639AU (roughly 2/3 the actual distance). This was more accurate than any other measurement previously recorded. Greater accuracy would require observations to be taken across the world. Horrocks' results were not published until 1661, long after his death in 1640 (aged only 22). Jeremiah Horrocks had shown that the transit could be observed and this enabled further studies to be completed in time for the next predicted transits of 1761 and 1769.

Transits and eclipses can tell us as much about the two bodies aligning as the distances between them. In 1761, scientists from Britain, Austria and France, in one of the earliest examples of an international collaboration, travelled across the world to various different points to view the next transit of Venus. These observations allowed Mikhail Lomonosov to predict the presence of an atmosphere on the planet. As Venus was passing across the edge of the Sun, a ring of light was observed around the edge of Venus that was not yet in contact with the Sun. Lomonosov predicted this was from light refracted through an atmosphere on the planet.

The second transit of the pair in 1769 was probably the most famous, viewed by British Astronomer Charles Green on board the HMS Endeavour with Captain James Cook in Tahiti. During this voyage, the French – who were fighting the British during the unrest following the Seven Years War – were instructed not to attack this vessel as it was on a mission for the good of all. This is a beautiful example of unity within the scientific community, and of international cooperation being promoted by science itself.

The 1769 transit calculated the distance to the sun to be 153 million km, compared to the 150 million km it is now know to be. Due to the Black Drop Effect, this was the most accurate measurement which could be made at the time.

The Black Drop Effect is found as Venus starts to move out of the Sun's disc. A teardrop shape appears, connecting Venus to the edge of the sun. This problem makes it difficult to determine the exact time Venus reaches the edge of the Sun's disc, making precise measurements difficult. (In fact, Green was originally blamed for bad observation as a result of this phenomenon. As he died on the voyage home, Cook had to step in and cleared his name). This effect is believed to be caused by Earth's atmosphere. Today's better optics means that, during the 2004 transit, the effect was not widely seen.

Observing eclipses and transits continues to offer decisive information for other aspects of physics. In 1915, Einstein theorised as part of his General Theory of Relativity that space became warped or bent in the presence of massive objects. During World War I, Sir Arthur Eddington and Astronomer Royal Frank Watson Doyle organised an expedition to prove this theory. In 1919, Eddington viewed a solar eclipse on the west coast of Africa on the island of Príncipe at the same time as others viewed the eclipse simultaneously in Brazil. General Relativity predicts that light travelling from distant stars, passing close to the sun, will be bent by it, therefore shifting their apparent position around the edge of an eclipsed disc when viewed from Earth. By observing this shift, the amount the light is bent can be calculated and Eddington was able to prove Einstein's General Theory. This was a giant step forward, not just for the observations but for an Englishman to be proving the theory of a German, so soon after World War I. Another example of science being used as a tool to promote international cooperation and the spirit of peace.[2]

Even today, eclipses are still viewed, not only as a source of amazement, but for scientific study. During an eclipse the corona, the Sun's outer layer, can be viewed. Normally the photosphere is too bright to allow this dimmer and less dense layer to be seen. The corona is the equivalent of the Sun's atmosphere and due to its extremely high temperature (the reasons for this are still unknown), it has some unusual properties and features astronomers are very interested in studying, in order to better understand our closest star.

Going back to Horrocks' achievement, it should be understood that determining exact distances to astronomical bodies (even those as close as our own sun) is vital to astronomy. Indeed it is one of the holy grails of cosmology. Jeremiah Horrocks was one of the first to do this and, for this alone, should be regarded as the forefather of astrophysics in the UK. For which I, and all my fellow astronomers, are deeply grateful.

1. Alan Chapman. *Jeremiah Horrocks, William Crabtree, and the Lancashire Observations of the Transit of Venus of 1639.* Proceedings IAU Colloquium No. 196, 2004

2. Matthew Stanley. *An Expedition to Heal the Wounds of War: The 1919 Eclipse and Eddington as Quaker Adventurer.* Isis, Vol. 94, No. 1, 50th Anniversary of the Discovery of the Double Helix (Mar., 2003), pp. 57–89

(University of Chicago Press)

Patience

Emma Unsworth

THE FLARED NOSTRILS at the base of a hooked nose, curving up to a pair of crinkled eyes and artfully penciled brows. Red lips curling in a smirk that pulled the long chin to a point. A thin, colourful body twisting into the beginnings of a jig,. arms high and legs akimbo.

Dmitri removed the cigar from between his teeth and scowled at the playing card on the windowsill across the room. He hated every last fibre of the Joker – from the bells on his boots to the prongs of his court jester's cap. The Joker was an anomaly; an American invention slipped into the pack and sent to mock Dmitri as he worked. He was a caperer, a master of chaos, a fool.

As Dmitri stood up from his chair, the grey woolen blanket around his shoulders slipped and fell to the floor. He walked over to the window, where the curtains were still open from the day. The Joker was propped up against the dark pane beside three portrait photographs that the maid arranged in descending height order every time she attempted to tidy his study. He looked along the row of photos, from his mother's face framed with glass jewels, to his wife's framed by steel, to his son's framed by wood. The Joker was at the end of the row, frozen in the obscene shape of his smug little victory dance.

Dmitri snatched the card and turned it over. A single

word was written on the blank reverse in his own neat, looping hand: *Hydrogen*. The lightest and the loneliest element. Hydrogen had an atomic weight of just one and seemed to be a law unto itself. Dmitri had banished it to the corner too. He looked at the card and nudged up his glasses. He couldn't decide which side irked him less: the brazen fool or the unclassifiable element. His fingers twitched and then he snorted and stomped back to his desk. The hinges on the chair base squeaked as he sat down.

The door of the study opened and his wife Feozva appeared, shadow first and then the solid reality of her, blank-mouthed, her dark hair strained back in a bun, her hand on her stomach. She looked between the tall stacks of yellow paper, over to where he sat hunched at his desk.

'Playing cards with yourself again, dear?'

Dmitri smiled at his wife and took a long suck on his cigar. Feozva walked across the messy room and picked up the fallen blanket. She moved slowly in her nightdress and shawl and he could see now that at four months she was starting to show. She folded the blanket over the crooked arm of his mahogany chair.

'You should have let me pick that up,' he said.

'Too slow.' Her voice was distracted. She was gazing at the playing cards on his desk, the only orderly feature of the room, laid out in their mesmerizing, maddening rows. 'What do they mean?'

'That's what I'm trying to work out.'

'There are so many.'

He had split open two decks of cards as he needed sixty-three in total, one for each element. Dmitri knew them all like old friends. He knew their predispositions, their habits and their quirks – from flighty fluorine, which reacted with almost everything, to steadfast gold, which could sit against skin for years without changing what it touched, or being changed. The cards were spread over the surface of his desk, alongside paperweights, a pen pot and a concertina of mathematical rulers. He had dealt the cards the way he always did: down in rows according to their atomic weights, then across in groups based on their chemical properties. Dmitri knew that it was the beginnings of something beautiful: a natural law governing the whole of chemistry. The stuff scientists' dreams were made of.

Feozva turned to face him, one hand on her hip and the other on her stomach.

'I'm going to bed,' she said. 'Are you coming?'

It was the first time she had asked in months. Cigar smoke hung in the air between them. Dmitri looked up at the window, where the ruched white nets shivered below red velvet, like a French cancan dancer's bloomers. He shook his head. Work. Work was all.

'I'll be another hour or so.'

As she walked towards him he removed his cigar for a goodnight kiss but when she only pecked his cheek he knew that she was annoyed. His wife was a mutable creature – one minute as bright as phosphorous, the next as sullen as lead.

His mother and his elder sister Olga had advised him to marry and Dmitri hadn't wanted to disappoint them. They were the wisest, most industrious people he had ever known. Before they died he had chosen Feozva, the daughter of a well-known writer, because she was creative and patriotic. She illustrated her father's fairytales with spidery pen and ink drawings of children and monsters, a fact that was kept secret within the family. Dmitri felt privileged when he was told. Olga and his mother approved of Feozva, but even before the wedding Dmitri wasn't sure he was doing the right thing. Had he just done what was expected of him? And, if so, who was he doing it for? His family? Russia? What scared him the most was the idea of surrendering the solitude that had become so precious to him as a child. Would his wife expect his company constantly whenever he was at home? The youngest of fourteen, he had spent much of his time in the library of the rough-and-tumble family home in Tobolsk, creeping there late at night to get some peace. That time crouched amongst the musty shelves became his sanctuary, and he learned to treasure those blank spaces for contemplation between the clamour of the days.

Feozva reached down, picked up the card on the windowpane and turned it around. Her long fingers were stained with ink. She still drew occasionally, mostly pictures of their son, in the housekeeping book that his mother had given her as a wedding present.

'I prefer this side,' she said, smiling at the Joker. 'He reminds me of you, over here just pleasing himself.'

Dmitri tucked a piece of hair behind Feozva's ear. 'I hope I don't remind you of him too much,' he said, but his wife didn't answer, just smiled again, and left the room with an ambiguous flick of her shawl.

Dmitri sat back down at his desk and wrapped the blanket around his shoulders. He stared at the cards, sucking on his cigar. Here they were, his beautiful patterns. A flush of alkali metals: lithium, sodium, potassium. A run of halogens: fluorine, chlorine, bromine, iodine. And then, the jaw-dropping reveal; the flip and gasp of a conjurer's trick: fluorine and chlorine side by side; related. And fluorine and chlorine weren't the only improbable bedfellows. His arrangement was slowly shaping up like a chart, with elements slotting into place next to one another, across and down, with episodic regularity. They constituted unlikely families, thrust together by nature to share properties.

He stubbed out his cigar on a saucer. Such suggestions of perfection thrilled him but he wanted more; he knew there had to be more, because patterns didn't come out of nowhere. There had to be a simple, unifying truth.

The next morning he listened to the sound of the ticking grandfather clock as he combed his beard at the mirror in the hall. The clock sounded like a tapping foot and Dmitri found himself combing his beard in time, and becoming more agitated.

'You look serious, Daddy.'

Dmitri looked down to see Volodya tugging at the bottom of his winter coat. He scooped his son up into his arms.

'That's because I'm going to work.'

Dmitri turned with his son to face the mirror. Volodya had Dmitri's hazel-green eyes and Feozva's high Renaissance forehead, but he had a smile all of his own. Dmitri smiled too, but he knew that austerity suited him better. At thirty-six, his hair was already thinning on top and lupine grey hairs were sprouting more regularly from his chin. His desire for a natural law had been brewing nine years now – ever since the Karlsruhe Conference of 1860. That early intuition left him with a fire in his belly; fire that came in handy when Tsar Alexander II closed the university and Dmitri was left jobless and hungry, with holes in his boots. His belief in his work had got him through, but he wasn't the only one obsessed with the science of substances, and the presence of rivals like Meyer was an irritating spur to his progress. Meyer, Bunsen's other protégé, was Dmitri's German nemesis. When his arrangement was finished he planned to send a copy to the university in Karlsruhe – that should put paid to the competition. People had suggested he and Meyer work together to speed up the process of discovery, but Dmitri couldn't think of anything worse than collaborating – especially with a rival. He had got this far alone – he would make it all the way.

Volodya picked at the chain of Dmitri's pocket watch, which was pinned to the front of his coat, precisely halfway between two buttons. Feozva appeared behind them in the archway that separated the hall from the dining room, his hat in her hands. When Dmitri caught sight of her he set Volodya down on the gleaming wooden floor. Apart from his study, the apartment was immaculate.

'I'm thinking of putting a sock in that clock.'

Feozva raised an eyebrow and handed him his hat. 'You

haven't forgotten you're at a concert later, have you?' she said.

'Of course not.'

His heart sank – he *had* forgotten about the concert. There would be no brooding and shuffling for him tonight.

'Don't look like that, dear.'

He banged his hat onto his head. 'Hopefully it won't last all night.'

'You never know, a change of scene might help.'

'I don't need a change of scene. All I need is time.'

He felt a slap on his knee and looked down to see his son's panicked little face looking up at him. Volodya had started slapping Dmitri whenever he or Feozva raised their voices; he hated it when they argued. Feozva sighed and spoke very gently.

'My father swore by regular breaks. If he got stuck he would take a long walk. He said he solved as many puzzles in the park as he did at his desk.'

'I'm a scientist, not a storyteller.'

Feozva shrugged. He buttoned up his overcoat. As he opened the front door he steeled himself for the inevitable blast of icy wind. St Petersburg in February was bitterly cold, sometimes dropping to minus ten, and it was only his sense of duty to his students that propelled him out of the house.

It was a short walk to the university – just long enough for Dmitri to take in the rapidly changing cityscape, where every day another mansion was demolished to make way for more multi-storey rental houses. It was as though St Petersburg was being compressed. A city getting denser.

'Professor Mendeleev!'

Dmitri turned to see his assistant Menshutkin hurrying towards him over the frosted pavements.

'Morning, Nikolai.'

'Any new developments?'

'No.'

Menshutkin handed Dmitri a stack of papers. It was his

own textbook: *The Principles of Chemistry*, from where he took most of his lecture material. Menshutkin stepped back, slipping, and Dmitri caught him and held his arm until he was steady on his feet. Menshutkin was an excellent chemist, methodical and careful in his conclusions, but he had a nervous air in public. Feozva said it was because he was scared of Dmitri, like most of the students, but Dmitri found that hard to believe, not to mention disappointing. Long gone were the days of sturdy, rigorous, gloriously emotionless teaching like that instilled by his own great mentor, Bunsen.

'I was wondering,' Menshutkin hesitated. Dmitri grunted.

'Don't wonder, Nikolai. Speak.'

'Are you free for a beer after class?'

'No, not today,' said Dmitri. 'I'm meeting Tchaikovsky.'

★

In the foyer of the Mariinsky Theatre he caught sight of Tchaikovsky's white hair and waved him over. His former colleague regularly invited him to his son's recitals and Dmitri always agreed – after all it was Ilya who, as head of the Technological Institute, had taken him on without a Doctor's degree. Dmitri continued to express his gratitude by inviting Tchaikovsky to the regular Wednesday gatherings at his apartment.

'Big night!' said Tchaikovsky, shaking his hand.

'Of course,' said Dmitri, racking his brain. What was the occasion? Ilya must have mentioned it. Then he remembered: it was the first recital of Pyotr's music since his graduation. 'Can't wait to hear how he's progressed.'

'He's much improved,' said Tchaikovsky. 'You know how determined he is.'

Dmitri recalled Tchaikovsky's words from the previous year, when he and Pyotr's mother had been trying to dissuade their son from pursuing a career in music. *Pointless vulgarity,* was how they had described it. Now they seemed to be right behind their son. Parenting was a messy, inconsistent business, thought Dmitri. Families weren't neat because people weren't neat; only the elements had true integrity.

'Then some Strauss,' Tchaikovsky continued, 'to keep the critics happy.'

But even the mention of a well-known composer didn't excite Dmitri. Music didn't move him in the way that visual arts did. He felt the most when he was around things he could actually see: paintings, sketches, glass bottles, cheese. His mind darted about for the entire length of Pyotr's symphony, and every time he thought of the cards on his desk at home he felt a pang of longing.

It was only when the opening bars of Strauss' 'Blue Danube' began that Dmitri found himself back in the concert hall. Had he heard this piece before? He couldn't remember. He didn't think so. It was unlike any other music he had heard – starting out so simple and moving through to complexity, but carrying him along with it, and so beautiful. Each flurry of woodwind, each shimmer of strings took him to a lucid place. He breathed deeply. This was more like it. This was what people meant when they said that music had the power to soothe. He realised that he was perched on the edge of his seat, hands clasped, attentive, waiting.

Then five minutes into the waltz the pauses began. Up and up went the music and suddenly – stop. A half-second of silence before a rush of notes flooding back to fill the void. He smiled. Oh clever, it was so clever. He never knew that the sound of nothing could be so meaningful. And there was an ebb and flow to the tune, it moved like bubbles through water, and the pauses weren't simply empty – they were about space. They were rich, bloated moments, full of anticipation and possibility. As each swell of silence arrived, Dmitri felt an intense sense of expectation as he wondered which of the four themes would return. Soon, the pauses became as satisfying as the crescendos. They showed such restraint, such subtlety, such patience.

★

When he got home he went straight to his study, sat at his desk and scraped all the cards together into one pile, ready to be laid out again. He stared at the moon through the open curtains. The craters on its surface were like the pauses in the 'Blue Danube', like the distance between himself and his wife in bed, like his unborn child's place in the family, like the spaces left by his mother and sister. They were tangible omissions; absences that were felt.

That was how he would create perfection. He would leave gaps for those elements yet to be discovered but which had to be there for everything else to make sense. He had drawn out three more cards: Eka-Aluminium, Eka-Boron and Eka-Silicium, and slotted them within the existing arrangement.

Dmitri looked over to the windowpane and saw the Joker card propped up in his usual place. But something was different. Someone had given the Joker a full beard and round glasses, the inky additions glistening in the lamplight. Dmitri lit a cigar and watched the blue smoke spool over his hand.

Afterword:

1869: Dmitri Mendeleev and the Periodic Table

Dr Zoe Schnepp

THE CREATION OF the periodic table arguably marked the
emergence of chemistry as a science from centuries of
alchemy and mysticism. At last, the jumble of unique and
diverse elements had found an order. Patterns became clearer
and through these patterns, undiscovered elements could be
predicted. Many people had struggled to discover this
exquisite order but the final answer came from the Russian
scientist Dmitri Mendeleev.

The importance of the periodic table is best put into
perspective by considering what was known at the time. Our
understanding of the world was changing rapidly and
primitive ideas such as the four elements – earth, air, fire and
water – were gone. Antoine Lavoisier had defined an element
as a substance that cannot be broken down into other
components, and new elements were being discovered every
year. We knew about atoms; that gold was made of gold atoms
and lead from lead atoms. We had also worked out that atoms
of different elements had different masses and the concept of
'atomic weight' was born. However, the world was still many
years away from the idea of the atom being divisible; that
something even smaller might exist.

Throughout history, scientific research has followed
trends and fashions, with many people or groups competing
for a single goal. Whether sequencing the human genome or
discovering a new form of carbon, publishing a major
breakthrough promises eminence and renown. It also requires

strength of character, since a new idea is bound to challenge existing opinion and naturally invites uncertainty and disbelief. At the time of Mendeleev, the big race was to be the first to create a periodic table and there were many contenders. Some looked for physical patterns, such as elements with similar properties. Others began by arranging all of the elements in order of their atomic weight. However, all ran into problems since some of the elements didn't seem to fit. Most people were so intent on finding the universal order that they forced these difficult elements into patterns despite logic telling them that it didn't work. This was where Mendeleev took a step that marked a real eureka moment. He left gaps for elements that had not yet been discovered and even predicted their properties, an incredibly bold move at a time when simply discovering a new element brought great fame! It was a move that generated skepticism and ridicule from many of Mendeleev's scientific peers. That is, of course, until these new elements were discovered with remarkably similar properties to those predicted.

The importance of the periodic table today is difficult to describe. Chemistry has moved so far from the days of discovering new elements and unlocking their patterns. Now we are able to image and manipulate individual atoms, or assemble thousands of atoms into molecules for specific applications. We are discovering that very small particles of an element or compound can have entirely different properties to their bulk counterparts. We are also attempting to mimic the fantastically complex systems in nature, such as photosynthesis. Through all of this however, most researchers will keep a periodic table close to hand. The exquisite ordering of the elements explains and classifies many trends in chemical behaviour and is still a valuable predictive tool. Of all the scientific advances of the last few centuries, few can claim such a fundamental and lasting effect.

Swan, 1914

Sean O'Brien

LADIES AND GENTLEMEN, I shall not be here for long; and nor will you. Nature has taken its course. For many of us the mortal span is ended; for others death approaches swiftly. It must be so. I speak to you from my desk and those of you who live are, many of you, scattered across the globe, but let us entertain the notion that we are all present to each other this evening in the lecture theatre of the Literary and Philosophical Society – as we were present (numbering, it is said, seven hundred) on the night when I addressed you in this very room on 20th October 1880, Lord Armstrong in the chair. At the conclusion of my address I asked for the seventy gas jets which at that time illuminated the room to be turned off. Let us suppose that; let us endow ourselves with temporary immortality. Turn off the gas. Here we are, then, in the dark, are we not? – As in the darkness that lay on the face of the waters. Now then. Bear with my story. I shall be brief.

When I was a boy the poor went to bed at sunset and frightened their children with the bogeyman Bonaparte. My family was never quite poor, but our fortunes declined by stages because of my father's generosity and improvidence and his trusting nature. I most remember our house in Pallion looking down on to the wooded slopes and shipyards of the Wear. We children would sing our adaptation of a Methodist hymn:

And then we'll shout and shine and sing
And make the Pallion arches ring
When all the Swans come home.

I think I have spent my life attempting to come home.

We had to leave that house, and then another and at last up sticks to Newcastle, but not before my curiosity led me into all the yards and workshops of the banks of the Wear to pursue my fascination with the physical processes of God's creation. 'And the light shineth in darkness; and the darkness comprehended it not,' as John's Gospel states. It was often a dark world, but at that early date science gave me means to light my way.

As to my incandescent lightbulb, it was a process of many years of thought and experimentation that led me at last to solve the fundamental problem of the device: how to create a bulb that would not only convert electricity into light but do so over a sustained period, thus making the bulb a useful domestic object. As I remarked before, there is no invention that does not possess a history, none that does not build on or learn from or owe a debt to the work of others. Fame, as we know, accrues to whoever makes the decisive step. Much labour and argument has been expended on the matter of who came first – myself or Mr Edison. I did, ladies and gentlemen, of course, as the record shows – but that is not really the point; neither are the fame or the money. The point was the illumination – the light for people to read and work and think or simply sit companionably by, to drive the darkness outdoors at least.

The means to achieve this, we theorized, was by producing a vacuum in the glass bulb and allowing the filament to heat until it generated light. Why then did this for so long prove to be such a brief candle in practice? As the poet Marvell wrote, you will recall, in his great ode on Cromwell:

> Nature that hateth emptiness
> Allows of penetration less...

Our problem was that our 'emptiness', our vacuum, was no such thing: the glass chamber was imperfectly purged of atmospheric gas. When I discovered this, I ensured that the vacuum was improved, and the seals around the filaments tightened. But still the bulb would blacken and the light would die.

At length I realized that what I faced was what might be considered an example of 'penetration', of two things occupying the same space – an impossibility, of course – on the one hand the vacuum, on the other the unpurged residues attaching to the filament itself. Until then the instrument of light had tended to produce darkness. But now I saw. And I could account for the processes involved: if the carbon filament were heated to extract the residual gas before being sealed in the bulb, sustained illumination would be achieved. Thus we and our children live in a world of light. Eureka! As the journalists would have us declare.

But the world of light was not the work of a moment, or an accident.

As you also know, what became known as my carbon process enabled the making of photographs of unprecedented quality: the world would not only be illuminated, it would be preserved against the passage of time. This is, of course, the function of art, to preserve, to make, as the poet Horace said, a monument more lasting than bronze. Immortality, or its image, is what all of us long for, and the image of immortality that I myself have constantly before my mind's eye is a family photograph taken indoors with the benefit of electric light, at the house in Pallion, impossibly. Another case of 'penetration'. It is a crowded picture, for I sit with my two families and my two wives, Fanny and Hannah, all our children and my friend, colleague and brother in law John Mawson. The picture is perfect, but as I say, it is impossible.

The disaster which befell us made no sense, I have told myself. It was simply something that must be borne, a part of the pains of the human lot. And of course we are never free of our losses; and why should we wish to be, since they are evidence of the durability of love? Had I seen John Mawson on the day, perhaps at an early meeting in my house at Leazes Terrace, what might we have said?

'Have you everything you require, John?'

'I have my equipment; there will be men to help on the site and to carry the material away to the Town Moor.'

'And is there still no explanation of why the material has been found?'

'None. It was simply discovered in the stable.'

'I feel disquiet at this task you have undertaken, John.'

'Likewise. It is the cost of being both a Chemist and the Sheriff.' We might have laughed at that coincidence. I would not have mentioned that Nobel's own brother Emil had died at twenty-one in an explosion of nitroglycerine at the family's factory in Sweden, or the fatal explosion in San Francisco the previous year. It would not have been necessary to do so.

John and a party of helpers including a police constable and several local youths entered a cellar in Old Swan Yard off Cloth Market where a store of nitroglycerine had been discovered. How it came there and for what intended use seems never to have been satisfactorily determined. The party went by carriage and cart to dispose of the material, John having chosen the Town Moor as an appropriate site. It seems that John and some of his party carried away some of the opened canisters from the place where their liquid contents had been poured away into the earth on the Town Moor, intending to dispose of the remaining crystalline deposits in another spot a little way off. It was then that the disaster occurred. Witnesses said that when the explosion took place the earth shook and that human limbs were seen to be hurled into the air. Now that you have all seen photographs and moving images, you can the better imagine this cruel catastrophe for yourselves: the world is able to turn its attention to its own seeming impossibilities. We can see what cannot and should not be seen.

John Mawson and several others were taken away to hospital, but he died that night of his injuries. My guide and partner, my great encourager, my friend, was snatched away. But this was not all. John Mawson's death seems to have produced what Herr Bodenstein later described as a chain reaction, whereby 'if two molecules react, not only molecules of the final reaction products are formed, but also some unstable molecules, having the property of being able to further react with the parent molecules,' and so on.

Even now I say this as if the impartial language of science might mitigate the subsequent sickness and death of my wife Fanny and then our twin sons, which occurred within a few months of John Mawson's accident. The task of science is to illuminate, is it not? It is possible, though, that there are times when the world it brings into view seems impossible to contemplate, when our sustaining beliefs and the optimism by which I myself had always previously been marked fall away, as into a void without form or meaning. This was my state for a year or more after these several bereavements. My thoughts stagnated and wandered away in a vagrant manner almost without control, and I was left with a painful sense of having neglected to fulfil a duty.

> And then we'll shout and shine and sing
> And make the Pallion arches ring
> When all the Swans come home.

There would be no such homecoming, it seemed.

Later and at different times I wrote the two following sharply contrasting comments in my diary. Firstly: 'the passing of genius through life is like the passing of a shooting star through our atmosphere – coming out of darkness, and quickly re-entering it again; and do what we may, we cannot but repine at this hard law.' Was John Mawson a genius? There was not time even to discover it. But I repined; oh, I did.

Then a little after that I wrote to my second wife, Hannah: 'Thank God for his goodness to us! So far from our deserts.' Is this not also a form of 'penetration', the impossible simultaneous presence of two things – unbearable grief and exalted joy – in the same space? Science seeks to uncover the facts of nature, but what is a fact when the spirit has fled?

After my time of mourning I applied myself once more to my researches until at length (with the aid of steadfast colleagues and German glassblowers) I succeeded in the task of making an incandescent electric light bulb. In that moment – and I do not say this out of vanity – the world changed. Where hitherto darkness had impatiently awaited its hour, now the light could govern all the hours of the day and night. The light might flicker but it would not fail, you might say. Mechanisms have no sense of irony, of course.

Scientists are often taught to be and are often temperamentally inclined to be wary of metaphor: that way magic lies; or poetry. But the human imagination is surely a unity: it can hardly be its own enemy. I immersed myself in poetry from childhood and would quote it throughout my life when the occasion arose. At the death of John Mawson I thought of Milton's 'Lycidas':

> For Lycidas is dead, dead ere his prime:
> Young Lycidas, and hath not left his peer:
> Who would not sing for Lycidas?

And the nature of the scientific events we are able to witness, with their sudden connections and their power to generate new realities, can fairly be viewed as a kind of poetry, just as the poet Coleridge in his great *Biographia Literaria* characterized the poetic imagination as 'a living power and prime agent of all human perception, and… a repetition in the finite mind of the eternal act of creation of the infinite I AM.' It was in this spirit, as part of the God-given process of discovering and forming new unities, that in 1871 I came to seek the hand of Hannah White, Fanny's sister, in marriage. The law of the land was against us, forbidding me to marry my deceased wife's sister, and it would remain so for almost forty years more. But the Swiss order matters differently, and it was to Neuchatel that we travelled to be wed in the eye of God at the Reformed Church in the town. And from this date my happiness began once more, as a result, perhaps, of a chain reaction, in which we could only play our parts in good faith to the best of our ability.

You see what I am doing – making sense, inferring meaning. Meaning, you might say, is not the sphere of the scientist: an observable fact is its own meaning, and its connection to the mind of the creator is not ours to divine. Metaphysics has largely ceased to be part of the empire of science. You might say I am making a category error, or trying to speak one language with the mind of another. Why could I not be happy with electric light and photography and the discovery of artificial fibre? Could they not be enough? Let me affirm that often I was happy, and more than happy, with my second wife and a family to which we added, and with our home, with research and the discovery of items and processes useful to my fellow creatures, with friends and worldly success and the world's applause. But at the edge of things there waited always that realm of restlessness and doubt where it seemed impossible to – to accommodate the spirit to the material nature of things – to glass and metal and filament and vacuum pump and the light that in combination they produced. The light I shed might be only the *image* of the greater light that must, surely, lie behind and beyond all our earthly endeavours; for if that was not so (though it must be so) what was our case, our situation but that of falling through a void, without a solid ground of being?

I was of my time as all men are. I stood for liberal

hopefulness, reform, improvement, the harnessing of the productive power of science to the common good. I followed the light faithfully, but could not but be aware of the dark. It may be strange to some that it should be a hymn by John Henry Newman, who was to convert to Catholicism, that seems best to convey these tensions and suggest that faith is continually in the presence of doubt:

> Lead, kindly Light, amid th'encircling gloom, lead
>   Thou me on!
> The night is dark, and I am far from home; lead
>   Thou me on!
> Keep Thou my feet; I do not ask to see
> The distant scene; one step enough for me.
> So long Thy power hath blest me, sure it still will
>   lead me on.
> O'er moor and fen, o'er crag and torrent,
>   till the night is gone,
> And with the morn those angel faces smile, which I
>   Have loved long since, and lost awhile!
> Meantime, along the narrow rugged path,
> Thyself hast trod,
> Lead, Saviour, lead me home in childlike faith,
>   home to my God.
> To rest forever after earthly strife
> In the calm light of everlasting life.

May it be so. I have come to doubt it, but I cannot abandon the possibility, and I know that to some that might make me the less a scientist. All I can do is admit to my ever-present questioning. I was a Victorian optimist, as I have said. I survived terrible loss. I hope I have been of help to others. Yet I speak now in the New Year of 1914, when it is clear to all serious observers that Europe is on the threshold of a great and terrible conflict which may bring the world we know wholly to destruction. How can it be that Christendom permits and even nurtures such a menace to humanity? Can it be that the great imaginative energies of science and industry have brought us into the light only that we may see the better to kill one another before plunging back into the darkness, like so many spent Lucifers into the ruined cities of Hell?

Put on the lights, in any case. I have no answer, of course, and perhaps you are laughing at me, a man past his time, and one without the armour of irony or cynicism or knowingness to help him on his way. But ladies and gentlemen, in the teeth of the present evidence I end with an affirmation by a poet who himself knew doubt on intimate terms.

> that which we are, we are;
> One equal temper of heroic hearts,
> Made weak by time and fate, but strong in will
> To strive, to seek, to find, and not to yield.

I say again: put on the lights. What else can we do, after all? Good night.

Afterword:

1880: Joseph Swan and the Electric Light Bulb

John Clayson

IN SEAN'S STORY Joseph Swan remarks:

> *There is no invention that does not possess a history, none that does not build on or learn from or owe a debt to the work of others.*

The principle of illumination by the resistive heating of an electrical conductor was demonstrated by Humphry Davy in about 1802, using a platinum wire connected across the powerful battery that he used for his electro-chemical investigations. Davy's glowing metal wire soon gave out, but others were inspired to experiment including W.E. Staite, whose lecture at the Sunderland Athenaeum in 1847 was attended by a youthful Joseph Wilson Swan. Between then and about 1860 Swan developed potentially viable thin conductors made from carbonised paper strips. However, the expense of obtaining power from a battery and the impossibility of achieving a sufficiently high vacuum caused him to set aside his work on the incandescent lamp.

In 1864, Hermann Sprengel invented his mercury vacuum pump. The Sprengel pump was a simple and elegant device that could evacuate from a closed vessel all but one thousand millionth of the gas present in the atmosphere. It was not, however, a piece of equipment that, today, we might call a 'plug and play' device. It could give of its best only in the hands of one who understood it and had perfected the technique.

As we have heard, the tragic chain of events which began in 1867 with the death of his business partner, John Mawson, left Joseph Swan much preoccupied with business and family life. By 1877 'dynamo-electric machines' had become a cost-effective source of electrical power, and Swan seized the opportunities presented by high vacuum science. He established a working partnership with bank clerk and amateur scientist Charles Stearn of Birkenhead. Stearn had developed a facility with the Sprengel pump, and he was willing to work with Swan to help to realise the vision of sustained incandescence of a carbon conductor. Prepared carbon strips were sent by Swan to Birkenhead; they were returned to Tyneside having been connected to wires and enclosed in expertly evacuated glass bulbs.

Yet still the inside of the bulbs shortly became obscured by a dark coating, and the filaments broke. Was the cause of this phenomenon the 'volatisation' of the incandescent carbon? If it was, there seemed to be no future for the carbon filament lamp, because volatisation would take place no matter how near-perfect the vacuum. Or, was some alternative mechanism at work? On the evidence before him Swan believed the latter, and the quest continued.

Early in 1879, Swan demonstrated in public the principle of the electrical incandescence of carbon in a vacuum during three general lectures on electric lighting, at Sunderland on 17th January (in the Subscription Library), at Newcastle on 3rd February (at the Literary & Philosophical Society) and at Gateshead on 12th March (at the Town Hall).

During 1879 Swan and Stearn discovered that setting a lamp aglow at the very end of the evacuation process drove off residual gases from the filament. These gases had previously evolved on the lamp's first ignition, poisoning the vacuum. The agent of destruction being now removed from the bulb before it was sealed, the durable incandescent lamp was born. It was as if the invention craved an initial spark of life from its maker before being sold for a life of usefulness.

Following Swan's demonstration of incandescent electric lamps ready for practical application at the Lit & Phil library on 20th October 1880, the chairman of the gathering, Sir William (later Lord) Armstrong, arranged with Swan for the new lamps to be installed at his home. Armstrong was president of the Lit & Phil and he had also been in the chair for Swan's lecture in February 1879. A Tyneside scientist, inventor, engineer and industrialist, his house at Cragside, near Rothbury in Northumberland, already had an electricity supply, generated by water power and supplying arc lamps. By December 1880 it was fitted up with incandescent lamps – the world's first domestic installation – apparently to Armstrong's entire satisfaction:

Each single lamp is about equal to a duplex kerosine lamp well turned up, and this I believe is equivalent to twenty-five candles, so that my 6-horse power in supporting thirty-seven lamps gives me an illuminating effect equal to 925 candles. The same power applied to the production of light by the 'electric arc', instead of by incandescence, would give vastly more light, but the arc light being only divisible to a small extent, could not be made nearly so serviceable for the distributed lighting of a house. Besides, the light produced by incandescence is free from all the disagreeable attributes of the arc light. It is perfectly steady and noiseless. It casts no ghastly hue on the countenance, and shows everything in true colours. Being unattended with combustion, and out of contact with the atmosphere, it differs from all other lights in having no vitiating effect on the air of a room. In short, nothing can be better than this light for domestic use.[1]

The improvements in comfort, convenience and cleanliness that the incandescent electric lamp brought, to such homes as could afford to install it, is further summed up in the following newspaper extracts. They relate to the family home of a young electrical engineer, John Henry Holmes, who was another of those present at the Lit & Phil on 20th October 1880. We should bear in mind that in those days, 'town's gas' was an impure fuel contaminated with noxious residues which would, in later years, be removed at the gas works as 'by-products': raw materials for the chemical industry.

Newcastle Journal, 5 September 1883
For several days past Messrs J.H. Holmes & Co., who have recently commenced business as electric light engineers at Stepney, Newcastle, have been engaged in placing in the residence of Mr. W.H. Holmes, Wellburn, Jesmond, Swan's incandescent light...

Newcastle Express, 5 September 1883
The new light has been in use for about two or three weeks, and has given great satisfaction, the illumination being both much brighter and much purer than gas. There are in all forty of Swan's incandescent lamps distributed throughout the house, the power being supplied by a half-horsepower Otto silent gas engine working a Siemens electric machine in conjunction with... batteries. The drawing room is brilliantly illuminated by ten 12-candle lamps, while the five 20-candle lamps, which light up the dining room, and which are enclosed in ground glass globes, shed around a soft, mellow and pleasing light. The hall, library, staircase, landing, bedrooms, dressing rooms and all parts of the house are similarly lighted. A very clever contrivance has been invented by the firm in the form of a switch which is placed at the door of each apartment, and by means of which any person entering or leaving a room can turn illumination on or off at pleasure.

The cost of gas for working the engine is about the same as was previously paid for illuminating with gas, but as a set-off against this there is the increased comfort and the absence of the noxious sulphuric fumes which are so detrimental to health − not to speak of works of art, plants and house furnishings. The engine, dynamo and batteries have been fitted up in an outhouse at the rear of the premises [and] are attended to by the gardener.

So, all you gardeners − away to your outhouses and turn on the gas. Then we shall flick the switch and there will be light!

And what of Edison? We have not time here to run through the arguments as to priority of invention. Part of the problem is that there was no specification of the properties of a successful incandescent electric lamp. What balance was demanded of longevity, light output, power consumption, robustness, cost, ease of manufacture?

In 1978, Neil Brown of the London Science Museum carefully researched and weighed the available evidence.[2] He found that the record of when this breakthrough, or that, took place in Swan's and Edison's experimentation on each side of the Atlantic Ocean is frequently inconclusive, and sometimes contradictory.

However, Swan's demonstration of 20th October 1880 at the Lit & Phil may well have been the first public showing of practical and commercially viable incandescent lamps, using his parchmentised thread filament. During November both men appear to have been manufacturing successful lamps 'for the market', small as it then was.

In conclusion, Brown wrote:

> Surely it does not detract from the stature of either man, Swan or Edison, to admit that the other also produced a successful filament lamp independently and practically simultaneously...
> The electric lamp was a product of the age of its invention as much as a product of any one man or group of men

Swan moved on to perfecting and improving filament material and manufacturing techniques, producing the first artificial thread along the way. In later life his skills as a chemist drew him to the concept of the fuel cell – a chemical device for the production of electricity directly from fuel, without combustion, and now much used in space travel.

Edison became intrigued by one of the idiosyncrasies of the incandescent lamp. The blackening of the inside of bulbs and the breakage of filaments continued, though much reduced. Edison noticed that these effects conformed to a pattern. His investigation introduced a second electrical element inside the bulb, independent of the lamp filament. He discovered that, in some circumstances, a flow of electric current occurred across the vacuum inside the lamp, without spark or arc. How *could* a current flow smoothly, imperceptibly through empty space? This unexplained phenomenon became known as the 'Edison Effect'.

If Edison *had* understood the effect he might have given his own choice of name to the negatively–charged particles which were carrying the current. Instead, he moved on to other work, leaving the Anglo-Irish physicist George Johnstone Stoney[3] to suggest the term 'electron' in 1891.

Later, in 1904, investigation of the Edison Effect inspired John Ambrose Fleming, who had once worked for Edison, to invent the thermionic diode valve, considered to be the first useful device conceived by application of the new science of electronics.

Thus the imperfect characteristics of early incandescent filament electric lamps, recorded and investigated by Edison, foreshadowed the thermionic valve, a technological key to the worldwide proliferation of 'wire-less' communication and broadcasting in the 20th century.

So we return to the remark of Swan's with which we began:

> There is no invention that does not possess a history, none that does not build on or learn from or owe a debt to the work of others.

1. From *Swan's Electric Lamps* in *The Engineer*, 21st January 1881.
2. C N Brown, BSc. *J W Swan and the Invention of the Incandescent Lamp* [Science Museum, London, 1978, ISBN 0901805238], page 63.
3. As a young man, Stoney had been the first regular Astronomical Assistant to William Parsons, 3rd Earl of Rosse, at Birr Castle, County Offaly, where Parsons had built the world's largest telescope. William Parsons' and George Johnson Stoney's sons were Charles A. Parsons and George Gerald Stoney. Together they directed and managed an internationally influential Tyneside industrial enterprise to develop and manufacture the steam turbine for electricity generation and ship propulsion.

The Special Theory

Michael Jecks

ANNE-MARIE SAW him as she served two other customers, a pair of gossiping women in their thirties. He arrived just as she was setting down their plates of gateau, a shambling man, perhaps forty, but looking older.

He had the seediness of a man without a wife. His coat was a green mackintosh, which once must have been expensive, but was now shabby, stained and worn. Beneath she caught a glimpse of a blue suit – surely clear proof that he was single, or that his wife had lost interest in him. Anne-Marie sighed. Blue suit, with a green coat, and suede shoes of a pale brown. Comfortable, perhaps, but not in keeping with the rest of his clothing. Perhaps he was weird, a geek or something. He had the look of a computer technician, she reckoned.

Anne-Marie pocketed the women's money in the leather purse at her belly, and fixed a welcoming smile to her face as she walked outside. This was the interesting part of the job, she always said, when she met a new customer, and could assess them. When at college she had studied psychology, and in her present job she enjoyed exercising her mind with the clients.

'Guten Morgen, und...'

He looked up, panic in his eyes. 'I'm sorry, I... er...'

She smiled. He didn't look too scary. His pale brown eyes were kindly, and there was an intriguing anxiety in them.

She was so used to having blatantly lustful stares from single males, that this was a refreshing change.

'You are English? So sorry. Please, what can I get for you?'

He stared past her, over to the huge face of the Zytglogge over at the top of Marktgasse. 'I — could I have a coffee, please? Bitte, I mean.'

'Ja,' she smiled and left him to place his order.

Jan in the bar was cleaning glasses. A skinny, pimply youth, he was always gaping at her cleavage when she bent down. Lately she had begun to turn away so he couldn't goggle so obviously. Glancing around, there were few people in. She had all too few customers in the bar, and rather than evade Jan's clumsy attempts at charming her, she resorted to looking out at the man at the table outside in a reverie.

He sat outside, staring at the clock with a kind of desperate misery that was terrible to see. His thin features, pallid and lined, seemed to point to a great sadness, and she couldn't help but wonder who he was, where he had come from, and why he was here, staring at the old tower. Many tourists would come to look at it, but only in the Japanese 'I've seen it so I've snapped it, what's next?' touristy state of mind. Anne-Marie and most Berners hated that. They were proud of their city, the ancient democracy, the sense of time standing still that pervaded it.

When Jan called, she was lost for a moment, and then recalled the man's order. She collected the tray and went outside.

Delivering the coffee, she was about to return to the bar, but her curiosity got the better of her. 'You like the Zytglogge?'

'Hmm?'

'The clock, yes? You like this clock? It is very old.'

'It's been the source of my life and work,' he said.

He looked almost ready to burst into tears.

'Why? You are not from Bern, are you?'

'No, no. But it was here that Einstein had his moment

of... well, it was his Eureka moment, I suppose. And because of his marvellous vision, so much of our lives has been changed. All because of a vision on a tram.'

'On a tram?'

'Yes. It was a miracle, really. Well, if you consider him as an academic, it was. He was a dreadful scholar. At school, when his father asked the headteacher what sort of career his son should consider, the teacher shook his head and said, 'It doesn't matter. He'll never make a success of anything.' Well, he proved them wrong.'

'Einstein lived here?'

'He was German, but he came here to get to the polytechnic. I think he wanted to teach, or to study physics, but he failed the arts part of the entrance exam, so he went to live in Aarau, and he passed with the next intake. But he was always questioning and probing. Even with his teachers. He took nothing for granted. Not physics. Not *people*.'

The man's eyes welled up suddenly, and Anne-Marie was shocked to see him put his hand to his brow. She put her hand on his shoulder. 'Please? Are you all right?'

'I'm sorry. I was just thinking. He and I were similar in so many ways. But I learned to take people for granted. Never again!'

She had a call from inside, and served a new customer, took a bill from another table, wiped two more clean, polishing away rings left by dirty coffee cups, before returning to the strange, scruffy man. She found him intriguing. He looked like an example of a man who had seen his homeostasis eroded to nothing, like a man who had passed through the levels of Maslow's Triangle. He was a case study for a phsychologist.

'It was on the tram, you say?' she asked.

'Einstein had a brilliant idea one day, sitting on the tram heading away from that clock there.'

She looked at it. A large face painted onto the medieval tower. Not hugely tall, but imposing in its squat solidity.

Figures adorned the wall: on the left a knight holding his sword, point down, his left hand held up as if in benediction, while a man and woman cowered at the other side. Over them a cloaked man loomed. The great clock hands gleamed gold, their symbols of sun and moon catching the light.

'You know, he'd always struggled with the idea of light. That was his first revelation, if you like. He had been having a miserable time. He married young, and he and his wife had already had a little girl, I think called Lieserl, and she died very young. Two or so. Just imagine it: young Einstein had a wife to support, he had this little girl die, and his wife became pregnant again, and he had no idea what to do for money. There was one job, which was a six day a week job in the patent office, but it wasn't what he wanted. He was always determined to make his name as a physicist, I imagine. All his life he had been fascinated with how things worked. And physicists can be quite single-minded. Focused, you could say.'

'Really?' she smiled.

'I used to be like that. I remember I was intrigued from an early age. In my case it was seeing a torch that first inspired me. I wanted to know how a self-contained device like that could bring light. It seemed so... miraculous.'

'He didn't have torches, did he?'

'Not at the turn of the century. But he saw a compass, and that enthralled him as a child. He wanted to know how that could work. And then later he began to be interested in pure theoretical physics. He wasn't bothered by mundane devices. His fascination was with the secrets of the universe. But he was only a man. An ordinary man.'

'So,' she said. She cast a glance behind her at the people in the bar, but there was no one seeking her attention. This really was a slow day.

'And then he had the idea on the tram. You see, he had been thinking for years about light.'

She nodded, but couldn't help a chuckle. 'Light? He was

a real, how say you? Geek?'

'Yes, I suppose so,' the man said. He had an apologetic smile on his face now, as though he realised how he must have sounded. 'I am sorry. I have spent my entire life thinking of him, trying to improve on his work. Please, I am sorry.'

He was about to rise from the metal table and leave. There was a sense of ineffable sadness that had engulfed him, and Anne-Marie felt it was her fault, as if she had slapped him down. His enthusiasm for Einstein had been so all-consuming, she saw.

'Please,' she said. 'You have not told me of his dream.'

'I am boring you,' he said, without accusation, only a gloomy certainty. 'I bore everyone. I used to bore... but I won't talk of them.'

'No. Please, I would like to hear.'

He looked about him. A tram rattled slowly on its way past them, and a spark flared from the overhead catenary lines. 'You see that? It's only the energy you see there. Pure; simple. No one realised that before Einstein.' He looked at her almost questioningly, and then sighed and sat again. There was a look of quiet desperation about him.

'He saw that?'

'Not with the electricity, no. It was light that caught his imagination. He was a teenager, I think, when he began to wonder about it and how it worked. You see, everybody believed that light must be like sound, that its energy depended on something filling space. They even had a term for it: 'The Luminiferous Ether', they called it. They believed something must be there in space, because, after all, nature abhors a vacuum. That was what they used to say. But Einstein thought about it on a different level. He began to think, if he was flying through space at the speed of light, holding a mirror in front of his face, would he see his reflection?'

'He would not see his reflection presumably, since the light could never reach the mirror from his face if the mirror is receding from it at the same speed. He would be invisible, like a vampire!'

'Ah, but no!' he said, and turned to face her. 'You see, what Einstein realised was that, even if he were travelling at the speed of light, he would *still* see his reflection. The light would take the same time to reach the mirror and get reflected back into his eyes as it would if he were standing still. Because 'standing still' is *relative* when it comes to light.'

'My English, perhaps, is not so good.'

'I am sorry. But, you see, what Einstein realised was, light was *different*. While everyone else was looking for their "luminiferous ether" that allowed light to be transported (and not finding it because it didn't exist), Einstein proposed that light itself always moved through space at a constant speed. So as an observer approaches the speed of light, the flow of time itself changes. If the tram was moving fast enough, he thought that the clock, relative to him, would be counting the seconds more slowly. You see? *All* motion is relative. And an observer, like him, holding his mirror before his face, would still see himself. Because light itself cannot be constrained. It must always move at a constant speed, no matter what the velocity of the observer. It was,' he said, gazing at the clock with that sadness returning to replace his brief animation, 'a remarkable achievement. A philosopher's conception, not a mathematician's or physicist's. As if a man could travel that fast, as if he could slow down time to hold it in his grasp!'

He reached out as if to clutch at the moment, and Anne-Marie stood very still, very alert, unwilling to break the spell that had swallowed them both.

'And you came all this way to see his clock?' she said after a moment.

His hand fell to the table. 'Sort of. I had to see the clock before I die.'

She smiled. 'You have finished your coffee. Would you like another? We have cakes, and apfelstrudel.'

'I should be going,' he said. There was again that air of shy desperation about him that she had noticed before.

'You must spend a little longer looking at the clock that inspired your hero, yes?'

'Why not?' he said, and he did try to smile at her, but the effect was too much for the sadness in his eyes. It made him look ghastly.

'I will bring you strudel,' she decided.

It took some minutes to make the coffee and fetch the strudel. He eyed the slice of rolled pastry without enthusiasm, but picked up his fork and tasted a little.

'You are hungry?'

'Not really. Not for a long time,' he said.

'You have studied Einstein for a long time, yes?'

'I became a physicist like him because of his wonderful genius. I thought for a while that I might be capable of achieving the same glory as him. But it wasn't to be.'

'You are a scientist, yes?'

'Of a sort. A poor sort,' he agreed.

'What, you are in a university?'

'A small English university. I am a professor.'

'You are young to be a professor, yes?'

'I was young when I began,' he smiled.

'Oh. But you are still working at the university?'

'Not just now. I have a holiday.'

'Oh?' She was surprised. This was not the time of year for holidaymakers. Most visitors here were locals like the two fraus in the café.

'I had a hard time,' he said, and his fingers were suddenly twining themselves about each other. His eyes had that haunted, terrible fear in them again. 'A crash. A bad accident.'

'Oh, and you were hurt?'

'Not me, no!' he said. 'My wife and son. They were in the car behind me. I was the observer, you see. Moving fast, up in front. I saw the crash behind me, in the mirror. Like Einstein's vision. And then... then I saw them. The car was very small. The lorry driver said she must have swerved into

45

him, but there were so many cars there, we all saw it. He was dozing at the wheel. Dozing? You understand? He had been late for a delivery, so had not slept when he had been supposed to. So my family was killed.'

'Oh, I am so sorry.'

'It's not your fault,' he said, shrugging, staring at the clock again. 'So, I wanted to see the clock, just this once.'

Before I die, he had said, she remembered.

'How was Einstein,' she asked. 'When his little girl died?'

'He must have been distraught. Devastated. To lose your child. It is hideous. The worst thing you can imagine. You are young, but believe me, to lose your little... it is enough to make a man's mind break.'

'Did Einstein stop work?'

'He couldn't. He had to bring in the money. He still had his wife and the new baby to think of. At least I don't have that problem,' he said without mirth.

'And then, when his daughter was dead, that was when he had his moment of Eureka?'

He looked up at her. 'You think I am being foolish? Perhaps I should work harder now that the distractions have been taken away from me? Do you think I am weak?'

'No. But you should be thinking of men like him who passed before you, with their own traumas.'

'Perhaps.'

He was silent for a moment. 'That clock. It is ancient. A fitting memorial to the passage of time. Perhaps as Einstein would have liked it.'

'You think so?'

'I don't know what I think any more. My life was empty before I married. And then we had our little boy, Stephen. Meg and he were there one moment, and the next, they were tangled with the metal of the car. God, it was horrible!'

'I am sorry,' she said softly. 'I cannot imagine how horrible it would be to see your family killed like that.'

'I will soon forget it,' he said absently.

It was a shocking statement. To see the man so distraught one moment, and then to hear him make such a cold, unfeeling statement, that was chilling to her blood. She shivered.

He continued: 'You are right, I suppose. Einstein must have been single-minded. You know in one year, in 1905, he published five major works? The Special Theory, that was the one he thought up here. His concept of synchronising clocks to show that time was relative, that was one of them, then there was the Theory of Relativity. That was considered equal in importance to Newton's *Principia*, and it was written by an unknown. A patent clerk, working in his spare time. He must have been incredibly single-minded. Truly determined to work away at such concepts.'

'A man with great commitment.'

'Yes. A complete anorak, or rather, a man high on the autistic spectrum. Like me, perhaps.'

She studied his face again. The lines of woe on his brow had eased a little. He had hardly touched the strudel or his coffee, and she suddenly realised that she must have been the first person to have expressed interest in him since his wife's death.

'Was it a little time ago, your wife?'

'She died two months ago. I've been trying to get my head in order ever since. But work... the thought of going back to teaching all those young, eager, enthusiastic students, looking at their faces, and thinking my little boy could have turned out like any of them...' the bitterness in his voice was vile. 'I couldn't do that. I would hate them all. My memories of my little Stephen would come back every day.'

'You said that Einstein had another child?'

'Yes. Two sons. But soon after that, he separated from his first wife. He married his cousin.'

'So, life continued.'

'For him, yes.'

'He did much good.'

'I suppose so,' he agreed.

'He looked at the clock and saw order, the logic of a solution. His observer on the tram was his first great thought.'

He smiled. 'Perhaps it was. I don't know which ideas he had first. But if it was his first, it was not his last.'

'But the clock inspired him.'

'It did.'

She heard a call from the café. 'I must go.'

'Of course. I am sorry to have held you up so long. Please, let me...'

'I will come back.'

She returned inside, and every time she looked through the window, she saw his eyes upon her. It was warming in a way. Devastatingly depressing in quite another. She served five more customers, and when she was done, he was gone.

Walking out, she looked up and down the road to see him, but there was no sign. For an instant she thought his face was there on the tram hurrying away along the road away from the clock, but whether it was him or not, she couldn't tell.

Where he had been sitting, pinned to the table by the plate with the strudel upon it, he had left a small envelope, and she wondered whether it meant he would return. It was a thought that was almost attractive. She took the envelope inside to keep it, just in case, and gave it to Jan for safekeeping, before hurrying to serve a trio of businessmen with beer.

'Anne-Marie, that letter. I think you did some good.'

She was back at the bar, and now she frowned at Jan. 'What do you mean?' she demanded.

'I opened it to see if there was anything inside.'

'You were going to see if there was money?' she spat with contempt.

'No! It was just that I thought he might need it. A passport, his insurance – it could have held anything. Maybe told us where to post the letter.'

'What did it say, then?' she asked, thinking again of the pale eyes, the quiet, restrained despair.

'It was a letter, confirming a meeting with Professor Stephen Baxter. From a clinic. You know the sort. A one-way clinic.'

'He was going to kill himself?'

'He had picked his place and time of death. Perhaps he was unwell? Many cancer sufferers want to kill themselves before the pain starts, eh?'

She nodded, but her mind was elsewhere. After what happened to the professor, who could blame him for wanting to end his life, she thought.

She thought about that as she cleared tables. He had come to Bern to see where his hero had achieved his life's greatest works, perhaps, hoping to see the source of his genius before he went to kill himself. A life dedicated to his hero, and then he saw his wife and family die in the mirror, just as if he had been racing away from them with Einstein.

But he had left his letter behind. She hoped he had decided to return to his life, just as Einstein had after the death of his little girl.

That was Anne-Marie's theory. Her special theory.

Afterword:

1905: Albert Einstein and Special Relativity

Professor Jim Al-Khalili

THIS SAD TALE of a man grieving the loss of his family is one that highlights the unforgiving, relentless march of time: in one direction, from past to future. But Einstein, who gave us a far more interesting and complex view of the nature of time, once used the implications of his own special theory of relativity to comfort the grieving widow of a friend. His old teacher, Herman Minkowski, had taught him how his discovery of the constancy of the speed of light for all observers, regardless of their relative motion, leads inexorably and unavoidably to the conclusion that we cannot view three-dimensional space and one-dimensional time as separate, but must combine them into a more beautiful and complete picture of reality: four-dimensional space-time.

You see the old view of space and time, and the one that our common sense still desperately clings to, is that of space being the stage on which events happen, while the passage of time is marked by some imaginary external cosmic clock that ticks off the seconds, minutes, hours and years, at the same rate everywhere in the Universe (even if our puny subjective view of the rate of flow of time changes depending on what we are doing, or how old we are). But if time is itself just another axis, said Einstein, which points (utterly counter-intuitively I might add) at right angles to our normal three spatial axes, then it becomes just another line frozen on a 4-D graph of reality that we can never imagine other than mathematically.

And yet, we now know this to be true. Einstein referred to this picture as the 'block universe' and used it to explain how our present moment, our 'now', is nothing more than a point on this time axis. The constantly changing present instant we are conscious of is no more 'real' or important when viewed from 'outside' the Universe (a vantage point reserved for an omniscient God if you wish) than any other point in time, whether in our past or our future. This was the argument used by Einstein when consoling the widow: that her dead husband still existed at other times within the block universe.

I have no idea if this was of any comfort to her of course.

But is this all just theoretical nonsense? After all, it sometimes seems to me that every Tom, Dick and Harry has his own version of a theory of time; so what makes Einstein's picture of reality so valid? Could this not just be the misguided theory of a crazy genius? It goes without saying that most people do not have a comfortable working understanding of Einstein's special relativity. Indeed, if you ask the average person to state something they know about Einstein's work, they are likely to quote his famous equation, $E=mc^2$. They may even know what the symbols stand for and what the equation means (a given amount of mass, m, can be converted into energy, E, equivalent to the amount of mass multiplied by the square of the speed of light, c).

Anyway, it doesn't matter, since this equation is not the most important thing about relativity. Indeed, it was an afterthought as far as Einstein was concerned and only appeared in a follow-up paper to his paradigm shifting one on the nature of space and time. More specifically, it is his description of the property of light that was so revolutionary, since this is what led, following a series of utterly beautiful and watertight logical and mathematical steps to the overthrow of our old views of space and time.

In his story, Michael Jecks refers to the 'Luminiferous

Ether', that mythical medium believed to be the carrier of light waves. Einstein's genius was to show how this invisible 'stuff', that would pervade all of space, is unnecessary. Light can travel from one place to another without any medium to carry it along – unlike sound waves, for instance, which cannot travel through the empty vacuum of space. But without the ether as an anchor in space, how do we fix the location and timing of events? If you measure a beam of light to have a particular speed, how can you then convince everyone else that you were standing still when you carried out your measurements? After all, the earth is spinning on its axis, orbiting the Sun, which is itself slowly circulating around the Milky Way galaxy, which is in turn on a collision course with Andromeda within our local cluster of galaxies drifting through the infinite cosmos. What does 'standing still' mean? Einstein explained that there is no such thing; all motion is relative. And yet... we would all, incredibly, measure a beam of light to be travelling at the same speed even if we are moving relative to each other at almost light speed ourselves. Clearly something has to give, and it is the nature of distances and time intervals that has to change. If I see two flashes of light a mile in space apart and one second apart in time, then you, whizzing past me in a high-speed rocket, might measure the distance between the two flashes to be only half a mile and happening two seconds apart. Which of us is right?

The answer of course is that we both are, within our own frames of reference.

These ideas are difficult to comprehend when first encountered. It takes a bit more effort and dedication to convince oneself of the unavoidable logical conclusions one is led to. The fact that we still have trouble with these ideas today only highlights Einstein's remarkable genius. But it turns out he was right.

Everything is Moving, Everything is Joined

Stella Duffy

LEWIN MINKOWSKI AND Rachel Taubmann were married beneath the chuppah in the small, light synagogue. Rachel, fully veiled (though Lewin had seen her face already, checked in the ante-room that she was the bride she promised to be, not a substitute ugly stepsister), walked seven times around her bridegroom, the glass was smashed beneath Lewin's foot, they were married. Mr and Mrs Minkowski. Two people, one name.

We were married, my love, remember? We smashed glasses when we cheered our union too forcefully, smashed teeth, bones, body, when we came together not too forcefully, but just forcefully enough. Two into one, two as one.

Lewin and Rachel Minkowski came together and out of the shards of broken glass; away from Germany where they themselves had begun, Mr and Mrs Minkowski began their sons. Oskar was born in 1858, Hermann a long, wanted, waiting time later in 1864. He was a summer baby, born the same year that the Governor General of Vilna, according to the wishes of the Tsar, ordered that all school books be printed only in the Cyrillic alphabet; the banning of the Lithuanian language had begun.

In Cyrillic, letters have numerical values, A equals 1, B equals 2; words and numbers are joined.

In 1872, when Hermann was eight years old, one of the works of fiction that later morphed into part of the infamous Protocols of Zion was first translated into Russian and appeared in St Petersburg; several different fictional works, combining, uniting, presenting as one truth. This was also the year that the Minkowski family returned to Germany, Lewin and Rachel's homeland.

Then. There. Hermann was eight, Oskar was fourteen. They were in Königsberg, Prussia. It was 1872. It was not yet called Germany. It would be.

Here. Now.

Because the Earth is always in motion, because the Earth moves around the Sun, because the Sun moves in the galaxy, the galaxy in the Universe and on and on – and in and in, because the thing, anything, you, me, an apple, is made of atoms, is made of electrons, is made of so much we have yet to know – because everything is moving, there is no true co-ordinate for here. Because time is also moving, there is no true coordinate for now. We cannot measure here and now because we cannot name the one place to begin our calculation, to say let's start here.

We started here.

And yet we like to think we can do this naming, name the moment, that one point of realisation, of understanding, of love. We like to play with this/now and that/then, and we make plans and determine and build on what is always moving, as if it is stationary, as if it will not change. It's all about perception.

I built on what is always moving when I said yes to loving you.

As a boy, Hermann's mathematical aptitude was noticed at the Gymnasium in Königsberg; he started university in the city in 1880 and also studied at the University of Berlin in the winter that bled from 1882 to 1883. It was during that winter the first permanent street lighting was installed in Leipziger Strasse and Potsdamer Platz. Warm electric light for the cold winter nights of Hermann Minkowski's studies.

Albert Einstein was born in Germany in 1879. His family were secular Jews. His father's name was Hermann. His father worked for a company manufacturing electronic equipment.

Everything is moving, everything is joined.

An apple falls from a tree. In the foreground a train travels along a track. In the distance another train, on a parallel track, travels in the same direction. The apple tree is located between both trains. From the train in the foreground it appears that the train in the background is stationary, that it is the tree that is moving, the tree and the falling apple receding, travelling away, travelling back, behind, travelling to where we've been. It's all about perception.

The trains are moving forward in time and in space. An apple has fallen. The trains have passed on. Past? Present.

You love me. Past.

An apple falls from a tree. I give it to you. Present.

In 1883, the French Academy of Sciences awarded the mathematics Grand Prix to both the nineteen-year-old Hermann Minkowski for his manuscript on the theory of quadratic forms and also to Henry Smith, an Irish mathematician who would have been fifty-six, had he not died two months before. The time and the place were good for Minkowski, the timing less so for Smith.

An apple falls from a tree. A man is near that tree. From the first train the man on the ground appears to walk slowly, while on the ground the man perceives himself to be walking quickly. If the train is heading east, the apple tree appears to be heading west at an equivalent speed. Close up the apple tree appears stationary. Nothing is stationary, it is all moving. Both move in reality and in time; it's all about perception. Light is the only constant. See? C. Let there be light. Let c be light.

Hermann Minkowski and David Hilbert became friends at university in Königsberg.

We were friends and then we were lovers. I was married to you, became related to you, our wedding day was an event in space and time, but the only constant is the speed of light in a vacuum, and I was not fast enough to keep up with the bright light of you. Our life was no vacuum.

When Minkowski applied for a job at the University of Bonn, his interview was an oral explanation of a paper on positive definite quadratic forms. He got the job. Years later, this oral presentation became the basis of his ideas on the geometry of numbers. And there is a geometry to love, an equation that is always the same.
(Without, with, with, with.)
(With, without, without, without.)

Back to the trains. The trees alongside the track appear to be passing the east-bound train incredibly fast, they go by in a blur; a distant cow, lumbering slowly, ever so slowly, in the opposite direction, appears stationary. But when the train stops, the cow is moving, the tree stationary. Time passes.
Two clocks. One stationary, one moving. The passage of time appears to slow down for the moving clock.
A thirty-year-old man on Earth ages a day. A thirty-year-old woman, with the exact birthday as the man, in the (non-existent) spaceship travelling at light speed also ages a day. Individually, time is a constant for both people. Separately, the man on Earth and the woman in space are now different

ages. Time for each has passed in the same way. Relative time – his to hers, hers to his – has not.

A thirty-year-old man loves a thirty-year-old woman. She loves him. Love is a constant for both people. His love for her, her love for him, these things are not constant. It's all about perception.

There is space and there is time. Had we world enough and time. We do. And we don't. Relatively speaking. It's all about perception. And an apple falling not mattering as much as it once did. And time passing.

In 1902, Hermann Minkowski, having taught in Zurich (where Karl Jung gained his PhD that same year), and in Königsberg (where Kant held the chair of metaphysics and mathematician Leonard Euler's work led to graph theory) and in Bonn (where Beethoven was born) returned with his family to Göttingen – where the goose girl is kissed by graduating students. David Hilbert had created a position for him in the mathematics department. The old friends, once more in the same time and place, began working together.

I located you, in time, in space. We were once an event, we came together at that place – space – in that time. There are two ways of looking at us, the event of us.

There is this way: with, without, without, without.

And there is this way: without, with, with, with.

I am time-travelling.

Forward, forward, forward, away from you.

In 1905, Albert Einstein, the theoretical physicist, working in the patent office in Bern, introduced the theory of special relativity in a paper he published on the electrodynamics of moving bodies. Six hundred and forty seven kilometres to the north–north–east, Minkowski and Hilbert were working on mathematical physics, Minkowski particularly interested in the simplicity of equations, the elegance of mathematics.

David Hilbert said of this time, working with his friend, 'Our science, which we loved above all else, brought us together; it seemed to us a garden, full of flowers. In it, we enjoyed looking for hidden pathways and discovered many a new perspective that appealed to our sense of beauty.'

There is no moment. No eureka moment. No overflowing bath, no hypotenuse to square, no apple falling. There is just time. And space. And it was noticed, noted, united. Made a moment and another moment and another moment. Time. A moment of time. A moment of time and space, four – not three – points, to measure all points.

Hermann Minkowski and David Hilbert walk through a garden together. They look at the flowers, a train goes by. A man in the train sees that Minkowski and Hilbert appear to be passing him. The garden (if it could see) would see both the train and Minkowski and Hilbert moving. The train (if it could see) would see the train tracks as moving. The train tracks (if they could see) see the train and the men pass by. And what do the flowers see? The flowers that are the ideas in the garden of science? They see time.

Hermann Minkowski is a mathematician. He wants the equation that makes sense of what is. And what is, is that space and time are linked. Have always been linked. It's just that Minkowski sees this. It's all about perception.

There is this way to write it : $(+, -, -, -)$

And there is this way : $(-, +, +, +)$.

Length, breadth, depth… and time. Together. Spacetime. Simple. Revolutionary. Quiet.

Mr Newton's law believed it could be possible, if we travelled fast enough, to catch up with a beam of light, with a point in that beam. Mr Maxwell's law of electromagnetism told us we can't; that point of light is travelling at a constant speed away from us, always away. And then Mr Einstein's special relativity found a way through the problem – time and space are not immutable concepts, identically experienced by everyone. In special relativity, time and space become mutable ideas, their appearance and form depending on the observer's state of motion.

A man travels at ten miles an hour is irrelevant unless we know what he is travelling past, from, toward. Simone de Beauvoir quoted Goethe, 'I love you, is it any of your concern?' Lennon and McCartney wrote, 'She loves you'. Yeah yeah. Yeah. 'I love' is irrelevant unless we know who or what is loved. You were loved. Are loved. Light travels at six hundred and seventy million miles an hour whether anyone is watching or measuring or not, regardless of where from or where to. I love, regardless of you.

Hermann Minkowski and David Hilbert are walking in a flower garden in Göttingen in 1905. It is a sunny day, probably. It is perhaps 11am. Maybe they are taking a break from thinking about mathematical physics, maybe they are talking about their wives or their children or their jobs, the business of academia, maybe they are not talking about science at all. Maybe they will soon stop walking and sit for *kaffee und kuchen*. They have been friends and colleagues since they were undergraduates in Königsberg; they know each other well. Maybe Hermann Minkowski is thinking he might buy some flowers for his wife Auguste, maybe he is pondering the geometry of numbers. Certainly the flowers have their own geometry.

Perhaps the garden is 20 metres from the university office. Maybe the garden is quite small, only 100 metres by 100 metres. Maybe it is spring, there are plants, but they are not yet fully grown, somewhere between ten and one hundred centimetres above the earth. Some of them will become bigger – higher, wider, deeper – in time.

It is 11.10am. It is time to leave the garden and go back

to work, away from the work that is the discussion of ideas in the garden to the work that is the discussion of ideas inside. Different spaces, same work.

It is time to leave this time and space and go on to another time and space, inside the building. Maybe Hermann Minkowski, walking in a flower garden, in Göttingen, Germany, with his friend and colleague David Hilbert, understands, as he checks his watch, that time has passed as they walked in this garden. Maybe the mathematician Hermann Minkowski, who taught courses attended by the young Albert Einstein, is thinking of Euclidean geometry – the measuring of space, of things in space – and maybe Hermann Minkowski, who has been married to Auguste Adler for eight years, and is the father of two young daughters, Lily who is seven, and Ruth who is three, maybe, this German Jew who was born in Russia a quarter century before Adolf Hitler, who is walking with David Hilbert just four years before he himself will die at only forty-four of a sudden appendicitis, maybe Hermann realises, looking at the time that has passed, in this garden, with his friend with whom he talks about ideas, that young Albert Einstein's theory of special relativity can be easier explained – far more simply, cleanly, beautifully explained – if time and space (11.13am, the flower garden, outside his office in Göttingen, Germany) are considered together. The three dimensions of space, and the one of time, four dimensions as one. Spacetime.

In 1908, Hermann Minkowski wrote a new paper and gave a speech to the Assembly of German Natural Scientists and Physicians. It was their eightieth such assembly. Minkowski explained that the work of Lorentz and Poincaré, which in turn led to Einstein's special relativity, could be better understood, more clearly, more elegantly, by bringing time to space and space to time. By taking the three dimensions of space and adding the fourth that is time.

And with spacetime, the (relatively) young Albert

Einstein developed the general theory of relativity.

In 1909 Hermann Minkowski died of a ruptured appendix. He was forty-four.

Here's a thing: before spacetime, before Einstein and Minkowski and Lorentz and Poincaré, and all the others, before them, back when, back then, with Newton, we believed gravity was all. We believed it held us, elliptically, to the sun. We believed that if the sun were to collapse in on itself, to explode, to otherwise die, then we too, our planet, this little Earth, that we here would be simultaneously – at the same time – thrown out, thrown off course, away forever. (Or in forever, forever in.) Now we know better, we know that it takes eight minutes for the light of the sun to reach us. Eight minutes for that light, travelling at light speed, to find our Earth. The Sun could die and we would only find out eight minutes later, when the light failed. It might feel as if we found out at the same time as it happened, because we wouldn't know it had happened until we saw it, but it would already have happened.

I didn't know you had gone until long after the fact. I didn't know you had left me until I saw the evidence – you, the body of you, the cold, waxy body of you. You had, of course, left much earlier. We always do.

We are not held by gravity to the Sun, we are held in gravity, in the warp and weft of it, with the Sun. Not to or from but with. Not one and the other, but together. And if that Sun, our Sun, fell, collapsed, exploded, imploded, died, it would be the ripple of that disturbed, rolling, roiling weft we felt as much as the absence of light.

I feel the absence of you. I feel the loss of you as much as I see that you are not here. Like those who first understood spacetime, I know our gravity is much bigger than just the pull of me to you, you to me. It surrounds me and holds me up, over, under, in. It holds me through and through. Without you, I am not held.

Hermann Minkowski said, 'Henceforth space by itself, and time by itself, are doomed to fade away into mere shadows, and only a kind of union of the two will preserve an independent reality.'

Two meaning far more as one than as their separate two. Two mattering far more together than apart. Two as one to make sense of both two and of one.

I am a shadow and there is no light to make me.

There is a Buddhist concept, *esho funi,* it translates as 'two but not two, one but not one.' That's spacetime my love, that was us. And in time, because of time, because neither space nor time can ever part again — it is us still.

Everything is moving, everything is joined. It's all about perception.

Afterword:

1908: Hermann Minkowski and Space-time

Dr Robert Appleby

THE IDEA THAT our point of view changes how we see the things around us, and yet certain things are the same for all observers, is the heart of how we view the space-time structure of our universe.

Minkowski had a simple idea. To treat space and time on the same footing, as though they are equal and entirely equivalent. All well and good, and easy to say, but what does it mean?

Think of a room, which has width, length and height. These three quantities are all that's needed to identify a single point in the room. We would say that a certain point, for example the tip of a lampshade, is located 3m from the wall, 5m along the wall and 2m in the air and this uniquely identifies this point in the room. These three numbers specifying the location in space of the point are equivalent to an arrow pointing at the tip of the lampshade and locating it. So the three numbers, let's call them components, are wrapped up inside a single arrow (or vector) pointing at the lampshade, and wholly equivalent to each other in terms of mathematical status. Of course we need to choose a starting point for this arrow, which is the same as specifying the point where the three numbers are equal to zero. Distances are measured from this starting point (or origin).

Minkowski, taking the ball from all the people who developed these ideas of arrows and vectors, and from Einstein who formulated the special theory of relativity, thought of the arrow to a point in space-time in terms of not three but four numbers. Three of these numbers tell us where the point is in space, just like the three numbers we needed to locate the tip of the lampshade, and one number tells us where the point is in time. These four numbers sit together to form an arrow in four-dimensional space-time. There is no special distinction between these four numbers – space and time are treated the same – and they sit with equal status inside the same arrow. The collection of all these points, all described by four equally important numbers, is called space-time. The hyphen is important. It's not space, and so needing three numbers to identify a point, or time, needing one number to identify a time, but space-time.

There is a fascinating feature of these arrows in four-dimensional space-time that comes about because the universe we live in is causal. Causality is a fancy scientific word for the everyday experience of cause and effect, so a person is born before they die, or gets into a car before driving down the street. This idea of causality has a deep and profound relationship to the length of our arrow in four-dimensional space-time and it all comes down to the old school favorite of the theorem of Pythagoras. Going back to the lampshade, if we decided to calculate the length of the arrow pointing at it, we take the square of each of the numbers in the vector, add them and then find the length of the arrow is the square root of this number. So when we said a certain point is located 3 m from the wall, 5m along the wall and 2m in the air, the distance to this point (from the origin) is the square of 3 (9), added to the square of 5 (25) and added to the square of 2 (4), which gives 38, and we then take the square root of 38 to get 6.16m. This means the distance to the point from our origin, or equivalently the length of the arrow, is 6.16m. To do this, we intuitively added the squares of all the numbers.

If we now think about our arrow in four-dimensional space-time, and decide to calculate the distance to a point in the space-time (from the origin) then we would start by squaring all the numbers making up the arrow and then add them. This sounds sensible, and is just what we did in the example of the room. However this is wrong, and it's wrong because if we do this we may violate causality. Or, equivalently, somebody would be able to think that someone else died before they were born. We don't want causality to be violated. To make everything work out and naturally build causality into our ideas of space-time, we still square the components of the arrow but instead of adding them all we need to add some of them together and subtract one of them. This ensures causality. To help us remember which squared components to add and which squared components to subtract we can write down a 'metric', which is simply a recipe to do just that. In the space-time of Minkowski this metric looks a little like '+ – – –', with some bits a plus sign and some bits a negative sign. It's the time part that we add if we subtract the space part, but what matters is we do a different thing for space and time. So there's a difference between space and time in space-time, but not an obvious one.

A remarkable thing about points in space-time is that the separation in space or the separation in time between any two space-time points depends on your point of view. But the separation in space-time, or doing Pythagoras's Theorem on our four dimensional vector, does not. We say that this four dimensional length which separates two points is space-time (or 'Lorentz') invariant and has a length which does not depend on your point of view. So some things depend on your point of view but some things do not. And that is our universe, and it comes down to simple geometry.

And what's more, to find out how people in different states of motion view the space and time separation of two space-time points we need to make a rotation in four dimensions through an imaginary angle.

But that is another story.

The Woman who Measured the Heavens with a Span

Sara Maitland

Magellanic Cloud (Great) so bright. It always makes me think of poor Henrietta. How she loved the 'Clouds'... Very, very, sad. -- Annie Cannon. unpublished diary 1923

Miss Leavitt inherited in a somewhat chastened form, the stern virtues of her Puritan ancestors. She took life seriously. Her sense of duty, justice and loyalty was strong. For light amusements she appeared to care little. She was a devoted member of her intimate family circle, unselfishly considerate in her friendships, steadfastly loyal to her principles, and deeply conscientious and sincere in her attachment to her religion and church. She had the happy faculty of appreciating all that was worthy and lovable in others, and was possessed of a nature so full of sunshine that, to her, all of life became beautiful and full of meaning.
[1] *(Solon Bailey. Obituary notice.* Popular Astronomy *1922)*

She tries to focus on the pain. Even for her this is difficult.

Once upon a time a little girl — *how old had she been? About ten perhaps, still small enough to have to reach upwards to hold her father's hand...* once upon a time a little girl was walking home from evening service holding her father's hand. It was early evening but already winter-dark and the snow piled on the street sides sparkled in the moonlight. She had a brand new pair of button boots and a little rabbit-skin muff of which she was inordinately proud, and inordinately anxious that her parents should not notice the pride or they might take the muff away. To set against these delights were the horrible mittens, lumpy and two different sizes. She had knitted them on her mother's instruction for her little brother's Christmas present, but her knitting was so bad and clumsy that her mother made her wear them herself. When she thought about her pride or the mittens she briefly felt both aggrieved and guilty. But she did not think about them much because there were all the other nicer things to think about: the muff and the boots and Christmas coming only next week and how large and warm her father's hand was and how firmly but kindly he was holding hers, despite the ugly lumpy mittens and what a good mood he was in and how the tune of 'While Shepherds Watched their Flocks by Night', which they had been singing in Chapel, danced in her head and seemed to hold all the other bits and pieces into one happiness.

And then, suddenly, there was an extra, bonus happiness. She looked up and there, above the Boston street, was a sharp streak of light, and then another, as though someone had suddenly scratched the sky with a sharp knife. And a couple of moments later, another.

'Papa,' she said, 'is it angels?'

'What?'

'Look. Oh, do look up, Papa.'

He looked up. They both stood still for a moment and then another vivid streak rushed overhead.

'No,' he said smiling, 'it's not angels. It's shooting stars. But it might almost be angels, because they always appear just before Christmas. Another work of Our Good Lord, and just as praiseworthy. They are called the Geminids.'

Her father knew everything – or nearly everything. He didn't know about her pride in her muff. At least she hoped not. She liked it when he told her things, especially if they were things her mother did not know, which covered more or less everything interesting. She wanted to keep his attention.

'What makes them, Papa?'

'God makes them.'

She draws in her breath, and is careful now, 'Yes of course, Papa, but *how* does God manifest his glory in them?'

She had got it right; he gave a bark of genuine laughter and said, 'Oh Ettie,' very affectionately. 'I understand they are little bits of dust and rock burning up out there in space.'

'How far away?'

'We don't know. We can't tell. We can't measure out there; we don't know how to.'

'Why not?'

'Well,' he paused. 'Think about it. See that big bright star up there, the one in the line of three. Now can you see there is a little one just beside it, not bright at all? How can we tell if it is smaller and less bright or further way? We can't. So we can't measure how far away anything out there is.'

'Is it God's secret? Or would He like us to be able to?'

'Ettie,' he says solemnly as she knew he would, 'God likes us to know things. Whatever anyone tells you, never forget that God always likes us to know and understand more about His mighty works and deeds. He wants us to have knowledge so that we may have wisdom. Everything we know is to His glory, so the more we know, the more we can give Him glory. He is a great force of intelligence, and especially in his creation. We must never be afraid to learn and to know.'

She knows her mother doesn't think that and is gratified by his trust in telling her.

'Well,' she says, as still more Geminids shoot away overhead, 'I think that's what I'll do when I'm big; I'll glorify God by finding a way to measure up to the stars.'

'That would be excellent, Ettie; but you will have to learn to pay better attention. Once there was an astronomer, a star man, called Mr. Herschel. He made his own telescope and looked and looked and he wrote down all the new things he saw. And other astronomers did not believe him and said to him, in angry letters, 'We do not see what you see.' But he was ready with an answer, 'Perhaps you do not take the care in your observations that I do.'[2] He took great care; he would leave his telescope out in the cold for hours so it would be the right temperature; sometimes he even stood out in the cold himself so his warmth wouldn't get in the way and that's how he was able to learn so much. If you want to glorify God through learning about the stars you'll have to learn to concentrate. Your mamma tells me, I am sorry to say, Ettie, that you don't always pay good attention, or take enough pains.'

'I'll try to learn,' she muttered.

'Good. Mr. Herschel had a sister who was his assistant; perhaps you too could be an assistant to an astronomer. I believe that would please God very much.'

So she had learned to pay attention, to concentrate, to focus.

Now, nearly half a century later, she tries to focus on her pain; to angle the mirror of her mind so as to cast the clearest possible light on the black spots of pain, sharp against the smooth white surface of her belly. It is her job to calculate their brightness and record their relationship to each other and to herself. If she could still sit up and write she would, in her tiny immaculate handwriting, list them one by one, their position, their colour and their magnitude, in numbers and with annotation.

This is what she had done for her North Polar Sequence, the 96 stars which she had recorded with such authority that the magnitude of every other star in the sky was graded by her standard. Her very high standard. When, for just a few moments, she can leave the careful study of her pain she occasionally thinks of her North Polar Sequence with some modest pride, but not often. The pain is her data now and she has always found it difficult to break her intense concentration on the data, which is why she was good at her job. Whatever they may say, she knows it was the concentration that made her deaf, not deafness that made her concentrate. Compared to the distant silence of the stars there is nothing else much worth listening to, not since her father died. But even when she takes a little time off from measuring the pain, she does not really care very much about the North Polar Sequence. She prefers to think about the Magellanic Clouds – *Nubecula Major* and *Nubecula Minor* – those beautiful drifts of shining sidereal smoke that had guided Magellan round the world, once he had sailed too far south to see the Pole Star; and about the 1777 Cepheid Variables within the clouds, which she discovered and which will guide the astronomers to the size of the universe once they have sailed too far out for parallax and for which she will always be remembered. Her pride here is less modest.

If she could find the energy, she could push away the pillows, lie flat on her back, stretch her arms out and use parallax to measure the distance to the pain. From fingertip to fingertip her physical span is 64 inches. If she can then measure the angle from her fingertips to the points of pain, she can triangulate and work out how far away the pain really is, because it is the pleasing nature of a triangle that it can be fully drawn on the information provided by the length of one side and two angles, or the lengths of two sides and one angle. That is why they know how far away the Moon is, and Venus measured when it transited the Sun. Then they had widened the length of the baseline, doing the sums at either end of the year – a base line of 186 million miles. This is easier for her to think about than it is for some of them because she still believes that God's glorified in measurements and that 186 million miles is not that much in relation to the infinite glory. They had pinned down Alpha Centauri, and Vega and 61 Cygni. Nearly 100 stars have been measured now, but most of them, like the points of her pain, are too far away, the shift is too small and parallax fails. It is huge out there, she knows that, as huge as the pain.

Then, gradually, after paying perfect attention through drawn-out, pain-filled nights and wearisome pain-filled days, she perceives that the points of pain pulse, variable and rhythmic. The intensity of blackness deepens and expands; then slowly it greys out a little, narrowing and paling on the white background of her belly. It gives her a strange joy that her pains should be periodic, should wax and wane on a steady beat, on a rhythm. Like her stars. For Henrietta Leavitt, head of Stellar Photometry at the Harvard Observatory, stars come black on white, dark on light. Occasionally Edward Pickering, the Observatory Director and her boss, had led her off to the telescope itself and let her look at flaming white stars on the deep black sky. She had never really cared for it – there was too much mess, of weather and technology; it kept her up late and her doctor had warned her that the cold night air would hurt her ears. She prefers her stars as neat columns of numbers, black on white paper or as tiny marks, black on the white photometric plates. She prefers them at her own desk and in her own time. She likes to be able to compare yesterday's stars with how they were last month or last year or today. She likes to feel intimate with them and in control. The photographic plates were her own black stars. Certainly now the black pains are her own pains. And they pulse.

She can still laugh at herself. She knows that her pains are not the stars at all; that the pain is here, contained neatly within her tired body and that when she dies, which will be soon, they will die with her. Meanwhile the stars will burn on. Her finely observed and immaculately measured Cepheid Variables will continue to pulse in a preordained and constant rhythm; the period of their pulsations will always be a measure of their intrinsic brightness. If any two Cepheid Variables pulsate at the same speed they will have the same intrinsic brightness. If one of the two seems to be dimmer then it *is* further away. You can tell how much further away using an elegantly simple, completely reliable aspect of light itself: light spreads and diminishes according to the Inverse Square Law: so if one of the two variable stars is four times dimmer than the other but has the same pulse rate then it is twice as far away. If it is nine times dimmer it is three times as far away. She found 1,777 Cepheid Variables in the Magellanic Clouds where no one had ever seen any before.

She smiles. They had laughed at her. 'What a variable-star fiend Miss Leavitt is – one can't keep up with the roll of new discoveries,' wrote a colleague to Edward Pickering. Even the *Washington Post* had commented flippantly 'Henrietta S. Leavitt has discovered twenty-five new variable stars. Her record almost equals Frohman's [the famous theatrical agent].' It was admiring laughter, teasing like her brothers'; she knew that and liked it. But her mother had been embarrassed – being in the papers was not ladylike.

'Mother,' she had said gently, 'it is astronomer-like.'

'I don't care about that,' her mother had said pettishly.

That is how it is. Always. She had not even been able to go and hear Pickering presenting her paper, because single ladies ought to go home for Christmas. Their widowed mothers are more important than measuring the stars.

She always takes very great care in her observations, measures very precisely, and writes very clearly so that people can see what she has seen. She had tabulated 25 of the new variables on a graph on axes of periodicity and brightness. There is undeniably, as she wrote, 'a remarkable relationship.' So now they can measure the distances and darling – though she has never met him – darling Ejnar Hertzsprung, a European astronomer has proved it. He has made a 'very pretty use' of her discovery and begun to calculate the size of the Universe. It is the first time anyone has been able to measure space, to begin to calculate how big it all might be. She, Henrietta Swan Leavitt, computer at the Harvard Observatory, has found a way to measure the vast distances out beyond the reach of parallax. She has lit the first 'standard candle' to the glory of the Lord. It will never be put out. Once upon a time she told her father she would and she has.

And if she had been given time perhaps she would have been able to calibrate her Cepheid yardstick and turn the theory into actual numbers, real distances. Someone will do it anyway now she has given them the tools; already the debate about the size of the Universe is hotting up. This fills the spaces in between the pains with white joy. It did not really matter who, though she likes to think she could have contributed; it would have been good fun and God would have been glorified again.

She has never been given the time. Pickering and her pain have had other agenda and she is the servant of both. Once upon a time her father had told her that she could be an assistant to an astronomer. He had been right. Her mother is still winning. She is not a real astronomer; she is one of Pickering's computers, one of his girls, cheaper than men, than graduates, than real astronomers. She is employed, at rock-bottom wages, to measure and record the precise brightness of each star in the North Polar Sequence, or anywhere else in the sky that Pickering is minded to attend to. He was kind, he was respectful, he was knowledgeable and he was her boss. She represses the thought that as slave owners go he was a good slave owner, but that slavery had been abolished elsewhere. All his girls had laughed and chafed to an equal degree under his benevolent despotism.

She had liked him because he was a meticulous observer. She chafed because that was all he believed in; he never asked what they were observing so carefully *for*. He never encouraged theorising, convinced that the job of the Harvard Observatory was purely to accumulate facts. And... *she does not know, she still does not know and it is better not to think about it, especially now the pain may warp her charity*... from the day he read out her paper, her beautiful groundbreaking paper on the *Nebecula Minor* and its Cepheid Variables he never found time to set her to work on that again, even though she knew, because the other computers told her, that other astronomers all over the world wrote to him begging for more. Even after she completed the immaculate North Polar Sequence he had thought of other projects for her. So 'she had hardly begun work on her extensive program of photographic measurements of variable stars.'[3]

Finally Pickering died, after over forty years as Director. They have appointed Harlow Shapley to succeed him. She may have doubts about the carefulness of his observations, but none about his willingness to theorise. And none about the admiration in which he holds her work. He was one of those who had asked Pickering for more:

> Her discovery of the relation of period to brightness is destined to be one of the most significant results of stellar astronomy, I believe. I am quite anxious to have her opinion.

He had arrived in the Spring and was treating her like a colleague. But it is too late now; the pain has become her new slave owner. She is laid out like a nebula on the sea of pain focused on the slow rhythmic pulsing. Everyone knows. When Shapley, as the new director of the Harvard Observatory, as her new boss if she still needs a boss, comes to visit her, he brings her flowers not anxiety for her opinion. She will never have time or opportunity to measure any more stars, their pulse rates and their intrinsic brightness.

It really does not matter very much. All the Cepheid Variables in the lovely Magellanic Clouds will go on pulsing, in their subtle elegant way, go on revealing what they have to reveal of the glory of God and the knowledge of his ways. Shapley's flowers are beautiful too. Everything seems beautiful now. Perhaps death will be beautiful and will certainly bring new knowledge so that she may get wisdom, new wisdom. Now it is a different hymn that dances in her mind:

> Out beyond the shining of the furthest star
> God is ever spreading, infinitely far.

So she is smiling when she dies. She sees the glory of God coming like a shooting star to greet her. God judges gently, questioning her humility.

'Who has marked off the waters in the hollow of a hand?'

'Only you, Lord.'

'Who has weighed the mountains in scales and hills in a balance?'

'Only you, Lord.'

'Who has measured the heavens with a span and called each star by its name.'

'You have, Lord.'

'And who else?'

'I have.'

'Well done thou good and faithful servant. Come enter into the joy of your Father.'

Her last moments are filled with modest pride, which turns out to be very acceptable.

She is buried on the 14th December. It is a grim day, bitterly cold. Because of the dark clouds the biting wind and the general desire to get inside as quickly as possible, no one even remembers that this is the day of the Geminid shower.

Afterword:

1912: Henrietta Leavitt and the Period-Luminosity Relation

Dr Tim O'Brien

YEARS OF CAREFUL measurement of photographic images of the sky led Henrietta Leavitt to a discovery that is fundamental to how astronomers measure the scale of the Universe.

Distances in space are so vast that we don't write them down in kilometres, there'd be too many zeros. We use units called parsecs or sometimes light years. Light travels at 300,000 kilometres per second. At this speed, it takes eight minutes to reach us from the Sun (a distance of about 150 million km or 93 million miles). This same light, passing by the Earth, would take a further 4.2 years to reach the nearest other star, 40,000,000,000,000 km away. We call this distance 4.2 light years. Our galaxy, the Milky Way, contains several hundred billion stars and is about 100,000 light years across. Light from the most distant galaxies we can see has taken billions of years to reach us.

Since we can't just take out an extremely long tape measure we have had to adopt some ingenious ways of measuring their distances.

The most accurate and direct way is called parallax. It relies on measuring the apparent change in position of a star as seen from different points on the Earth's orbit around the Sun. The closer the star the more its position appears to move relative to stars in the background. However, the change in position is tiny. So, although fundamental, its use is limited to relatively nearby regions of space. It is used however as the first rung on a 'distance ladder', calibrating other techniques that work at greater distances.

One of the most common methods of estimating much greater distances in the Universe is the use of 'standard candles'. Imagine two identical candles which shine with equal brightness. If one is placed farther from an observer than the other, then it would appear fainter. In fact the brightness follows an inverse square law: so for example if it appeared 100 times fainter this means it is 10 times farther away (10 squared = 100). In practise, of course, the candles are replaced by stars or other objects which are thought to be of the same intrinsic brightness. The technique then allows their relative distances to be estimated. If the distance to the nearer one is known by some other method, say parallax, then the actual distance to the farther one can be calculated.

At the time that Henrietta Leavitt was working at the Harvard Observatory, we did not know the scale of the Universe. Indeed in 1920 there was a 'Great Debate' on the subject between astronomers Harlow Shapley (who later replaced Pickering as Director of Harvard Observatory as described in Sara's story) and Heber Curtis. Curtis argued that the 'spiral nebulae', the most famous of which was the Great Nebula in Andromeda, were galaxies in their own right, lying outside our own Milky Way galaxy. Shapley however thought that the Milky Way was itself huge and that the Universe was essentially one large galaxy. Objects like the Andromeda Nebula were simply clouds of gas inside the Milky Way. Leavitt's work proved crucial to resolving this debate.

Leavitt worked as a 'computer' at the Observatory. Before iPads and PC's, a computer was a human being who carried out calculations by hand or with the aid of mechanical devices. Commonly the computers were educated women who found it one of the few ways into a scientific career. Observatories and other organisations would often employ teams of computers at rather low salaries. Problems would be organized so that they could be fed into the 'computer' room, worked on by a team of people and the answer fed out at the other end. Beginning with astronomical calculations of the orbit of Halley's comet in the 1700's, this practice continued through to applications such as atomic weapons development during World War II.

Leavitt's work focused on the detailed analysis of photographs of the sky taken with Harvard's 24-inch Bruce Telescope in Arequipa, Peru. Large glass plates covered in photographic emulsion were used to record the images. These were then returned to Harvard. Her job was to take each plate, mount it on a device which illuminated it from behind and, with the aid of a magnifying eyepiece, carefully measure the sizes of the black dots representing each star on the negative image. The larger the dot, the brighter the star. Each plate would contain many thousands of stars. This was a painstaking task, requiring patience, attention to detail, accuracy and stamina.

Sara's story makes clear how the Observatory Director, Edward Pickering instructed her to work on the North Polar Sequence and other important tasks in calibrating the brightness of stars. However, her major contribution and lasting legacy was her work on the Cepheid variable stars in the Small Magellanic Cloud.

Many stars change in brightness. Some because of flares or explosions, others because of eclipses by an orbiting companion star. The Cepheid variables repeatedly brighten and then fade with periods ranging from a few days to a few months. They are named after the prototypical example, delta Cephei. Although the cause was not clear when Leavitt was studying them, we now know that this variability is because the stars pulsate. The combination of changing size and temperature causes the variation in brightness.

The Large and Small Magellanic Clouds were of particular interest. Looking like small clouds in the night sky, we now know that these are actually two dwarf galaxies close to our Milky Way. Most easily viewed from the southern hemisphere, they are named after Magellan, the famous explorer who sailed the southern oceans.

Plates of the Small Magellanic Cloud were sent from Peru back to Harvard for analysis. Leavitt carefully measured the brightnesses of stars on repeated photographs over months and years. Since the stars in the 'Cloud' were grouped together, they were all approximately the same distance from us, and so there was no confusion caused by one star appearing fainter because it was much farther away. Like many of her colleagues, Leavitt was not simply a human calculator – she improved her measurement techniques, thought carefully about the data she collected and what it meant. In particular, she noticed that the brightest Cepheids rose and fell in brightness more slowly than the fainter ones. This has become known as the Period–Luminosity Relation. Pickering published Leavitt's statement of her results on 25 of these stars in a Harvard Circular of 1912.

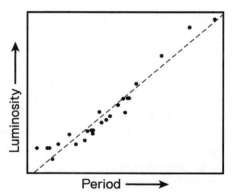

Leavitt's 25 Cepheid variables showing the Period–Luminosity Relation

By simply measuring the period with which the brightness of a Cepheid rises and falls, the relation can be used to determine its luminosity, the intrinsic brightness of the star. A comparison with its apparent brightness then allows the use of the 'standard candle' technique to determine its distance.

Leavitt's discovery has proved crucial to measurements of distances in astronomy.

In the mid-1920's Edwin Hubble found Cepheid Variable stars in the Andromeda Nebula and was able to use Leavitt's relation (as calibrated by Shapley) to measure the distance to the Nebula. This showed that it lay at much greater distances than previously thought, outside our Milky Way. It was therefore a galaxy in its own right, contrary to Shapley's earlier views in the Great Debate on the scale of the Universe.

Working with Milton Humason, Hubble went on to use Cepheids and other indicators to gauge distances to other galaxies. They found that the distant galaxies were all moving away from us, the most distant moving the fastest. This is now a cornerstone of our understanding of the expanding Universe and its origin in the Big Bang.

Even today, Cepheid variables remain a major rung on the cosmic distance ladder. However, developments in technology mean that modern equivalents of Leavitt's painstaking measurements have been massively expanded. For example, OGLE (the Optical Gravitational Lensing Experiment) uses a robotic telescope in Chile to study the Magellanic Clouds and the centre of our Milky Way. Each clear night, about 100 images are automatically taken with CCDs (similar to those in domestic digital cameras, albeit of better quality). These are processed through pipeline software (the modern equivalent of the old 'human computer' room) resulting in huge databases of the changes in brightnesses of hundreds of millions of stars.

The OGLE survey is used to study stellar variability including Cepheids as well as variability caused by the warping of space-time as predicted by Einstein. Other similar automated surveys are used to find planets orbiting other stars or study the explosions of stars which map the expansion of the Universe.

Modern astronomy and our understanding of the

Universe owes a great debt to Henrietta Leavitt and her dedication to the measurement of variable stars in the Magellanic Clouds.

1. Solon Bailey. Obituary notice. *Popular Astronomy* 1922.
2. Not much is known about Henrietta Leavitt's family; but her father, George Rosewell Leavitt, was a Congregational Minister and in 1885 gave a sermon containing this story about Herschel.
3. Obituary notice *Reports of the President 1921-2* Harvard University. Celia Payne-Gaposchkin, an important woman astronomer of the next generation, believed that Leavitt had been 'done a great wrong': 'It was a harsh decision, which condemned a brilliant scientist to uncongenial work and probably set back the study of variable stars for decades.' To the best of our knowledge Leavitt never once complained.

What Kind of Dog

Annie Clarkson

I

THERE IS A *bang bang bang* at the door. Ivan is in bed, asleep with Sara, and it's still dark, six perhaps. Sara tries to light the lamp. 'Do you think it's Vladimir?' she asks with panic in her voice. He fumbles to fasten his gown. There are still moments where she worries about one or other of their children.

'Dr Pavlov,' a voice shouts from outside, and Ivan hurries down the stairs. He finds Pyotr on their doorstep, wet and shivering. Pyotr is one of his assistants from the Institute, one of the men who supervise the kennels.

'What is it, man?'

'The river.' Pyotr struggles for breath. 'It's been rising since yesterday, we can't reach the dogs.'

By now Sara is downstairs with the lamp. She can see that the man's clothing is soaked through. 'My god, what happened to you?'

She brings him further into the house and shouts for their daughter Vera to bring blankets.

They are used to floods in Petrograd. Every September the Neva swells, backed up with water from the Gulf.

'How high is the water there?' Ivan asks.

Pyotr shakes his head and shrugs. 'Worse than I've seen before. Five feet perhaps, or more? It must be flooded inside and the dogs are in their cages.'

83

LITMUS

II

Unwanted dogs. Dogs bought for fifteen kopeks. Laboratory-bred dogs. Dogs raised in isolation. Caged dogs. Free dogs. Working dogs. Non-working dogs. Litters of puppies separated and raised in different environments. Dogs on operating tables. Dogs that died. Dogs that survived. Melancholic dogs with their weak nervous systems that cower in corners or stand passive and unresponsive. Sanguine dogs with their yapping, jumping, yelping, licking. Dogs that are eager to please. Aggressive dogs. Phlegmatic dogs. Choleric dogs. Everyday dogs. Strong dogs. Weak dogs.

III

First they fail to find a boat, then in their battle against the currents, wind and waves, they collide with debris in the water, and with whole trees that have crashed down and are carried along with window frames, milk pails, lost belongings. They argue about which way and how and whether it's safe. There are quiet arguments expressed with tense jaws, tense fingers gripping the oars.

This is the first time Pyotr and Artur have no instructions, either from Dr Pavlov or one of his researchers. There was no Wednesday meeting where they could stand with praktikanty, assistants and doctors to hear what they should do, which dogs would be the subject of which experiments, how such-and-such a dog is progressing, and with what skills and methods such-and-such a doctor is learning about what type of nervous system.

Pyotr's journey to work has never been so physically exhausting. His shoulders ache from pulling so hard on the oars over and over. His hands are wet and sore, and a sickness ebbs and rises with the boat's surging motion as water slaps hard against its sides. He can tell that Artur is finding it difficult as well. He pauses between strokes, resting for the briefest time, before using the whole weight of his upper body to pull back against the flood again.

It has been three days since anyone last saw the dogs.

IV

Sara urges Ivan to sit down, to read or focus on some task or another. 'You are seventy-five years old, Ivan Petrovich, a little old to be going on rescue missions.'

He might have snapped at her a little.

How convenient that she can continue with her creative work, writing in her office between visits to church and the neighbours to see what help she can give. She was bailing water from flooded shops yesterday. How good for her that she has been useful and of purpose to others.

While all he can do is pace around, wait for news, listen to his sons report back from the city about damages to buildings, how Vladimirsky Avenue is blocked with trees and rubble, how the loading bay has been washed away near Tuchkov bridge.

He has heard from Mariia Petrova, and Andreyev Speransky, and Gantt.

But he still can't reach the laboratory. And there are five new dogs that need operations to their parotid glands. Ongoing experiments with forty-seven dogs. New experiments to begin. There are two praktikanty due to start who need assistants to familiarise them with procedure. He needs to assign research topics. Write lectures.

Sara tries to be patient with him, responds with silence or quiet suggestions. She should be used to him by now, know his mood will soon give way to kindness.

V

Artur fastens the boat to a railing and wades towards Pyotr. It takes them a minute or more to unlock the door. Once inside, they head straight to the kennels, hoping the water hasn't reached a critical level.

In the first room, they find all the dogs drowned. The water is above cage-height, and these dogs have not survived. Their swollen bodies are held under water by the roof bars of their cages.

Pyotr finds three surviving dogs in the second room. He's seen dogs die or ill many times, after operations or experiments, but this. Seeing them swim in terror, fighting to keep their heads above the water. He swims to their cage and ducks under the surface to slide the bolt. He comes up for air and then into their cages, pulling each dog down underwater and through the cage door. Paws claw at him and scratch his skin. But he guides them out into the corridor, and goes back into the room for more.

Pyotr and Artur move from cage to cage. They find most have died. Milford. Bek. Max. Avgust. Tuzka.

They gather the surviving dogs in the corridor. The water is still too deep for them. They paddle wildly, their nostrils barely above the water.

'What now?' Pyotr asks.

They need to get them to safety. The laboratory is the closest place, but is still a half-mile from the kennels.

'We could swim with them?' Artur is holding two dogs under their bellies to support them in the water.

'Stupidity,' Pyotr replies, but has no better ideas.

So they take them in two groups on the laboured half-mile swim. By the time they reach the end of their swim with the second group of dogs, they are exhausted.

The animals are dragged out of the flood by waiting researchers from the laboratory. They huddle together in the middle of a first-floor room, while assistants rub them dry with towels, fill bowls with food.

VI

Ivan arrives at the laboratory and ignores his usual routine of checking the coat hooks to see which of his assistants are already in work. He is expecting to find the laboratory in chaos. But there is no barking. No fighting or quarrelling amongst the animals. Remarkable considering these dogs are not all familiar with each other or this room.

Pyotr waves him over to one side. 'They were starving,' he says. 'In utter terror, and so many dead.'

It is a most unusual scene for Ivan. The quiet attention his workers are giving to these dogs, and the way the animals respond. The state these animals have been found in, that they were rescued in possibly their last moments. This is more stress than they have ever been able to subject them to in controlled environments. Ratmir, a most excitable dog, shows no response to being stroked. Postrel, normally a friendly dog, wagging his tail, jumping up to lick the nearest person; now he lies apathetic, head on paws, eyes staring straight ahead.

Ivan gathers his team. 'Notes must be taken immediately. Artur. The kennels prepared. Pyotr, as soon as the flood waters wane. Mariia, Andreyev. Your dogs. I want all of you ready. Dogs will be prepared. We need to test their responses, the reflexes we have been conditioning in these animals for months. Such severe inhibition in these dogs. These floods are beyond any stimuli we have been able to introduce in our experiments.'

He fires out questions. How did this dog appear, how has another one responded, what observations have been made so far, how have they reacted to one another? He gives instructions about how they will proceed for the next few days.

He waits in his study afterwards, for one of his assistants to report to him about the losses, which dogs haven't survived.

There is a quiet knock. He clears his throat and leans back in his chair.

It's Mariia. She has been with him for twelve years now, his most invaluable researcher. She shuts the door behind her and perches on the chair opposite him. 'Ivan, this is disastrous.'

He tuts and smiles. 'Not disastrous, Mariia. No. An opportunity.'

VII

Ratmir is prepared by Pyotr, brought to one of the experiment rooms and put in his stand. Pyotr leaves the room and Mariia watches through the glass. Ratmir struggles against the binds holding his legs. He twitches his head, pulls, twists. He was never usually this restless, eager yes, but not restless. His eyes dart left, right. He yelps and seems irritated by the rubber tube attached to his salivary gland.

Mariia introduces basic stimuli. Metronome. Light. Whistle. Food is provided. No drops of saliva. Ratmir will not touch his food, in fact turns his head away.

Mariia enters his room, and stands next to him. 'Tsh, Ratmir. What is this?'

Ratmir responds by pushing his nose against her arm, but turns away again.

'Seven months of conditioning wiped from this dog's brain.' She shakes her head and attempts her experiments again.

Metronome. Flash of a bright light. Buzzer. Appearance of a circle. Whistle. Metronome. Flash of a bright light. Buzzer. Appearance of a circle. Whistle. Metronome. Flash of a bright light. Buzzer. Appearance of a circle. Whistle.

She sends Pyotr to find Ivan, who, like most days, is giving each of his workers attention, focusing in on experiments of particular interest, observing, assisting, questioning.

'Leave him without food. Let's see how Ratmir responds then.'

Pyotr is instructed to bring Ratmir back after three days without food. But it's still the same.

'Right,' Ivan instructs. 'We start again. We condition him from the beginning. Start with basics. Work with him as he needs to be worked with. Mariia, this is your expertise. If it's necessary to be in the room with him, then you will be in the room with him. We start with the metronome. We work slowly, with patience. When possible you leave the room, if necessary, you return to the room. We build up the sequence of stimuli as you did all those months ago.'

It takes forty seven days.

'Right, now we introduce a new stimulus. We trickle water beneath the door, let it form a pool. We see how he responds.'

'Like the flood.'

'Yes! Like the flood. We re-introduce his trauma. Observe. Measure. Record. Analyze. Observe. Measure. Record. Analyze.'

VIII

Metronome tick tick tick tick. Salivary gland drip drip drip drip. Flash of a bright light. Drip drip. Buzzer. Drip drip. Appearance of a circle. Drip drip drip. Whistle. Drip. Animal takes the food with avidity. Slow down the metronome. Tick. Tick. Tick. No drips. Speed up the metronome tickticktick. Saliva drip drip drips.

Pyotr lets water from a jug trickle through the crack under the door to Ratmir's room.

Metronome. Tick tick tick. No drips. Buzzer. No drips. Light. No drips. Circle. No drips. Whistle. No drips.

Ratmir is shaking. He stares at the pool of water on the floor, trying to escape his binds, pulling and twisting against them, obviously making noises but they can't be heard from outside the soundproof room. He refuses the food, stares at the floor, shaking, stares at the floor.

IX

Ivan has finished for the day, his coat fastened. There are still a few people in the laboratory. He can hear a buzzer, the barking of a dog.

Mariia is downstairs, fastening a pin into her hat.

'Can I walk with you?'

He holds the door open for her. It's been a while since she asked to walk with him. She lives in the opposite direction, so he knows she must want to talk. He sets the pace and she keeps level with him, their strides matching.

'I keep forgetting this is Leningrad now,' she says.

He laughs. It's true, it has been difficult to get used to the change, and he still says Petrograd every time he refers to the city.

'What was he like, Lenin?'

It's a difficult question for him to answer. 'You know as much as I do, Mariia.'

'Yes, but when you met him?' There are not many people who know he met Lenin, and she's unaware of the circumstances.

'I had no difficulties with the man himself.'

'But you didn't like his methods?'

'Mariia, you already know my political views. So, is this what you want to talk about? Or is there another matter?'

Their footsteps resound against the cobbles. She appreciates his candour. It's true. She hoped to talk with him about her experiments with Ratmir, ask for his agreement to push forward her ideas.

'Well, I want to extend our use of sodium bromide. I thought perhaps we could use it with the flood dogs.'

'Bromides. Yes.'

'And then, use some more extreme stimuli? Erofeeva used electric currents and acid, am I right?'

'In what way, more extreme?'

'I was thinking of castrations. Push the limits with the stronger dogs.'

He frowns. 'You certainly have some strong ideas, Mariia.'

'But?'

'I will consider it.'

They walk together side by side, not touching or looking at one another, but rather keeping their attention on the streets around them. People hurry home, heads down, hats dipped to the ground. They are wary of footsteps that approach, cross over to avoid passing too closely to others. It's a suspicious way to walk around the city, but necessary.

He invites her in for dinner, and as usual she declines. But as they get nearer the house, she agrees to just a small drink.

Mariia feels self-conscious talking about herself or Ivan or the laboratory, worrying that this will exclude his wife. But Sara is interested in their work, and is always keen to know their progress with the dogs. She likes to know their names, temperaments, what kind of dog they are and how they are different from one of the other dogs she knows about.

As always, Ivan offers to accompany Mariia home, and Sara insists. 'It's not safe on the streets for a woman alone, and I'm sure you have more work matters to talk about.'

X

There are matters which Dr Pavlov does not talk about:

1. The meeting between himself and Lenin. It's not clear when this took place. In fact, it's not clear whether it happened. Ivan told a man in London who told another man who wrote this down. He stayed with Lenin for three months. He may have been obliged to stay. Lenin asked him to write a manuscript of everything he had learned so far in his research with animals, his whole life's work. He may have been asked to expand and expostulate on how his findings might be applied to humans. He wrote 400 pages and gave this to Lenin. He told a man who told another man who wrote this down. It is not clear whether this story is true. If it does exist, this manuscript has not been seen outside the Kremlin.

2. The film. It's not clear whether Dr Pavlov saw or was part of making *The Nervous System*. A silly, amusing film for the most part, with learning and information for the audience. Ducklings totter down to a lake for their first swim. A bird tries to hatch wooden eggs. A lion is trained to lie down and roll over.

There is a dog in a harness, standing on a table in an experiment room. A container has been inserted into the side of the dog's lower jaw. A light flashes and food is provided. The dog salivates. Each drop is counted. The dog learns to associate light with food, and so salivates when the light flashes even when there is no food.

There are other scenes in the film.

A man sits in a chair. There is a rubber tube from the man's mouth. He is given food. A light flashes. Drip drip drip. The man is lying on a bed. Biscuits are dropped into his mouth. The light flashes. Drip drip drip.

It is not certain why this film exists.

3. There is a man Dr Pavlov has never met. Let's say his name is Sergei.

At some hour of the day, in some house in a rundown part of the city where it isn't safe to walk at night, there is a splintering of wood as a door is forced and five men take Sergei away.

He may have been arrested. He may sit before a troika to be sentenced to time in the labour camps. He may have been detained for political reasons. It's not clear.

Sergei is left in a room alone. He does not know when someone will come into the room, whether they will be pleasant or unpleasant, give him food or deprive him of food. He does not know whether he will feel pain, or when the noises will start again. The deafening siren, the bright light, the drip drip drip the siren the bright light the drip drip drip the siren the bright light.

He is a strong man.

But he will confess. Or they will bring in his wife for questioning, or his son perhaps. It's not altogether clear.

XI

Ivan returns home late. The house is in darkness. Sara has left him a supper of sweet tea, black bread, and Ukrainian bacon in the kitchen. He eats in the study, leaning back in his chair and reading over and over the analyses written by his doctors from their research these past weeks.

'What is this? What have you scribbled there?' he mutters to himself, and reads the data again.

These prolonged neuro-pathological disturbances in their dogs since the flood. The results are quite definite. How some dogs switched from being in a state of acute excitement to severe protective inhibition, how conditioned reflexes disappeared. It is taking months to restore their old behaviours.

They were wiped away, washed away by the flood, as if some protective mechanism in the brain makes the animal shut down. Rather like the mental breakdowns Ivan has observed in patients in hospitals.

It is quite definite. They are starting to show evidence that these animals respond to completely new conditioning. Almost starting again, like newborns.

And yet, some animals stayed strong, their higher nervous system resisted total breakdown. Somehow, he knows that every dog has his breaking point. Would it be possible, perhaps to induce sufficient stress or trauma or pain so that each dog would reach that point where the brain would shut down to protect it?

Castration would be sufficient for even the strongest dog, perhaps.

He bites into his bread, and sighs. There's much work to be done yet.

XII

He shuts the door to their bedroom quietly, and slips under the blankets so as not to wake Sara. But she is already awake.

'What kind of woman is she? Mariia, I mean.'

He answers quietly, 'You know Mariia as well as I do.'

'Yes, but what kind of woman is she? How you describe your animals, strong and weak, of the moderate type and so on. Is she a strong woman? I imagine her a strong woman.'

'Yes I should think so.'

'What about me, Ivan? Am I a strong woman?'

He looks towards her, but can't see more than her outline in the dark of their room. He reaches for her hand.

'Why are you asking this, silly wife?'

'It's just the way you classify and group, say one animal is one type and another different.'

'Yes, but we can change weak from strong, strong from weak, it is all a matter of time, strengthening, weakening.'

'Like after Mirchick died?'

He cannot answer straight away. She still astonishes him, his wife, with the way she can say things so directly, address them without hesitating. Of course, it's easier to say these things in the dark, as though the dark holds the words for you. Yet somehow the dark makes them so much larger than they are. He almost cannot answer.

'Why are you saying this now, Sara, after all these years?'

She is quiet for a moment before answering. 'Do you remember how ill I was, Ivan?'

Yes, he remembers. How the pain of losing their son was like a fever that prevented her from eating or sleeping, and all desire to live emptied from her.

'Any person can be made weak,' he says, 'by extreme stress or pain. I am sure of it. But you are a strong woman Sara. You always have been.'

She seems satisfied with this because she says no more. He is left in the silence, the dark still holding her words, until he falls asleep.

Afterword:

1924: Ivan Pavlov and Transmarginal Inhibition

Professor John Wearden

Pavlov's concept of 'transmarginal inhibition', illustrated by observations of the behaviour of dogs traumatized by the rising waters of the St. Petersburg flood, as the story so nicely describes, has fascinated researchers, therapists, writers and film-makers, and even politicians, for many years. The basic idea is that subjecting an animal or person to extreme stress produces a kind of 'protective' reaction, which both changes the habitual way in which the organism behaves and, perhaps more tantalizingly from the point of view of potential applications, some of them sinister, renders the person's or animal's behaviour particularly susceptible to change.

In a normal Pavlovian experiment, a dog might be conditioned to salivate to a bell by repeatedly presenting the bell followed by food. After a number of pairings, the dog will salivate when the bell is rung and, in most cases, increasing the loudness of the bell will increase the quantity of salivation produced. Pavlov claimed that the traumatized dogs showed unusual effects, often following a course of three phases. One was an 'equivalent phase', where all stimulus intensities produced the same effect, the second a 'paradoxical phase' where weak stimuli produce strong reactions, and vice versa, and the third an 'ultra-paradoxical phase' where unpleasant stimuli evoke positive reactions and pleasant ones negative reactions. Clearly, highly stressful events produced quite profound alterations in the way that organisms reacted to stimuli.

However, as the story shows, there were differences in the way that individual dogs were affected by the trauma of the flood, and Pavlov used observation of these differences to construct a 'typology' that accounted for them, where different 'types' of nervous systems were supposed to explain why one dog showed one sort of reaction and another dog a different one so, for example, different dogs might vary in the balance of 'excitation' and 'inhibition' in their brains. Gray (1964) provides an accessible account of Pavlov's ideas, and their development by others, about how 'temperament' might be related to nervous system properties, using mostly Soviet literature.

In fact, the idea that the way people react to events might be determined by different 'types' of nervous systems has been extremely influential, even among theorists who did not follow an explicitly Pavlovian line. For example, Eysenck's well-known explanation of personality differences between extraverts and introverts is based on the idea of 'arousability' of their cerebral cortex: extraverts are supposed to be under-aroused, thus seek new and exciting sensations to increase their arousal level to optimal, whereas introverts already have highly-aroused cortices, so exciting sensations are generally avoided to control 'excessive' arousal. Eysenck proposed that differences in arousability were genetically determined, so extravert and introverts were 'born not made'. The details of Eysenck's work remain controversial, but scales measuring personality based on his ideas are commonly used, and others have also agreed with the notion that personality differences are based, in part if not wholly, on differences in nervous system activity. Eysenck published many books and articles during his lifetime discussing relations between personality and brain activity, but perhaps the best starting point for his views on relations between personality and brain activity is Eysenck (1967).

Ideas linked to Pavlov's typology of the nervous system have thus been important in developing a systematic, and scientifically-based, approach to understanding human personality. Another aspect of Pavlov's notions about transmarginal inhibition, the idea that the stress had left some of the flood-traumatized dogs particularly susceptible to rapid 're-conditioning' has had less respectable consequences, based on the claim that deliberate induction of stress might aid 'mind-control' or 'brainwashing'. The 1962 John Frankenheimer film *The Manchurian Candidate*, based on a 1959 novel by Richard Condon, is perhaps the best-known fictional portrayal of brainwashing based on imagined Pavlovian techniques. The story of the film is too complex for retelling here but, in essence, members of a US platoon are captured during the Korean War and taken to Manchuria in China for brainwashing, resulting in one of their number becoming a programmed assassin, with commands triggered by seeing the playing card the Queen of Diamonds.

The idea that brainwashing techniques, based on Pavlovian methods, were developed by Soviet and Chinese scientists has been the subject of much speculation. Certainly, captured soldiers during the Korean War were frequently exposed to stresses such as sleep deprivation and solitary confinement, conditions perhaps conducive to the development of transmarginal inhibition, but the 're-conditioning' that followed often seemed to have little to do with Pavlovian methods, and usually involved readings from Maoist works, forced discussions of political issues, and so on. The CIA, ever-present in conspiracy theories about 'brainwashing', likewise is said to have experimented with 'mind-altering' methods, mostly involving drugs like LSD or barbiturates (sometimes administered without the recipients' knowledge), as part of their project MKULTRA, with the research largely being carried out in the 1950s.

Cults, likewise, may often subject newcomers to stressful periods of induction, involving fasting, drugs, isolation, or traumatic and humiliating initiation rituals, which must be undergone to gain standing in the cult, but whether the subsequent 'mind-control' methods used have much direct relation to Pavlovian conditioning techniques as they are technically understood is much more questionable. Inducing stress, both physical and psychological, as part of the questioning of suspects obviously has a long history, with the modern version being the Bush administration's 'enhanced interrogation' methods, which included convincingly simulated drowning ('waterboarding', disturbingly reminiscent of the experience of Pavlov's dogs during the St. Petersburg flood), sleep deprivation, slapping and shaking, hypothermia, and forcing subjects to stand in uncomfortable 'stress positions'. Obviously, debate about the morality and effectiveness of such methods has been widespread in recent years.

Pavlov's enduring contribution to psychology has not been his work on exotic phenomena such as transmarginal inhibition, even though some aspects of research in this area have fired the popular imagination, but rather his influence on the study of how associations between events are formed, and what properties these associations might have. Associating two stimuli, such as the bell and food in the prototype Pavlovian study, seems to be one of the simplest psychological processes imaginable, and as such might be considered fundamental to understanding how some types of learning occur. Dickinson (1981) gives a clear and comprehensible account of work carried out in the 1960s and 1970s, as well as discussing Pavlov's legacy of research in this area.

References:

Dickinson, A. *Contemporary Animal Learning Theory.* (Cambridge University Press, 1981).

Eysenck, H.J. *The Biological Basis of Personality.* (Thomas, 1967).

Gray, J.A. *Pavlov's Typology.* (Elsevier, 1964).

Crystal Night

Zoe Lambert

'"The Jewess endangers the institute." That's what Kurt Hess has been saying.' Otto Hahn was pacing back and forth in front of Lise's desk. She ignored him and continued writing up the results; she'd already heard what Hess had said, what they were all saying about her.

Otto leant on her desk, perspiration pricking his forehead. 'Lise. Are you listening? I lost my nerve and talked to Horlein about this foolish situation. Something needed to be done about you and Hess.'

Lise dipped her pen in the ink. She couldn't account for their results with thorium any more than she could with uranium. The reaction of fast neutrons with thorium resulted in three different decay series. It didn't seem possible.

'Horlein said you may have to resign. Perhaps you could stay on in an unofficial capacity. He even said you may have to vacate your apartment!'

'What?' Lise pushed back her chair and placed her hands on her knees. 'I don't know why you had to say anything to Horlein at all.'

'I'm sorry, Lise, I'm worried about the Institute.'

'I know you are.' She pretended to sort through her papers till Otto had left the room and his footsteps had disappeared down the corridor. She couldn't believe he had spoken about her. The air in her office felt still and empty; she was alone in this institute. Utterly alone. She couldn't just sit there, so she gathered her coat and walked through the grounds towards her apartment, picking her way over the patches of snow. The trees and greenery were usually calming and blocked out the street vendors and trams of Dahlem, but she could still hear a parade.

She had managed to hold on till now at the Institute, putting up with the party members vying for her position and twittering on about the greatness of Aryan Physics, but now Austria had been annexed and for this she was supposed to gracefully resign after thirty years? As if she had done something wrong?

Her boots sank in a deep patch of snow, so she lifted her skirts and stood under a tree where the grass was dry. Here, she took her Austrian passport out of her bag and flipped through the pages. This document was defunct, like an outdated theory.

She was, in effect, back where she had started in 1908 when the entire Kaiser Wilhelm Institute for Chemistry had been off-limits to women. *What if you set fire to your hair in the laboratories?* Emil Fischer had asked, not unkindly. It had been dear Otto who had suggested that they work together in the old carpenter's shop in the basement, where he had set up equipment to measure radiation. It had a separate outside entrance, so she could go to a restaurant down the street to use the toilet. She had liked Otto immediately; his sociability and willingness to work with a woman. Even his upturned moustache. They had always worked well together. In 1918, with Otto returning from the front and Germany in chaos, while it seemed as if the crazy socialist ideas of the Spartacists would take hold, Lise and Otto had discovered the radioactive element protactinium, the element just before uranium in the periodic table. Now the race was on to explain various strange observations that seemed to indicate still heavier elements – out in the mysterious zone beyond uranium: the 'transuranes'.

She found a packet of cigarettes in her bag, lit one and leaned against the tree. She could have left when Albert and everyone else had, five years earlier, but Otto had promised her that this department would be different, they could keep working together despite the race laws, and she'd supposed things would calm down eventually. They had even managed to get a small stipend for Fritz Strassmann to join their team. He had been unemployable and virtually starving after refusing to join National Socialist organisations.

But now, Otto, dearest Otto, had in effect kicked her out.

In June, Lise was sitting in her room in Hotel Adlon, which, she had told herself, was only a temporary adjustment. To make do, she had turned the dressing table into a desk, with her books piled in front of the three-way mirror. She was re-reading Bohr's article on 'Neutron Capture and Nuclear Constitution' in *Nature*, and still trying to interpret the results with uranium, when Carl Bosch, president of the Kaiser Wilhelm Society, phoned.

'Lise,' Carl said. 'I've asked the Ministry of Education about getting you a passport.'

'I'm sure that won't be necessary...'

'Well, in any case, they're determined not to give you one. Let me read it to you.'

16 June 1938

'It is considered undesirable that well-known Jews leave Germany to travel abroad where they appear to be representatives of German science, or where their names and corresponding experience might demonstrate their inner attitude against Germany. Surely the KWG can find a way for Frau Prof. Meitner to remain in Germany even if she resigns, and if circumstances permit she can work privately in the interests of the KWG. This statement represents the particular view of the Reichsführer-SS and Chief of the German Police in the Reichsministry of the Interior.'

Lise scribbled it down in shorthand. 'Well, perhaps I can just keep working here in an unofficial capacity.'

'You must listen to me, Lise. I've spoken to Coster and Bohr and they are both adamant you must leave. They're making enquiries for you. I thought about speaking to Himmler himself, but Bohr advised against it.'

'No, please don't speak to him.'

Lise replaced the phone and dabbed at her face; the days were getting hotter and her situation more and more ridiculous. What did they mean? Her 'inner attitude against Germany?' After she had lived here all her adult life. Anyway, she'd converted to Protestantism when she was a girl. Everyone knew that. Since she was only allowed to work in an 'unofficial capacity' their team had made little progress, and the transuranes seemed to be even more of a puzzle. Otto and Strassmann were still bombarding uranium with neutrons, and trying to detect the new elements forming in the precipitate. It was well known that if a neutron was captured, the new element created was unstable and quickly decayed to a lighter element, but there seemed to be more than one species forming. Curie and Savitch had failed to interpret the so-called '3.5 hour activity' they had detected, eventually claiming it must be a transurane. Lise and Otto had nicknamed it 'Curiosum', and privately doubted that it was any such thing.

And here she was stuck in this airless hotel room. She tried to open the window, but the latch was stiff, and outside there was another rally in Pariser Platz. Above the marching soldiers and cheering crowd, Brandenburger Tor shone a beautiful, gleaming white in the sunshine, despite the swastikas hanging limp between the columns.

On the 12th July, the plan was to pretend it was a normal day. Lise worked till eight in the Institute, correcting a young colleague's paper, then she went to Otto's to pack what she could into two small suitcases and stay the night. Everything had been arranged by Dirk Coster and Niels Bohr. She wouldn't be going back to Hotel Adlon, though she hadn't checked out.

Bohr had tried to find her a position in Copenhagen, but he'd said it was quite impossible on account of the great number of foreigners already working in the institute; he'd already found places for numerous refugee scientists, including Lise's nephew, Otto Robert Frisch. Coster was trying to raise funding for a position in Amsterdam, but Lise had heard there was a new physics institute in Stockholm. The director, Manne Siegbahn, seemed open to offering her some kind of position. Perhaps she could be of some use there.

Lise was in Otto's spare room, packing her few summer clothes. She hadn't been able to bring her books and journals, her notes and writing materials, but hopefully they could be shipped later on. She closed the cases and sat wearily on the bed.

'Lise, I've got something for you,' said Otto, coming to sit beside her. 'Here, it was my mother's.' He placed a small blue box in her hand in which sat a diamond ring. 'Edith and I want you to have it. In case you need to sell it.'

'I'm sure I won't need to do that.' Lise slipped it on her finger. 'But it's beautiful. Thank you.'

The ring – a simple gold band with a small diamond – seemed out of place on her fifty-nine year old hand. Even so, she would wear it.

In the morning, Lise struggled to climb onto the packed train at Lehrter Bahnhof. She was wearing her ring under her glove and carrying a suitcase in each hand. She squeezed down the corridor till she saw Coster sitting by the window in one of the compartments. Her seat was opposite. A woman with a small boy pushed in with a suitcase, which Coster lifted onto the top rail. Then he turned to help Lise with hers. He smiled, but didn't say hello; they weren't supposed to speak till they were safely over the border, so Lise sat down with her handbag and tried to make herself comfortable, but under her dress and coat she had a cold sweat and her mouth was dry.

On the other side of the carriage, Coster looked pale, as if he had developed a fever; he must be as nervous as she was. He reached up and wiped his forehead with a handkerchief, then gave her a quick wink and closed his eyes. Next to him, the woman laid her boy's head on her lap and stroked his hair.

As the train drew out of Berlin and into the countryside, Germany started to look like it used to − fields growing sunflowers and rye, then valleys dotted with cottages − until they reached the stations when swastikas swarmed into view again.

Lise took the newspaper from her bag and flicked through the pages. She hardly read the papers these days; they were full of ridiculous ideas. However, on her final day in Germany she'd wanted to know what she was leaving. There was more of the usual nonsense: pages and pages on the mass rallies:

The Jewish Problem is the Background to World Politics
To a tightly packed Vereinshause, Suendermann highlighted the fact that recognition of the Jewish threat must be spread to all the nations. He added that no people or leader longs for war, but we know that the question 'peace or war' is not to be decided by the will of the nations but through the might and influence of the Jews. Only when domination by the Jews is done away with will world peace be possible...

Lise sighed, dropping the paper on the seat beside her. People would see reason, that all this was foolish nonsense, she was sure of it. Coster was staring out the window, while the woman was fussing over her little boy. Lise rested her head in her hand and focused on the rhythm of the train, its soothing whoosh and chug, as if she was only visiting Gusti and Jutz in Vienna and she would return in a few days to the laboratory.

She woke to the train halting at a station and the sounds of voices. They were at the border town of Nieuweschans, and the woman had gone.

'Look,' said Coster.

Lise peered out of the window to see uniformed Nazi officers and Dutch border police getting on the train.

'Don't say anything. Just show them your entrance permit.'

Lise didn't have a passport or a travel visa, only a permit from The Hague that Coster had obtained for her. The day before, he'd travelled to meet the border police and they had assured him a permit would be enough. From the corridor, she could hear the barking commands of police checking documents. Coster was watching the compartment door and turning his passport over in his hands. Then they were crowding into their compartment, the Dutch policeman gesturing for her document, and the German soldier saying 'Heil Hitler!' over his shoulder.

'Heil Hitler!'

The Dutch policeman handed her permit back, and gestured for Coster's.

Lise stared straight ahead till they reached the University town of Groningen, breathing in short sharp breaths.

There was no reception in the foyer of Stockholm's Nobel Institute for Experimental Physics and no one to speak to. The new building was white and vacant; Lise's shoes echoed on the smooth floors, and the foyer was a gaping space with several corridors stretching outwards. At the end of one were two men in white coats. 'Excuse me?' Lise called, but they disappeared up the corridor, leaving an echo of their Swedish voices. She clenched her hands at her sides and followed the signs to Manne Siegbahn's room, peering through windows into empty laboratories and rooms that didn't seem to have any function at all.

The place seemed deserted and Siegbahn wasn't in his office, so she walked round and round the corridors and then back down the hill, where she caught a tram to her hotel in downtown Stockholm. Her room was narrow, with murky white walls, a bed and washstand. There wasn't even a desk where she could work.

She sat on the bed and began writing to her sister, Gusti Frisch, in Vienna. In the morning she would apply for visas for Gusti and Jutz, though it was only a precaution, really.

Lise finally met Manne Siegbahn two days later. He was rushing down the hall with papers in his arms – a grey, tired looking man, hardly the youthful physicist she'd worked with in Lund, nearly twenty years before.

'Prof. Siegbahn.'

'Yes? I'm sorry, you are...?'

'Professor Meitner.'

'Frau Meitner, how wonderful. We meet again. Good, good.'

'I was wondering where I was to work. Which laboratory space I may use.'

'Ah... yes. Well, I can find you somewhere, of course. I'll be right back.' Siegbahn hurried into a room and closed the door. She sat on the chair in the corridor, perching her bag on her knee and shivering in her dress. Finally, a young assistant came out, saying, 'I'll show you to your room.' He couldn't have been more then twenty-five and spoke to her as if she was a student.

He led her down the stairs to a small, narrow room, holding out his hand to indicate she should enter.

Inside, there were tables and empty bookshelves. She placed her bag on a desk and looked at the assistant. But he had already gone.

By September, Lise still hadn't managed to get hold of any equipment for her laboratory. No counters, sources, capacitors or ammeters. Not a fraction of what, for years, she'd taken for granted in Berlin. For an institute in experimental physics, it was quite impossible to do any experiments at all. The days were growing chilly and she was constantly cold in her summer clothes. On an assistant's stipend – the kind of wage she had received thirty years previously – she had only enough to cover limited food and travel. Her pension and bank account had been frozen in Germany, and it was proving difficult for Otto to send her belongings. In her letters, she pleaded with him to send her the rest of her library. 'I hope it is understood that I will receive my journals, card-files, slides, diagrams of my experimental apparatus and so forth,' she wrote. But hitch after bureaucratic hitch came up.

Thankfully, there was an overnight mail from Stockholm to Berlin, so she could keep in touch with Otto and her lawyer. Lise's mail was delivered to her room every morning. It seemed cruel that the most treasured moment of her day should come so early. She would lie in bed, waiting to hear the shuffle of the porter placing the envelope on the mat outside her door. Then she'd reach for the spare blanket, wrap it around her and dash to retrieve the envelope and climb back into bed. It was still dark when the post arrived; she was dreading winter when it went dark by three in the afternoon.

At the university she would set up a few separation experiments and stare at them, but it was no use. She needed a chemist to work with, a source of neutrons, and a Geiger counter for her to do anything remotely like the work she was doing in Berlin. If only she had organised her departure earlier and been able to bring some equipment with her.

She would listen as someone walked past her office, their shoes echoing up the hallway. There was hardly anyone in the Institute other than the four young physicists in Siegbahn's group, but she wasn't invited to participate. They would blink at her when she attempted to speak to them in Swedish, so that she stumbled over her words, nervous, as if she were a shy young woman again.

Back when she had first arrived at the Kaiser Wilhelm Institute and they were only just letting women into universities, she'd walk next to Otto, fearful of everyone who spoke to her. The chemistry students ignored her, greeting Otto with 'Good morning Dr Hahn,' as if by not acknowledging her existence they could make her go away. It was the same when Siegbahn stared over her shoulder. He had done the honourable thing in helping her, but he didn't want a woman in his laboratories.

She shouldn't have come to this institute. It had been a mistake.

On quiet days, when there nothing to be done, she would re-read Otto's letters.

25 October 1938

Dear Lise,

Despite dreadful weariness, I want to answer your letter. Toward the end of last week a new paper by Curie and Savitch about the 3.5 hour substance appeared. We are now working on reproducing the experiments and we do now believe in its existence. According to Curie's results we have found the substance, perhaps even better than Curie and Savitch. The properties do in fact appear to be remarkable. But we still have to identify it. (Perhaps a radium isotope has something to do with it. I tell you this only with great caution and in confidence). A great pity you are not here with us to clear up the exciting Curie activity!

A great pity indeed. She could see Otto and Strassmann in their laboratory on the first floor of the institute, completely silent as they lifted the lead shielding between the tube of beryllium-radium powder and the uranium compound. The source would be inside a paraffin wax cylinder, in order to slow down the neutrons, and for a whole minute, the powder would shoot neutrons at the uranium. Otto would keep his eye on the clock, and after this minute, slide the lead shutter down to stop the bombardment.

The uranium would be dissolved in hydrochloric acid. Then the work of separating these substances from the solution would begin.

Lise carefully folded up the letter, and placed it in the envelope. She had replied to this letter saying she had obtained the Curie paper and found many statements hard to understand. The 3.5 hour substance was very intense and she wondered why they hadn't found this substance in thorium when they'd repeated the Curie experiment last January.

She opened Otto's reply and smoothed back her hair.

30th October 1938
Dear Lise!
With thorium as carrier we could not find it. It isn't thorium of course. At most thorium is gradually produced from it. If anything definite turns up next week, I'll write again.

This reply had been so brief and enigmatic that she had written asking him again how the experiments were going. She had hoped that after thirty years of work and friendship together in the Institute he could at least tell her what was happening there. But his most recent letter had been the most puzzling of all. Otto and Strassmann no longer seemed to think there was a single 3.5 hour activity, but a number of different activities involving radium.

2nd November, 1938

Dear Lise,

I am certainly not keeping secrets from you about work or Institute matters. We really could not say anything definite about the 3.5 hours substance in two weeks, despite working day and night, when Curie has been at it for 1 ½ years. We are now almost convinced that we are dealing with several – or 2 or 3 – radium isotopes, which decay to actinium. Perhaps we can feel sure enough by Sunday so that on Monday we can write a letter to *Naturwissenschaften*. Because the finding of radium is really so interesting and improbable that we would like to publish it before Curie gets to it, and before she hears of it from anyone else. That was the reason I wrote to say that you should please not say anything about it.

Naturally, we would like it very much if you could think about the situation, how an alpha transformation can come about, probably also with slow neutrons and at the same time produce several radium isomers.

Love Otto.

On the 13th November, Lise stood in Copenhagen Central Station, hugging herself against the wind that whipped down the platform. It was barely seven and there were only three other people waiting for the express train from Berlin. Niels Bohr had managed to organise her permit to come to Copenhagen while Otto was visiting to give a lecture. She was wearing the shawl, hat and thick underwear that Margrethe Bohr had given her, but the cold inside her, the shivering, the clenching of her stomach wasn't because of the wind. Yesterday, Bohr had showed her a newspaper, and translated from Danish that Jewish property had been destroyed all over Germany and the former Austria. Synagogues ransacked; shop windows broken, people had been attacked and thousands of Jewish men imprisoned. And as Lise looked at the photo of broken windows on the front of the paper, she knew it wasn't the spontaneous event they claimed it was; it had been planned. It was a strategy.

All morning, Lise had tried to phone her sister in Vienna, but the operator had not been able to put her through. That afternoon, she hadn't gone to the colloquium at the university, but instead walked round Copenhagen till she was lost in the backstreets, and then returned to Bohr's to find a telegram from Gusti saying that her husband Jutz had been arrested and sent to Dachau.

Otto's train drew into the platform. The carriage was packed and Lise strained to see him as the passengers brushed past her. Finally, there he was with his wonderfully familiar moustache under a brown trilby. They hugged, her head against his coat. 'Lise,' Hahn said, pulling back to look at her. 'You're a bag of bones!'

'Four months! It's been four months!'

They hurried to Otto's hotel, where they took breakfast in the dining room. He picked up his napkin and then put it down again. 'You've heard, haven't you, what's happened?'

'Yes.'

'And you've heard from Gusti? I was in Vienna to speak to Mattauch. I saw them on the ninth and they both looked well. Then I took the overnight train to Berlin. Gusti sent a telegram about it yesterday.'

'Did you not see any of it?'

'Not till I arrived in Berlin and I was going to Dahlem on the tram.'

'You have to do something, Otto.'

'What? What can I do?'

'Speak to someone. Try to get him released.'

Otto sat back in his chair. 'It's getting more and more difficult in Berlin, Lise. It's hard keeping Strassmann in the Institute when neither of us are party members.'

'You and Strassmann are fine. It's us who aren't.' Lise

picked up her cup, spilling the tea onto the white tablecloth. She dabbed at it and then left the napkin over the stain. 'Why aren't you doing anything? Why aren't any of you doing anything?'

'Why are you being like this?' Otto said, lowering his voice. 'I've come all this way to see you when Edith is in the sanatorium again, and my son has been conscripted to the Hitler Youth.'

'I know, I know, I'm sorry,' she said, dabbing at the stain again.

'I'll speak to Carl Friedrich von Weizsacker. Maybe his father, the Baron, will be able to intervene.'

'Thank you.'

They both stared out the window, at people bent against the wind and the newsvendor across the street, holding up copies of the daily.

Lise reached across the table and grasped Otto's hand. 'Please, speak to Weizsacker.' He gave her hand a squeeze. 'I will. Now, let me cheer you up and tell you about the radium results.' He poured her some more tea and went over his and Strassmann's experiments, and how they'd even taken to sleeping in the laboratory.

'I just don't understand,' Lise said, 'how uranium's decay to radium is enhanced when it is bombarded by slow neutrons. Everything we have done has shown that slow neutrons are captured by the nucleus. You need fast neutrons to chip off an alpha particle.'

'I don't know. But that's what the results were. If only you were still with us, Lise, and it was like it used to be...'

Lise poured herself another cup of tea. 'If only,' she said.

Later, when Otto was about to board his train, Lise grasped hold of his hand. 'Repeat the experiments. Test for radium again.'

19 December 1938

Dear Lise,

We are working on the uranium substances. It is now practically 11 o'clock at night. Strassmann will be coming back at 11.45 so I can get home at long last. The thing is: there is something so ODD about the 'radium isotopes' that for a moment we don't want to tell anyone but you. The half-lives of the three radium isotopes are pretty well determined; they can be separated from all the elements except barium: all processes are correct. Except for one — unless there are some very weird accidental circumstances involved, fractionalization doesn't work. Our radium isotopes behave like barium.

Now, last week I fractioned the radium isotope thorium-x on the first floor. Then on Saturday Strassmann and I fractioned our radium isotopes with mesothorium-1 as indicator. The mesothorium-1 became enriched, our radium did not. It could still be an extremely strange coincidence. But we are coming steadily closer to the frightful conclusion: Our radium isotopes do not act like radium but like barium! I have agreed with Strassmann that for now we shall tell only *you*. Perhaps you can come up with some sort of fantastic explanation. We know ourselves that uranium can't actually burst apart into barium, which is almost half its size. But we must clear it up.... So please think about whether there is any possibility — perhaps a barium isotope with much higher atomic weight than 137? If there is anything you could propose that you could publish, then it would still in a way be a work by the three of us!

We intend to write something for *Die Naturwissenschaften* before the Institute closes because we have achieved some very nice decay curves.

Yours, Otto

Very cordial greetings and best wishes also from me, Fritz Strassmann

On December 23, Lise travelled to Kungälv, where she was meeting her nephew, Otto Robert Frisch. In the hotel foyer, Lise waited for him in an armchair, smoking and re-reading Otto Hahn's letter.

It was a cosy hotel, with wooden beams and a large log fire. Outside the window, the grounds were thick with snow, which reached up to the hills and down to the sea. Lise touched where the ink had blotted on the letter. She could see Otto at his desk, writing these words, dashing back to the apparatus, leaving the pen nib resting on the paper.

She wanted to be there more than anything; to observe these experiments, working all night, taking shifts, focused solely on the activities in the beaker.

Late at night, with the rest of the Institute in darkness, Otto would be standing over the beaker of radium solution, adding a small amount of barium chloride with the burette. This barium salt would solidify into crystals, locking up the tiny quantities of radium in its crystal structure.

Lise could see Otto quickly filtering the solution through one of the porcelain funnels, the minute crystals catching in the filter paper. Then he'd set the Geiger counter, listening to the click-click-click that, when measured, would plot out his beloved curves. He'd add the same amount of barium salt and wait as it crystallised again. But then he must have paused, checking the Geiger counter.

The reading was the same. Click-click-click. It should be slower, showing that with each dose of barium salt there was less radium to capture. No, the reading was about the same, as it would be if the salt was capturing ordinary barium into its lattice, and not radium. He would have added more barium salt, and repeated the fractionalisation, but the result was the same. She could see Otto calling Strassmann over, and them both bending down next to the Geiger counter: click-

click-click. Baffled by the results.

Lise smoothed the letter flat on her knee. She had written to Otto, saying that a reaction with slow neutrons that supposedly led to barium was very startling. The idea of such a thoroughgoing breakup of the nucleus seemed very difficult. But in nuclear physics they had experienced so many surprises that she could not unconditionally say that it was impossible.

'Aunt Lise!'

Robert walked into the foyer, holding wooden skis and wearing a fur hat.

'Robert! Look at you, you're so handsome!'

He put his skis down and hugged her, her face only reaching his chest. She always forgot he was so tall and grown up.

'Your father. Have you heard anything?' Lise said, pulling back to look at him.

'They said he can be released if he leaves the country.'

'And your mother? She hasn't replied to my last letter.'

'She's stopped leaving the house. She's scared she'll be attacked by Hitler Youths.'

'I just don't understand it all. I just don't...' She got up from her chair and looked about her. 'I need some air.'

'You'll catch your death.'

'I'm fine. I have my coat.' She buttoned it up and held out her letter. 'I've got something to show you.'

'I've been dying to tell you about my graphs.'

'First you must read this.'

He took the letter and scanned it. 'Have they made a mistake?'

'What? No. Hahn and Strassmann are too good. They don't make mistakes.'

She slipped the letter in her bag and walked outside, grasping the rail for the stone steps were icy. At the bottom of the steps, Robert fitted his feet into the wooden skis and tied the straps. He waded forward and Lise laughed, 'Don't fall!'

'I *won't* fall, Aunty.' He pushed himself through the snow on the grass, while Lise kept to the cleared path, the cold seeping through her thin soles. They walked for a while, Lise glancing at Robert lurching on his skis, his face tense with concentration and looking for all the world like he once did as a little boy, learning to ride a bike. Finally, Lise said, 'I think it can be explained by the fact the nucleus is not just shedding a mere flake. A bit does not chip off, and barium is so much smaller.'

'Bohr,' said Robert, out of breath. 'Do you remember Bohr's idea about the nucleus being like a liquid drop, which might elongate and divide itself?'

'Yes, the uranium nucleus could be a wobbly, unstable drop, ready to divide itself at the slightest provocation,' she said, pointing to a tree trunk lying on the ground. 'Let's sit on there.' She wiped the snow off and perched on the wood.

'Like the impact of a neutron,' Robert said.

Already, Lise's hands were shaking with cold as she searched in her bag for a scrap of paper and started writing down the packing-fraction formula to work out how much energy was needed to break the surface tension of the atom.

Robert sat beside her, watching her writing, waiting, so attentive, as he used to do when she visited Gusti and Jutz in Vienna. She'd sit him on her knee and tell him about the periodic table; how the elements fitted together, and showing him where there were spaces for elements yet to be found. With pride she'd pointed out the element protactinium, just before uranium, the element that she herself had found.

And then in no time at all he was applying for a position in Hamburg, and she had tried to be professional and objective with his reference. Too professional, perhaps. The director of the Institute wrote to her demanding to at least know whether Robert was 'a disagreeable person' or not, and she'd had to reply saying, 'No, he isn't a disagreeable person.'

'Like the impact of a neutron,' Robert said again.

'Hmm?' Lise said, looking up. 'Oh no, not like the

impact of a neutron, like the slow sidling up of a neutron, Robert, like a tiny bead of condensation beside a larger one. You see the charge of a uranium nucleus is large enough to destroy the effect of surface tension almost completely. The problem is that the two drops once separated would be driven apart by their mutual electric repulsion and breaking fully would require a lot of energy, approximately 200 MeV.'

'But where would that energy come from?'

'According to the packing-fraction formula,' she said, waving her piece of paper, 'the two nuclei formed by the division of a uranium nucleus would be lighter than the original uranium nucleus by about one-fifth the mass of a proton,' Lise said. She looked out at the snow covering the fur trees, and beyond to the grey basin of the sea; she thought of her sister in Vienna, unable to leave the house and Jutz in Dachau; and Otto saying that the large numbers of Jews would surely be better treated in the camps than the political prisoners had been; of Albert congratulating her on finally leaving their 'dear and grateful fatherland', and here she and Robert were, in this icy, frozen place, so far from everyone.

'$E=mc^2$,' she said suddenly. 'According to Albert's $E=mc^2$, when mass disappears energy is created.' Lise began to write down the equation as snow fell onto the paper. She shook it and tried to wipe the flakes away.

'Here,' Robert said, shielding the paper with his hat as she added figures to the equation. He shifted his legs to lean over her. Snow had already coated the glossy wood of the skis, and as he moved, a lump of snow slid down the rounded end to join the snow on the ground.

'200 MeV!' Lise said. 'One-fifth of a proton mass is equivalent to 200 MeV. When mass disappears energy is created. $E=mc^2$. There it is. There is the source of energy!'

Lise stared at the dampening paper as the wind picked it up, and blew it from her knee to land on the ground and disappear under the falling snow.

'Do you know what this means? This means there were

no transuranes.' She pressed her hands together; she could hardly bend them now. She needed to warm herself by a fire, so she slowly stood up, every part of her aching from the cold, and walked back to the hotel, Robert following her awkwardly on his skis.

'But Aunt Lise, think about it…'

'Four years' work,' she said, turning to him. 'You don't know what this loss would mean to me.'

At New Year, Lise waved goodbye to Robert at the station as she boarded the train to Stockholm. Back in her hotel room, she switched on the paraffin heater and sat on the bed with her notes. Uranium nuclei could divide with varying proportions of neutrons and protons to form a variety of fragments including barium. There, it was clear in the equations. She was sure of her interpretation. But all that time – three, no, four years – and she had thought they had found higher elements. But there weren't any. Instead, they had found ordinary elements of middling weights. Hardly exotic. She had been so, so stupid. She had not seen what was really happening in the solution; she had not been able to interpret the results that were right in front of her. And all her life she had put her faith in the Institute and in their search for higher elements; she had ignored what was happening in Germany so she could continue their experiments, and now people were destroying homes and businesses and killing in the street.

Lise rifled through the papers and articles on the bed until she found a piece of notepaper. She rested it on the bedside table and wrote:

1 January 1939
Dear Otto,
I begin the year with a letter to you. May it be a good year to us all. You understand, of course, that the question of the transuranes has a very personal aspect for me. If all the

work of the last four years has been incorrect, it cannot be determined from just one side. I share the responsibility for it and must therefore find some way to participate in the retraction. If the transuranes disappear, you are in a much better position than I, since you have discovered it yourselves, while I have only four years of work to refute — not a very good recommendation for my new beginning.

In the morning, Lise received a letter from Robert in Copenhagen, saying that he had just talked to Niels Bohr about the discovery. Bohr was astonished he had not thought earlier of this possibility, which followed so directly from the current conception of nuclear structure. Bohr was on his way to America this week and was so excited about the results that he had installed a blackboard in his cabin.

Lise couldn't think clearly in the dank little room, so she left the hotel and walked down to the quayside. For once, the winter light wasn't murky; it was so sharp she had to shield her eyes. The river was unevenly frozen; the ice must have thawed and refrozen to form plates, but on the bank of Gamla Stan, the water still flowed and boats bobbed up and down. Further along, people were walking outside the Parliament buildings and she could hear their voices echoing across the ice. She walked along the quayside and then over the bridge to the island. Halfway across, she stopped to stare down at where the river was frozen and where it flowed. Here, as the sun melted the ice, she could see that despite the loss of the transuranes, the splitting of uranium made perfect sense; with the energy mass equation she could calculate the uranium nucleus fragmenting across the periodic table in intricate, beautiful patterns. And if she and Robert quickly published a note about their interpretation — just a page in *Nature*, then Otto could refer to it in his publication. If he wished to.

Yes, it was a drop. The atom was a drop, which could swell and swell into two, and its loss of mass would turn into energy. She dipped her gloved finger into the snow on the bridge wall and held up the flakes to her face. After the hours and days of separation and fractionalisation, Otto and Strassmann would be left with barium crystals, pure and steady in the world.

Lise shielded her eyes: over the water she could see the white orb of the sun, its fierce rays igniting the ice and quayside; merciless, searing light, blinding and burning from a fiery ball of incalculable energy that scorched and left parched whatever lay in its path.

Afterword:

1939: Lise Meitner and Nuclear Fission

James Sumner

SCIENTISTS BEGAN ATOM-SMASHING around the end of the First World War. Firing various tiny particles at particular chemical elements seemed to chip off parts of the atomic nucleus, often transmuting it into a different element: carbon, for instance, could become nitrogen. To identify and explain these transformations, chemists and physicists had to collaborate. In Berlin, a world centre for atomic chemistry, Otto Hahn had worked since 1907 with Lise Meitner, head of his institute's physics section, and one of the few senior female scientists in Germany (or, indeed, anywhere).

In 1932, James Chadwick at Cambridge had found a new particle, the neutron, which offered intriguing possibilities for atom-smashers. A group led by Enrico Fermi in Rome set to work systematically bombarding each of the chemical elements with neutrons, purely to see what would happen. This process, like all new research, was full of confusing complications. Neutron bombardment created many different products at once: most of these were themselves unstable and transmuted again, often repeatedly.

As all these processes happened together, at wildly different rates, the result was what we might think of as a nuclear jungle, buzzing with exotic species. Chemists worked to make sense of the situation by reacting, dissolving and crystallising their samples until particular products could be filtered out. Physicists had their own tricks, using cloud chambers to examine the reactions, and Geiger counters to plot the products' radioactive behaviour. Often, however, the new species bore no obvious resemblance to any known substance.

In mid-1934, Fermi's group bombarded the heaviest known element, uranium, and found some exceptionally exciting new products. Although almost all the holes in the periodic table had been filled in by the 1930s, it had never been obvious why the table ground to a complete halt at uranium. Many were tempted to believe that the neutron bombardment was creating 'transuranes': unknown elements, heavier than uranium, too unstable to exist in nature.

The Berlin group responded keenly to this remarkable prospect against an increasingly grim political backdrop. The Meitner-Hahn-Strassmann collaboration overrode significant gender and discipline boundaries, but Meitner's enforced exile in 1938 threw up a geographical barrier. Absurdly, yet doggedly, the collaboration persisted through the strikingly efficient Stockholm-Berlin overnight mail. If Meitner could no longer see the experiments, she could still use her theoretical expertise to guide her colleagues.

Following up work by Irène Curie's rival group in Paris, the chemists had found what seemed to be three different forms of radium (element 88), a metal similar in size to uranium (element 92). Meitner found this result confusing in many ways. In particular, the new products were most often produced by 'slow', low-energy neutrons, which should, if anything, be poorer at bashing fragments out of the uranium nucleus. She urged the chemists to look again.

Strassmann used a clever chemical trick to test for radium species. Vertically above radium in the periodic table was the much lighter barium (element 56), conveniently non-radioactive, but chemically much like radium. Deliberately adding barium to the solution, then crystallising it out, should leave traces of unfamiliar radium locked up in the barium's crystal structure. Indeed, radium was slightly more attracted to the crystal structure than barium itself. Given repeated doses of barium, much of the radium would come out in the first crystallisation, while the others would be progressively less 'enriched'.

This was exactly what Hahn and Strassmann did *not* find. Across four crystallisations, the proportion of 'radium' coming out in the crystals remained the same. Its radioactivity meant it must be something new, but chemically it behaved exactly like its barium carrier. After endless trials, there was only one conclusion left: the 'radium' wasn't radium. It was barium.

The chemistry was clear, but the physics was baffling. Uranium turning into a medium-sized element? It would somehow have to slough off nearly half its nucleus, meaning a huge series of reactions which nobody had noticed. And for this to be triggered by docile slow neutrons, and in three different ways? The chemists were completely lost. So was Meitner − but not for long, as she pictured the uranium nucleus splitting, more or less neatly, into *two* medium-sized parts. A nucleus of barium, for instance, and... what would the other part be? Perhaps a new form of another well-known element like krypton.

Fission, as Meitner and Frisch called the splitting process, cast doubt on all recent nuclear theory, and in particular the mysterious 'transuranes'. They seemed, as far as anyone could tell, to be chemically *similar* to well-known, medium-sized elements, which made sense if they belonged in the blank spaces vertically below those elements on the periodic table. But what if they simply *were* medium-sized elements? The chemists set to work re-testing old discoveries, reinterpreting them for the new framework.

Another realisation was more startling. The uranium did not split perfectly into two parts: it usually released a few spare neutrons, too. What if these neutrons, in turn, struck other uranium nuclei? Under the right conditions, the fission process would multiply, 'like rabbits in a meadow', as Frisch put it. Each fission involved a slight loss in mass and, by Albert

Einstein's mass-energy equation, a release of energy. Carefully controlled, this chain reaction meant a steady power source; carefully *un*controlled, a terrifically violent explosion.

Nuclear scientists, who responded to the same basic human hopes and fears as everyone else, had been talking of 'hell bombs' for years, but it had begun to appear that there was nothing suitably fearsome among the fauna of the nuclear jungle. Uranium fission proved otherwise. The stakes were suddenly very high indeed. At the end of 1938, it was still possible to tell the world about fission, but Germany was gearing up for a major expansionist war, hugging its assets to itself. It would soon be impossible for colleagues like Meitner and Hahn to communicate, even by letter. Exiled physicists thought gravely about what they had left behind: the brilliant nuclear chemistry, the strength of German industry, the corporate lunacy of the Hitler regime.

By March 1940, Frisch was in Birmingham with another refugee physicist, Rudolf Peierls, trying to calculate the practicalities of the superbomb. Less than a kilogram of fissionable uranium, they decided, might destroy a city. The British Government began research, and in 1941, following British pressure, the US commissioned the vast Manhattan Project to develop the bomb at any cost. Meitner, still stuck in Sweden, was asked to help but refused: 'I will have nothing to do with a bomb!' Frisch and Peierls contributed; so did Niels Bohr.

The consequences hardly need description: the 1945 destruction of Hiroshima and Nagasaki, and the beginnings of the technological race which defined the conduct of the Cold War. Public fear, in turn, triggered governmental drives to convince populations that the power of fission could be harnessed for peaceful purposes, including nuclear energy production. The discovery of fission, then, changed the world if anything did. It is one of the most tempting 'Eureka moments' in the history of science. But the temptation is one we should resist.

As any historian of science will tell you, Eureka

moments are made, not lived. They are stories, distillations, tools to teach and promote scientific ideas; but they do not capture how the ideas actually arose. Treating 'the discovery of fission' as a moment in history means confining it to one of two places: Hahn and Strassmann's laboratory in Berlin, or Meitner and Frisch's confab in snowy Kungälv. Which should it be? The question is misplaced. The discovery was complex and dispersed, smearing out across the Hahn–Meitner letters, the Copenhagen meeting, and a clutch of earlier and later work, some of it by other people. (The revolution in established assumptions was not quite as drastic as Meitner first feared. By 1940, others had established that there really were elements heavier than uranium, such as plutonium.)

Yet the Eureka myths of fission are almost as old as the discovery itself. In 1946, during a visit to the United States, Meitner found herself a celebrity. The Women's National Press Club made her Woman of the Year; she was introduced to President Truman and celebrated as the 'Jewish mother' of the atom bomb, still widely accepted as the technological triumph that had ended the war. The most extreme version, based on a confused newspaper report, had Meitner smuggling the bomb itself out of Germany in her handbag. Meitner was appalled by this connection, and by the limelight in general.

Meanwhile, an alternative myth took shape. Emerging from the ruins of war, occupied Germany desperately needed non-Nazi public figures, particularly in fields which could offer non-military routes to renewal, like science and technology. Otto Hahn fitted the bill. By 1946 he had a senior role in German scientific administration, and was particularly influential in establishing, in Allied minds, which of his fellow scientists were untainted by Nazism. He was thus able to shape the story of German science more generally, particularly where his own work was concerned.

Immediately after the war, Hahn received a Nobel Prize for 'his discovery of the fission of heavy nuclei.' Meitner was not cited (and nor, for that matter, was Strassmann). For obvious reasons, the Hahn-Meitner collaboration had been excluded from German fission stories under Nazism, but afterwards Hahn did nothing to revive it. In fact, he positively promoted the division. 'The discovery of fission' meant the chemists' barium result; Meitner and Frisch, as he put it in 1958, 'came out independently with their historic publication' shortly afterwards.

In later life, Meitner and Hahn remained friends – distantly. Meitner never accepted her former colleagues' silence on the horrors of Nazism. To Hahn, Meitner failed to understand the reality of life inside Hitler's Germany; to Meitner, Hahn failed to understand the consequences for the outsider. The partnership itself had fissioned. Hahn remained in Germany; Meitner became a Swedish citizen, later moving to Cambridge. Both died in 1968.

Influential discoverers are often lost entirely to the public memory. In her legacy, as in her life, Meitner was luckier than most of the unlucky. In 1966 the Enrico Fermi Award, a prestigious US governmental prize for energy research, acknowledged Hahn, Meitner and Strassmann jointly for 'extensive experimental studies culminating in the discovery of fission.' Physicists, of course, understood Meitner's significance. So did some chemists, including Ruth Sime, whose 1996 biography, *Lise Meitner: a life in physics*, provoked new interest in Meitner's role in the discovery.

Negotiation of the myth continues. In one place, at least, Lise Meitner stands above her former colleague. Since the 1950s, several scientists have been commemorated in the naming of heavier-than-uranium elements. The name *hahnium* was proposed at different times for two elements, numbers 105 and 108, but a formal settlement of competing proposals in 1997 accepted neither. It did, however, enshrine the widely supported suggestion for element 109, which you will find on any up-to-date periodic table today: *meitnerium*.

Morphogenesis

Jane Rogers

HE'S 10 YEARS old, hot, with itchy grass seed sticking through his socks. The glittering loch is behind him; up here he's surrounded by a sea of purple heather. He's come to a standstill by the bothy, which is at the intersection of 52 bee flight paths and now his body is pinging his still-computing brain with messages: lungs gasping for oxygen, stomach empty, left heel sore where the new shoe rubs; ears tuning in to the intensifying buzz; eyes – scanning... yes! Fix on the crack beside the corner post where bees are alighting, crawling in, crawling out, taking flight. It's at shoulder height. He can get the honey, easy. As he watches their angular dances, the thudding of his heart recedes, and his bladder gives a plaintive twinge. Unbuttoning his flies with his right hand and grasping his penis with his left, he aims at the base of the corner post, drilling a hole in the dust with his pee, splashing darkly up the wood. The hot ammonia smell rises intensely for a moment then mingles with the heather and dust, dilutes, diffuses, fades into the summer air. When the pee has evaporated, it will leave that little ridged circle in the dust which it has turned to mud. Like a volcano crater. It was part of him, that pee. Cells from inside him will be left there in the mud. And when it dries completely, and the dust gets blown by the wind, and a speck of the dust falls to the ground by this heather plant, and the heather drops a seed which sprouts from that dust which was partly made by his pee, will the heather have his cells in it? Will the honey, made by the bee who collects the pollen from the flower that has grown from the pee-dust? And if he came back and ate that honey, would a bit of it recognise it had come home?

He buttons himself up and crouches to look at the shape of the pee-crater; now the heather is at eye level and he notices a white flower. 5 petals, veined and tender as eyelids: fairy flax. A white star against the dark peat. He stares at its perfect shape. 5 petals equally spaced around the yellow centre; how does it *know*? How does it know to grow like that? And not dark and knobbly-secret like the heather? How does it know to grow its simple open face; how, when it is nothing but green mush in the stem, does it know to unfold in the same perfectly recognisable pattern, every time? For each petal to be narrow at the base, swelling to roundedness at the middle, tapering away finely to a point? How does it know not to be longer or thicker or wider or darker? Not to be round or square or one of 7? What makes it grow that shape? A human being, with all the cleverness in the world, couldn't make a thing that grew to that shape. It would be utterly impossible. Unless he planted a seed. Alan laughs. So the seed knows all that. In miniature. In code, probably. He recites to himself from his new book, *Natural Wonders Every Child Should Know*. It is the best book he has ever read, but the things it doesn't know are the things that echo for the longest. 'We are made of little living bricks. When we grow it is because these living bricks divide into half bricks, and then grow into whole ones again. But how they find out when and where to grow fast, and when and where to grow slowly, and when and where not to grow at all, is precisely what no one has yet made the smallest beginning at finding out.'

Yet. He scrambles up. Now he will get the honey.

★

He's 16. Sitting at the far end of the library, at the one table which can't be seen from the librarian's desk; screened by Reference. Their table, his and Chris's. He's tearing through a Latin translation with the wretched pen splattering and blotching all over the page as per usual, and focussing on precisely how many things the Stanster got wrong in Maths, and the door's swung open twice now but it's not Chris yet. His knee's jiggling and stomach a bit fluttery but under control, he will be able to tell when Chris opens the door without looking up, he'll sense him; *Compluribus expugnatis oppidis Caesar.* Caesar, having captured many of their towns, perceiving that injury could not be done to them, he determined to wait for his fleet. Injury to the enemy? Or his fleet? He needn't have bothered, it would have happened anyway, whatever it was. The idea that Caesar could have changed it is impossible – but that's the point, he didn't want to, he was only programmed to do exactly as he did – but is Alan? Only programmed to sit here waiting for Chris hardly daring to breathe because he's not here yet? And why is he so agonisingly jumpy when whatever happens was always going to happen anyway?

Every embryo develops from two cells into a precisely ordained human shape: history is no more than the unrolling of a prefigured series of events. The nerves and the illusion of choice are simply ignorance. Only in the gap of ignorance does free will exist. Thinking only happens through not-knowing. Yesterday evening, he and Chris sat here doing prep together and he put his fingertips (right hand, index and middle fingers) onto Chris's naked wrist to draw his attention to a diagram, and Chris glanced up and smiled into his eyes and left his arm lying carelessly on the table. So that if he wanted Alan could have slipped his fingers right around the marble-cool wrist and encircled it while he and Chris were looking into each other's eyes so that both of them really knew and didn't have to be breathless with panic anymore. But he didn't. Because he's so pathetically afraid of Chris jumping away in disgust – and because he's afraid, he never will touch Chris like that, and nothing will ever happen because his destiny is in his cells as much as his hair growing back the same sandy colour each time one falls out. So with hindsight it was inevitable, but the thinking happens now because his brain still pretends there are choices. That he still might manage to plan to touch Chris and not bottle at the last moment. That he might do it. And if he does, then the history will be different. Which it was always going to be. But he didn't know it in advance. He can't read his own writing. Although turrets were built, yet the height of the stems of the barbarian ships exceeded these... stems? Puppium, *sterns*, idiot.

He's here. Alan can feel him. A moving cohort of intensely dense matter, drawing in all around it through its gravitational pull. His own head, without his volition, tilts up like a puppet's to greet Chris. Who nods curtly and slips into the seat beside Alan, leading every cell in the right side of Alan's body to yearn towards his radiance, like a field of sunflowers turning their faces to the sun. After an interminable moment, 'Stanster!' Chris mutters in disgust, and they both laugh, shattering the impossibility.

'You know the Fibonacci numbers?' Alan spills it out before there's time for him to seize up again. '1, 1, 2, 3, 5, 8, 13 – you know?'

'Each one's the sum of the previous two?'

'Yes. They're replicated in fir cones. Look.' His fingers close around the cone in his pocket. It has half opened in the warmth. He sets it on the desk between them. This was this fir cone's destiny. Not only to grow its spiral patterning in exact Fibonacci sequence, but to be delivered as an offering unto the young god Chris, to sit upon this library desk alone of all its species, exemplar.

'Look, start at the top.' He turns the fir cone, counting, demonstrates. Chris takes it from him, holding it with his long cool fingers, turning it delicately as he inspects. Alan imagines Chris's long cool fingers touching him – there – no, no! Blocking it blocking it desperately blocking it and edging his chair closer under the table to hide himself.

He has control. But something has shifted in his head.

Something has shifted into its rightful place. Knowledge. Recognition of the inevitable, bringing joy. He won't be afraid any more. Because it will happen. As surely as that fir cone grew into a fir cone. This is what he, Alan Turing, is.

★

He is seventeen. One week ago, on Thursday February 13th 1930, Chris Morcom aged 18 died of bovine tuberculosis. Now it is 3am.

Alan kneels by the dormitory window, balancing his telescope on the windowsill. Behind him the syncopated breaths of the other boys rise and fall, Bates always with a gentle snort. The sky is clear, stars pulsing. Alan puts his right eye to the eyepiece and has the swimmy sensation of falling out through the black cylinder into space, as a star looms towards him. Which is it? He can't remember, the vast unknowability of the heavens lurches at him sickeningly as he shifts and tilts the telescope. Raising his face he looks again with the naked eye and the stars settle into their constellations, into the names and patterns Chris has taught him: Cassiopeia, Perseus, Ursa Major, Ursa Minor, Polaris – the Pole Star. He feels Chris's confident presence at his shoulder. 'There, Turing. Work from left to right. Use the church spire as your direction finder. Slow down, you are always in such a tearing hurry, you mad oaf.'

Chris is here; Alan's brain reports that as objectively as it notes the sharp brilliance of the stars; the dull glow behind trees of the early-setting moon; the grainy chill of the dormitory floorboards impressing their patterns on his knees through his old pyjamas. It is fact enough for him to assert it both to his own mother, and to Chris's; and for it to drive him, in a few weeks' time, to a scientific explanation:

'As regards the actual connection between spirit and body I consider that the body by reason of being a living body can 'attract' and hold onto a 'spirit'; whilst the two are alive and awake the two are firmly connected. When the body is asleep I cannot guess what happens but when the body dies the 'mechanism' of the body, holding the spirit, is gone and the spirit finds a new body sooner or later, perhaps immediately.' In Chris's case the spirit is attracted – by reason of their similarity – to Alan's. 'I feel sure that I shall meet Morcom again somewhere and that there will be some work for us to do together, as I believed there was for us to do here. Now that I am left to do it alone I must not let him down.'

But a spirit is not a body. Kneeling stiffly on the cold floorboards Alan feels as ancient and distant as the stars he's watching. He must hold his course and shine, even though there is nothing around him but cold black void. He must do his best to shine. Because what else is life for?

★

He's 51. This is the idea that has been coming – moving towards him through the mists of unknowing – all his life. It follows a pattern; as all ideas must. Since it is a theory, in which that which we term real (by the evidence of our senses, which are themselves a system of invisible electro-chemical reactions) is represented by mathematical formulae, it is capable of proof: it is able to be true. Here is a shell, brown and creamy white, striated in wave patterns of deeper and paler colour. He cups it in his hand, then touches its cool curve to his cheek. Passes it under his nostrils and takes in the faintest breath of the sea. Sight, touch, smell: three of his senses bear witness. His theory explains the mechanism by which the striations occur. And in grasping this, he sees, he has grasped the mechanism which gives shape to all living things.

It is not a discovery: it is not new. But to give it a mathematical proof will be new, and will create a space for other thinkers, chemists and biologists who do not like to mingle, to explore in search of physical proofs. They can devise experiments to provide all the evidence the literal-minded need.

He does not think it is *his* idea. Well, it is not an idea, but part of the truth lying out there waiting to be uncovered. If it is anyone's maybe it is Eddington's. And Chris has been at his side in this, this is what Chris would have discovered; should have discovered; no, through the agency of Turing, *has* discovered. Though Alan no longer fully believes in the inevitable – as was, perhaps, inevitable.

He read Eddington a long time ago – when Chris was still alive. *Science and the Unseen World* – they sparred at it together, unwilling to be convinced by Eddington's religiosity. There are sentences he absorbed; words and images laid down in his memory, in chemical sequences in the grey tissue inside his skull. Buried treasure, strings of cells which were able to shift to the surface of his consciousness a knowledge which they had held dormant (or simply uncalled-upon) for thirty-odd years, and which they have now delivered: Eddington's description of the formation of the universe.

'The void is sparsely broken by the tiny electric particles, the germs of things that are to be... The years roll by, million after million. Slight aggregations occurring casually in one place and another drew to themselves more and more particles, until the matter was collected round centres of condensation leaving vast empty spaces from which it had ebbed away. Thus gravitation slowly parted the primeval chaos.' From homogeneity to shape and not-shape. From diffusion to concentration. From smooth to lumpy. From chaos to pattern. From nothing to something.

And the earth was without form, and void; and darkness was upon the face of the deep. And the spirit of God moved upon the face of the waters; And God said, Let there be light.

It is a metaphor which has been used before. And will be reused again when he is gone. But he is here in this moment in time and able to formulate it in this precise way. Which is a raid on the unknown. He has turned the opening sentences of his paper in his mind for days. The claim is so large the language must be modest.

'The purpose of this paper is to discuss a possible mechanism by which the genes of a zygote may determine the anatomical structure of the resulting organism.' A chemical and mathematical explanation of the *mechanism* which permits a bundle of tissue to develop in this direction, and that, and that, and that, forming the buds of four distinct limbs: and not to develop (in the case of a human being) four more; but only to do that in the case of an octopus.

'We are made of little living bricks. When we grow it is because these living bricks divide into half-bricks, and then grow into whole ones again. But how they find out when and where to grow fast, and when and where to grow slowly, and when and where not to grow at all, is precisely what no one has yet made the smallest beginning at finding out.'

But now he has. And he's right. He knows it in every living brick of his body. Which, like every other living form, has obediently grown into its correct predestined shape thanks to the controlling genius of the reaction and diffusion of morphogens, as he has named them; those chemicals which inhibit growth here, foster it there, by switching on or off the potentialities within each individual cell.

'Each morphogen moves from regions of greater to regions of less concentration, at a rate proportional to the gradient of concentration, and also proportional to the diffusability of the substance.' Because nothing is perfectly homogenous. And the slightest disequilibrium, the slightest imbalance or intrusion of an external factor – heat, gravity, motion, anything – generates an appropriate instability, enabling diffusion and reaction, triggering that slow and never-ending process, the tendency of all living matter to shape and form, the tendency of chaos to become order, of an homogenous random mass of tissue to stratify, cluster, and morph into a recognisable shape.

Morphogenesis. The budding and flowering of a shape

from an indistinguishable mass of cells. Not by the hand of God, but by the simple, mechanical reaction and diffusion of chemicals. Moving into the cells, flicking switches, as a man might enter his house and turn on the lights.

★

He's 52. He's brought Arthur back to his room and now there's the tremendous awkwardness, as ever, of how to proceed. Arthur's a good-looking chap but now he seems disgruntled, peering into the jars and bottles on the shelves, picking up shells and cones from the mantelpiece and examining them as if he expects them to be something more than they are. Sniffing. It does still smell, even Alan can detect that. The gas. But also ammonia, formaldehyde, cyanide, iodine, there's a lot of admixture in the air he breathes. The thought of it in Arthur's lungs makes his own breath quicken.

'What's this?'

'A mixture of chemicals. I'm waiting for them to react – they react very slowly – to form a pattern.'

'Why?' asks Arthur.

Is he interested? Playing for time? Does he want to be here, or is it just the thought of the money? He's got the kind of looks women go for too.

'I'm not stupid you know,' says Arthur in an aggrieved tone. 'You can explain it to me.'

'Alright, I will.' Kneeling, Alan puts a match to the fire Mrs Clayton has laid. The flame nibbles at a corner of newspaper, leaps forward into the nest of dry twigs, and begins to crackle through them. He picks up a shiny lump of coal and sets it in the centre of the blaze, relishing the wash of heat over his bare hand. 'I've written a paper on morphogenesis. Which means, how things get their shape.'

'I know what it means,' says Arthur sulkily, and Alan wants to laugh. Laugh and put his arms around the boy. No one knows what it means. Only him.

'Well then. If you take an egg – a human egg – that's just been fertilised, it grows into a sphere. The cells multiply and they grow into a sphere.'

'Right.'

'But when you are born – when one is born, one is not spherical.'

'Bleedin obvious.' He's turned away from the jars and is moving towards Alan and the fire. The firelight makes his handsome face glow.

'So the question I wanted to solve was, what makes the sphere grow into a different shape?'

'What does?'

Alan hasn't been expecting another question. Nor that Arthur will fling himself into the armchair to ask it, rather than continuing his advance upon Alan, who has held his position, weak with desire, on the hearth rug. 'Do you really want to know?'

'Yeah.' There is something in his tone of frank acknowledgement, almost surprised acknowledgement, and gruffness at himself for acknowledging it, and within that gruffness a gentleness of concession to Alan, so that the 'yeah' has a wondering as well as a rude 'it's obvious' quality: so many slender and contradictory threads of meaning intertwined in the utterance that Alan quite looses his heart.

'Well then. There are chemicals – I call them morphogens – within the cells. They diffuse through the cell walls and react with one another. The reactions cause some of them to intensify, others to diminish. This affects the genetic content of the cells, so that some develop and multiply and others are inhibited. Does that make sense to you?'

'Yeah.' A single note to this one. Defiance. Which means he probably doesn't understand. Alan puts more coal on the fire.

'Do you know what gastrulation is?'

'No.'

'Within the sphere, the first development of the zygote – the tiny tiny baby – is that a groove develops. There's a perfect sphere, then a groove. The groove determines which end the head is. It's not a sphere, it's not even symmetrical, so what makes that happen? What makes a sphere change shape? The individual motion of molecules, caused by the triggering of the morphogens: all those cells in the sphere were the same, but now they're changing, some are replicating and some are not, they've been given their instructions – chemically.'

'Right you are.' Now he sounds unconcerned. Alan wonders if it's enough. The fire is beginning to make heat. He allows himself to topple onto all fours and crawls to Arthur's chair.

'Lesson over?' he says.

After a tiny pause, Arthur smiles. He puts his Judas hand on Alan's head.

★

He's 54. If he is meant to die he will be dead. The illusion of choice is simply lack of knowledge. Living cells at death transform into another state. Christopher has been in that state for 36 years, and has remained a constant companion. There is nothing shameful in joining him now. There is nothing shameful in staying alive but he'll never be able to pick up another Arthur, now Her Majesty's Government are so interested in his private life. His body is an oldish mechanism and has been ill-treated; now even cycling makes him out of breath. At death it will degrade and metamorphose into a range of other useful substances. The knowledge generated by his brain will continue to diffuse through the lectures, papers and computing machines he has authored. Diffusion continues long after the agent has ceased. The diffusion is complex, containing many elements of other men's thinking (Eddington, Chris, all those living and dead with whom his brain has engaged and reacted) and the diffusion will – in the nature of diffusion – continue to spread and be altered by the reactions of other men, until it is so dilute as to be scarcely recognisable as anything of his. One cell in a pot of honey. He smiles. There will be a meteorologist called Edward Lorenz who will discover that the tiniest alteration in initial conditions can drastically change the long-term behaviour of a system, who will ask, 'Does the flap of a butterfly's wings in Brazil set off a tornado in Texas?' knowing consciously – or maybe not knowing, except by background diffusion – Alan's vision of appropriate instability, and the way that leads to the disappearance of homogeneity; to the incremental growth into a specific shape. And after Lorenz there will be all the exponents of Chaos theory, and after them another wave of seekers after truth, and the waves will lap on and out in regular irregularity through time towards an end he cannot fathom. His own physical part in this pantomime is done. The law will not allow him to be the man his own cells tell him he is, so now he will offer those rebel cells the chance of escape, which they will probably prefer to the chemical restraints recently imposed upon them by HMG. He will try the effects of cyanide upon his system.

A radical alteration occurs when, through reaction and diffusion, a tipping point is reached, and the changes which have been occurring one light switch at a time, one room at a time, in one single street, are multiplied across cities, countries, a continent, as a million million lights go on and in one mighty flash, blow the grid, and fade to black.

1952: Alan Turing and Morphogenesis

Dr Martyn Amos

I often drive right over a memorial to Alan Turing. A section of the Manchester ring-road is named in his honour, and that – together with a pigeon-spattered statue by the University – is all that commemorates the existence of one of the city's most influential figures. His death in 1954 came at the end of a sustained period of persecution by the authorities.

It's been said that Turing contributed more to the defeat of the Nazis than Eisenhower. Certainly, it's believed that his contribution to cracking the German Enigma code system was a decisive point in the war. Yet, as Jack Good, a contemporary of Turing's pithily observed, 'It was a good thing that the authorities hadn't known Turing was a homosexual during the war, because, if they had, they would have fired him – and we would have lost.'

Although Turing is best known for breaking the German codes, and thus helping to bring the war to a close, he is also celebrated for his seminal work on the nature of computation, and non-specialists might even recognize his eponymous Test – the method for evaluating whether a computer can truly be 'intelligent', by engaging it in conversation. Yet few will know of his contribution to the study of the natural world, which Jane Rogers describes so eloquently.

The modern world is a dense network of interactions, both embodied and virtual. Connections are everything, yet Turing was profoundly disconnected from the world. We know very little about his thoughts on human events, yet it is

141

clear that he yearned for connection – to the universe, to his dead childhood friend and first love, and to the deep, deep patterns of nature.

Turing's connections were intellectual, and spanned several disciplines. In the modern era, when 'inter–disciplinary' science is almost de rigueur, we take such thinking for granted. Yet, in his time, Turing was one of the very few pioneers who could see the commonalities between seemingly disjoint areas.

He grounded mathematical logic in the physical world of engineering, with the creation of what would become known as the 'Turing Machine'. By defining the notion of a computation, as well as the limitations on what computers could achieve, he laid the foundations for modern computer science and gave it a rigorous framework.

Later on, he would be captivated by the idea of artificial intelligence, and defined the criteria by which a machine (or computer program) could reasonably be called 'intelligent'. His motivation was clear when he explained, in 1951, that 'The whole thinking process is still rather mysterious to us, but I believe that the attempt to make a thinking machine will help us greatly in finding out how we think ourselves.'

In his childhood, Turing was fascinated by nature, inspired by a copy of *Brewster's Natural Wonders Every Child Should Know*. His experiments were in chemistry, not mathematics. Towards the end of his life, he focussed on the problem of morphogenesis. How can a single fertilized cell grow and develop into a fully-fledged organism? What processes can take such a tiny seed and convert it into an animal? Or, as Ian Stewart puts it, 'How do you cram an elephant into a cell?'[1]

In 1952, when Turing published his seminal paper 'The Chemical Basis of Morphogenesis'[2], Watson and Crick were still a year away from publishing their structure of DNA. Yet it was clear, even then, that the body was somehow an emergent form. Turing was inspired by the Fibonacci sequence observed in many plant structures (for example, the branching of trees, or the arrangement of a pine cone). He wanted to know how complex biological growth and development could be achieved via simple, natural mechanisms.

Of particular interest to Turing were the patterns observed in animal markings. He sought a scientific explanation to Kipling's question of how the leopard got his spots. Stripy zebras and spotty cows; each presented the same mystery. Turing started from the assumption that markings were laid down in the developing animal as an embryonic pre-pattern, or a 'template'. Over time, as it grew, this template would be 'filled out' by pigment on the embryo's surface (that is, the skin). Colour by numbers.

Turing therefore set out to understand precisely how this pre-pattern could be sketched out using chemicals. He imagined two different processes working together: reaction and diffusion. He coined the term morphogen ('generators of form') to refer to chemicals which could react together to make other molecules, and which could somehow influence tissue development. These morphogens and their products could also 'spread', or diffuse, across the embryonic surface, and whether or not a particular skin cell produced pigment depended on the relative level of morphogen in the cell.

Within such a system, Turing proposed the existence of two substances, one a catalyst (or 'activator') that stimulates the production of both chemicals, and the other an inhibitor, where the latter slows production of the former. The concentrations of each chemical can oscillate between 'high' and 'low' as the chemicals spread over the surface, giving rise to complex patterns (corresponding to the pre-pattern) if the inhibitor diffuses much faster than the activator.

By bringing to bear a combination of analysis and computer modelling on problems in the natural world, Turing pioneered the study of computational biology. His morphogenesis work was largely ignored by experimental biologists, though, who argued that his model was founded on a number of untested hypotheses. Very soon, however, evidence for the existence of natural 'Turing patterns' came in the form of the BZ reaction (named after its co-discoverers, Belousov and Zhabotinsky). This reaction proved that, by mixing a handful of specific chemicals, one could spontaneously obtain rings, spirals, spots, and other patterns – in a dish. Even then, observers were sceptical, pointing out that BZ patterns moved across the dish, unlike the static markings on animals. When the experiments were later repeated in gels, the patterns became more 'realistic', but by this time, as Ian Stewart explains, 'biologists had lost interest in the debate',[3] and Turing was long dead[4]. Recent work in fish, chicks and mice has leant increasing support to the relevance of Turing's model[5], but its real power lay in the demonstration of how order could arise spontaneously from disorder. It suggested an entirely new approach to the understanding of living systems.

Turing's contributions (both scientific and historical) will endure forever, and his vision lives on in a diverse range of research fields, from artificial intelligence to self-organization and chaos theory. As his biographer[6], Andrew Hodges explains, Turing's philosophy '...depends upon a synthesis of vision running against the grain of an intellectual world split into many verbal or mathematical or technical specialisms. He preached the computable but never lost natural wonder; the law killed and the spirit gave life.'[7]

1. Ian Stewart, *Mathematics of Life*, p. 198. Profile Books (2011).

2. A. M. Turing, 'The Chemical Basis of Morphogenesis'. *Phil. Trans. Roy. Soc.* London B, 237:641 (August 1952), pp. 37-72.

3. Ian Stewart, *Mathematical Recreations*. Scientific American (November 2000).

4. The story of the BZ reaction and its sceptical reception by the scientific community would be a good subject in its own right. Belousov was so disheartened by resistance to his discovery that he effectively withdrew from science. See A. T. Winfree, 'The Prehistory of the Belousov-Zhabotinsky Oscillator'. *Journal of Chemical Education* 61:8, p. 661-663 (August 1984).

5. S. Kondo and T. Miura, 'Reaction-diffusion Model as a Framework for Understanding Biological Pattern Formation'. *Science* 329, p. 267-275 (2010).

6. Andrew Hodges, *Alan Turing: The Enigma* (Vintage, 1992).

7. Andrew Hodges, *Turing* (Great Philosophers series, Phoenix, 1997).

The Heart of Denis Noble

Alison MacLeod

As Denis Noble, Professor of Cardiovascular Physiology, succumbs to the opioids – a meandering river of fentanyl from the IV drip – he is informed his heart is on its way. In twenty, perhaps thirty minutes' time, the Cessna air ambulance will land in the bright, crystalline light of December, on the small landing strip behind the Radcliffe Hospital.

A bearded jaw appears over him. From this angle, the mouth is oddly labial. Does he understand? Professor Noble nods from the other side of the ventilation mask. He would join in the team chat but the mask prevents it, and in any case, he must lie still so the nurse can shave the few hairs that remain on his chest.

No cool-box then. No heart on ice. This is what they are telling him. Instead, the latest technology. He remembers the prototype he was once shown. His new heart will arrive in its own state-of-the-art reliquary. It will be lifted, beating, from a nutrient-rich bath of blood and oxygen. So he can rest easy, someone adds. It's beating well at 40,000 feet, out of range of all turbulence. 'We need your research, Professor,' another voice jokes from behind the ECG. 'We're taking no chances!'

Which isn't to say that the whole thing isn't a terrible gamble.

The nurse has traded the shaver for a pair of nail-clippers. She sets to work on the nails on his right hand, his plucking hand. Is that necessary? he wants to ask. It will take him some time to grow them back, assuming of course he still has 'time'. As she slips the pulse-oximeter over his index finger, he wonders if Joshua will show any interest at all in the classical guitar he is destined to inherit, possibly any day now. According to his mother, Josh is into electronica and urban soul.

A second nurse bends and whispers in his ear like a lover. 'Now all you have to do is relax, Denis. We've got everything covered.' Her breath is warm. Her breast is near. He can imagine the gloss of her lips. He wishes she would stay by his ear forever. 'We'll have you feeling like yourself again before you know it.'

He feels he might be sick.

Then his choice of pre-op music – the second movement of Schubert's Piano Trio in E-Flat Major – seems to flow, sweet and grave, from her mouth into his ear, and once more he can see past the red and golden treetops of Gordon Square to his attic room of half a century ago. A recording of the Schubert is rising through the floorboards, and the girl beside him in his narrow student bed is warm; her lips brush the lobe of his ear; her voice alone, the whispered current of it, is enough to arouse him. But when her fingers find him beneath the sheet, they surprise him with a catheter, and he has to shut his eyes against the tears, against the absurdity of age.

The heart of Denis Noble beat for the first time on the fifth of March, 1936 in the body of Ethel Noble as she stitched a breast pocket to a drape-cut suit in an upstairs room at Wilson & Jeffries, the tailoring house where she first met her husband George, a trainee cutter, across a flashing length of gold silk lining.

As she pierced the tweed with her basting needle, she remembered George's tender, awkward kiss to her collarbone that morning, and, as if in reply, Denis's heart, a mere tube at this point, beat its first of more than two billion utterances – da dum. Unknown to Ethel, she was twenty-one days pregnant. Her thread dangled briefly in mid-air.

Soon, the tube that was Denis Noble's heart, a delicate scrap of mesoderm, would push towards life. In the dark of Ethel, it would twist and grope, looping blindly back towards itself in the primitive knowledge that circulation, the vital whoosh of life, deplores a straight line. With a tube, true, we can see from end to end, we can blow clear through or whistle a tune – a tube is nothing if not straightforward – but a loop, a *loop*, is a circuit of energy understood only by itself.

In this unfolding, intra-uterine drama, Denis Noble – a dangling button on the thread of life – would begin to take shape, to hold fast. He would inherit George's high forehead and Ethel's bright almond-shaped, almost Oriental, eyes. His hands would be small but unusually dexterous. A birthmark would stamp itself on his left hip. But inasmuch as he was flesh, blood and bone, he was also, deep within Ethel, a living stream of sound and sensation, a delicate flux of stimuli, the influence of which eluded all known measure, then as now.

He was the cloth smoothed beneath Ethel's cool palm, and the pumping of her foot on the pedal of the Singer machine. He was the hiss of her iron over the sleeve press and the clink of brass pattern-weights in her apron pocket. He was the soft spring light through the open window, the warmth of it bathing her face, and the serotonin surging in her synapses at the sight of a magnolia tree in flower. He was the manifold sound waves of passers-by: of motor cars hooting, of old men hawking and spitting, and delivery boys teetering down Savile Row under bolts of cloth bigger than they were. Indeed it is impossible to say where Denis stopped and the world began.

Only on a clear, cloudless night in November 1940 did the world seem to unstitch itself from the small boy he was and separate into something strange, something other. Denis opened his eyes to the darkness. His mother was scooping him from his bed and running down the stairs so fast, his head bumped up and down against her shoulder.

Downstairs, his father wasn't in his armchair with the newspaper on his lap, but on the sitting room floor cutting cloth by the light of a torch. Why was Father camping indoors? 'Let's sing a song,' his mother whispered, but she forgot to tell him which song to sing.

The kitchen was a dark place and no, it wasn't time for

eggs and soldiers, not yet, she shooshed, and even as she spoke, she was depositing him beneath the table next to the fat yellow bundle that was his sister, and stretching out beside him, even though her feet in their court shoes stuck out the end. 'There, there,' she said as she pulled them both to her. Then they turned their ears towards a sky they couldn't see and listened to the planes that droned like wasps in the jar of the South London night.

When the bang came, the floor shuddered beneath them and plaster fell in lumps from the ceiling. His father rushed in from the sitting room, pins still gripped between his lips. Before his mother had finished thanking God, Denis felt his legs propel him, without permission, not even his own, to the window to look. Beneath a corner of the black-out curtain, at the bottom of the garden, flames were leaping. 'Fire!' he shouted, but his father shouted louder, nearly swallowing his pins – 'GET AWAY from the window!' – and plucked him into the air.

They owed their lives, his mother would later tell Mrs West next door, to a cabinet minister's suit. Their Anderson shelter, where they would have been huddled were it not for the demands of bespoke design, had taken a direct hit.

That night, George and a dicky stirrup pump waged a losing battle against the flames until neighbours joined in with rugs, hoses and buckets of sand. Denis stood behind his mother's hip at the open door. His baby sister howled from her Moses basket. Smoke gusted as he watched his new red wagon melt in the heat. Ethel smiled down at him, squeezing his hand, and it seemed very odd because his mother shook as much as she smiled and she smiled as much as she shook. It should have been very difficult, like rubbing your tummy and patting your head at the same time, and as Denis beheld his mother – her eyes wet with tears, her hair unpinned, her arms goose-pimpled – he felt something radiate through his chest. The feeling was delicious. It warmed him through. He felt light on his toes. If his mother hadn't been wearing her heavy navy blue court shoes, the two of them, he thought, might have floated off the doorstep and into the night.

At the same time, the feeling was an ache, a hole, a sore

inside him. It made him feel heavy. His heart was like something he'd swallowed that had gone down the wrong way. It made it hard to breathe. Denis Noble, age four, didn't understand. As the tremor in his mother's arm travelled into his hand, up his arm, through his armpit and into his chest, he felt for the first time the mysterious life of the heart.

He had of course been briefed in the weeks prior to surgery. His consultant, Mr Bonham, had sat at his desk – chins doubling with the gravity of the situation – reviewing Denis's notes. The tests had been inconclusive but the 'rather urgent' need for transplantation remained clear.

Naturally he would, Mr Bonham said, be familiar with the procedure. An incision in the ribcage. The removal of the pericardium – 'a slippery business, but routine'. Denis's heart would be emptied, and the aorta clamped prior to excision. 'Textbook.' The chest cavity would be cleared, though the biatrial cuff would be left in place. Then the new heart would be 'unveiled – voilà!', and the aorta engrafted, followed by the pulmonary artery.

Most grafts, Mr Bonham assured him, recovered normal ventricular function without intervention. There were risks, of course: bleeding, RV failure, bradyarrhythmias, conduction abnormalities, sudden death...

Mr Bonham surveyed his patient through his half-moon specs. 'Atheist, I presume?'

'I'm afraid not.' Denis regarded his surgeon with polite patience. Mr Bonham was widely reputed to be one of the last eccentrics still standing in the NHS.

'A believer then. Splendid. More expedient at times like this. And fear not. The Royal Society won't hear it from me!'

'Which is perhaps just as well,' said Denis, 'as I'm afraid I make as poor a 'believer' as I do an atheist.'

Mr Bonham removed his glasses. 'Might be time to sort the muddle out.' He huffed on his specs, gave them a wipe with a crumpled handkerchief, and returned them to the end of his nose. 'I have a private hunch, you see, that agnostics don't fare quite as well in major surgery. No data for *The*

Lancet as yet but' – he ventured a wink – 'even so. See if you can't muster a little… certainty.'

A smile crept across Denis's face. 'The Buddhists advise against too much metaphysical certainty.'

'You're a Buddhist?' A Buddhist at Oxford? At Balliol?

Denis's smile strained. 'I try to keep my options open.'

'I see.' Mr Bonham didn't. There was an embarrassment of categories. A blush spread up his neck, and as Denis watched his surgeon shuffle his notes, he felt his chances waver.

The *allegro* now. The third movement of the Piano Trio – *faster, faster* – but the Schubert is receding, and as Denis surfaces from sleep, he realises he's being whisked down the wide, blanched corridors of the Heart Unit. His trolley is a precision vehicle. It glides. It shunts around corners. There's no time to waste – the heart must be fresh – and he wonders if he has missed his stop. Kentish Town. Archway. Highgate. East Finchley. The names of the stations flicker past like clues in a dream to a year he cannot quite summon. Tunnel after tunnel. He mustn't nod off again, mustn't miss the stop, but the carriage is swaying and rocking, it's only quarter past five in the morning, and it's hard to resist the ramshackle lullaby of the Northern Line.

West Finchley. Woodside Park.

1960.

That's the one.

It's 1960, but no one, it seems, has told the good people of Totteridge. Each time he steps onto the platform at the quaint, well swept station, he feels as if he has been catapulted back in time.

The slaughterhouse is a fifteen-minute walk along a B-road, and Denis is typically the first customer of the day. He feels underdressed next to the workers in their whites, their hard hats, their metal aprons and steel-toed Wellies. They stare, collectively, at his loafers.

Slaughter-men aren't talkers by nature, but nevertheless, over the months, Denis has come to know each by name.

Front of house, there's Alf the Shackler, Frank the Knocker, Jimmy the Sticker, Marty the Plucker, and Mike the Splitter. Frank tells him how, years ago, a sledgehammer saw him through the day's routine, but now it's a pneumatic gun and a bolt straight to the brain; a few hundred shots a day, which means he has to wear goggles, 'cos of all the grey matter flying'. He's worried he's developing 'trigger-finger', and he removes his plastic glove so Denis can see for himself 'the finger what won't uncurl.'

Alf is brawny but soft-spoken with kind, almost womanly eyes. Every morning on the quiet, he tosses Denis a pair of Wellies to spare his shoes. No one mentions the stink of the place, a sharp kick to the lungs of old blood, manure and offal. The breeze block walls exhale it and the floor reeks of it, even though the place is mopped down like a temple every night.

Jimmy is too handsome for a slaughterhouse, all dirty blond curls and American teeth, but he doesn't know it because he's a farmboy who's never been further than East Finchley. Marty, on the other hand, was at Dunkirk. He has a neck like a battering ram and a lump of shrapnel in his head. Every day, at the close of business, he brings his knife home with him on the passenger seat of his Morris Mini-Minor. He explains to Denis that he spends a solid hour each night sharpening and sanding the blade to make sure it's smooth with no pits. 'An' 'e wonders,' bellows Mike, 'why 'e can't get a bird!'

Denis pays £4 for two hearts a day, a sum that left him stammering with polite confusion on his first visit. At Wilson and Jeffries, his father earns £20 per week.

Admittedly, they bend the rules for him. Frank 'knocks' the first sheep as usual. Alf shackles and hoists. But Jimmy, who grasps his sticking knife – Jimmy, the youngest, who's always keen, literally, to 'get stuck in' – doesn't get to slit the throat and drain the animal. When Denis visits, there's a different protocol. Jimmy steps aside, and Marty cuts straight into the chest and scoops out 'the pluck'. The blood gushes. The heart and lungs steam in Marty's hands. The others tssk-tssk like old women at the sight of the spoiled hide, but Marty is butchery in motion. He casts the lungs down a chute, passes the warm heart to Denis, rolls the stabbed sheep down the line to Mike the Splitter, shouts 'Chop, chop, ha ha' at Mike, and waits like a veteran for Alf to roll the second sheep his way.

Often Denis doesn't wait to get back to the lab. He pulls a large pair of scissors from his hold-all, grips the heart at arm's length, cuts open the meaty ventricles, checks to ensure the Purkinje fibres are still intact, then pours a steady stream of Tyrode solution over and into the heart. When the blood is washed clear, he plops the heart into his Thermos and waits for the next heart as the gutter in the floor fills with blood. The Tyrode solution, which mimics the sugar and salts of blood, is a simple but strange elixir. Denis still can't help but take a schoolboy sort of pleasure in its magic. There in his Thermos, at the core of today's open heart, the Purkinje fibres have started to beat again in their Tyrode bath. Very occasionally, a whole ventricle comes to life as he washes it down. On those occasions, he lets Jimmy hold the disembodied heart as if it is a wounded bird fluttering between his palms.

Then the Northern Line flickers past in reverse until Euston Station re-appears, where Denis hops out and jogs – Thermos and scissors clanging in the hold-all – down Gower Street, past the main quad, through the Anatomy entrance, up the grand, century-old staircase to the second floor, and into the empty lab before the clock on the wall strikes seven.

In the hush of the Radcliffe's principal operating theatre, beside the anaesthetised, intubated body of Denis Noble, Mr Bonham assesses the donor heart for a final time.

The epicardial surface is smooth and glistening. The quantity of fat is negligible. The aorta above the valve reveals a smooth intima with no atherosclerosis. The heart is still young, after all; sadly, just seventeen years old, though – in keeping with protocol – he has revealed nothing of the donor identity to the patient, and Professor Noble knows better than to ask. The lumen of the coronary artery is large, without any visible narrowing. The muscular arterial wall is of sound proportion.

Pre-operative monitoring has confirmed strong wall

motion, excellent valve function, good conduction and regular heart rhythm.

It's a ticklish business at the best of times, he reminds his team, but yes, he is ready to proceed.

In the lab of the Anatomy Building, Denis pins out the heart like a valentine in a Petri dish. The buried trove, the day's booty, is nestled at the core; next to the red flesh of the ventricle, the Purkinje network is a skein of delicate yellow fibres. They gleam like the bundles of pearl cotton his mother used to keep in her embroidery basket.

Locating them is one thing. Getting them is another. It is tricky work to lift them free; trickier still to cut away sections without destroying them. He needs a good eye, a small pair of surgical scissors, and the steady cutting hand he inherited, he likes to think, from his father. If impatience gets the better of him, if he sneezes, if his scissors slip, it will be a waste of a fresh and costly heart. Beyond the lab door, an undergrad class thunders down the staircase. Outside, through the thin Victorian glass panes, Roy Orbison croons 'Only the Lonely' on a transistor radio.

Denis drops his scissors and reaches for a pair of forceps. He works like a watchmaker, lifting another snipped segment free. A second Petri dish awaits. A fresh bath of Tyrode solution, an oxygenated variety this time, will boost their recovery. If all goes well, he can usually harvest a dozen segments from each heart. But the ends will need to close before the real work can begin. Sometimes they need an hour, sometimes longer.

Coffee. He needs a coffee. He boils water on the Bunsen burner someone pinched from the chemistry lab. The instant coffee is on the shelf with the belljars. He pours, using his sleeve as a mitt, and, in the absence of a spoon, uses the pencil that's always tucked behind his ear.

At the vast chapel-arch of a window, he can just see the treetops of Gordon Square, burnished with autumn, and far below, the gardeners raking leaves and lifting bulbs. Beyond it, from this height, he can see as far as Tavistock Square, though the old copper beech stands between him and a view of his own attic window at the top of Connaught Hall.

He tries not to think about Ella, whom he hopes to find, several hours from now, on the other side of that window, in his room – i.e., his bed – where they have agreed to meet to 'compare the findings' of their respective days. Ella, a literature student, has been coolly bluffing her way into the Press Box at The Old Bailey for the last week or so. For his part, he'd never heard of the infamous novel until the headlines got hold of it, but Ella is gripped and garrulous, and even the sound of her voice in his ear fills him with a desire worthy of the finest dirty book.

He paces, mug in hand. He can't bring himself to leave his fibres unattended while they heal.

He watches the clock.

He checks the fibres. Too soon.

He deposits his mug on the windowsill and busies himself with his prep. He fills the first glass micro-pipette with potassium chloride, inserts the silver thread-wire and connects it to the valve on his home-made amp. The glass pipette in his hand always brings to mind the old wooden dibber, smooth with use, that his father used during spring planting. Denis can see him still, in his weekend pullover and tie, on his knees in the garden, as he dibbed and dug for a victory that was in no hurry to come. Only his root vegetables ever rewarded his efforts.

Soon, Antony and Günter, his undergrad assistants, will shuffle in for duty. He'll post Antony, with the camera and a stockpile of film, at the oscilloscope's screen. Günter will take to the darkroom next to the lab, and emerge pale and blinking at the end of the day.

Outside, the transistor radio and its owner take their leave. He drains his coffee, glances at the clock, and checks his nails for sheep's blood. How much longer? He allows himself to wander as far as the stairwell and back again. He doodles on the blackboard – a sickle moon, a tree, a stick man clinging to a branch – and erases all three.

At last, at last. He prepares a slide, sets up the Zeiss, switches on its light and swivels the lens into place. At this magnification, the fibre cells are pulsing minnows of life. His 'dibbers' are ready; Günter passes him the first and checks its connection to the amp. Denis squints over the Zeiss and inserts the micro-pipette into a cell membrane. The view is good. He can even spot the two boss-eyed nuclei. If the second pipette penetrates the cell successfully, he'll make contact with the innermost life of the cell.

His wrist is steady, which means every impulse, every rapid-fire excitation, should travel up the pipette through the thread-wire and into the valve of the amplifier. The oscilloscope will 'listen' to the amp. Fleeting waves of voltage will rise and fall across its screen, and Antony will snap away on the Nikon, capturing every fluctuation, every trace. Günter, for his part, has already removed himself like a penitent to the darkroom. There, if all goes well, he'll capture the divine spark of life on Kodak paper, over and over again.

Later still, they'll convert the electrical ephemera of the day into scrolling graphs; they'll chart the unfolding peaks and troughs; they'll watch on paper the ineffable currents that compel the heart to life.

Cell after cell. Impulse upon impulse. An ebb and flow of voltage. The unfolding story of a single heartbeat in thousandths of a second.

'Tell me,' says Ella, 'about your excitable cells. I like those.' Their heads share the one pillow. Schubert's piano trio is rising through the floorboards of the student hall. A cellist he has yet to meet lives below.

'I'll give you excitable.' He pinches her bottom. She bites the end of his nose. Through the crack of open window, they can smell trampled leaves, wet pavement and frostbitten earth. In the night above the attic window, the stars throb.

She sighs luxuriously and shifts, so that Denis has to grip the mattress of the narrow single bed to steady himself. 'Excuse me, Miss, but I'm about to go over the edge.'

'Of the bed or your mental health? Have you found those canals yet?'

'Channels.'

'Precisely. Plutonium channels. See? I listen. You might not think I do, but I do.'

'Potassium. Potassium channels.'

'That's what I said.'

'I'm afraid you didn't. Which means…'

'Which means..?'

He rumples his brow in a display of forethought. 'Which means – and I say this with regret – I might just have to spank you.' He marvels at his own audacity. He is someone new with her and, at the same time, he has never felt more himself.

'Cheek!' she declares, and covers her own with the eiderdown. 'But I'm listening now. Tell me again. What do you do with these potassium channels?'

'I map their electrical activity. I demonstrate the movement of ions – electrically charged particles – through the cell membranes.' From the mattress edge, he gets a purchase by grabbing hold of her hip.

'Why aren't you more pleased?'

'Tell me about the trial today.'

'I thought you said those channels of yours were *the* challenge. The new discovery. The biologist's New World.'

'I'm pleased. Yes. Thanks. It's going well.' He throws back the eiderdown, springs to his feet and rifles through her shoulder bag for her notebook. 'Is it in here?'

'Is what?'

'Your notebook.'

'A man's testicles are never at their best as he bends,' she observes.

'So did The Wigs put on a good show today?'

She folds her arms across the eiderdown. 'I'm not talking dirty until you tell me about your potassium what-nots.'

'Channels.' From across the room, his back addresses her. 'They're simply passages or pores in the cell membrane that allow a mass of charged ions to be shunted into the cell – or out of it again if there's an excess.'

She sighs. 'If it's all so matter of fact, why are you bothering?'

He returns to her side, kisses the top of her head and negotiates his way back into the bed. 'My supervisor put me on the case, and, like I say, all's well. I'm getting the results, rather more quickly than I expected, so I'm pleased. Relieved even. Because in truth, I would have looked a little silly if I hadn't found them. They're already known to exist in muscle cells, and the heart is only another muscle after all.'

'Only another muscle?'

'Yes.' He flips through her notebook.

'But this is something that has you running through Bloomsbury in the middle of the night and leaving me for a date with a computer.'

He kisses her shoulder. 'The computer isn't nearly so amiable.'

'Denis Noble, are you doing interesting work or aren't you?'

'I have a dissertation to produce.'

'Please. Never be, you know...take it or leave it. Never be bored. Men who are bored bore me.'

'Then I shall stifle every yawn.'

'You'll have to do better than that. Tell me what you aim to discover next.' She divests him of his half of the eiderdown, and he grins, in spite of the cold.

'Whatever it is, you'll be the first to know.'

'Perhaps it isn't an "it",' she muses. 'Have you thought of that?'

'How can "it" not be an "it"?'

'I'm not sure,' she says, and she wraps herself up like the Queen of Sheba. The eiderdown crackles with static, and her fine, shiny hair flies away in the light of the desk-lamp. 'But a book, for example, is not an "it".'

'Of course it's an "it". It's an object, a thing. Ask any girl in her deportment class, as she walks about with one on her head.'

'Then I'll re-phrase, shall I? A story is not an "it". If it's any good, it's more alive than an "it". Every part of a great story "contains" every other part. Every small part anticipates the whole. Nothing can be passive or static. Nothing is just a part. Not really. Because the whole, if it's powerful enough that is, cannot be divided. That's what a great creation is. It has its own marvellous unity.' She pauses to examine the birthmark on his hip, a new discovery. 'Of course, I'm fully aware I sound like a) a girl and b) a dreamy arts student, but I suspect the heart *is* a great creation and that the same rule applies.'

'And which *rule* might that be?' He loves listening to her, even if he has no choice but to mock her, gently.

'The same principle then.'

He raises an eyebrow.

She adjusts her generous breasts. 'The principle of Eros. Eros is an attractive force. It binds the world; it makes connections. At best, it gives way to a sense of wholeness, a sense of the sacred even; at worst, it leads to fuzzy vision. Logos, your contender, particularises. It makes the elements of the world distinct. At best, it is illuminating; at worst, it is reductive. It cheapens. Both are vital. The balance is the thing. You need Eros, Denis. You're missing Eros.'

He passes her her notebook and taps it. 'On that point, we agree entirely. I wait with the utmost patience.'

She studies him with suspicion, then opens the spiral-bound stenographer's notebook. In the days before the trial, she taught herself shorthand in record time simply to capture, like any other putative member of the press, the banned passages of prose. She was determined to help carry their erotic charge into the world. 'T.S. Eliot was supposed to give evidence for the defense today, but apparently he sat in his taxi and couldn't bring himself to "do the deed".'

'Old men – impotent. Young men' – he smiles shyly and nods to his exposed self – 'ready.' He opens her notebook to a random page of shorthand. The ink is purple.

'My little joke,' she says. 'A sense of humour is *de rigueur* in the Press Box.' She nestles into the pillow and relinquishes his half of the eiderdown. He pats down her fly-away hair. 'From Chapter Ten,' she begins. '"Then with a quiver of exquisite pleasure he touched the warm soft body, and touched her navel for a moment in a kiss. And he had to come into her at once, to enter the peace on earth of her soft quiescent body. It was the moment of pure peace for him, the entry into the body of a woman."'

'That gamekeeper chap doesn't hang about,' he says, his smile twitching.

'Quiet,' she chides. 'He is actually a very noble sort. Not sordid like you.'

'My birth certificate would assure you that I'm a Noble sort.'

'Ha ha.'

Denis lays his head against her breast and listens to the beat of her heart as she reads. Her voice enters him like a current and radiates through him until he feels himself almost hum with it, as if he is the body of a violin or cello that exists only to amplify her voice. He suspects he is not in love with her – and that is really just as well – but it occurs to him that he has never known such sweetness, such delight. He tries to stay in the moment, to loiter in the beats between the words she reads, between the breaths she takes. He runs his hand over the bell of her hip and tries not to think that in just four hours he will set off into the darkened streets of Bloomsbury, descend a set of basement steps and begin his night shift in the company of the only computer at the University of London powerful enough to crunch his milliseconds of data into readable equations.

As a lowly biologist, an ostensible lightweight among the physicists and computer guys, he has been allocated the least enviable slot on the computer, from two till four am. By five, he'll be on the Northern Line again, heading for the slaughterhouse.

Ella half wakes as he leaves.

'Go back to sleep,' he whispers. He grabs his jacket and the hold-all.

She sits up in bed, blinking in the light of the lamp which he has turned to the wall. 'Are you going now?'

'Yes.' He smiles, glancing at her, finds his wallet and checks he has enough for the hearts of the day.

'Goodbye, Denis,' she says softly.

'Sweet dreams,' he says.

But she doesn't stretch and settle back under the eiderdown. She remains upright and naked even though the room is so cold, their breath has turned to frost on the inside of the window. He wonders if there isn't something odd in her expression. He hovers for a moment before deciding it is either a shadow from the lamp or the residue of a dream. Whatever the case, he can't be late for his shift. If he is, the porter in the unit won't be there to let him in – which means he has no more time to think on it.

He switches off the lamp.

In his later years, Denis Noble has allowed himself to wonder, privately, about the physiology of love. He has loved – with gratitude and frustration – parents, siblings, a spouse and two children. What, he asks himself, is love if not a force within? And what is a force within if not something *lived through* the body? Nevertheless, as Emeritus Professor of Cardiovascular Physiology, he has to admit he knows little more about love than he did on the night he fell in love with his mother; the night their shelter was bombed; the night he felt with utter certainty the strange and secret life of the heart within his chest.

Before 1960 drew to a close, he would – like hundreds of thousands of other liberated readers – buy the banned book and try to understand it as Ella had understood it. Later still in life, he would dedicate himself to the music and poetry of the Occitan troubadours. ('*I only know the grief that comes to me, to my love-ridden heart, out of over-loving...*') He would read and re-read the ancient sacred-sexual texts of the Far East. He would learn, almost by heart, St. Theresa's account of her vision of the seraph: '*I saw in his hands a long spear of gold, and at the iron's point there seemed to be a little fire. He appeared to me to be thrusting it at times into my heart, and to pierce my very entrails; when he drew it out, he seemed to draw them out also, and to leave me all on fire with a great love of God. The pain was so great that it made me moan; and yet so surpassing was the sweetness of this excessive pain that I could not wish to be rid of it.*'

But *what*, he wanted to ask St. Theresa, could the heart, that feat of flesh, blood and voltage, have to do with love? *Where*, he'd like to know, is love? *How* is love?

162

On the train to Totteridge, he can still smell the citrus of Ella's perfume on his hands, in spite of all the punched paper-tape offerings he's been feeding to the computer through the night. He only left its subterranean den an hour ago. These days, the slots of his schedule are his daily commandments.

He is allowed 'to live' and to sleep from seven each evening to half past one the next morning, when his alarm wakes him for his shift in the computer unit. He closes the door on the darkness of Connaught Hall and sprints across Bloomsbury. After his shift, he travels from the Comp. Science basement to the Northern Line, from the Northern Line to the slaughterhouse, from the slaughterhouse to Euston, and from Euston to the lab for his twelve-hour day. 'Seven to seven,' he declares to his supervisor. He arrives home to Connaught Hall for supper at seven-thirty, Ella at eight, sleep at ten and three hours' oblivion until the alarm rings and the cycle starts all over again.

He revels briefly in the thought of a pretty girl still asleep in his bed, a luxury he'd never dared hope to win as a science student. Through the smeared carriage windows, the darkness is thinning into a murky dawn. The Thermos jiggles in the hold-all at his feet, the carriage door rattles and clangs, and his head falls back.

Up ahead, Ella is standing naked and grand on a bright woodland path in Tavistock Square. She doesn't seem to care that she can be seen by all the morning commuters and the students rushing past on their way to classes. She slips through the gate at the western end of the square and turns, closing it quickly. As he reaches it, he realises it is a kissing-gate. She stands on the other side but refuses him her lips. 'Gates open,' she says tenderly, 'and they close.' He tries to go through but she shakes her head. When he pulls on the gate, he gets an electric shock. 'Why are you surprised?' she says. Then she's disappearing through another gate into Gordon Square, and her hair is flying-away in the morning light, as if she herself is electric. He pulls again on the gate, but it's rigid.

The dream returns to him only later as Marty is scooping the pluck from the first sheep on the line.

He feels again the force of that electric shock.

The gate was conductive...

It opened... It closed.

It *closed*.

He receives from Marty the first heart of the day. It's hot between his palms but he doesn't reach for his scissors. He doesn't open the Thermos. He hardly moves. Deep within him, it's as if his own heart has been jump-started to life.

In the operating theatre, Mr Bonham and his team have been at work for three-and-a-half hours, when at last he gives the word. Professor Noble can be disconnected from the bypass machine. His pulse is strong. The new heart, declares Mr Bonham, 'is going great guns.'

His dream of Ella at the gate means he can't finish at the slaughterhouse quickly enough. On the train back into town, he swears under his breath at the eternity of every stop. In the lab, he wonders if the ends of the Purkinje fibres will ever close and heal. He has twelve hours of lab time. Seven to seven. Will it be enough?

Twelve hours pass like two. The fibres are tricky today. He botched more than a few in the dissection, and the insertion of the micro-pipette has been hit and miss. Antony and Günter exchange looks. They discover he has amassed untold quantities of film, and he tells Antony he wants a faster shutter speed. When they request a lunch break, he simply stares into the middle distance. When Günter complains that his hands are starting to burn from the fixatives, Denis looks up from his micro-pipette, as if at a tourist who requires something of him in another language.

Finally, when the great window is a chapel arch of darkness and rain, he closes and locks the lab door behind him. There is nothing in his appearance to suggest anything other than a long day's work. No one he passes on the grand staircase of the Anatomy Building pauses to look. No one glances back, pricked by an intuition or an afterthought. He has remembered his hold-all and the Thermos for tomorrow's hearts. He has forgotten his jacket, but the sight of a poorly dressed student is nothing to make anyone look twice.

Yet as he steps into the downpour of the night, every light is blazing in his head. His brain is Piccadilly Circus, and in the dazzle, he hardly sees where he's going but he's running, across Gordon Square and on towards Tavistock... He wants to shout the news to the winos who shelter from the rain under dripping trees. He wants to holler it to every lit window, to every student in his or her numinous haze of thought. He wants to dash up the stairs of Connaught Hall, knock on the door of the mystery cellist, and blurt out the words. Tomorrow at the slaughterhouse, he tells himself, he might even have to hug Marty and Alf. 'They *close!*'

He saw it with his own eyes: potassium channels that *closed*.

They did just the opposite of what everyone expected.

He assumed some sort of experimental error. He went back through Günter's contact sheets. He checked the amp and the connections. He wondered if he wasn't merely observing his own wishful thinking. He started again. He shook things up. He subjected the cells to change – changes of voltage, of ions, of temperature. Antony asked, morosely, for permission to leave early. He had an exam – Gross Anatomy – the next day. Didn't Antony understand? 'They're not simply open,' he announced over a new ten-pound cylinder of graph paper. 'They *opened.*'

Antony's face was blank as an egg.

Günter suggested they call it a day.

But the channels opened. They were active. They opened *and*, more remarkably still, they *closed*.

Ella was right. He'll tell her she was. He'll be the first to admit it. The channels aren't merely passive conduits. They're not just machinery or component parts. They're alive and responsive.

Too many ions inside the cell — too much stress, exercise, anger, love, lust or despair — and they close. They stop all incoming electrical traffic. They preserve calm in the midst of too much life. They allow the ion gradient to stabilise.

He can hardly believe it himself. The heart 'listens' to itself. Causation isn't just upward; it's unequivocally downward too. It's a beautiful loop of feedback. The parts of the heart listen to each other as surely as musicians in an ensemble listen to each other. That's what he's longing to tell Ella. *That's* what he's discovered. Forget the ensemble. The heart is an *orchestra*. It's the BBC Proms. It's the Boston Pops. Even if he only understands its rhythm section today, he knows this now. The heart is infinitely more than the sum of its parts.

And he can prove it mathematically. The super computer will vouch for him, he feels sure of it. He'll design the equations. He'll come up with a computer model that will make even the physicists and computer scientists stand and gawp.

Which is when it occurs to him: what if the heart doesn't stop at the heart? What if the connections don't end?

Even he doesn't quite know what he means by this.

He will ask Ella. He will tell her of their meeting at the kissing-gate. He will ask for the kiss her dream-self refused him this morning. He'll enjoy the sweet confusion on her face.

Ella at eight.

Ella always at eight.

He waits by the window until the lights go out over Tavistock Square and the trees melt into darkness.

He waits for three days. He retreats under the eiderdown. He is absent from the slaughterhouse, the lab and the basement.

A fortnight passes. A month. The new year.

When the second movement of the Piano Trio rises through the floorboards, he feels nothing. It has taken him months, but finally, he feels nothing.

As he comes round, the insult of the tube down his throat assures him he hasn't died.

The first thing he sees is his grandson by the foot of his bed tapping away on his new mobile phone. 'Hi Granddad,' Josh says, as if Denis has only been napping. He bounces to the side of the ICU bed, unfazed by the bleeping monitors and the tubes. 'Put your index finger here, Denis. I'll help you... No, like right *over* the camera lens. That's it. This phone has an Instant Heart Rate App. We'll see if you're working yet.'

'Cool,' Denis starts to say, but the irony is lost to the tube in his throat.

Josh's brow furrows. He studies his phone screen like a doctor on a medical soap. 'Sixty-two beats per minute at rest. Congratulations, Granddad. You're like...alive.' Josh squeezes his hand and grins.

Denis has never been so glad to see him.

On the other side of the bed, his wife touches his shoulder. Her face is tired. The fluorescence of the lights age her. She has lipstick on her front tooth and tears in her eyes as she bends to whisper, hoarsely, in his ear. 'You came back to me.'

The old words.

After a week, he'd given up hope. He realised he didn't

even know where she lived, which student residence, which flat, which telephone exchange. He'd never thought to ask. Once he even tried waiting for her outside The Old Bailey, but the trial was over, someone told him. Days before. Didn't he read the papers?

When she opened his door in January of '61, she stood on the threshold, like an apparition who might at any moment disappear again. She simply waited, her shiny hair still flying away from her in the light of the bare bulb on the landing. He was standing at the window through which he'd given up looking. On the other side, the copper beech was bare with winter. In the room below, the Schubert recording was stuck on a scratch.

Her words, when they finally came, were hushed and angry. They rose and fell in a rhythm he'd almost forgotten. 'Why don't you *know* that you're in love with me? What's wrong with you, Denis Noble?'

Cooking smells – boiled vegetables and mince – wafted into his room from the communal kitchen on the floor below. It seemed impossible that she should be here. Ella. Not Ella at eight. *Ella.*

Downstairs, the cellist moved the needle on the record.

'You came back to me,' he said.

His eyes filled.

As his recuperation begins, he will realise, with not a little impatience, that he knows nothing at all about the whereabouts of love. He knows only where it isn't. It is not in the heart, or if it is, it is not only in the heart. The organ that first beat in the depths of Ethel in the upstairs room of Wilson & Jeffries is now consigned to the scrap heap of cardiovascular history. Yet in this moment, with a heart that is not strictly his, he loves Ella as powerfully as he did the night she re-appeared in his room on Tavistock Square.

But if love is not confined to the heart, nor would it

seem is memory confined to the brain. The notion tantalises him. Those aspects or qualities which make the human condition human – love, consciousness, memory, affinity – are, Denis feels more sure than ever, *distributed* throughout the body. The single part, as Ella once claimed so long ago, must contain the whole.

He hopes his new heart will let him live long enough to see the proof. He'll have to chivvy the good folk at the Physiome Project along.

He wishes he had a pencil.

In the meantime, as Denis adjusts to his new heart hour by hour, day by day, he will demonstrate, in Josh's steadfast company, an imperfect but unprecedented knowledge of the lyrics of Jay-Z and OutKast. He will announce to Ella that he is keen to buy a BMX bike. He won't be sure himself whether he is joking or not. He will develop an embarrassing appetite for doner kebabs, and he will not be deterred by the argument, put to him by Ella, his daughter and Josh, that he has never eaten a doner kebab in his entire life.

He will surprise even himself when he hears himself tell Mr Bonham, during his evening rounds, that he favours Alton Towers over the Dordogne this year.

Afterword:

1960: Denis Noble and Mathematically Modelling the Heart Cell

Professor Denis Noble

Can fiction be truer than truth? As I first read this story my pen itched to correct some (actually, surprisingly few) of the imagined details. But, of course, my pen misunderstood. Fiction can capture truth that is beyond the truth itself. If she could read it, the 'bedroom girl' would have the last enlightened laugh on this one.

But, to turn to the science – the discovery itself – why do those potassium channels close during each heartbeat? Well, in doing so they save precious energy. The heart can beat away for 70 or more years (that's over 2 billion beats) without draining the body of more energy than necessary. Moreover, by closing during each electric excitation, they allow tiny trickles of other ions, sodium and calcium, to have much larger effects than would otherwise be the case. That trick must have been discovered during evolution more than half a billion years ago in one of those 'pacts with the devil' (Noble, 2006 page 109) that litter the archives of the evolutionary process. The intelligence of life doesn't lie in genes, those dead bits of DNA that we pass onto our progeny much as we pass CDs of our music to others who wish to hear it. It lies in delicate oily membranes in which the protein channels float as they talk to each other by varying the electrical potential across the membrane, and so generate electrical and mechanical rhythm. The genes know nothing of those oily membranes. Not being proteins or RNAs, there are no DNA templates for them. Not everything we inherit is determined by DNA.

That kind of 'membrane intelligence' is used everywhere in living systems, even at the beginning of life itself when a successful spermatozoon triggers an electric potential across the full expanse of the egg cell's membrane to tell any other, still hopeful, competitors that this egg cell is his and his alone.

At each level, life forms a metaphor for itself at other levels. In triggering an electric signal, that spermatozoon uses the same force that draws oppositely charged fundamental particles to each other. And why is a first sensual kiss so electric? Those protein channels yet again, in the membranes of highly sensitive nerve cells in the lips and tongue.

But that also misses the point. I still have no idea what love is, but whatever else it is, it isn't just electric kisses and orgasms, however exciting those may be! The troubadour Bernart de Ventadorn (c 1180) put it well in the second verse of his *pastorela*:

Ai las! tan cuidava saber
d'amor, e tan petit en sai.

Alas, so much I thought I know
of love, and so little do I know.

But I do know a little more than I did about the mechanism of the heartbeat, and I owe the privilege of access to that knowledge to an extraordinary supervisor, whose full story I did not know for nearly 40 years. It was Otto Hutter at University College London who introduced me to electrophysiology and to working on the heart. He had already done some pioneering work on how the heartbeat is controlled by its nerves and hormones and was later to become the Regius Professor of Physiology in Glasgow.

I shall never forget the electric feeling that I had when

I first found that those particular potassium channels close during excitation. We called them the i_{K1} channels, the name they still carry today. He was teaching a practical class at the time so I rushed downstairs to the classroom to tell him. That was the eureka moment. Just a few months later, we published a short article together in *Nature* (Hutter & Noble, 1960) announcing what we had found, and I had meanwhile coded up my equations to run the computer simulations to show the role this mechanism played in the generation of cardiac rhythm. This also was published in the same issue of *Nature* (Noble, 1960). That was how I came to have two references in *Nature* even before I received my PhD.

There are many strange aspects of this story, not least that I didn't even have A level (school-leaving) qualifications in mathematics, let alone a degree in the subject. It was not just the slaughterhouse, the lab and the big basement computer that kept me away from my bedroom. I was also busy rapidly teaching myself as much mathematics as I could absorb.

And Otto's story? About 20 years earlier he was almost the last boy to travel on the *Kindertransporten* train from Vienna as the Nazis closed in on Austria. He told me nothing about that when I was his student. I learnt that story 40 years later when he sent me a treasured copy of his own account of those terrible pre-war years and the loss of loved ones to the holocaust.

50 years on from those *Nature* papers, we met again to celebrate the half-century at a great meeting held in Oxford. In 1960, there were just the two of us in the UCL laboratory. In 2010 at the Oxford meeting, there must have been close to 100 people, many of them working on what is now called the Cardiac Physiome Project (Bassingthwaighte *et al.*, 2009), an international project to build whole organ computer models of the heart.

In some recent recollections (Noble, 2011) I wrote:

> 'So, if I could ask the 23-year-old walking down the worn steps to the basement room where the *Mercury* computer lived in 1960 the question where did he think this was leading, what would he have said? Not much probably. How many students see much beyond their thesis when they are writing it?'

True enough, which may be why the student in the story could not even convey his excitement to his girlfriend! Fortunately, he grew up enough to stimulate many others to join the project and in later years to produce the world's best-studied computer model of an organ of the body.

So could one mathematically model love? Forget it! Some things, those not-"its" in the story, indeed the story itself, just are. Too much reduction destroys their very existence.

1. Bassingthwaighte JB, Hunter PJ & Noble D. (2009). 'The Cardiac Physiome: Perspectives for the Future.' *Experimental Physiology* 94, 597–605.

2. Hutter OF & Noble D. (1960). 'Rectifying Properties of Heart Muscle.' *Nature* 188, 495.

3. Noble D. (1960). 'Cardiac Action and Pacemaker Potentials Based on the Hodgkin-Huxley Equations.' *Nature* 188, 495–497.

4. Noble D. (2006). *The Music of Life*. OUP, Oxford.

5. Noble D. (2011). in *Journey toward Enlightenment* (Editors, Auffray, Chen, Noble & Werner). Imperial College Press, London.

We are all Made of Protein but Some of us Glow More than Others

Tania Hershman

AT FIRST WHEN she looks down the eyepiece she sees nothing, only blackness. 'Mum,' he says, and moves her hand to show her how to focus. Sarah turns the knob and suddenly there's a pulsing: the fish's heart! Her own beats up in time. So small, so magnified. She sees a swarm of tiny dots, all glowing green. One dot moves, it makes a dash along. 'Immune cells,' he whispers by her ear. She's watching like it's television. The creature's inner workings. 'Beautiful,' she says, her boy, her son, standing proud as if he built this microscope, made this tiny zebrafish. 'How?' she says, as the green dots shift and shuffle. 'How?'

The jellyfish's name is *Aequorea victoria*. When the young scientist hears this, he thinks of the old English queen. He wonders if the current queen, the one who was crowned only a few years before, would like her own jellyfish. He is in Princeton, listening to his new supervisor, hearing words like 'squeezate'. Squeezate, he thinks, from, squeeze, squeezed, squeezing. A squeeze expanded, lengthened out; an old word moulded into novelty. The young scientist hasn't yet met one of these jellyfish, let alone thousands. He hasn't yet made the seven-day journey with his wife in the back of his supervisor's new car across so many states, or lain in the rowboat on the harbour, looking at the clouds. The young scientist tries to listen again to the older man, not to think about all that might be, all that he doesn't know, the questions he might ask.

Sarah giggles and shrieks because her friends do. Giggling, shrieking, as they lift each one from the bucket. That first summer, hauling each creature out with both hands, whispering, twitching. Her friends shriek and giggle as they do this but Sarah doesn't find them odd or cool or creepy. She likes the heavy weight, as if it is a pudding or a pillow, but living, or once lived. As she lifts it gently out and holds it there, she imagines something passing between it and her, and while it does she doesn't make a sound. She stands quite still and lets it pass.

The young scientist is watching them as he lifts from his own bucket. He hopes the girls obey his guidelines; he is paying them, he is expecting that, he is hoping that they take some care. This is no outing to the shopping mall, he hopes they understand. His own small children do it well. They are younger, but they are slow and careful, cutting only what should be cut and not missing anything that must be there. The scientist has wished that he could do this alone, at one side of the quiet laboratory. But he needs such quantities, so many creatures, just to get the smallest part, some drops to test; he requires an army of assistants. His mouth turns down slightly. He picks up his scissors and reaches into the bucket.

The young scientist lies back in the rowboat and dreams. He dreams himself under the water and among them. Why do they glow? And why not just use the blue light they absorb, why that next step which turns it into green? The *Aequorea victoria* do not answer him. One dream he has: tiny fireflies upon each jellyfish, sitting on the creatures' skin, waking up when agitated. Another dream: the glow is like a match being struck, an underwater match. Perhaps the glowing ones are like beacons guiding in errant flyers like an airport runway. Perhaps they are marking places of great importance. He does not dismiss these as nonsense, he doesn't laugh at anything. This is his thinking, this is how it works. He looks up at the clouds and continues to dream.

She has seen him, the young scientist, in the rowing boat. Sarah has stood on the jetty on her way back from school and seen him lying there, just floating, bobbing, floating. At first she thought the boat was empty, out there on its own. She moved to where she had a better view and then she saw him, eyes maybe open, or maybe not. She stood for a long time: what is he doing, what is he thinking about? But he was thinking nothing, emptying out his mind as far as possible. What he wasn't thinking about: his wife, jellyfish, the tension in the lab, the blue light, the green glow, how.

Another man, in another time, thinks only: worms. Worms are his field, *C. elegans*, a lovely name for something unlovely. A transparent worm. He is thinking of them as he walks towards the hall in which the seminar will be held, wondering about them as he sits in his place, at the end of a row in the middle. He is not expecting much from today. This is what he is not expecting: glowing, insight, protein, green, revolution. When he hears what he hears, he stops listening and begins to imagine.

There is a boy who wants to take Sarah to the movies. This is the first boy to ask her. The first time. Her friends giggle at this and nudge and tickle her and she likes that they giggle because she can too and inside her is a big shriek waiting to come out. A boy and the movies and a boy in there with her, sitting by her! It will be this Saturday, her mother and father have allowed it, after some discussion, after some questions regarding the boy. The discussions did not happen in front of her, they were in the kitchen while she sat still on the sofa, not thinking. What she was not thinking about: Simon, his hands, his funny smile, his arm next to hers, her stomach, the big shriek inside.

In the rowing boat, he is trying again not to think. Of *Aequorea victoria*, of blue and green and glowing. So instead he thinks of his daughter, how she is enjoying school, how she is speaking like an American already, using words he doesn't know, and this makes him happy. His son is not so forward, and the young scientist smiles at this too, because it was like that for him. He closes his eyes and there in his mouth is that taste, his wife made it for their dinner, after the fried chicken. A recipe from the friendly neighbour who thinks perhaps they eat the jellyfish, who is worried for them. This makes the young scientist almost laugh, he knows it is what many of them think. Eating the jellyfish! But what they had last night was like meringue but not so hard, and then − the sweetness! The lemon sweetness, and he can taste it again, filling his mouth. Wait. And he sits up, the boat rocking.

Simon has chosen the movie and Sarah is happy about this because she doesn't want to have to do anything. He has kept his hands in his pockets and then, when he stands by the end of their row and lets her walk down first, his arm hovers slightly as if he is going to touch. Sarah slides along, her legs rubbing the seat backs as she moves to the middle of the movie theatre, then two more along so there is no-one in front. She sits and Simon is still standing, and she looks up towards him and his mouth is turned in an odd way that makes her think he is happy and her skin is tingling and in her stomach is a glow.

There is tension in the lab air. The young scientist doesn't know the expression about cutting it with a knife, but if he did he would repeat it to himself because this is how it feels. He has a new theory but it is not agreed with. This has not been the expectation, that the younger disagrees with the older, that there is disharmony. This has not been said in words, but it has been implied strongly and the young scientist is disappointed. This is not how science is, following along, agreeing. Of course, he cannot say this, he is here on someone else's invitation, an invitation that comes with money, that comes with certain assumptions. But he is not being blocked. Just disapproved of, and that is something he can live with. So the supervisor carries on grinding tissues, with his assistant, sticking to the path already known, while across the room, the young scientist walks another road, in darkness, looking for some small light to justify rebellion.

Sarah is on her own today. Her friends decided not to come, they tried to make her join them, they teased and prodded but she didn't want to go where they were going. So it is just her and her bucket, no giggles or shrieks, just quiet perseverance. Take one out, carefully, carefully cut around its edge, its fringe. She has instructions, what to do, was not told the why of it, but doesn't mind. The small amount they pay her makes her feel grown-up, she's saving it for something special. While she holds the jellyfish and cuts around, she thinks of pearls, her mother's, that she is not allowed to touch but only sometimes, when her mother has a party. When she was small, she tried to grab and got a slap on her hand, which hurt. When she's older, will she be allowed? Sarah looks down at where she's cutting. 'I'm sorry,' she whispers, as the scissors slice.

It works! The young scientist has done it, and now he shows his boss, the man who brought him here, who drove them across so many states, that long long drive of seven days. The young scientist has found what they were trying to isolate, thanks to lemons, to thoughts that began with lemons, citric acid, pH difference. It is not what anyone imagined. Back in his home country, he had researched lights and glows in other creatures but this one is different. Differently luminous, and now he has found it, isolated what makes it shine. He needs more samples to study it, this new protein, which he will soon call 'aequorin'. He needs buckets of jellyfish, armies of assistants at the docks, scooping them up. The young scientist makes sure not to grin at all when he shows his results to the older man, but inside he is smiling so much that there is an ache. Lemons.

Sarah is pregnant, a great roundness already so that she is slightly off balance. Her husband, who is not Simon, who came a while after that first one, the scratchy movie seats, the first lookings up and down, is away a great deal and Sarah is mostly on her own. She stands in front of the bedroom mirror and cups her hands underneath her stomach, feeling something pass between her and herself. 'Come on,' she says, waiting for it, waiting for emergence.

The man who thinks only of worms has tried it once; it took several weeks and many steps, but something didn't work and under the microscope: darkness. He shone the blue light, strained his eyes for something, but only black. So he began again, with new worms, breeding them up with the protein, tagging the cells. And then, weeks later again, more weeks, he slides the tiny creature under, focusses, shines the blue light, and it's there. Green glowing cells, dashing about. For the first time, he sees inside. He sits there quietly, watching his living worm.

Sarah is behind her easel in her studio, which is really just an extension of the kitchen. Her paintings are bought and sold often enough; someone has called them 'silently luminous', although to her they are very loud. She is creating this one for her son, to go in his new apartment. She stares for a while, then puts the brush down, pushes back her chair with some effort and goes into the kitchen. It is early, the morning show is playing, with muted sound, on the television on the counter, and as she switches on the kettle, she sees it: jellyfish. She stands quite still, and feels it again in her hands, sees them in the buckets, hears her friends giggling. An old face on the screen, but something speaks to her, of rowing boats and scissors, of hours in laboratories cutting. They're saying that he's won, and she's not convinced the face is him, but she thinks that it just might be. She turns up the volume, forgets about the tea, the kettle. They talk about his prize, what he has done, and as they do they show the pictures, little green glowing cells, and Sarah watches, listens and remembers.

The jellyfish's name is *Aequorea victoria*. When the young scientist hears this, he thinks of the old English queen. He wonders if the current queen, the one who was crowned only a few years before, would like her own jellyfish. He hasn't yet met one of these jellyfish, let alone thousands. He hasn't yet made the seven-day journey with his wife in the back of his supervisor's new car across so many states, or lain in the rowboat on the harbour, looking at the clouds. The young scientist tries to listen again to the older man, not to think about all that might be, all that he doesn't know, the questions he might ask.

Afterword:

1961: Osamu Shimomura and Green Fluorescent Protein

Nick R. Love

In 'We are all Made of Protein', Tania Hershman explores the work of a young scientist, Osamu Shimomura, and the unique circumstances in which a large portion of his Nobel Prize winning work took place, namely, on a row boat off the west coast of the USA. There, Osamu and colleagues collected bucketful upon bucketful of a glowing, mouse-sized jellyfish called *Aequorea victoria*, and from a specific organ found in the jellyfish's translucent and delicate bodies, a ground-up jellyfish goo or 'squeezate' was meticulously prepared. From the squeezate, and with a bit of serendipity, Osamu Shimomura was the first person to isolate the proteins that enabled *Aequorea victoria*'s light emitting behavior.

As it turned out, there were two different proteins in the jellyfish squeezate preparations that enabled the green glow of *Aequorea victoria*. One of these proteins was 'bioluminescent', and the other, 'fluorescent'. Bioluminescence, for example, allows fireflies and other organisms to utilize chemical reactions to release light – one can see these bioluminescent organisms glow or light up in a dark room. Fluorescence works differently, however, in that it does not actually produce light. Instead, fluorescent entities absorb a wavelength of light (or range of wavelengths) and then release light of a different wavelength. In technical terms, fluorescent entities are 'excited' by an absorbed wavelength of light and then release or 'emit' a different wavelength of light back.

Osamu Shimomura and colleagues found that in his

Aequorea victoria jellyfish preparations, there existed a bioluminescent protein called aequorin that produced blue light, and a fluorescent protein that converted this blue to green light. These two proteins work in tandem to give the *Aequorea victoria* its characteristic green glow. Unbeknownst at the time, however, it was the isolation and discovery of this latter 'Green Fluorescent Protein' (or GFP) that would have far-reaching consequences nearly thirty years later. After all, when Osamu Shimomura moved from Japan to Princeton to embark upon his study of *Aequorea victoria* in 1960, it was less than 10 years after the structure of DNA had been discovered. Biologists were only beginning to really understand the relationship between DNA and proteins. And thus, it took nearly thirty years of laboratory technology and know–how to develop before the true power of GFP became apparent.

The magic of GFP is this: the biological information or instructions to construct the GFP protein are found in a DNA sequence approximately 700 bases in length ('bases' being the A, T, C, or G 'letters' of DNA) which can be inserted into other organisms, making them 'fluorescent green'. This is because the genetic instructions that encode GFP in jellyfish can, amazingly, also be read in other organisms. The first animal to be genetically engineered to express GFP was a small, translucent worm called *Caenorhabditis elegans*, reported in 1994 by the lab of Martin Chalfie (co-recipient of the Nobel Prize). Soon after, almost every imaginable creature that possessed laboratory protocols for genetic manipulation had a GFP expressing member of its species, including bunnies, frogs, fish, mice, cats, dogs, monkeys, and pigs. Since the development of GFP as a research tool, a veritable rainbow cornucopia of other fluorescent proteins have been isolated from nature or engineered in the lab. In the context of modern biological research, GFP and its derivatives have become ubiquitous and absolutely essential tools in probing biological systems.

So, why are fluorescent proteins like GFP so powerful?

One reason is that they allow the 'tagging' of biological entities (like certain tissue types or parts of the cell), and consequently enable scientists to watch the dazzling complexity of living systems unfold in realtime, *in vivo*. For example, by painting biological systems with proteins like GFP, researchers gain admission to watch biological activities such as: 1) restless axons (the 'branches' of nerves) migrating from the spinal cord, sniffing 'growth factor' gradients towards final targets of enervation; 2) ravenous white blood cells homing in on and engulfing pathogenic agents; 3) a highly coordinated and enigmatic 'dance' that dividing nuclei (where the DNA is held in the cell) undergo during cell division. These activities would be practically unseeable without GFP. And asides from simply marking entities in biological systems, more recent and fancy fluorescent proteins can even act as biological sensors, for example, by changing light emission properties depending on biological conditions such as pH.

In 'We are all Made of Protein' Tania Hershman weaves a provocative story of a human who went jellyfishing and netted a Nobel Prize, and whose painstaking scientific pursuit of understanding bioluminescence continues to excite scientists in laboratories worldwide.

In Search of Silence

Adam Marek

At the Holmdel Science Fair, Bob Dicke's frustrated gesticulating was so wild that his watch flew from his wrist and skidded across the parquet floor. 'This isn't fair!' he said. 'They stole my idea!'

'We never even met you before today!' said Arno, a much shorter boy, on the stand beside his.

'And yours doesn't even work!' said Robert, Arno's companion, making a face.

'You're like... ten, there's no way you came up with this by yourself, no way!'

'I'm eleven,' Arno said, pushing his glasses up his nose.

The head of the three judges waved the first prize certificate and envelope like a fan to calm them down. 'Boys, these are both great projects –'

'But they weren't even looking for the Big Bang!'

'But we found it!'

'You found it by accident!'

'But we still found it.'

'Come on now, Mr Dicke,' said another of the judges, wearing a suit despite the heat and sweating in it. 'You're all scientists. A great discovery has been made, whoever made it. Your theory about the remnant heat signature of the Big Bang has been proved correct, even if the proof came from these two.'

'It's a stupendous discovery,' the first judge added. 'The

185

papers will want to talk to all of you.'

'But look,' Dicke said, 'They've even copied my horn-shaped antenna! No one has done that before. No one! So how did they know if they didn't copy me?'

'We didn't use a horn,' Robert said. 'We used a cone.'

★

It began with a bang. On New Year's Eve, all the boys on the Cunard liner *Georgic* gathered around the three-inch gun on the aft deck, waiting for the captain. Tonight would be the first time Arno, or any of the hundreds of passengers, had seen the gun fired.

Arno had spent many hours over the last week sketching the gun's long barrel, its wheels and wires. He imagined that he had x-ray vision and could see through the armoured housings, to the pistons and components inside – in his vision, a brilliant hybrid system of steam and electrical engineering.

Everyone was on deck, wearing shiny hats that the crew had unpacked from crates at the start of the evening. They were cheering and drinking and shivering, holding candles with paper hand guards that made the deck blaze in a way that Arno thought was most magical.

At just two minutes to midnight, the captain turned one of the gun's hand-wheels, and the barrel's elevation increased. 'The new year is almost upon us, my friends,' he said.

On this ship, gossip and rumour about their destination were rife. They said that in America, everyone was free to behave outrageously, that their wealth was so obscene they ate from plates as big as serving platters, that their cars were more like rocket-ships than cars.

The captain cleared a space around the gun, and he looked about the crowd, as if he'd lost something. His eyes settled on Arno. 'Son,' he said. 'Would you like to pull the trigger?'

He installed Arno in a place that was safe from the barrel's recoil, set both his hands on the cold trigger, and told him not to fire until the count of zero.

The first twinkling lights of New York Bay were just coming into view when the collective countdown of every mouth on board reached 'five, four, three, two, one, zero!' Arno pulled the trigger. The explosion made a drum of his chest, emptying his lungs so that he had to gasp quickly for air. The cloud of smoke shot out behind the boat was caught by the wind and dragged back across the deck, reeking of tangy metal.

There was singing. The captain ruffled Arno's hair, leaning in close to his ear so he could be heard above the tumult, and said, 'Welcome to the future my friend.'

Arno wiped his feet on the doormat, while Mrs Wilson stood at the bottom of the stairs calling out, 'Robert! Robert where are you?'

After the longest time, Robert's voice could be heard faintly saying, 'I'm here.'

'Where here?' Mrs Wilson said. She tilted her head to the side, to make her hearing more sensitive.

'Here!' Robert's voice came again.

Arno struggled to pull his eyes away from the thin black line running down the back of Mrs Wilson's stockings, appearing from beneath the hem of her skirt, tracing the fine hump of her calf, and disappearing into the red cup of her shoe.

'I think he's over that way,' Arno said when Mrs Wilson set off in the wrong direction.

Mrs Wilson's heels were tapping out a faster, heavier beat on the floorboards now. She stood at a door to the left of the stairs, one which had four locks on it, and it was here that she really lost her rag. She spouted all kinds of threats about the retraction of pocket money and sweets and radio privileges.

Arno stepped back to look again at the enormous fibreglass ice cream cone on the roof of the Wilson's house-cum-shop.

The cone was cracked at the top, where the ball of chocolate ice cream was missing, leaving only scoops of vanilla and strawberry. Two pigeons were perched on the metal brackets that held this cone aloft by its pointed end. The top of the cone was the tallest thing around, a beacon at the edge of this widely scattered town of short buildings and big lawns.

Even stranger was the circular track on which the house sat. Each corner of the house was borne up on great wheels, black at their axles with globs of oil. Arno put his fingers on the track, and it was only when they were almost crushed that he noticed the wheels were slowly turning, creeping round at a speed imperceptible from any distance but this.

A sign above the entrance to the ice cream shop read 'Scooped', except the second 'o' had fallen off and was leant up against the front of the house.

'What are you doing in there!?' Mrs Wilson's voice shot out from inside the house, alarming the pigeons, driving them up and away over the telephone wires.

Arno went back inside, through the Wilson's hallway, and into the shop. Mrs Wilson was standing in front of the freezer room, holding the door open with one hand, massaging her forehead with the other.

Coming fully into the room, Arno could now see Robert, a boy a couple of years older than he was, sitting on a cardboard box in the freezer. He was surrounded by big tubs of ice cream. The many collars of different colours around his neck suggested that he was wearing at least five jumpers.

'Robert,' Mrs Wilson said, 'This is Arno. He's from Germany and he can't read. I've told his guardian you'll help him out, okay?'

Robert's teeth chattered. He rubbed his knees together.

And when he said, 'Oh great, thank you very much,' the words came out in an explosion of frozen breath.

Robert pointed at the word again, tapping his finger on each of the letter sounds 'Sm-a-ll.' He rolled his eyes.

'What?' Arno said. 'So I can't read. Have you always been able to read?'

Robert said nothing.

On Robert's bookshelves, all of the books were arranged by height. His shortest, a collection of Tarzan paperbacks, were on the left hand side of the bottom shelf. The tallest, a set of encyclopaedias, were on the right hand side of the top shelf.

This same fastidiousness of arrangement was repeated everywhere, in the shoes waiting under his bed, his shirts and trousers on the rail, his boxes of toy soldiers, cars and planes. Everywhere there were rising scales of size and colour spectra.

'You like Flash Gordon?' Arno said, patting Robert's duvet cover. 'Me too. So how come you were in the freezer? Were you doing an experiment?'

'It's the only place that's quiet,' Robert said.

'Are you kidding? This whole town is quiet. You should come to Munich.'

'Can we just finish this book so you can go home?' Robert said, jabbing again at the word Arno had become stuck on.

'This is a terrible book,' said Arno. 'I'm not interested in talking elephants. It's nonsense. Can we read something else? Can you help me read this?' From his back pocket, Arno took out an envelope which was now crumpled and stained denim blue at the edges from his new jeans.

'No way!' Robert said when Arno unfolded the letter and he saw its length and density. 'If you can't read *Horton*, you'll never read that. Not ever.'

Downstairs, the bell above the shop door rang as someone came in.

'What's it like living above an ice cream shop?' Arno

said. 'Are you allowed to eat ice cream whenever you like? And why is your house on wheels?'

Robert scowled at him. 'We have to stop now,' he said. 'I've had enough. I have a headache.'

Arno was kneeling beside the small nest of tables in his room when the telephone rang. For one excited moment, he thought that the ringing had come from the handset he'd brought from home. He even reached out to answer it. On the train from Munich, and then on the *Georgic*, and every day since he arrived, Arno had been disassembling and re-assembling this handset, undressing its screws and wires – a process from which he took great comfort.

Mrs Lassiter, his guardian, called upstairs that Robert was unwell, so Arno could not go round to his house today. 'She says Robert'll be fine tomorrow though,' she added, coughing with the effort of projecting her voice.

On the largest of the three tables was the letter, all three pages flattened out and held in place by batteries stood on their ends. Arno stared at it, willing the wild tails and aerials and loops to sit still, for just a second, but the only word that behaved itself was the second word on the page, and that was his own name.

When Mr Wilson let Arno in the next day, he said, 'Sorry about this,' and gestured with his thumb to upstairs, where Mrs Wilson and Robert were arguing. Robert was saying his head was killing him, and Mrs Wilson was telling him to stop being a hypochondriac, and Robert said, 'You don't even care that I might have a tumour!' and Mrs Wilson said, 'We've already wasted the doctor's time looking for tumours.'

'You want an ice cream, Arno?' Mr Wilson said.

This was the first time he'd been offered an ice cream in the house, even though it was his third visit. Arno made a grin so big he got self-conscious and pulled it back. 'I would, Sir,' he said.

On the high stool at the bar, his feet miles above the chequered linoleum, Arno pushed craters into his raspberry ripple ice cream with his tongue. He asked Mr Wilson if Robert was sick again.

'He's not sick,' Mr Wilson said. 'He'll be okay in a minute. He's just a bit too sensitive, worries about things a bit too much.'

'Sir,' Arno said. 'I've been wondering... why is your house on wheels?'

'So the shop always faces the sun,' he said. 'That box over there on the wall controls it.'

Arno looked outside and saw that the sun was indeed straight ahead.

A big black car hummed past, sunlight sparkling off its elegant curves, an emissary from the future. Something about the heat, and the sweet ice cream in his mouth, the moment of kindness from Mr Wilson, the flag fluttering on top of a faraway house, and the swing of the stool on which he sat, made Arno feel more complete than he'd felt for a long time.

'So when are your folks coming over?' Mr Wilson said. 'I see things aren't so good back there right now.' He tapped his finger on his newspaper's front page photo, which showed uniformed men outside a building dressed in flags.

Arno shrugged. He sank his front teeth into the ice cream, and a sudden cold flash of pain travelled up through the roof of his mouth, into the top of his head. He squeezed his eyes tight against it.

'Head freeze?' Mr Wilson said. 'Occupational hazard.'

Mrs Wilson pushed at Arno's back, ushering him into Robert's room and said, 'Just ignore Mr Grumpy Face,' before closing the door behind him.

Robert was lying on the bed with two blue plastic bags of ice either side of his head.

'Does it still hurt?' Arno said.

Robert looked away, out of the window, where nothing was happening but clouds.

'You know, I don't think I've ever had a headache,' Arno said. 'My eyes sometimes hurt when I've been working on an experiment for a long time. Do your eyes hurt?'

Robert did not look away from the window, but said no, and adjusted the position of the ice cube bags.

'So what does it feel like then?' Arno said.

Robert said nothing for the longest time. Arno did not move from the doorway where he stood holding the *Horton* book Mrs Wilson had given him. But then Robert did speak, and he said, 'It crackles.'

'Like how?' Arno took a couple of steps towards the bed. 'Like when you screw up a paper bag?'

'No.' Robert turned his head to look up at the ceiling. 'It's more like when the radio is in between stations, only I can't tune it out. It's there all the time. A constant background crackle.'

'Radio?' Arno said, coming right to the edge of the bed. 'I once heard about a man in Berlin who heard the radio all day in his head, except he heard music and talking and things.'

Robert shifted his body over onto its side and looked directly at Arno. He rested his head on one of the ice bags and balanced the other on his upper ear, so that his face was sandwiched between them.

'Did he manage to get rid of it?' Robert asked.

'No one believed him at first. They just thought he was mad. But then he had to go to the dentist and have a filling replaced, and when the dentist drilled the filling out, the radio sounds disappeared. It was the filling that caused it, like an antenna.'

'But I don't have any fillings,' Robert said.

'Oh.'

'So no one else could hear the radio in his mouth?'

'Not that I know of,' Arno said. 'But I suppose if he'd

been able to boost the signal somehow, maybe by biting on something metal, and attaching it to an amplifier, the whole city could have had a party round his mouth.'

Robert laughed, and Arno was glad to hear it.

'You know,' Arno said, 'if it's not just in your head—'

'I'm *not* making it up!'

'Then we could try and amplify the sound so other people can hear it too.'

'You could do that?'

Arno smoothed his black hair down, looked at the floor with precocious intensity, and said, 'I could try.'

'I thought you were supposed to be stupid or something.'

'I just can't read yet. The words jump around. But electronics is easy.'

When Robert's mother came into his room two days later, she made a yell that turned her face white. Robert was sat on his chair wearing her new colander on his head. There were wires taped around its circumference that joined onto a metal chain-link collar around his neck, the collar that had belonged to Albert, their long-dead cocker spaniel. Also round his neck was the plastic cone-shaped collar that Albert had worn in the days after his unsuccessful operation. The inside of this collar was lined with cut open and rolled flat soda cans, held together with insulating tape. From this collar sprang two more wires, a red and a green one, which went all the way down to Robert's bed, where they were connected to a disembowelled radio.

The yelling that Robert's mother did was mainly an exclaimed list of objects: your radio! My colander! And so on. She launched across the room, arm stretched out to rescue her kitchenware from this abuse, stumbling and almost breaking her ankle when the tiny heel of her shoe pressed down on and cracked a circuit board which lay on the floor amongst various electrical debris.

'Don't!' Robert said. 'We're nearly done!'

At the moment Mrs Wilson had flung open Robert's bedroom door, Arno had frozen, his fingers applying the last bit of tape to the last wire to hold it in place on the dog's veterinary collar. And there he waited, even while Mrs Wilson came for them with her bright red nails and lipstick, looking so fresh and ferocious.

'Just let him finish!' Robert said.

Unfinished questions and accusations tumbled out of Mrs Wilson's mouth as she advanced on them.

'Switch it on! Switch it on!' Robert said.

'Don't!' Mrs Wilson said, her fingertips just inches away from the rim of the colander. 'You're going to electrocute him!'

Arno opened his mouth to reassure her that Robert was not plugged into the mains, just a pair of nine-volt batteries, but before he could get any of that out, Robert commanded him to 'Flick the switch!' again, and in compliance, he flicked.

Robert pushed his palms out towards his mother to keep her at bay. From the radio there came a soft crackling sound, which grew louder as Arno turned up the volume. Mrs Wilson was jabbing with her finger at Arno, demanding that he switch it off. Robert flapped his hands to extinguish her noise. 'Ssssh!' he said. Arno and Robert tilted their ears towards the radio, and when the dial was turned all the way to 10, another sound was discernable. The exploding particles that made up the static were interlaced with a high hum that set everything in the room aquiver.

'That's it!' Robert said, pointing at the radio. 'That's what I always hear! See, Mum! I told you, that's it! My head is a radio!' Robert's expression of excitement was mixed with deep relief. The skin around his eyes reddened, like he might cry, and Arno was shocked at this display. So shocked he worried for a second that the gear affixed to Robert's head might be causing it. He moved his hand towards the off switch, but Robert batted it away.

Mrs Wilson blew out a long plume of exasperation. 'If you know what's good for you,' she said, 'you'll have all this back where it was before your father gets home from New York.'

For a while, the only sounds in the room were of disassembly, and of rubber soles squeaking on boards, until Robert said, 'I've been thinking. Do you reckon this would make a good project for the Holmdel Science Fair?'

'I suppose. If we could work out what the sound actually is.'

'If I've got to live with this damn buzzing all the time, it can at least do something for me and get me that prize money.'

'There's prize money?'

'Only *two thousand* dollars! I've never entered before because it always goes to the nerdy seniors, but you're like... like a *super*-nerd.'

'Oh thanks.'

'No, that's a good thing. With my head and your brains... just think what we could do with that money!'

'You know,' Arno said. 'I think there might be a way to stop your noise.'

'Well how?'

'I think your whole room, maybe your whole house, is acting like a radio antenna, feeding radio waves in through that cone on your roof. That's why it gets quieter when you get cold.'

'You're gonna have to give it to me slower than that, Einstein.'

Arno rubbed his hands together. 'Everything above absolute zero gives off radio waves,' he said. 'Your body, that chair, the ground outside, New York City all the way over there. The radio waves make molecules in an antenna jiggle about. It's that jiggling about that gets turned into sounds in the radio, or in your head.'

'Soooooooooo,' Robert dragged out a sound of incomprehension.

'So when something's really cold, it doesn't give off so many radio waves, so it gets quieter. That's why your freezer is so quiet.'

'How does this help me?'

'Let me try something.'

Mr Wilson's college sweatshirt came all the way down to Arno's knees. His nose was running with the cold, and he sniffed frequently.

'Well?' Arno said, the word emerging in a cloud of vapour.

'It's quieter,' Robert said. 'But it's still there. Can it go any colder?'

The light in the centre of Robert's ceiling flickered as Arno turned the thermostat down the whole way. While they waited, they did half an hour of reading practice on one of Robert's X-Men comics, which Arno was much more excited to decode than *Horton*. Throughout the half hour, their breath became more and more dense, the beads of condensation on Robert's window more opaque with frost.

The maze of copper pipes with which Arno had constructed a crude extension to the freezer room directly below was complaining. It coughed and rattled, tugging at its tape fastenings behind the big poster of Sean Connery in *Dr No*, which did a hugely inadequate job of concealing it.

'I can refine it a bit if it works,' Arno said. 'Make it a bit quieter. I don't think you'll sleep any easier with this noise than the buzzing. So, how is it now?'

'Still there,' Robert said.

Arno could already see that this was the case from the chart recorder he had rigged up from a toaster, the movement mechanisms from a Robbie the Robot toy, a disassembled model of the George Washington Bridge, and a tank, the caterpillar tracks of which did the job of pulling in the old envelopes that Arno fed into the machine's slot. The machine was connected via two wires to a halo of taped-together chewing gum wrappers around Robert's head. The pencil in the graph-plotter drew a slow wave, never varying more than a degree up or down, just a few notches above perfect silence.

'Well, don't give up yet,' Arno said. 'There are other things we can try. This is just stage one.'

'Stage one?' Robert said. 'What's next?'

Arno looked up at the roof. 'The pigeons,' he said.

Arno had never known a sound as terrifying as that of Mr and Mrs Wilson's truck braking so suddenly outside their house. He had one foot either side of the roof's apex and was supporting a dining chair on which Robert stood, on his tiptoes. With his arms fully extended, Robert could just reach the very top of the enormous fibreglass cone to scrub away the accumulated pigeon shit with the foamy business-end of the broom he was holding.

As soon as Robert heard the car approach, he stuck the end of the broom into the bucket between his feet on the chair, sloshing frothy water out over the edges in his hurry to get down. The bubbles burst into steam the instant they hit the hot roof tiles.

Throughout the exasperated screaming that followed, Arno stared down, his face swollen with shame, at the few remaining feathers still idling across the driveway. He could only think how lucky it was that Robert's parents had not come home earlier, before they had returned his Dad's air rifle to its hiding place in their wardrobe.

The last straw for Mrs Wilson was the aluminium foil. She bellowed at Robert about how she was running out of punishments for him. She was at her limit. She'd taken away his pocket money, his comics, his desserts. She'd advanced his 'lights out' time by 10 minutes, then 20, then an hour. 'You're out of control!' she screamed. And then she said that Arno had to go, and he couldn't come back.

'But he hasn't finished learning to read yet!' Robert begged her.

She said that as polite as Arno might be, and as deep as her sympathies ran for his and his family's predicament, the truly naughty behaviour had only begun when he arrived.

'He brings out something in you,' she said. 'Something I don't like.'

Arno sat on the end of Robert's bed with his hands in his lap while Robert fought for his right to stay.

Mr Wilson arrived home and called out from downstairs, 'What on Earth is going on?' when he heard the crashing and bashing of Robert making his case by kicking his chair, his toys, and his metal bin. Robert blew the case for his defence with an ill-aimed baseball, which hit one of the copper pipe mazes hiding behind the James Bond poster and made it ring like an alarm bell.

Discovering that Arno and Robert's antics had now extended into the very plumbing of the house set her storming from the room with a frustrated wail. She'd been crazy enough ten minutes before when she discovered that Robert, with Arno's assistance, had used all of the aluminium foil she'd bought just last week to cover the heads of all the screws in his room 'to stop them singing'. But the freezer pipes were so far beyond the limit they made the limit look conservative.

She stood back, her hand covering her mouth while Mr Wilson pulled out Robert's chest of drawers to follow the pipes down through the removed floorboards, all the way to the crudely soldered joins to the pipes above the freezer room.

'You'd better go now,' Mr Wilson said.

Back at Mrs Lassiter's, Arno rehearsed the apologies he wanted to make to Mrs Wilson, detailed explanations of his line of scientific enquiry, which had been aimed only at helping her son. He wished he had the capacity to write a letter, and he filled his wastepaper basket with naive attempts. He picked flowers for her that wilted, undelivered.

Shame even drove Arno from his experiments. He rounded them up from his bedroom, put them in tangerine packing boxes and slid those boxes under his bed. When he washed the dishes after supper, he applied himself to them with such self-loathing that the bubbles spilled over onto the draining boards, engulfing the clean crockery on one side and the dirty on the other.

No one had ever asked to speak to Arno on the phone before, and so he moved down the stairs, towards where Mrs Lassiter held out the handset, with a nervous solemnity. She put her hand over the mouthpiece and said, 'Hurry up!'

Her tone made him sure he knew who it was, and he couldn't help but smile. Before he reached the bottom step, he'd already imagined the whole scene at the other end of the phone: his mother standing at the dock, holding one hand over her ear against the rain and the deep hooting of ships. He could imagine the thrill that would slip into her voice when she heard him, telling him she loved him, that she'd missed him, that she and his father were leaving Germany now, would be with him in just a few days in fact, that she was so proud, that he'd been so brave, but now they were coming and he didn't have to be so brave any more.

But when Arno put the phone to his ear, the voice that said his name was not his mother's. It was Robert's, and he was whispering.

'Arno,' he said. 'Do you still want to win that two thousands dollars?'

Arno turned his back to Mrs Lassiter, who was watching him from the kitchen. 'But we still don't know what the sound is.'

'That doesn't matter. When it's all hooked up it looks really impressive. Even if we don't get first prize, we might still win the book vouchers.'

'But I still can't read.'

'I know and that's my fault. If you help me with this, I promise we'll do your reading every day till you've got it, okay?'

'Okay, but only if you do one more thing for me.'

'Sure, what?'

'My letter,' Arno said. 'Will you read it for me?'

★

When Bob Dicke's parents told him to be a good sport, to put his things away gently, that they'd cost a lot of money, he told them to buzz off.

Holding the envelope, which was fat with notes, Robert couldn't shake the grin from his face.

'Are your parents not here?' The first judge said.

'No, Sir,' Robert said.

'Well, make sure you take that money straight home and give it to them for safekeeping.'

'We will, Sir,' Robert said.

As Arno and Robert put their wires and soda cans, colander and tin foil into boxes on the back of Robert's old brick trolley, Arno felt conscious of the looks he was getting from the other students and their parents. These were looks of suspicion. But he hadn't cheated. He hadn't. This was all his own work. True, they wouldn't have known what they'd discovered if the fair organisers hadn't set them up on the table next to Bob Dicke. But the discovery was still his and

Robert's, even if they had discovered it by accident. Science was full of happy accidents.

'Hold still,' Arno said to Robert, 'You have a piece of duct tape on your head.'

'You know,' Robert said, 'I guess it's like my super power, that I can hear the universe exploding billions of years ago.'

'I guess,' Arno said. 'Would you read my letter now?'

'Of course!' Robert said. 'But not here. Let's go back to mine and have something to celebrate.'

'But I'm not allowed over to yours any more.'

'When they see this,' he said, waving the fat envelope in the air, 'you'll probably get free ice cream for life.'

Robert sat on top of the newspaper vending machine, in the shadow of the cone. Arno handed him the letter. 'It's from my mum,' he said. 'So you mustn't laugh if she says anything mushy.'

'Mushy? You didn't tell me there'd be mushy stuff,' he said, pretending he was going to jump down, but he stopped teasing when he saw the graveness of Arno's face.

'Why'd she send you a letter if she knew you couldn't read, anyhow?'

'She gave it to me when she put me on the train back home. And she didn't know about my reading.'

'How could she not...'

'I pretended I could. Will you just read the letter?'

'Okay okay, sorry.'

Robert held the pages in both hands and began. 'Dearest Arno. My heart is breaking because I have something dreadful to tell you.' Robert stopped. 'Are you sure you want *me* to read this?'

'Go on,' Arno said.

'As I write this, you are asleep in your bed next door.

This is the last night you will ever spend in your own bed. It is the last night you will ever spend in Munich. We have saved for years, hoping that one day, we would be able to move out into the country and escape the city, but alas everything we saved has only just been enough to buy the ticket that will get you to America, and safe. There, the war will be long over. Here the whole country is shutting down around us, sealing us in. The windows of opportunity for escape are becoming fewer in number and smaller in size every day. Your father will do what he can to buy tickets for us too, but it is unlikely we will be able to travel as far ahead as 1965 to find you. But hopefully we'll be able to get away just far enough. Arno, the only thing that matters is that you are safe. You are a big leap ahead of us, and it is unlikely we will ever meet again.'

Here, Arno's sniff stopped Robert reading. 'Do you want me to stop?'

Arno shook his head, and Robert continued, softening his voice somewhat. 'It is unlikely we will ever meet again. Please be brave, and be strong and good. Tell no lies and only make friends with people who make you proud of yourself. Work hard, and know that wherever and whenever we are, we will always be proud of you. With all our love forever.'

Robert re-folded the letter.

'But listen,' Robert said, waving the prize envelope again, 'you have this now! You could buy their ticket. Couldn't you? How much would it cost? Less than this I bet. I'll even lend you some of mine if you really need it.'

Arno wiped his face on his forearm. 'You can't go back in time,' he said, 'Only forwards. You should know that. This isn't Metropolis and I'm not Superman.'

Robert hopped down from the vending machine and put his arm around Arno's shoulders. He asked if Arno wanted some ice cream, and Arno said that he did.

When Arno left Robert's it was late. He stood outside and listened to the wheels of the house slowly turning, still following the sun, even though it was on the other side of the world. There were crickets making merry, and big old frogs and nightbirds far off. There were bugs courting in the streetlights. Above him, at first, there were just a few stars, but the longer he looked, the more he saw. The sky bloomed for him, filling up with light upon light, a billion freckles on its sleeping face. He imagined that he could hear the faint echoes of plane-dropped bombs felling houses in Europe, the sounds of the explosions oscillating as they were pulled through time to his ears.

But then a real noise, from within the ice cream shop, distracted him, and now that his eyes were fine-tuned from sky-gazing, he could see movement behind the front windows. For one frightful moment, he thought it was a burglar, and wondered how best to raise the alarm without drawing attention to himself, but then, creeping closer, he could see that whoever was inside was not stealing anything, but rocking from side to side, a most eerie movement.

Only when his face was pressed right against the glass could he see two people embracing, shuffling softly from foot to foot, turning circles on the floor, orbiting each other, their heads resting on each other's shoulders. Mrs Wilson wore a dress that pinched in tight at her calves. Her shoes were discarded at the side, bare feet padding lightly around Mr Wilson's big shoes.

Even with his ear up against the glass, Arno could hear no music. They were dancing to nothing but silence. And then they saw him, and were obviously afraid for a moment, until he waved to them and they realised it was him. They laughed together and came to the front door to unlock it.

'You still here?' Mr Wilson said.

'Sorry,' he said. 'I didn't mean to scare you. I'm just leaving.'

'Come on,' Mrs Wilson said, 'we'd better get you home.'

'I'll lock up,' Mr Wilson said. 'Don't be long.'

Mrs Wilson left her shoes on the table, and walked barefoot beside Arno.

'Can I take my shoes off too?'

'Sure,' she said.

Arno held his plimsolls in one hand. Mrs Wilson took his other hand. They walked together on the cool grass beside the road, and it was good.

Afterword:

1965: Arno Penzias, Robert Wilson and the Cosmic Microwave Background

Dr Tim O'Brien

IN 1965, TWO radio astronomers working at the Bell Laboratories in Holmdel, New Jersey, made a discovery that revolutionised our understanding of the origin of the Universe.

At that time radio astronomy was still a relatively new science. For thousands of years we have looked up into space with our eyes. Since the 1600s, our vision has been improved with the use of telescopes. But we first began to study the *invisible* universe in the 1930s when radio waves arriving from outer space were detected.

With radio eyes we now see the Universe as never before. The sky is covered with bright points of radio light – not stars but quasars, distant galaxies powered by super-massive black holes. The steady flashing of pulsars, the spinning collapsed cores of exploded stars, stand out from the crowd of radio sources. Even the warping of space-time predicted by Einstein can be seen in the distorted images produced by massive gravitational lenses.

But one of the most amazing discoveries to be made by radio astronomers – by Arno Penzias and Robert Wilson – was the cosmic microwave background. A discovery for which they were awarded the 1978 Nobel Prize in Physics.

Light emitted just 380,000 years after the Big Bang still floods the Universe. Stretched and cooled by the expansion of space, this light exists now as a faint glow in the microwave radio part of the spectrum. We see it all around us, coming from all directions and appearing almost exactly the same wherever we look. It has been travelling for almost 14 billion years and by studying it we can see right back in time almost to the Big Bang itself. It is the oldest light we'll ever see.

Penzias and Wilson were using a radio telescope in the form of a large horn (looking a little like the ice cream cone in Adam's re-imagining of the story). The power of this telescope was not its size. The parabolic reflector at the wide end of the cone was only 20 feet across. It collected far fewer radio waves than the giant telescopes like the 250-foot dish at Jodrell Bank. But its particular design and special electronic amplifiers made it the best in the world for accurate measurements of the brightness of the larger astronomical sources of radio waves.

For Penzias and Wilson, this was crucial to their plans. They wanted to measure the brightness of both individual astronomical objects and the outer parts of our Milky Way galaxy. It was predicted that this background emission from the Galaxy would be very weak and probably not detectable even with the excellent horn antenna at Holmdel. In order to detect or put stringent limits on this background radiation they needed to push the capabilities of the telescope to its limit.

The signals arriving at radio telescopes from astronomical objects can be very faint. They are also mixed in with background noise from various sources: the atmosphere, the ground, the structure of the radio telescope, the connecting cables, the amplifier and other electronics in the receiver. This noise looks almost exactly like the noise produced by a warm resistor. The higher its temperature, the more noise is produced, as the typical speeds of the electrons jiggling about in the resistor are higher. These random thermal noise fluctuations in the receiver electronics can therefore be reduced by cooling them down to very low temperatures. In the case of Penzias & Wilson's system the amplifiers were cooled with liquid helium to an extremely low temperature, about 4 degrees above absolute zero (4 degrees Kelvin, or minus 269 degrees Celsius).

In order to remove the sum of these sources of background noise, the telescope is often pointed at the object of interest and then at a nearby reference position which hopefully just contains background. This can then be subtracted. But if we want to measure the absolute brightness of an astronomical source we need to calibrate the whole system by making observations of a source of known brightness. Penzias built a special 'cold load' cooled with liquid helium to a known temperature. Wilson then connected this to the telescope in a way that allowed them to switch between the signal arriving at the telescope and that from the cold load. In this way they could compare the two signals and accurately calibrate the signal from the telescope.

In Adam's story, the boys' unauthorized use of the ice cream refrigerators was inspired by both the requirement to cool the electronics to reduce the added noise and the need for a cold load to calibrate the results.

By the summer of 1964, the Holmdel system was producing excellent results in which the random noise fluctuations had an equivalent temperature of less than 0.2 degrees Kelvin. They pointed the telescope at the sky and found a signal equivalent to a temperature of about 6.7 K. This was a worrying result. Their careful calculations showed that the sum of contributions from the sky, the ground and the telescope structure should only be about 3.2 K. Somewhere there was an extra signal amounting to about 3.5 K (give or take a degree).

The excess signal couldn't be radio emission from our Milky Way – other observations showed this could be no brighter than about 0.02 K. Neither could it be radio interference – they experimented by pointing their telescope towards New York City and other places around the horizon, the signal was never strong enough to account for the 3.5 K residual background. Famously, they even evicted a pair of nesting pigeons from inside the horn and, just like the protagonists in Adam's story, carefully scrubbed off their deposits (Wilson's Nobel Prize lecture referred to this as 'a white material familiar to all city dwellers') – it made little difference.

They now had no idea what might be causing the excess. A colleague, Bernie Burke at MIT, told them about some work being carried out just 25 miles away at Princeton University by Bob Dicke's research group. Penzias telephoned Dicke and he sent over a pre-publication copy of a theoretical paper by one of his group, Jim Peebles. This paper predicted the existence of the remnant radiation from the Big Bang: radiation whose properties were consistent with the signal detected with the Holmdel telescope. It also described how Dicke's group had begun to build a telescope designed to detect the signal but hadn't yet got it working. After Penzias' phone call, Dicke announced the serendipitous discovery of the cosmic microwave background to the rest of his group with the famous words 'Boys, we've been scooped.'

The two groups agreed to publish the results jointly in back-to-back papers in the July 1965 issue of the *Astrophysical Journal*. First the Princeton group of Dicke, Peebles, Roll and Wilkinson, described their theoretical calculations of the properties of the remnant radiation from the Big Bang. Then Penzias and Wilson described its detection with the Holmdel telescope.

The cosmic microwave background (CMB) is one of the main pieces of evidence for the origin of the Universe in a hot, dense state – a key feature of the Big Bang. Since its discovery, its properties have been subjected to intense scrutiny. For example, spacecraft observations with COBE (Cosmic Background Explorer) and WMAP (Wilkinson Microwave Anisotropy Probe) have allowed us to map out tiny variations in the temperature of the CMB. These fluctuations, famously described by George Smoot as 'like seeing the face of God,' are caused by ripples in the density of the Universe which led to the formation of structures like stars and galaxies. Smoot and John Mather shared the 2006 Nobel Prize in Physics for the COBE observations of the CMB.

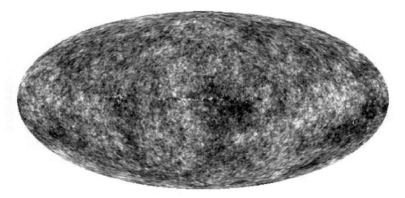

The all-sky view of the cosmic microwave background showing its tiny fluctuations in temperature (white = hot, black = cold).
Credit: NASA/WMAP Science Team.

The last decade has been referred to as the 'era of precision cosmology'. WMAP measurements of the CMB have determined the age of the Universe to be 13.73 billion years to within 1%. We have been able to measure the curvature of the Universe and show that it is almost exactly 'flat'. Perhaps most bizarrely, CMB observations and other studies have shown that ordinary atoms make up only 4.6% of the mass–energy of the Universe. Dark matter, something that has mass and hence gravity but is as yet unidentified, makes up 23.3%. The remaining 72.1% is the mysterious dark energy: also unexplained and, rather shockingly, causing the expansion of the Universe to accelerate counter to the expected influence of gravity.

At the time of writing, we are awaiting the publication of results from the European Space Agency's Planck spacecraft. Its location in space removes the noise contribution from the Earth's atmosphere and some of its receivers are cooled down to just 0.1 K. Carefully designed to be able to subtract the contaminating foreground emissions from the Milky Way, it will produce the most exquisitely detailed map ever made of the CMB. The challenge now is to use the CMB to study not only the aftermath of the Big Bang but how the Bang happened.

The story of the detection of the CMB and its identification with the Big Bang is interesting in many ways. In one sense you could claim Penzias & Wilson were lucky. They hadn't set out to find the CMB and didn't know what it was when they did find it. However, they did set out to build a radio telescope which would be capable of making extremely precise measurements of the background radio emission from space – exactly what was required to detect the CMB. The story demonstrates the value of careful experimental design and of keeping our minds open to the possibility of application of our research work well beyond its originally intended scope.

Living with Insects

Maggie Gee

i

From The Lives of Famous Scientists, *by Dr Simon Smith, Chapter 5, 'W.D. Hamilton and 'Hamilton's Rule'':*

Ants and beetles. They fascinate me. I welcome them in my accommodation. They are company, and you do not have to feed them.

Sometimes I have felt alone. This is partly to do with my temperament. I give most of my attention to social insects, which does not make me sociable. With them, I am a scientist, and through studying them I found my Rule (I did not mean to make rules for my fellows.)

And yet, I can see, as others do, that my work on altruism has human applications. It's these, of course, that cause all the fuss. Strange that altruism makes us quarrel.

People don't want to hear things that shock them. But scientists can't always anticipate that. A new idea has its own weight. We are pulled towards it over years of struggle. Partly because we have wrestled with it, tested it, finally found something that fits what we know, fenced with observations, underpinned by equations – we are surprised when perfectly rational people go red in the face and rage at it.

I have often made people red with rage, some of them other scientists.

But faces redden, then return to normal. I have always tried to take the long view.

I was lonely for years in my postgraduate work, shuttling

between LSE and UCL, not fitting post-war pigeonholes. I never had a desk: I had a lunch box, and sat and worked in parks and gardens. That didn't bother me. I liked to be outdoors. The birds pecked at my papers at Kew. A lot of my thinking was on Waterloo Station, sitting on the benches long after midnight. I liked it because there were always people. I walked everywhere, from Chiswick to King's Cross, pretending, perhaps, that I still lived in the country, for I loved the Kent countryside in which I grew up, and looked with longing for the maverick plants that cheeked their way up through cracks in the pavement, from dank basements or crumbling walls. Yellow ragwort, shining out like stars.

(I think plants can be altruistic too. This is the sort of statement that gets me into trouble.)

I read Ronald Fisher in my last year at Cambridge. His work was so much more interesting than undergraduate Natural Sciences. R A Fisher was a genius, but his ideas about evolution were incomplete. I was young, and alone. Of course, I had no children. Would I ever have 'the maximum number of offspring'?

It seemed there was no place for me in Fisher's pattern. I was left outside his Fundamental Theorem. But the problem wasn't a personal thing. The theory's view of altruism was... too narrow.

Yes, deeds that benefit one's own offspring improve their reproductive chances, which helps the spread of genes for performing deeds that benefit one's own offspring. It's sound enough, but it's a closed world. It reminded me of my mother's greaseproof-paper packets at home, which had a tormenting picture on the front of a woman smiling and holding up a packet of greaseproof-paper, on which there was another, smaller picture of a woman smiling and holding up a packet of greaseproof-paper, on which there was ANOTHER picture, even more constricting... No one could escape them, forever and ever, the smug housewives in the family kitchen. No one could escape, no one could get in.

The Hymenoptera were also left outside, huge swarms of insects buzzing purposefully, most of them infertile workers busy caring for the offspring of their sister, the queen. They had no children of their own. They spent their lives serving others. Admittedly, close relatives.

And I thought about Haldane's unsolved conundrum. 'Would I lay down my life to save my brother? No, but I would to save two brothers or eight cousins.'

So in the end, we are all related. Everything that lives is related. So it isn't just about one's own children.

And instead of the doctrine of Survival of the Fittest, we get Hamilton's Rule of Inclusive Fitness. The Rule I found that let everyone enter. The Rule I found that let me in, and the wasps and ants by the Brazilian high-road. Which is where I was the day my paper was published, bumping in my jeep towards Brasilia, dazzled by the white kapok trees, the snowy silk pompoms of the Ceiba flowers, screwing up my eyes to see, in the sun, in 1964, when I was young.

ii

Lincolnshire, 2011

Lisa stares at it blankly: ants on snow. The afternoon sun is sharp on the page. In fact, three letters and a 'less than' sign:

$$c < br$$

It was Hamilton's Rule (– who is Hamilton? Is he an actual man, or that town in Australia? Or was it New Zealand? – she hasn't a clue. If it's a man, she doesn't know the first thing about him).

But Hamilton's thingy was 'the most important thing in biology for the last 30 years', her teacher said.

But she doesn't understand it, and her mouth opens slightly, like a fish, like the symbol between the 'c' and the 'b', which means 'less than', she does know that much, and just now everything in life is getting less.

There were only three in her family to start with. Now it was going to be less than. Less than, less than, less than before.

Since yesterday, the world has changed.

Yesterday evening, Dad left home.

He's a scientist and knows everything, but he's left home in her A-level year, even though she said to him in September, joking but meaning every word, 'Dad, Dad, it's your A-level year.'

It's her A-level year, but Dad has gone.

'Sorry the pig had to leave in your A-level year; he never could choose his moment, could he?' her mother had said, almost spitting with bitterness as they sat together on the carpet on the landing, tears running down both their cheeks, and even in her grief and pity for her mother, Lisa had found time to dislike her, because she couldn't bear it when Mum slagged him off, slyly begging Lisa to love her more.

And instantly her mum said sorry. 'I shouldn't have called him a pig,' she mumbled.

'Dad isn't a pig,' Lisa said, blank. There was a sheer black wall of misery she couldn't see past.

'Forgive me, I'm desperate,' her mother said.

I'll never forgive them, Lisa thinks now as she stares blindly at her A-level textbook, re-reading the equation, not taking it in.

What was Hamilton's Rule of Inclusive Fitness? Something to do with evolution.

But on TV she'd seen a grey-jacketed professor say that in the 21st century, evolution had stopped, because even the unhealthiest babies were saved – (although that wasn't true, Lisa knew for a fact) – so there wasn't any actual survival of the fittest.

Then perhaps evolution only mattered now in a historical way? So it was just... shit. Lisa hated history.

The past disappeared and let you down.

Lisa needed to know, and understand, the future. The fearsome long gallery that opened up beyond that blank wall that blocks her view. It stretched away from her into the darkness. Heat, floods, global warming. Every now and then a window appeared, a fearful oblong blazing red with terror. She and her mother would be alone, without Dad, unprotected. Two of them until the end of time.

Then it shrank again into something pathetic. The future was just a set of empty boxes. A new, lonely, smaller home, her mother and father suddenly strangers. Strange to each other and stranger to her.

She'd taken them for granted, all her life, but the family has disappeared in an instant.

Nothing will be as it was before. Lisa sighs and goes back to her homework.

This Hamilton Rule, or whatever it was, was supposed to have changed evolutionary thinking for good. It was something about altruism. Lisa was crap at science but good at English, and she was the only person in the class whose hand had gone up when the teacher asked them, without much hope, what altruism was.

'It's when someone does something for someone else.'

'Example?'

'Like, well, at home, Dad makes tea. For my mum. Actually he does stuff for everyone.' It was true: her mother complained about it. He mended bikes, he hauled push-chairs off buses.

'That's right,' said Ms Terry, surprised someone knew. 'Does he? That's nice.' In the back row, people giggled and sneered, but unless they threw things, the teachers ignored it. 'The trouble is, there's always a cost. That is the point of Hamilton's Rule.' She scraped her black marker across the whiteboard.

$$c < br$$

Now the same equation stares from the page of Lisa's book. She makes an effort to remember.

c was the cost to the altruist. b was the benefit to the person. And r was... Yes. What WAS r?

Relatedness. Yes, that was it. Although of course Dad wasn't related to Mum. And did things for her all the same.

Not any more. Never again. They would be divorced and life would be over.

Now Dad might not be related to Lisa.

'Less than before,' she mumbled, agonised, trying to keep out the rush of pain. She stared at the equation, furious.

If Dad were here. If Dad were here...

But no, he wasn't the same Dad any more.

That was the most sickening thing of all, what Mum had dumped on her yesterday, so she crumpled to the floor, on the old blue carpet, and her mother knelt beside her, so they must have both looked as though they were praying, on the small square landing, as the sun went down. A kick of horror as her world turned over.

'What do you mean?'

'He might not be your father. Don't look at me like that, it's true."

'You're mad. You're... wicked. Of course he's my dad.'

'I told you I was pregnant when we married–'

'So?'

'I had another, you know, boyfriend as well–'

'–You're disgusting–'

'–who I actually liked better, he was less of a wet, but he felt too young to have a baby, whereas Simon didn't want me to have an abortion. You might as well know the whole truth.'

In that second on the landing, her world had changed. The wall in front of her was cold and brutal. She shivered, though the heating hummed.

'I don't believe you. You're mad. You're a witch.'

Her mum's big bony face had shuddered. 'And now he's off after someone else. That awful slut with the dirty children.'

'Tracy Butcher? Of course he isn't.' Tracy lived near them, at the end of the road. She had five children she couldn't cope with, and rent arrears, and a car that broke down. The rumour was they were travellers. The eldest boy rode a noisy motorbike. She had curly brown hair and cheap stilettos, and looked better in summer when she was tanned. Sometimes you saw the kids zooming round the pub forecourt 'like a swarm of flies', her mother said, eating crisps and laughing as they waited for Tracy. In spring their lawn was yellow with dandelions. Dad had lent Tracy their lawn-mower, and gone round with his power-tool to cut her hedges. She was always nice to Lisa, but Mum couldn't stand her.

Now Lisa had to hurt someone. 'No wonder he's leaving. You're... MEAN to him, I hate you Mum, I'll always hate you, my life is just SHIT, and it's your FAULT.'

Her mother's tired eyes were suddenly brightened by a rim of tears. 'We don't want to hurt you. Dad just wants... Simon says... we want different things, but we both still want what's best for you.' And her vein-ridged hand reached out for Lisa's, and Lisa let her take it, hold it. Then Lisa said 'Sorry' and lunged across to sit, ungainly and fat as she felt, on her mother's bony lap, her strong calves pressing down Mum's thin pale legs, and hugged her, and they clung there, awkward and hot, on the carpet, mewing with tears and stroking each other.

But afterwards Lisa felt vaguely cheated, because her mother cried more than her, and who was the mother, who was the daughter?

Just two of them, clumsy and absurd on the landing. And now it was almost a whole day later, and the new awful truth was beginning to settle. Settle and harden. We're less than before.

'What did you say?' her mother asked, startled, looking up into the light from the book she was reading, so the lamp made hammock-y bags in her cheeks, and Lisa realised she had spoken aloud.

'I said "less than before,"' she said. 'It's my homework. Biology.'

But her mother kept gazing and frowning, with the lamp making silver tracks on her hair, a grey greasy shawl on her shoulders. 'Are you OK?' she said. 'You look weird.'

'Well you always look weird, so?' Then Lisa felt sorry. Her mum looked old. 'I was just thinking. When Dad moves out, I mean for good. We'll be, you know, less than before.'

'Fewer than before,' said her mother. 'Or maybe it SHOULD be 'less', in this case... every so often, the rule breaks down.'

'Shut up always going on about grammar.'

'Don't be rude. Get on with your homework.'

'I could do it if Dad were here. It's biology. But with maths in it.'

'Can I help?'

'Unlikely.' Lisa scraped back her chair with an ugly vraark sound she hoped would mark the tiles, and went upstairs, clutching her work.

There's an ache in her throat, what her granny calls her 'craw', and a pain in her gut, but she has to do her homework.

If Dad were here. If Dad were here...

Had he stopped loving them years ago?

When she was 12, her newborn brother had died. Not that he was a proper brother. He was born too early, and not right. (They couldn't even give me a proper brother, she thinks now, bent on bitterness.) She didn't even get a chance to hold him. She'd glimpsed him, pale as a fish, in the casket, with hardly any chin and vein-y skin, stretched too thin across bulging eyes. After that, in her memory, they were less happy. There was more shouting, and more sadness. So it wasn't true that unhealthy babies didn't die, because their baby died, and that was all that mattered.

Instead of doing homework, Lisa looks at Facebook. Sighing, she clicks on her father's profile. Because she has forbidden her parents to be her Facebook friends, she can't check out his contacts. He would have thousands of friends, in any case, because he was a soft touch, as her mum always said. She searches the outline she can see for clues. 'Works as Professor of Evolutionary Biology, Faculty of Life Sciences, Grantham University.' His profile pictures are just his book covers — boring books about biology. Books by Dr Simon Smith.

There was the one he'd said she might enjoy reading. *Lives of Famous Scientists.*

'She doesn't like science, she's never going to read it,' Mum had snapped, when he told Lisa about it, and then, because Dad looked unhappy, 'You should, though, Lisa. It's fiction, really, Dad imagining what it would be like to be all these famous scientists.' Then she started putting him down again. 'Which is certainly fiction, because he isn't famous.'

'Fair enough,' Dad had said. 'I thought that book might make me famous… I did enjoy writing it, though. I sort of felt like part of them.'

'The title was a clunker, Simon, I did say so at the time.' Mum had always edited Dad's books, and Lisa suspected she was jealous of him, because she couldn't write, she could only edit, and cut things down, and go on about grammar.

'The title was ironic,' he said, gently. 'Referring to 19th-century certainties. Whereas I knew that really I was making it all up. Other people are a mystery. What do we know about each other?'

Now the words have a different, horrible meaning. He was the mystery man all along.

My parents are liars. I really hate them.

She was stalking her own father on Facebook. How sad was that?

If he was her father. The thought came with a stab of pain. She broke away and went back to her homework, the blind little ants of Hamilton's Rule.

c < br

It starts to make a glimmering of sense to her when her thoughts creep back to her own life. So, if Dad was a mentalist who cut other people's hedges, c, the cost to the helper (Dad) must be less than b, the benefit to the other person (Tracy Butcher), times r, which meant…what? She tried again. Oh yes, r was their relatedness – how closely they were related to each other. But – having sex – if they were – which was vile – wasn't actually being related, was it?

Though Dad once said everything alive was related.

That's bollocks, Lisa thought; he should be here to help me do my work, because he's Dad, and I'm his daughter. I hate other people for taking him away. He's useless, like Mum always said. Always wasting time helping idiots.

But love surges up like a physical pain and Lisa has to

get up off her chair and kick around the room, feeling like a bin-bag full of different, brawling people, and she snatches up the card he had sent on her birthday, 'All the love in the world to our beautiful daughter,' and kisses it, frantic, then rips it in two.

In the middle of it, she hears her mother shouting. 'He's here. He wants to talk to you.'

Her stomach convulses. 'I don't want to talk to him.' But she hides the torn pieces of card in her bin.

iii

He was suddenly there, in the doorway of the bedroom, astonishingly like the same old Dad, his pink round cheeks, his kind, worried mouth. 'Lisa. I'm sorry. We have to talk.'

She struggled to speak, her voice shaking. It started as a squeak, then ended too loud, sounding false and actor-ish, even to her. 'You're sorry, are you. Well that's just RUBBISH–'

'Hang on, Lisa. Let me explain.'

'I know everything. I know you're a liar.'

'Why am I a liar?'

'Mum told me.'

They looked at each other for a long moment. He tried to turn his body slightly away, but he said, 'I want to talk about whatever it is. Ask me anything you want.'

But when it came to it, she couldn't. She couldn't say, Are you my father? 'You have to help. I'm stuck with my homework.'

Science rushed in to fill the gap between them.

iv

From *The Lives of Famous Scientists*, by Dr Simon Smith, Chapter 5, 'W.D. Hamilton and 'Hamilton's Rule'':

And I thought about my godfather Charles Brasch, who had loved my mother, decades ago. He helped me to my first publication by asking me to write for his magazine, *Landfall*. I thought about all childless people. What was the point of the unmarried uncle?

Of course, he can benefit his nieces and nephews, whose genes are related to his. He can help other people's nieces and nephews.

So everyone can join the dance of evolution. There is a point to all of them.

That was the nub. We were all related. (Though some are more related than others.) Even the beasts of the field, and the bees, and the beetles, like my favourite Coprophaneus beetles, with their blue-green wing-cases flashing in the sunset, the hour when they feast upon the dead. And so the dead become the living.

v

Dad talked about Hamilton's Rule for over an hour, while Lisa gazed at him, trying to focus. The words blurred. She asked questions, but didn't hear the answers. 'So is it about insects, or about people?'

'Well...' His lips moved, and she focused on them. She needed to grasp this strange new person. '...Inclusive Fitness...' he kept saying. Bits of it were interesting. He gave examples from his own research, and some of it took her back into the past, to a time when they were still... normal.

'Do you remember when I brought home the ants? They were in sections of plastic piping. I picked them up in France, in the old Volvo. I told you, and made you promise not to tell Mum, but she heard something rustling when she opened the boot—'

At once Lisa was listening. 'Yes, and there was a horrible argument.' Mum's face had gone crimson with rage and fear, getting redder the calmer Dad had stayed. Now father and daughter smiled at each other, briefly remembering a row survived. 'I thought you would get divorced right then... But what will Mum do now if there are spiders?' she suddenly pleaded, agonized. Her mother had a phobia for insects, especially in the bedroom and bathroom. Dad always came and rescued her, carefully releasing the insect in the garden. Sometimes he showed it Lisa first. He'd always told her not to be frightened.

'If Mum's scared, I'll still come,' he said. 'I'll only be living up the road.'

'With Tracy Butcher?'

'Don't be ridiculous. Is that what Mum's been telling you?'

'I'm scared too,' said Lisa, urgently.

'I thought you were OK with them.'

'Just because I don't make a fuss like her... It's you who has to deal with spiders. Fathers have to do things like that.'

'Sorry.' He did look desperately sorry, and for a second she almost pitied him. There was a silence, and then he said 'So do you want me to go on explaining?'

'What?'

'The Rule of Inclusive Fitness?' He was begging her to give him a chance.

'Are you saying that most of these ants or wasps or whatever don't have children at all?'

'Yes. Of their own. That's right.' He became enthusiastic. 'In the species I study, the queen, or *gamergate*, terrorises the others. She goes all round the colony exuding pheromones, smearing sticky goo over everything, which stops the others ovulating. She sniffs out her chief rivals, grabs their antennae and rubs them over her stinky abdomen, pinning them down till they give up.'

Lisa thought she heard disgust in his voice. Did he hate females, her own dad? Maybe he just hated her mum. 'So this Hamilton. He is a person?' She didn't want to make a huge mistake.

'Yes, a fascinating one. But... he died, in fact. He caught malaria, being brave, in the Congo. He wasn't very old. He did risky things to help other researchers. He didn't believe you should fear death.'

'Why is his law so boring then?' She wanted to be rude,

and hurt him, and besides, talk of dying made her very afraid, because parents could die before you were ready, when they weren't with you, when they went away.

He looked at her, effortfully patient. 'If you're interested, read my book. *Lives of Famous Scientists.* You like reading. You could read it.'

'That's typical. It's what you always do. Try and teach me things I don't need to know.' All her friends had the same complaint. Fathers could never really help with schoolwork, because they kept trying to educate you.

'You did ask,' he said, mildly. 'The book's downstairs.' There was a hint of departure in his voice.

'That's it then. Now you're going to bugger off.'

'Not if you don't want me to.'

'Go. Because you're going to go in the end.' She didn't want to cry, but the tears pushed up. 'Are you having an affair with Tracy Butcher?'

He didn't deny it. His hands were in his pockets. The room around them was starting to get dark. 'I wanted to help her. Mum got jealous.'

'Are you even my dad?' she suddenly said, a little wail of misery. 'Mum was pregnant when she married you. Maybe my real dad was someone else. I don't look like you. I'm no good at science. I only did science A-level to please you.'

He was stung, then. 'Don't you want me to be your father?'

'But is it true? Is anything true? How can I trust you? You don't love us. You're leaving us. And Mum said you're not my father. I wish – I wish – I wish you were dead.' Then she began to cry in earnest, snot blowing out from her nose in a bubble, a stupid, empty, shameful bubble.

He came across the room and took her hand, matching the thumbs against his own. 'Mum said that? She doesn't know. She doesn't know any more than I do. I love reading, and writing, like you. In any case, you're mine, Lisa. Genetics doesn't change anything. I'll be your father till the day I die.'

'Everything's' (sob) 'changed. Everything's' (sob) '… over.'

'How could I ever stop loving you? I've known you every day of your life. I loved you even before you were born. I'd do anything – anything at all – to help you.'

'But you help everyone,' Lisa sniffed, but her hand in his began to relax, and she tucked two fingers through the gaps in his, and for a second, their two hands squeezed.

'I try. It's always annoyed your mum. It's all in Hamilton, actually.'

'Don't say another word about him.'

'I'm going now. You could read my book. I don't expect you to, it's all right. I'll be back tomorrow to see you're OK.'

After he went downstairs she heard quiet conversation, a grumbling noise that grew suddenly louder, then a brief bout of shouting involving Tracy Butcher, and the door slammed, after which she heard sobbing.

At 1am, she couldn't sleep. She felt cold as death, and she opened the curtains and shivered to see the cloudless night, the distant pale nets of stars. They were all so little. They would all die. Dad would die, and she wouldn't be there. He might go anywhere in the world. She just wanted to be close to him. And she had said, 'I wish you were dead.' *Please God please don't listen to me.* But there wasn't a God in evolution.

She crept down in the dark and fetched his book. The pages were already slightly yellow, as if it had grown tired of waiting. She stopped reading at 4am, just as the dawn began to creep around the curtains, a dim rectangle of something warm, and in the dream that followed, she was his child, though in the morning, there were only the words.

vi

From The Lives of Famous Scientists, *Chapter 5, 'W D Hamilton and 'Hamilton's Rule", p.236, 'My Intended Burial and Why', by W D Hamilton:*

I will leave a sum in my last will for my body to be carried to Brazil and to these forests. It will be laid out in a manner secure against the possums and the vultures... and this great Coprophanaeus beetle will bury me. They will enter, will bury, will live on my flesh; and in the shape of their children and mine, I will escape death. No worm for me nor sordid fly, I will buzz in the dusk like a huge bumble bee. I will be many, buzz even as a swarm of motorbikes, be borne, body by flying body out into the Brazilian wilderness beneath the stars, lofted under those beautiful and un-fused elytra which we will all hold over our backs. So finally I too will shine like a violet ground beetle under a stone.

'...I too will shine... like a violet ground beetle under a stone.' Lisa read it aloud, the very last sentence, as she sat in the garden the next afternoon. Then she wandered to the flower-bed, where yellow flowers grew, and wished she knew the names, as Dad did. And then she started picking up stones, not knowing what she was looking for. And under each stone, something was living. They were so many, she became dizzy.

'Teatime,' her mother screamed from the house. 'You don't want to stay out there on your own.'

'I'm not on my own,' Lisa called back, though when her mother looked, there was no-one in the garden, just her strange daughter staring transfixed at a stone.

Afterword:

1964: William Hamilton and Inclusive Fitness

Professor Matthew Cobb

BILL HAMILTON WAS probably the most important evolutionary biologist of the second half of the 20th century. As Maggie's story indicates, by introducing the idea of 'inclusive fitness', Hamilton changed our conception of natural selection. Previously the idea of 'survival of the fittest' (not a phrase coined by Darwin, though he did eventually use it) had focused on an individual's ability to survive and leave offspring. In a pair of very difficult papers published in 1964, Hamilton provided a theoretical basis for understanding 'inclusive fitness' – measuring the success of an individual in terms of the survival of itself and of its relatives.

Darwin had worried about exactly this problem in *The Origin of Species*, when he looked at what he called 'neuter' insects – sterile female ants, bees and wasps. Evolution by natural selection occurs where individuals have small differences in their behaviour, shape, colour and so on that lead to differential rates of survival and/or reproduction. If even a small part of those differences are inherited, then you get the evolution of adaptation. But in many species of social insects (bees, wasps, ants and termites), the vast majority of females do not reproduce, indeed they cannot. Their ovaries are shrivelled, and they may even lack the required genital parts. Darwin's problem – which he first thought would be 'insuperable, and actually fatal to the whole theory' – was to explain how natural selection could produce such sterile worker castes, which left no offspring.

Darwin's solution – as in so many of his examples – was to study how artificial breeding works. If you want to produce a breed of animal or plant that tastes good, in practice you will have to eat it before you can breed from it. Humans have selected some very tasty crops and animals, by breeding not from the thing that was eaten, but from its close relatives. This kind of selection is not direct, but the greater the relatedness between what you eat and the individual you breed from, the more likely you are to select the desired character. The same explanation, reasoned Darwin, could be applied to the social insects, which must use what he called 'family selection'. Natural selection did not act on the infertile worker ant, but on her mother or sister who was busy doing the reproducing – the queen.

Hamilton's papers turned this simple verbal explanation, which had satisfied everyone for over a century, into some rather complicated maths. Above all, Hamilton provided a theoretical framework to explain the evolution of one of the most mysterious and counter-intuitive of characteristics to have been shaped by natural selection: the performing actions that favour others, at a cost to oneself, or what can loosely be termed 'altruism'. Hamilton reasoned that if the two individuals share the genes that are involved in producing altruistic behaviour, then there was no contradiction in explaining why an individual would behave in such a way as to reduce its own fitness and benefit another. In this neat piece of dialectics, when viewed through the prism of inclusive fitness, such altruistic behaviour looks selfish rather than selfless.

This was the insight that Richard Dawkins was to popularise so brilliantly in *The Selfish Gene*. By shifting the way we look at the natural world to what Dawkins called 'a gene's eye view', Hamilton changed our perception of evolution, and produced testable hypotheses about how characteristics such as altruism evolved. His theory provided an explanation of the evolution of different sex ratios, of social and parental behaviour and, in another dialetical twist, of the conflicts that occur between parents and offspring in the apparent unity of the family.

At least partly inspired by Hamilton's work, another brilliant British mathematical biologist, John Maynard Smith, coined the term 'kin selection' to describe the same phenomenon, and this is the term that is often used today. In 1966, US biologist George Williams published *Adaptation and Natural Selection* in which he, too, focused on the gene to explain the evolution of complex behaviours. In fact, natural selection does not operate directly on genes. Although genes are passed from one generation to another, the way those genes affect fitness is generally indirect, buffered and filtered by the environment the organism grows and lives in, and indeed by the other genes in the individual's genome.

Hamilton's insight was not immediately recognised – it took over 10 years before it began to be cited with any significant frequency. This was probably due to the rather daunting maths it contained – even Maynard Smith admitted that he did not follow the mathematical details of Hamilton's earlier work. And today, while Hamilton's two 1964 papers are amongst the most highly cited in the discipline of behavioural ecology, I wonder how many of the people who cite his work have actually read those papers, let alone understood them (I have done the former, but could not manage the latter).

Most of us make do with the simplified version Maggie gives at the beginning of the story: $c < br$ (or, in words, altruism evolves in situations when the cost to the altruistic individual is less than the benefit to the receiver, multiplied by the relatedness of the two individuals concerned; do you see why Hamilton used an equation?).

If Hamilton's work is so difficult, why is it so influential? For the most mathematically-minded biologists, Hamilton's theory is attractive because it is elegant. There is an internal coherence, truth and beauty that means it *must* be true, they might say. But that kind of view, which is often used in physics or mathematics to underline the veracity of a given theory, has much less purchase in biology. Biologists study a very strange form of matter — stuff that is alive. Living organisms are a product of their history, and of the random and selective processes that constituted that history. As a result, all sorts of odd things have happened in the evolution of life, leaving their traces in all of us and resulting in life-forms that can be very inelegant, incoherent and ugly. As the French molecular biologist, François Jacob put it, evolution does not design but rather tinkers with what it has to hand.

Hamilton's work continues to be so influential because it explains the evolution of apparently bewildering characteristics such as altruism, or cooperative behaviour, or parent-offspring conflict, and leads to testable predictions that have been verified. In other words, it works. Kin selection underpins our understanding of the evolution of social behaviour and is accepted and used by the vast majority of evolutionary biologists. Recently, there have been some dissenting voices, who have created equally abstruse mathematical models and claimed these equations prove that kin selection is wrong. But models can be made to prove what you want them to prove — biologists are more impressed by experiments and observations than they are by Greek letters, no matter how elegant they might be. That probably explains why over 150 scientists have written rebuttals to this recent criticism, emphasising the explanatory power of Hamilton's work and giving many examples of predictions flowing from Hamilton's theory that have been verified in nature.

Like any great scientific contribution, Hamilton's work has two aspects: it has clarified and reinterpreted existing knowledge, and it has stimulated a vast amount of discovery. Future studies may eventually prove it wrong — or at least, less right — but for the moment, the amount of data that has been accumulated supporting his theory makes that seem very unlikely. For nearly half a century, Hamilton's insight has changed the way we view the world. Sadly, in the real world it is not explicitly studied at A-level, but whether students realise it or not, it forms the background for everything they learn about evolution.

Bride Hill

Kate Clanchy

MY HUSBAND HAS Alzheimer's disease and my daughter does not believe me.

If I ring her and say, he went out for ham and milk and he came back with an empty bag, she will say, oh, I do that all the time.

Or if I say, for example, he took the bus into town and then he walked back, she will say, that's the healthy option, and if I say no, it was because he couldn't remember where the bus stop was, she will laugh and say: he's a philosopher, what do you expect?

I say, today he bought *The Guardian* twice, and there are six reels of twine in the shed when we only need one, and she says, Mum, you have to take into account that you're both retired, now. You're in the house together, now, all the time. You're just *noticing* stuff. Normal stuff. Why don't you come here for a week, help out with the kids, give yourself some space? But, as she predicts, I do not do this.

Ordinary, says my daughter, over and over, *normal*. And of course it is *ordinary* for him to walk past the bus stop, *normal* for him to carry several full paper bags, or one empty one, and, yes, he has always liked shopping at the ironmongers. I am a materialist, after all, he will say to the neighbours, or their too-young children, and then he will explain at length what this means, philosophically. In the shed, everything is in order, to look at. Everything is *normal*. It would take me, the nagging, fault-finding wife, to notice the extra twine, or that he has twice left the shovel in the compost, and once on top of the car.

I think my daughter thinks we are too young for such a problem. I think that because Jeff is sixty-eight and I am sixty-five; because we are thin, brown, white-haired people with gold-framed glasses; because we are the *active retired* and favour a practical style of dress in modern fabrics such as fleece and colourful lace-up shoes and walking trousers which we buy from a German catalogue, because we often undertake long walks using Scandinavian metal poles: my daughter thinks our brains are equally wiry, equally up to the long coast-walks of the mind.

Or, she thinks I am making it up. My daughter has always thought I grudge her. It's not the war, my daughter says. There isn't rationing. My daughter's business, from the day she could get out the front gate on her own, the moment she got her fat hand on the hot tap, has been to defy me, to run the deep bath, to get first the parma violets and then the cheap clothes and the boyfriends and now the 4x4 and the widescreen telly for herself, despite me. I believe she discusses my phone calls with her friends, among whom it is well known that wives bear grudges, wives like me, *who gave everything up*, unlike the wives of Jennifer's generation who apparently *have it all*.

But if jobs are so much careers, then at least my daughter should respect my scientific training, when she has none herself. She often rolls her eyes at the antiquity of my degree, says times have moved on since sixty-five Mum, but in fact I have read about the new thinking in the area of Alzheimer's, and looked things up on the computer at which I am a dab hand. I have tried to bring my daughter up to date with my research. I rung and said, Jennifer, do you know what the *hippocampus* is? And she sighed and guessed, *horse field*, Latin was one of her O'Levels, and when I said no, hippocampus meant seahorse, she said: and you say *Dad's* senile?

Well. This sort of banter is part of our relationship. Many mothers and daughters behave like this. There is no point in taking offence or in writing a letter with a diagram enclosed because my daughter does not do letters. She calls them snail mail. She is incapable of buying a stamp.

So, after a day or two, I ring again, but this time I tell her, without preamble: Jennifer, the hippocampus is part of the brain. It is the shape of a sea horse, the size of a sea horse, has the very shine of that primitive marine creature, particularly when pickled; imagine a seahorse coiled underneath the cerebral cortex – and Jennifer says, Okay, Mum, I'm imagining the seahorse. And?

Well, I say the hippocampus is old, like the seahorse. Primitive, like the seahorse. All mammals have one.

In the brain? says Jennifer.

In the brain. I say, in the bottom of the brain.

What does it do? says Jennifer, sounding marginally interested.

Well, I say, one thing it does, is make new memories. The cells there have Neural Plasticity. They make new patterns, and they have something called Long Term Potention; it means the patterns they make have the potential to go into your long-term memory.

That's nice, says Jennifer, And?

Well, I say, in Alzheimer's, the hippocampus often goes first. The neurons become weighed down by plaques. They shrink. Their proteins tangle. *Sclerotic*, is the word.

Right, says Jennifer. The sea horse is sclerotic. Shrunk. Like the dried kind. You bought me one of those once, from Italy.

And then, I say, when the hippocampus is sclerotic, when it can't light up its neurons, you can't lay down new memories. You can't process new experiences through to your long term memory.

Umph, says Jennifer.

Your father, Jennifer, I say. The ham, Jennifer, I say. The

milk. The bus stop. The empty bag.

And Jennifer makes a scoffing noise like the paper bag crumpling and says, Wikipedia is a terrible thing.

But the next day, she calls back. She says does he do Sudoku it's good for the brain and I say, of course not, his subject is philosophy. And then she says, Look, the kids are back at school next week. I'll come over on Monday, and we'll take Dad to Bride Hill. And of course that is a lovely idea.

But over the five days before Monday, I think about Jennifer's choice of picnic location, and review the available web-literature on the subject of the hippocampus, and realize that the picnic, like for example my grandchildren's extravagant christening parties, is nothing but a trap designed by my daughter to make me look dry, over-analytical, mean. For Bride Hill is more than a nearby ancient monument appropriate to family outings: it is a maze, a ritual maze cut in the chalk. Jennifer, I am certain, has been reading of the performances of rats in mazes, and about the map-forming functions of the hippocampus thus discovered, and in her usual, hazy, unscientific, manner has concluded that if her father, Jeff, who indeed has grown whiskery and long-nosed with the years, is placed in the maze and succeeds in finding the path to the centre he devised so many years ago chiefly for her amusement, she, Jennifer, will have successfully demonstrated to me, her stupid mother without the outdated science degree, that there is nothing sclerotic about his hippocampus and that he does not have Alzheimer's Disease.

Once I have realized this intention, I strongly consider, over a period of three days, the possibility of telephoning my daughter and telling her that I have rumbled her. Also, that her test is thoroughly unscientific and based on a false principle. The hippocampus *does* form maps in our heads, it *is* the way that a new visitor to Bride Hill would turn his view of the twisting white paths, and his sniffs of the chalk and turf and his orientation to the sun and long shadows into a map in the mind, a concept of how to get to the middle of the maze, but it is a tool, a processing tool, not a repository of maps. And it isn't our only way of finding our way about either. We can also orient ourselves using our long-term memories, which is how Jeff is still perfectly well able to walk into the ironmongers. The bus-stop on the other hand, which moved this year, is beyond him. A map of Bride Hill exists, I am fairly sure, in Jeff's' long-term memory, for we have been there so often, and on Monday he may well be able to access that despite the probable state of his hippocampus. The bus-stop is the fair test, not the maze: but how can I ring and tell Jennifer that? She will simply deny the whole thing. On Sunday, I find the lawnmower out, abandoned on the half-cut lawn, but still, I do not call.

And so it is that on the Monday I put on the table several things which are in Jeff's long-term memory, already, things which do not need to go through the hippocampus and its LTP cells to be recognized and loved: the tartan thermos flask, the sandwiches, in grease-proof paper and elastic, his red cagoule, the picnic mat. Then his daughter comes, fat and forty, freckled and smiling, and she is safely in Long-Term too, mine and his. And if Jeff seems astonished, if he has forgotten the short-term arrangements for the picnic which I have gone over and over with him, well, we do not notice. Aren't we all surprised by joy? Isn't that what joy is?

So, Jennifer drives the car, Jeff sits in the front with his sun hat on, and I am in the back beside the baby-seat. Jennifer is wearing sunglasses and peers often to the left, checking the Sat Nav. I thought you'd know the way, I say, and she says, no, now I have my TomTom, I can't remember anything, and Jeff, who really is on top form, says it's all marvelous and there is an argument to be made for smart machinery actually being part of our brain, that we are all semi-cyborgs and perhaps have been ever since we invented the pocket watch or indeed the hand-axe.

Jennifer is smiling, tapping the indicator with a polished

nail, and I can tell she is thinking, not much wrong there, and I want to tell her: your Dad does this. His chat-track about semi-cyborgs was processed in the hippocampus years ago, and now it lives in his long-term memory and he can get it out and use it, on cue. It's *now* that can't go through there, down through the pipes to his long-term memory. Ask him where we're going Jennifer, he'll make a joke, because he won't remember what you told him an hour ago. The *now* of you, Jennifer, with all the new layers of you that I hardly recognize myself, which shock me when I see you – your great womanish hips, those glasses, the lines when you frown – he won't remember that this evening. But how would I even start to say such a thing? She looks so harmlessly smug and cheerful, so apparently in charge. My daughter loves to drive.

We drive. It is so flat, hereabouts, we can see Bride Hill miles off: a round egg of gold downland, and the maze on it outlined in white like a thumbprint or a silicon chip. The lines are trenches, really, dug deep into the hill and filled with chalk. It must have taken Neolithic man a long, long time, and then, what did they do with it, what was it for? A sacred path? A mnemonic for a ritual? A tribal sign? No one knows, exactly, though there are barrows everywhere around, and the design, as Jeff will say in a moment, when he is prompted by the sight of it, retains its own potency.

Look Mum, says Jennifer, Red kites. And I look up through the sun roof and there they are, so very many of them, wheeling directly above me in a spiral, like leaves whirling down a drain.

And then we are parking, and get out into the day, which is golden and bright. Jeff says, marvelous, simply marvelous, and Jennifer says it is, Dad, it is, and looks at him adoringly, as she always has, and she does not look at me. And suddenly I feel angry, and I let them go over the National Trust lych gate and up to the Maze and sit down instead on the bench that has been thoughtfully provided for the elderly and infirm.

There's always a wind up here. I listen to the dry noise it makes through the high grass, and smell the hay and chalk smell. For a long time, they thought the hippocampus was olfactory, that it dealt with smell, but this is not true, or rather it is not mainly true. Smell is part of the memories the hippocampus makes. The smell of this hill has passed through my hippocampus and linked itself with the perhaps hundred times I have made this trip with my children, and now the scent again releases my children for me: lounging teenagers in old-fashioned jumpers leaning on the lych gate; ten-year-olds in flares, chasing each other round the maze; toddlers tumbling, fat in nappies. All of these children are walking with Jennifer and Jeff up the hill, pacing the narrow pale paths of the maze, and Jeff the young father goes with them, his blunt dark fringe falling over his eyes, talking as he goes about the possible meanings of this pattern, about the perfectly simple, perfectly mathematical route he has worked out to the centre of the maze, and the smell lets the complicated release mechanism of my love for him slowly, reluctantly, click.

I know what is happening to Jeff by my chart of absences: by the spade not on the hook, the lawn not mown, by the empty bag. I have been telling them to Jenny so she too can shade them in, and also to confirm them to myself, because each absence is so small. If she would listen, I would tell her that that is how the hippocampus was found out too, by its absence. There was a young man called Henry, Patient HM. America, the fifties. He had epilepsy, seizures to the point he couldn't work, might easily die, and in 1953, the year I had a tonsillectomy and was sent away to school, a surgeon called Scoville performed an experimental operation on HM. Scoville cut away most of the hippocampus, and the rest of it atrophied, and that did cure HM's epilepsy, but when he woke up after the operation, he was amnesiac, and his amnesia was special: seahorse shaped.

It was a woman doctor who studied HM, a Doctor

Brenda Milner. Patiently, steadily, she counted up all the things HM couldn't do. HM could remember the first twenty-five years of his life well, but not the two before the operation. He could recognize people from his past, but no one new, not Dr Milner, not even carers he saw daily for twenty years. He could not remember new information: facts such as a new president, or man landing on the moon, would surprise him each time he was told, but he could learn new things without knowing he was learning them. His *procedural* memory worked, but not his *declarative* memory. So, Dr Milner asked HM to join dots on a piece of paper into a star while he looked only in mirror – a ticklish sort of job. HM obliged, and over three days he learned to get quicker and better at the task, but *without ever remembering that he had done the task before.*

Jennifer and Jeff are near the centre of the maze now: Jeff, ahead, Jennifer behind, both with their arms outstretched for balance on the narrow path, like children. I can see already that if Jeff started off following his secret system, his famous, code-cracking route to the centre, he has now forgotten it: they are heading for one of those infuriating twists of the maze which return you to the entrance. And I find I do not want Jennifer to notice this, after all; I find I want to be the fool here, I want her experiment to succeed, and so I start up towards them, thinking of something to say, goodness my old legs, perhaps, but Jeff has jumped over the grass to a different part of the maze, a big jump, like a little boy on a big ditch, and is turning to encourage Jennifer to cheat, too. Naughty Daddy! I expect he is laughing.

I keep walking. No doubt Jennifer would have it that I am jealous of women like Brenda Milner, women who are *fulfilled*, who used their brains to make a lasting impression on the world, but she is wrong. I like to think of her, older than me and cleverer, but still in those terrible clothes we had in the fifties, the roll-on and stockings, sitting opposite HM and his mirror with her notepad, as he struggled with his fiddly, heavy-breathing star-drawing. Him with his pencil, her with her pen, the two them shading into the field of human knowledge, stroke by stroke, the function of the hippocampus, the temporal lobes, the declarative memory, the procedural memory, steadily, calmly, filling in the hidden lines and pathways, the way the image of a memorial brass can be rubbed onto paper with black wax, the banana shapes becoming feet, the scattered uprights, legs. Besides, Brenda Milner was doing something for me. In his mirror, which I am imagining as my own mother's mahogany-framed dressing table mirror, under his own, frowning, unexpectedly aged reflection, HM traced a little map for the Alzheimer's patient, a map with all the awkwardness of mirror writing, a map with gaps in it, but the only one we have.

Jennifer and Jeff are making a game of it, now. They have abandoned the rules, and are leaping from path to path, recklessly, flinging up their arms. I can hear their laughter, thin ribbons. But when I reach the entrance to the maze, my declarative memory pops up like a butler with the news of how to tackle the puzzle. It says: And would you like to follow Jeff's Route, today? Jeff's declarative memory failed him today. His is a servant who has taken to drink, who takes longer and longer holidays, who appears, disheveled, in the middle of the night, talking nonsense.

And, to honour Jeff, I take his route, starting with the long, counter-intuitive swoop to the right. HM's mother lived with him for twenty years after the operation. Twenty years growing step by step, day by day, further and further from his recognition, as if he were docked in 1953, and she were passing away from him in a great ship. Did she dye her hair, perhaps, or dress in forties suits, to remain more the mother he knew from the first twenty—seven years of her life? Was there a morning when he simply didn't know her, when he asked, perhaps, her name?

Jennifer and Jeff are sitting in the centre of the maze, now, a worn, grassy spot surrounded by white hooks of chalk.

Jenny's head is up, her profile pulling clear of her flesh: she looks like a girl. Jeff is talking. The path takes me away from them, then back. I follow it. HM stayed in his lonely station, washed up in his island in time, for nearly eighty years. Jeff won't. In Alzheimer's, after the hippocampus, the whole brain shrinks, the frontal lobes, the long-term memory, the procedural memory, and all the time, insistently, the brain-stem remembers how to breathe.

When I arrive, no one congratulates me on solving the puzzle. Jeff doesn't even stop talking. I recognize the discourse: heaven, and the essential self. 'It makes my point, you see, that a personality only exists in reaction to others, that is, as a result in part of memories, but always in a forward trajectory in time. As I say to my students: what will you talk about in heaven? What will you do in a perfected world? And no one has ever given me a decent answer!

And suddenly I see that Jennifer is crying. I sit down beside her and pat the middle of her anoraked back, the place you touch when you mean to be kind. I hate to be right, in fact. And Jennifer sniffs and says, I think heaven is now, don't you think so, Mum?

Then we all sit on a while in the sun, and Jeff says again, it is so wonderfully warm. It is. If you shut your eyes, you could take it for real heat, the generative heat of spring. You could forget that September is just the afterglow of summer, the impression on the eyes after the candle is blown out.

Afterword:

1971: Brenda Milner, HM and the Hippocampus

Sarah Fox

Rather like an author, our brains work fastidiously collecting information and sketching out our autobiographies. Like any work in progress, these stories have a beginning, middle and an end; moreover we can scan back through our previous text, or memories, and often have an idea what we intend to write next. In her story 'Bride Hill', Kate paints a lucid picture of how Alzheimer's disease acts like an eraser initially obscuring newly written chapters before slowly working its way back in autobiographical time until all that remains are distant memories, a confusing present and an uncertain future.

The memory-related disturbances linked with the earliest stages of Alzheimer's can be traced back to a region of our brain known as the hippocampus. This structure first received scientific notoriety in the late nineteenth century, during which time a number of acclaimed anatomists pioneered detailed studies of the area's overall structure and cellular arrangement. This work spawned a wealth of theories concerning hippocampal function, ranging from a proposed role in attention to an involvement with our sense of smell. It was however, not until the mid twentieth century that the hippocampus first became conclusively linked with memory. This breakthrough arose from the study of psychological deficits experienced by patients with significant hippocampal damage. These patients showed varying degrees of amnesia for events experienced during the years leading up to their injuries and, more prominently, a striking deficit in transferring newly acquired information into long-term memory. These studies played a crucial part in demonstrating a specific role for the hippocampus in the formation of long-term memories for facts and events, a function referred to as declarative memory.

The hippocampus is formed from a number of separate processing units all of which work together like cogs in a machine. Alzheimer's disease causes a build-up of unwanted material within this system which, like in a machine, can act to interfere with the movement of these cogs, slowing them down and ultimately causing the entire system to fail. Interestingly, the damage caused by Alzheimer's during its early stages appears to specifically target certain hippocampal regions whilst leaving others relatively unharmed. Therefore, to gain a more thorough understanding of how Alzheimer's interferes with the memory system as a whole, it is first necessary to discern how these separate hippocampal regions contribute to the overall process of memory formation. Hence, although we can observe the damage caused by Alzheimer's through a microscope and document its effects on cellular communication, we cannot claim to fully understand the disorder until we are also able to discern how the individual hippocampal regions affected contribute towards memory formation.

My work focuses on studying, in healthy individuals, a specific hippocampal region, known to be targeted by Alzheimer's pathology. Different types of information originating from separate sources converge upon cells in this region. This means that these cells occupy an ideal position for combining these separate inputs into single memory events. Thus the overall function of this region is twofold, firstly it works 'on-line' to combine current experiences into new memories and secondly it can store these recently formed memories within its circuitry for access at a later point. Within this system, these two tasks must remain separate, ensuring new memories do not interfere with old.

For example, if you drive to work parking your car in a different spot every day, you want to be able to remember where you parked today without this information merging with your memories of previous trips, otherwise you may have to walk home! I am experimentally testing the theory that the formation of new memories and retrieval of previously stored memories are separated in time by a regular rhythm of waxing and waning cellular activity, present within the healthy hippocampus. Like the tides, patterns of activity within separate hippocampal regions oscillate rhythmically, perhaps 'binding together' pieces of information to form a remembered event. Specifically, during memory formation brainwaves show prominent oscillation in the theta frequency range (between 3 and 10 'beats' a second). My work analyses input at separate phases of this oscillation, allowing me to quantify how cellular activity changes throughout the cycle. It is my hope that as we build a better picture of how all the separate regions of the hippocampus work together to form memories, we will also become better equipped to understand the effects of devastating disorders such as Alzheimer's, and thus, be better prepared to treat them.

What If?

Christine Poulson

IMAGINE TWO STRINGS of beads each one and a half billion beads long. Imagine those two strings of beads twisted together into a double helix. Those beads are molecules, or nucleotides, and this is your DNA. It's unique (unless you are an identical twin) and every single cell in your body contains it. If these two strings of beads were stretched out they would each be a metre long. That's three billion beads, so tiny that they cannot be seen even with a microscope. Their presence can only be detected by X-ray crystallography.

Imagine that somewhere along that string of beads is a section that carries a faulty gene. That section is around 400 beads long. It is a tiny fraction of something that is already almost unimaginably tiny.

Imagine you want find out if someone is carrying the gene for sickle-cell disease or cystic fibrosis or any other genetic disorder. You will need a lot of that tiny, tiny section of DNA, far more than you can extract from a standard blood sample. You will have to insert it into the cells of living bacteria and they will replicate it along with their own DNA. It takes weeks to get enough for a diagnosis and it's the same if you want to amplify DNA to do research or to solve a crime.

Imagine some alchemy that would get the job done overnight.

On a Friday evening in May 1983, Kary Mullis leaves his home in Berkeley, California, to drive north to his cabin in Mendocino County with his girlfriend, Jennifer.

It's been a busy week in the lab – it's always a busy week in the lab – and it's been a blisteringly hot day. He's glad to be driving into the hills. The light of the setting sun filters through the giant redwoods. His hands move automatically on the wheel, following the twists and turns of the road. Jennifer has fallen asleep beside him.

He lets his thoughts wander. Maybe he thinks about that bottle of Anderson Valley Cabernet that he's going to open later at the cabin. Maybe he thinks about his children – he has a daughter by one marriage and two sons by another – or wonders what the future holds. He's thirty-eight, has a PhD in biochemistry, and for the last four years he has worked for a small biotechnology company. He's doing fine, but he hasn't set the world on fire.

Certainly at some point his thoughts turn to a problem that's been preoccupying him. He runs a lab that synthesizes oligonucleotides, short strings of nucleotides. They are the molecules that are the beads in the strand of DNA and they come in four types, adenosine, thymine, guanine, and cystosine (A, T, G, and C). Mullis and his team can produce strands of twenty to thirty nucleotides long in any combination. It is as if he has a string of only twenty beads, but he can arrange them in any sequence of four colours. Thanks to a new machine from Biosearch, Inc. across the bay in Marin County, the lab has become so efficient that it is making more than the company can use. Either he'll have to lose some of his staff or he'll have to think of another way to use these strings of nucleotides.

He yawns and winds down the window, lets in the dry heat of the California night. Californian buckeyes throng the verge of the road, their white and pink flower spikes luminous in the twilight...

Years later, in an office in a rain-spattered town in the Midlands, a man puts down the phone and punches the air. Twenty years ago he was just a sergeant when he worked the case of a young woman who was raped and left for dead. No-one was ever brought to justice. Through all those years he has rung her every few months just to let her know that the case is still open and that he hasn't forgotten, will never forget. He admires the way she has rebuilt her life, has a husband and a child now.

In his heart of hearts he never thought he would see this day. All these years that trace of semen, originally too small to be of any use, waited in a dusty evidence room. A few months ago a new technique allowed forensics to obtain enough DNA for a profile that went on the database. Then a month ago: a match. Just a run-of-the-mill breaking and entering, but the burglar left blood on the jagged glass of the window he broke to gain entry. The DNA in the blood matches the DNA in the semen. And he has just heard that they have the man in custody.

It isn't the first time he has heard of amplified DNA being used. A few weeks ago a man walked out of a cell on death row in Kentucky. He had been convicted of a triple homicide on the basis of blood left at the scene. He has the same rare blood type, but DNA profiling has proved conclusively that it belongs to a different man.

Into the policeman's mind comes a memory from his Methodist childhood – something from the Old Testament that he hasn't thought of in years: 'Let justice roll on like a river, righteousness like a never-failing stream.'

He stares out at the grey sky as he thinks about what this means for the young woman who was so badly damaged. What do they call it? Closure? No, that's too easy, too glib. But a world that was knocked badly out of kilter that day will be a little less so. That at least he can say.

He pulls the phone towards him and dials her number.

The scent of California buckeyes floats in through the open car window. The traffic grows sparser. The light of an occasional isolated house gleams through the trees. DNA chains uncoil and float before Mullis's eyes as though projected onto the road ahead. Adenosine pairs to thymine, cytosine to guanine, A to T, T to A, G to C, pair after pair after pair...

Mullis wonders if he can tie up the problem of having too many nucleotides with the bigger problem of replicating DNA. What if he can use one problem to solve the other? The problem of DNA replication is really two problems: how to select the piece of DNA that you want and how to amplify it when you've got it. Later he'll admit that as a chemist he didn't really appreciate the hugeness of the human genome in comparison with the smaller scale that he had been working on. If those three billion nucleotides that make up DNA were words, you'd have a book around 4000 times as long as the Bible. In that book Mullis's string of twenty nucleotides would be the equivalent of a single line.

Even so it is one of the properties of nucleotides that if Mullis puts these strings in a test-tube with a complete strand of DNA, they will search the entire vast genome and bind to their matching sequences. Suppose you want to reproduce a particular sequence of DNA, say, 400 nucleotides long, that you suspect could be carrying a faulty gene. If you know what sequence comes before it, you can design your little strand of nucleotides so that they will bind there and act as a marker for the beginning of your faulty gene sequence. But they'd also find maybe a thousand other places that were similar and you wouldn't know which was the one that marked your faulty gene sequence. You've only narrowed it down. If you could pinpoint that faulty sequence precisely, Mullis thinks, you could use a naturally occurring enzyme to replicate—

It just comes to him.

What if he makes a second, different string of twenty nucleotides, that will seek out and bind itself to the opposite strand of what comes *after* the faulty gene sequence? That would narrow it down to one place on the genome. The two strings would act like brackets or bookends and they would be pointed towards each other. That means that out of all those billions of nucleotides, he'd be able to select one sequence of DNA and–

'Holy Shit!'

Mullis pulls over to the side of the road. He finds an envelope and a pencil in the glove compartment and starts to make feverish calculations...

Black white black white. They run in wide solid blocks. The read-out usually looks like a barcode, narrow strips of black and white. But not this time.

Normally he loves his job. What he discovers from a patient's gene chip can provide a diagnosis that can indicate treatment, but then there are times like this when what he sees chills him.

He heaves a sigh.

His colleague at the next bench says, 'What's up?'

'Come and see.'

She gets up, comes over, and looks over his shoulder.

'Oh dear,' she says.

'"Oh dear" is right.'

They don't need to say any more. What they are seeing might assist the clinician in his diagnosis or it might have no immediate bearing. Either way to record this information in the patient's medical notes is to set a time bomb ticking. This DNA print-out tells them – literally in black and white – that this child is the product of a consanguineous relationship. He has been born as the result of incest between father and daughter, or brother and sister, or even mother and son.

In all likelihood no-one knows except the birth parents. But when the child reaches adulthood he can request to see his medical records and if he does...

The lab is still formulating its policy on the ethics of situations like this. Maybe they'll decide this information doesn't need to be formally recorded.

'Luckily we don't have to decide,' she says. 'Fancy a quick

drink before we head off?'

'Best idea you've had all day.'

Later that night lying in bed next to his sleeping wife, pregnant with their third child, he wonders what secrets lie hidden in his own DNA and that of his children. We all sail under sealed orders. To rip open that envelope and to discover where you have come from and where you are going — that is an awesome thing.

That night it is a long time before he falls asleep.

Mullis presses so hard that the point of the pencil snaps off. He rummages in the glove compartment for a pen.

Beside him Jennifer stirs and mutters a complaint.

'I've just thought of something incredible,' he says.

'Yeah, yeah. Let's get moving, can we?'

'Just wait.'

She yawns and goes back to sleep.

Mullis goes on scribbling.

What he has realised is this.

When you heat DNA to a temperature between 90 and 100 degrees the hydrogen bonds between the two strands of the double helix break and the strands melt apart. But the strands don't want to be separate. DNA has a natural tendency to pair up. When you add a short string of nucleotides, they will find their matching sequence in the larger strand and attach themselves to it. If you also add DNA polymerase — the enzyme responsible for replication — it will home in on those short strands of nucleotides. DNA polymerase is like a caretaker. It will sit on the paired section and move along the DNA looking for gaps, places where there is only a single strand of DNA. When it finds a gap, it repairs it, making a new strand to match the one that melted away. The key thing is that it will repair both strands of DNA, so that you'll end up with two copies of the original double strand. And if you do the exact same thing again, melt the DNA back to single strands, let the polymerase repair it, you'll have four copies. And if you do it ten times –

If you do it ten times, you'll have... you'll have...

Yes, you'll have over a thousand copies.

Do it twenty times, you'll have a million.

At a stroke, Mullis has solved both problems: how to select a sequence of DNA and how to amplify it. The weeks that it takes now to replicate DNA would shrink to hours. Of course heating would destroy the polymerase, so you would have to add new polymerase by hand between each cycle. That would slow things down. You'd have to find some way of automating it: heat it up, cool it, add the polymerase, heat it up, cool it... But hell, there'd be a way, of course there would...

In a lab in Manchester a young woman prepares the PCR machine to run overnight. Everyone else has gone home and the lab is quiet. It's such a simple mundane task and yet ten years ago this technique was so new that there was a question on it in her Oxford finals paper. The guy who invented the Polymerase Chain Reaction got the Nobel Prize for Chemistry – and he deserved it. The PCR machine has become such a standard piece of equipment that it was the first thing that she and her boss bought when they set up the lab.

She thinks no more of setting up the machine than of putting coffee on to percolate or throwing together a pasta sauce. At the same time she has to be meticulous. DNA is very stable, hard to destroy, but easily contaminated. She focuses on the job in hand. She divides the master mix, containing the polymerase, the primers, the nucleotides and so on into small plastic tubes. She adds mouse DNA to each one.

She's working on a group of metabolic disorders called Mucopolysaccharidoses or MPS. They are caused by the absence or malfunctioning of certain enzymes needed to break down long chains of sugar carbohydrates in human cells in order to build bone, cartilage, tendons, corneas, skin and connective tissue. It's a glitch in the DNA code that has devastating results. A child may be mentally disabled, they may have heart disease, or hearing loss, skeletal deformities... the list goes on and on. Children with these disorders rarely live into adulthood.

She slots the tubes into the PCR machine.

She sets the machine to run for thirty cycles. By morning the DNA will have been replicated a billion times. She will find out tomorrow which mice are carrying the defective gene and can therefore be used for her experiments into transplanting bone marrow to treat MPS. The bone marrow cells are healthy, their genetic code intact. They can supply the missing enzyme to the faulty cells. One day these diseases, which have ended the lives of countless children and broken the hearts of their parents, will be as much a thing of the past as polio and smallpox. One day, the diagnosis won't be a death sentence.

She presses the button and the machine begins a gentle whirring.

She has done enough for one day. Her husband has dinner waiting. She shrugs off her white coat, tosses it in the laundry bag, and heads for home.

Of course, Mullis thinks, there's no way it can work. There has to be something wrong somewhere. It isn't as if he's discovered anything new. Everyone knows that a string of nucleotides will search out matching sequences on the genome. Everyone knows that if you add DNA polymerase, it will copy DNA. And everyone knows that if you heat DNA you can get it to peel apart into separate strands. Hell, is it likely that no-one has put all this together and come to the same conclusion that he has? There must be a reason why it won't work or everyone would be doing it.

And yet it's so simple, so elegant, that it surely must be right.

There is a lot of hard work ahead, he knows that. There'll be problems he can't yet foresee. It might not be easy to make it work and it might take a while to convince people. The process will have to be refined and other scientists will become involved. Machines that will automate the process will have to be designed and developed... Maybe he can find a form of polymerase that won't be destroyed by the heat...

He drives on. It's dark now, but it's a clear night and stars stream across the sky.

When Mullis pulls up outside his cabin in Medocino County, it's only two and a half hours since he left Berkeley, but it has been long enough for him to think of something that will cause a revolution in biological research and touch the lives of billions and billions of people.

Afterword:

1983: Kary Mullis and the Polymerase Chain Reaction

Dr. Angharad Watson

WHILE THERE ARE many scientists whose work or lives have inspired me, when it comes to 'eureka moments', few, in my opinion, can come close to the invention of the polymerase chain reaction, known as PCR. It was a genuine lightning strike, a moment of revelation. But what really makes it so breathtaking is how completely invaluable PCR has become to Life Sciences. I have never been into a lab that doesn't have at least one PCR machine. Many have several, often in different varieties. The machine used by the clinical geneticist in the story is a different flavour from the one used by the basic researcher, and gives different information. The clinical geneticist was scanning hundreds of genes for possible mutations, while the researcher was checking for the presence of a specific, known mutated gene. The forensic scientists that identify criminals don't technically look for genes at all, they look for short stretches of non-coding 'junk' DNA that litter our genomes. Nobody knows why these stretches of apparently useless DNA are there, but we know that they are passed down from parent to child, and we know what they look like. They are like library stamps inside the cover of a book; they don't change the content or meaning of the book, but they allow you to identify one copy from another, and know where it's come from.

There's another kind, quantitative PCR, which can tell you not simply whether a gene is present or absent, but how many copies there are. This type of PCR is invaluable to gene therapy, which is what people in my lab are trying to do for the Mucopolysaccharidosis diseases mentioned in the story. Gene therapy is the idea that where a disease is caused by a single faulty gene, as in Mucopolysaccharidosis or Cystic Fibrosis or Haemophilia, you can supply the correct gene and therefore cure the disease. We are able to do this by incorporating the gene into a virus. Some viruses are able to insert their own genes into the genome of a human cell, and so can be engineered to insert therapeutic genes instead. With all that moving around of genetic information, there needs to be a way of tracing the genes, seeing how many cells get a copy, and whether each cell gets one copy or several copies. Quantitative PCR allows this to be done in a few hours. Although it sounds like science fiction, this experimental therapy has been used in the clinic, and offers real hope for many currently incurable genetic diseases.

You can also use PCR to tell whether a gene is switched on or not. This is very important in understanding things like cancer, when cells start to behave in ways they shouldn't. Every cell in your body contains your whole genome, the entire instruction book for you. But a skin cell on your elbow only needs to use the instructions for being a skin cell – it doesn't need to know how to be a blood cell or a neurone – so it files away all that irrelevant information in a process known as silencing. In cancerous cells, some genes that should be switched off are switched on, while others that are vital for normal function are silenced. Reverse transcriptase PCR can tell the difference between the silent genes and the active genes. This means that a cancerous cell can be compared to a normal cell, in order to see which genes have been incorrectly switched off or on, and so begin to understand how the cancer has formed. This sort of analysis has led to new kinds of specific targeted treatments for cancers.

Every single type of PCR, however, relies on Mullis's primers, the short sequences of DNA that he realised could be used to find and 'bracket' specific sections of DNA. This realisation revolutionised biochemistry by unlocking the genome. Prior to Mullis's discovery, the only way of identifying specific genetic sequences was using Southern blotting, named after Professor Ed Southern, who received an earlier Nobel Prize for his technique. Southern blots still have their place in today's laboratories, but their reliance on DNA tagged with radioactive isotopes makes it much more hazardous for the researcher than PCR. They do have the distinction, however, of immortalising their inventor in not one, but three techniques; related methods for examining RNA and protein have been named whimsically in homage to Prof Southern as Northern and Western blots, respectively (there is not, as yet, an Eastern blot). PCR, despite not having such a characterful name as Southern blots, changed the accessibility of the DNA code in much the same way that the invention of the printing press changed the availability of books. This may be something of an oversimplification (and one that is, I allow, unfairly critical of Southern blotting) but it does give some idea of the huge change that PCR brought about. For a scientist of my generation, life without a PCR machine is like life without a mobile phone, or the internet. Possibly slightly more so, as I can remember living without both those things, but the very first experiment I ever did was to run a PCR.

There is one more thing that deserves a mention in the story of PCR, and that is an obscure bacterium called *Thermus aquaticus*. In the story, Mullis had to add fresh polymerase after every cycle, but the modern researcher just switched a machine on and let it run while she went home for the night. How? By using a polymerase from *Thermus aquaticus*. This little beastie lives in thermal vents at the bottom of the ocean, and so has evolved special proteins that aren't destroyed by heat. Enzymes from these unusual organisms that live at the extreme edges of the environment pop up in all sorts of ways – in your biological detergents that work at very high or low temperatures, for example – and without the heat-stable polymerase, PCR may well have not become such a widespread technique. Imagine instead of switching something on and letting it run, having to sit next to it for several hours adding new material every five or six minutes. I'm not sure my husband would keep dinner waiting for me for that long!

When I tell people that I'm a biochemist, a frequent question is, 'So, you're going find a cure for cancer (or Alzheimer's, or AIDS, or maybe even the disease I work on, Mucopolysaccharidosis)?' Inventing a new technique that requires first year undergraduate Biochemistry to understand makes for much less impressive dinner party conversation, but in reality can be even more important and inspiring. Any scientist researching any of the diseases I've just mentioned, or any disease you can think of, will, in one way or another, use PCR to facilitate their research. Many discoveries would have been impossible or delayed for years, even decades, without it. Not bad for a late-night brainwave on a desert highway.

Monkey See, Monkey Do

Trevor Hoyle

NOT SURE WHEN I started to suspect that my friend Reece might be suffering from something called the Extreme Male Brain. It was a worry because his behaviour, especially towards me, changed a lot over a short time. I don't mind admitting it scared me.

Reece was the one I worked mostly closely with, roughly the same age as me. There were four of us altogether (including Lucy and Diane) in our particular lab team, and possibly several hundred support workers like ourselves throughout the university, all engaged in extremely important research. Personally neither Lucy nor Diane attracted me, though I got the idea that Reece fancied Lucy. It was the way he stared at her when he thought no-one else was looking. Mind you, Reece tended to stare at everybody, so maybe it didn't mean what I thought it meant, if you know what I mean.

Anyway, where was I? Oh yes, this discovery, the one I want to tell you about, happened one day in the lab, quite by accident. Out of the blue. I myself was an eyewitness that Tuesday morning, and I can recall what took place as if it were yesterday.

The team of neuroscientists, under the direction of Professor Rizzolatti, were studying the part of the brain which controls hand movements: reaching out, grasping, picking up, etc. The experiment was set up to record the activity of a single neuron in the brain of a monkey when it reaches out for a peanut. This was routine; it had been carried out countless times before. On that day something odd and totally unexpected happened. The device suddenly registered the triggering of a neuron stimulus in the brain when the monkey hadn't done anything. It was simply sitting there, motionless, placidly observing what went on around it in the lab. And what it had observed was one of the technical staff helping himself to a peanut from the dish of food in front of the cage.

What could this mean? The identical neuron being activated when the monkey watched a hand picking up a peanut as when the monkey performed the action itself? At its most basic, the scientists said, it was affirmation of the old saying, 'Monkey See, Monkey Do' – though, I have to admit, the saying made no sense to me.

And to be honest, I didn't have a clue what all this meant. I was pretty low down the research food chain, engaged in fairly menial lab duties. I wasn't expected to understand the theories behind what we were doing, merely to perform my function as best I could.

As well as Professor Rizzolatti, the team included Giuseppe Di Pellegrino, Luciano Fadiga, Leonardo Fogassi and Vittorio Gallese. I mention these because I'm unsure which one of them came up with the term 'mirror neurons'. A simple description, but those are often the best. The neurons, it seemed, were mimicking or 'reflecting' the perceived behaviour of another creature, and yet doing so without the action itself being performed by the brain's owner...

I hope this explanation makes sense. It's just from what I observed and overheard going on around me, lacking as I did the academic training of the researchers. Reece was just as much in the dark as I was, but he wouldn't admit it – competitive by nature, always restless, never happy unless he was poking his nose into something and causing trouble. Actually he got on my nerves. 'Can you make head or tail of any of this stuff, Mack?' he asked me one day in the lab. It was late afternoon and things were quiet. It had been a particularly hard day, I remember, and I had a thumping headache.

'Hey!' He flicked a peanut which only just missed my eye. 'You ignoring me?'

'I'm trying to,' I said.

'Why, what's wrong? Something bugging you, Mack?'

'I'm tired, that's all. And stop calling me Mack.'

'Don't you like it?'

'You know I don't.'

'—Don't be so touchy. It's only a nickname. So what about it?' Reece gave me one of his flashing stares and flicked another peanut when I wearily closed my eyes. 'Wake up there!'

'Leave it out.' I bit my lip. 'Don't know what you mean.'

'I mean this… stuff, this junk—' he waved at the benches and metal racks all around loaded with equipment and flickering screens and rows of dials with quivering needles. 'What do you think they're up to, these big brains, all day long? There must be something. A reason. So what is it?'

'How should I know? I'm the same as you – I just do as I'm told. No point trying to understand it, we're not trained to.'

Reece scratched his chin and looked round, as if deciding whether to ask Lucy and Diane what they thought, then dropped the idea. He didn't value their opinions anyway. 'Do you want to know what I think?' I didn't, as it happens, but whatever I said wouldn't stop him. 'They're not up to any good. That's what I think.'

'How do you work that out?'

'Because I'm not dumb like you. I watch what's going on.'

Though I didn't show it, there were times when Reece drove me mad. I got so worked up with his sudden mood swings and stupid questions and his irritating habits. I just wanted to be left alone, instead of playing silly mind games with a cretin. Perhaps that was the start of the Extreme Male Brain thing – or was he always that way and I hadn't noticed it?

There wasn't much of a fuss following the discovery of mirror neurons. It didn't seem to have a practical application, or even to lead anywhere that might be worth investigating. So what if a certain bunch of cells in the brain of a macaque monkey lit up when it observed a hand reaching out and picking up a peanut and transferring it from hand to mouth? No big deal. When they began to study the activity of mirror neurons in humans, all that changed. They didn't surgically insert electrodes in the frontal lobe system, of course. They used electromagnetic imaging scans instead to pinpoint very accurately where the mirror neurons were located, how they were being activated, and by what. The *what* was vital. Not just the sight of a lab technician eating a peanut, it turned out, or other physical stimuli, but in response to emotional behaviour too.

This was the breakthrough, apparently. The same group of mirror neurons was being stimulated by the emotions of others – their joy, their fear, happiness, disappointment, sadness, rapture – as when the subject himself was feeling them. Humans (and perhaps other creatures too) shared and communicated the same pain, the same joy, the same despair, the same anger.

They were in empathy with what they were observing.

The atmosphere in the lab was transformed. The researchers were becoming excited. They began to construct a theory. Several theories. Dozens of them. Might not this explain why humans become so immersed when watching a dramatic performance on stage or in a film, living vicariously through the actors and experiencing the same intense emotions? Or losing themselves in the turbulence and upheavals of characters in a novel, suffering their pain, rejoicing at their triumphs? Mirror neurons are at work, the theory proposed – simulating, imitating, then replicating those same feelings in the mind of the beholder.

Humans receive pleasure by watching the strength and grace of physical movement. The sight of a professional dancer or a highly-trained athlete stimulates the appropriate mirror neurons of those same actions all humans have performed – dancing, running, jumping – but enhances and elevates the feeling so that the passive observer shares the superior achievement of the dancer and the athlete.

This quality of empathy is more important, according to the theory, than mere shadow play. It allows humans, and perhaps all sentient creatures, to form bonds of friendship and dependence on others. When humans perceive happiness, their own joyful neurons respond and reproduce a simulacrum of happiness inside their own minds. They know what it feels like to be happy from their own reservoir of happiness. Just as they know that a hand reaching for a peanut is to anticipate the pleasure of tasting it, of chewing and swallowing and satisfying hunger.

So when humans empathise with one another they feel the warmth and closeness and comfort of shared experience. They feel they are not alone.

The exact opposite seemed to be happening in the lab. The most obvious signs were when Reece started behaving strangely and horribly to Lucy: nice to her one minute, playful almost, giving her a smile that without warning turned into a scowl, so she visibly recoiled. I guessed, in fact I knew, what this was all about.

Jealousy.

Reece had somehow got the notion into his head that Lucy and me were up to something behind his back, which definitely was not the case. Such a relationship held no interest for me.

As if worrying about Reece wasn't enough to be going on with (which made my headaches worse), there were rumours going around that our little team was to be broken up. One of us, possibly two, would be sent to another department on a new assignment, something to do with the study of vocal and facial imitation in primates. I was happy where I was. Several of my friends in the past had been sent on assignments in other departments and it hadn't done their job prospects any good. They ended up as faceless numbers, mere ticks and crosses, on the monthly lab roster.

Meanwhile the research went on. Some new studies came in that surprised everyone, suggesting that mirror neurons in the female brain are more responsive than those in the male. Females react more strongly and actively, which means an increased capacity for identifying with another's emotional state; in other words, more empathy.

At the opposite end of the spectrum, where emotions are not engaged as fully and mirror neurons fail to respond, it's as if part of the brain has been sealed off, isolated by a lead shield. The name given to this lack of empathy was the Extreme Male Brain.

That's what gave me this notion about Reece. Wasn't Reece a prime candidate for the Extreme Male Brain condition?

A few days later there was an interesting discussion in the lab with one of the professors and a group of students. By now I had picked up enough of the jargon to just about follow his line of argument. He wandered about as he talked, stroking his beard, as if a little lost in thought. 'The characteristics of the Extreme Male Brain are the same or similar to those found in cases of autism – a failure to interpret the gestures and expressions of others. To such people, body language is a mystery. They lack social skills and find it difficult to make friendships. They tend to shy away from close personal contact. This behaviour has similarities with psychopathic personality disorder. Suffering, or indeed any kind of distress,' the professor went on, waving his hand as if swatting away a fly, 'means nothing to the psychopath. Because his mirror neuron system is not functioning, he can harm others, even kill them, with complete indifference, not caring about the consequence of his actions.'

Even kill them...

I was getting more and more alarmed. If Reece had an Extreme Male Brain he might commit a violent act at any moment because he didn't know the difference between right and wrong. Didn't know and didn't care either. A violent act against anyone.

This was worrying of course, but it also got me thinking. The next day was pretty quiet in the lab. There were no experiments going on and we were left to our own devices.

Reece was in one of his jumpy, excitable moods, which presented an ideal opportunity. I knew the slightest thing could set him off: it didn't even have to be something real or actually happening. It could be imaginary.

I started it off by being nice to Lucy. Nothing too obvious, touching her arm, patting her shoulder and so on. Because normally I didn't bother much with her, Reece noticed this change in behaviour straight away, as I knew he would. I thought to myself, 'It's working. He's twitching already. He's getting suspicious.' I'd seen him react this way before, working himself up from nothing into a frenzy. Reece kept staring, or rather glaring, at me, as if challenging me to a fight. Then switched from me to Lucy, then back again to me, back and forth, probably imagining what we got up to when his back was turned. I didn't react. I stayed calm and in control. The calmer I was, the more agitated Reece was.

Lucy was the innocent party in all this of course. She and Diane were quietly minding their own business, so it came as even more of a shock when Reece suddenly turned on Lucy without any warning. Really tore into her, poor thing. That was Reece's big mistake. The lab was under constant surveillance and the incident was caught on camera. To prevent any more disturbances or disruption to the routine, Reece was temporarily transferred – given the new assignment in another department, as it turned out. Two problems solved at a stroke! My lucky day.

When he returned a week later, there was a definite difference. Reece was quieter, more withdrawn, and he no longer asked questions, even just to be annoying. No more staring, and he gave up teasing me and flicking peanuts at my eye. It was clear he'd also been told not to fraternise with his female co-workers. Actually he'd been given a final warning – behave himself or the researchers would find him another assignment to be sent on. It seemed that Reece wasn't keen to repeat the experience.

As Lucy said to me at the time, 'We've been very fortunate, you and me, Mack, to have had such long careers in neuroscience and still be here to tell the tale.'

Which is very true. And we're even luckier compared to Reece and Diane, who both ended up having their ventral premotor cortexes sliced into thin rashers for examination under the mircoscope. These are itsy-bitsy portions of brain tissue, smaller than a monkey's little fingernail, seared to an electrical device like a transistor so that single, individual neuron cells can be isolated and blown up on a screen for close scrutiny. All very useful I'm sure.

At the very least this solved the problem of Reece and his Extreme Male Brain. The silly chump ended up having no brain at all, extreme or otherwise.

As for the two of us left – Lucy and me – well, after the electrodes and four stainless steel retaining pins had been removed and the fur had grown again, leaving just faint scars on our scalps, we were given a warm, dry, secure environment with a regular and adequate supply of food and water. And even though we had plenty of opportunity, nothing much happened between us; to be honest, nothing at all happened. If truth be told I had as much feeling for Lucy as I did those pale blank faces shifting back and forth beyond the wire cage all day, forever busy with their own mysterious activities, probing this, measuring that, their pasty paws sneaking in to pinch our food when they thought no one was looking.

My mirror neurons were unaffected, as Professor Rizzolatti himself might have phrased it.

Yet thinking of the four us now – Lucy and Diane, Reece and myself – it takes me right back to the moment when the lab technician reached out for that peanut on our food tray and I saw Reece's eyes gleam with their usual, characteristic excitement. Poor Reece. Impressionable, as always.

Afterword:

2003: Giacomo Rizzolatti and Mirror Neurons

Professor Giacomo Rizzolatti

Trevor Hoyle's story about the discovery of mirror neurons is written by somebody 'pretty low down the research food chain, engaged in fairly menial lab duties'. The story is quite accurate. Yet it might be of interest, at least to some readers, to also hear an account of the discovery from the perspective of someone at the other end of that chain.

So, how did we discover mirror neurons? It was a matter of luck and merit. Luck, because we never expected to find these strangely behaving neurons. Merit, because we put ourselves in a unique condition to discover them. Several years before the events described in this story, I decided to test monkeys in what has been called a 'naturalistic' way. Contrary to most motor neurophysiologists who considered monkeys as equivalent to small robots performing precise tasks, I thought that we could learn more about their motor system by 'playing' with them: giving them food, observing them eating, and detecting which were the stimuli able to trigger their motor responses. Their actions were correlated with the discharge of the recorded neurons, and often videoed. This approach allowed us (my co-workers in those days were Massimo Matelli and Maurizio Gentilucci) to give a new and much richer description of motor neuron properties. For example, we found that many neurons in the sector of the ventral premotor cortex, where later mirror neurons were discovered (area F5), encode the goal of a motor act (e.g. grasping) and not the movements (e.g. finger flexing, arm extending) that form that motor act. We also found that other neurons, located in an adjacent sector of premotor cortex (area F4) encode the space around the monkey. We called this space 'peripersonal space', in spite of the protest of one reviewer claiming that we cannot use Greek ('peri') and Latin ('persona') words together. (We won the argument using as an example the word 'television' which also has 'mixed' origin).

We were often criticized at that time for being too 'qualitative'. This criticism was indeed correct. In fact, you cannot have the same precision when you test the monkey in a naturalistic condition as when you test it while immobilized in a cubicle in front of a computer screen. So I decided to be a bit more quantitative and to use a special apparatus given to us by Hideo Sakata, a highly creative Japanese scientist, with whom we collaborated at that time. This apparatus allowed us to better control the stimuli and the monkey behavior. The use of this apparatus required putting, from time to time, some food inside it. The monkeys watched us and, of course, also saw us grasping food before putting it in the apparatus. To our surprise, we noticed that some neurons, which were certainly 'motor' also, fired when *we* grasped the food. For a long time we thought this was evidence of some monkey movements that passed unnoticed by us.

Given, however, our ethological bias, we did not disregard the phenomenon. On the contrary, we became more and more interested in it. One day we found a neuron that fired exclusively when we grasped the food in a specific way. The monkey was completely still. We gave that food to the monkey and the neuron fired only when the monkey grasped it in the same way that we had grasped it. That day we became convinced that the phenomenon was real. This is probably the episode that Mack mentioned in his story. Mirror neurons were discovered.

We were very excited and sent, a few months after the discovery, a short, preliminary communication on these strange neurons to *Nature*. The article did not pass the first scrutiny. According to the *Nature* editors, the discovery was not of general interest. Thus, the first report appeared in *Experimental Brain Research*, a rather good, but strictly neurophysiological journal. Fortunately, the subsequent publications were accepted without difficulty by prestigious journals.

Mack also mentions that the great excitement caused by the discovery of the mirror mechanism occurred only later, when we found that this mechanism is also present in the emotional centres of the human brain. He is right as far as the general public and journalists are concerned. Indeed most of the questions I am asked at conferences, especially by the general public, concern this issue. Emotion, empathy, and how to control them or improve them are problems of great relevance and, not surprisingly, arouse a lot of interest. Personally, however, I preferred and still prefer thinking about the wider consequences of the mirror mechanism on cognition and conscious perception.

Finally, I want to express my gratitude to Mack for his help and to his friend Trevor Hoyle for describing so vividly our discovery.

That is the Day

Sarah Hall

At 7am Charles collected him from the Centre in the old white pickup and they left for Makowe. Town seemed quiet as they drove through. There were fewer people on the streets and at the market, and no one was queuing at the Post Office. Charles was not so talkative today. He was leaning heavily against the driver's door, in a classic hangover slump, one fist resting on the bottom of the steering wheel. He had on a faded KwaZulu Health Centre T-shirt and his elbows looked ashy. Sunday night was Kwamsane barbeque night. A couple of times he'd been along with Charles to the joint on the outskirts of town to play pool and drink beer, but it was hard working the next day.

The suspension of the truck boxed and bounced as it hit potholes in the road. The air conditioner was still broken and the ventilation panels smelled musty when they were open. He wound the window down all the way and hot air blew into the cab. The heat had felt immense all week, almost solid. Even the sudden, deluging rains in the mornings hadn't cleared it. For several nights now he'd woken up in a heavy sweat, the sheets saturated, the mattress damp. It was hard to ask people about night-sweats during screening, hard to define what was and wasn't febrile. The translator always came back with the same answer. Too hot, yes. At night. In the day. In the sky.

They passed the small district hospital. The gate was open but outside it a crowd had massed. Some women were clapping their hands and singing. The rest of the crowd wasn't making much noise and did not seem rowdy, but the entrance was blocked. Two policemen stood alongside the group, their rifles lowered, smiling and chatting. The ambulance was parked up inside the compound. He couldn't see any staff.

What's going on, he asked Charles.

Strike. It's the first day.

Striking for what?

Pay rise. What else? They want more than inflation. Double.

Right.

The truck turned onto the highway and sped up. They passed slow taxi-loads of people sitting and standing in the back of wagons and buggies. Women were walking with canisters half-full of water on their heads. Along the road were lacunas in the trees where the loggers had clear-cut. From the driver's seat came the occasional quiet groan. Evidently, Charles was still suffering.

He took an apple out of his bag and began eating it. When he was finished he tossed the core out into the scrub. He watched the flashing arboreal scenery for a while. He turned his iPod on, went through his notes, and scanned a paper sent to him from a colleague about latently infected, resting CD4 T cells. Then he took out his book. Makowe was an hour's drive. If Charles' company didn't improve he would keep reading. The novel was set in the Fens, a landscape of big skies and silty ditches, breweries and rusting dredgers. The central romance was doomed by the crimes of previous generations. It was diverting enough.

You like to strike in England?

There was the metal crack of a ring-pull being released, and fizzing. He glanced up. Charles was rubbing his face with one hand and holding a can of coke in the other. He had his knee jammed under the steering wheel and was sitting up straighter.

He shut the novel and put it back in his bag.

Sometimes. It depends if the Tories are in power.

Do the doctors strike?

They might soon, if the reforms go ahead. It's a difficult situation. The circumstances have to be pretty bad for medical personnel to protest en masse, usually. You're putting people's lives at risk.

Ya, ya.

What do you think?

I think I don't get paid enough. But today I'm driving.

He decided to play devil's advocate, to stretch the conversation out.

A.J. Cook said that strikes are the only weapon. Maybe public sector workers have no other way of pressuring the government.

Who's he?

British Trade Union leader in the 20s. He was a miner.

Gold?

Coal.

It's not the same thing.

They talked for a while about the virtue and limitation of industrial action. Then about democracy. They often talked about current affairs. Charles liked to debate. He liked to know what was going on in England and often asked him on their journeys together what the English would do in a given situation. Once he had tried to play Charles a podcast of a debate about Globalization during the drive, but Charles had not enjoyed it. There was no point in listening to other people argue if you couldn't join in. Sometimes they listened to music. After squabbling gently about which song to play next they would agree to set the device on shuffle.

They turned off the highway and drove towards the game park. The clinic was the remotest in the district and the views became austerely beautiful and expansive as altitude was gained. There were herds of zebra and giraffes, rhinos. In the river basin the truck slowed and he looked to the right. An elephant was standing between two bushes; its heavy crêped ears folded forward, shading itself. Though it was early there were already carloads of game-spotters parked on the road, windows wound down, binoculars glinting in the sunlight. The earth became redder as they drove. The road narrowed and rose up between hills. Eagles looped and rose on the updrafts. Charles took the turning out of the park, towards Makowe. The track was un-tarred, deeply rutted; the truck bounced and jolted and left a cloud of red dust behind it.

He liked this stretch of scrubland. It was not truly desolate. The earth was always brighter after the rain. Women would come into the clinic with earth smeared on their faces, like sunscreen. It was eaten during pregnancy; his patients often said they craved it. Sometimes, after clinic, while he was waiting for Charles to collect him, he would go for a short walk. There was always something interesting to see. Birds. Praying mantises with thick raptorial forelegs. Even the dung beetles were oddly attractive, the moment they stood back and lifted away their armour, revealing sheer elegant wings and a pulsating back.

They passed a few settlements, consisting of mud and concrete buildings. People were walking slowly up the track. Children waved at the familiar vehicle and he waved back. Charles was drinking another can of coke and humming. He looked out of the window. Here and there on the red mounds of earth were snowy specks. He tried to make them out. Flowers perhaps. Some kind of blossom. Or ash from a fire.

Hey, could you slow down a minute?

Charles braked and stopped and idled the truck at the side of the road. In their weeks together a system of understanding had developed. Slow down meant stop, it meant exotic curiosity. He opened the door and climbed out. He walked away from the road. Butterflies. There were dozens of them, a grounded rabble spread across the earth, their wings flickering and twitching. They must all be hatching, he thought. As he approached they lifted gracefully from the ground and flitted away. He went back to the truck and they continued on. Two miles later Charles slowed again. One of the nurses, Thiliwe, was walking up the track. She had on a lab coat with brown lapels and loose green trousers.

You want to give her a lift?

Sure, why not.

Charles pulled over. They greeted each other in Zulu. She gestured towards the clinic, said a few words, and then shrugged. Charles asked her something. The two spoke for a minute. He couldn't follow any of it. Then Charles turned to him.

Might not get in. There are some people protesting up there too.

Really? From a union?

What do you want to do? Go back?

Is it going to be a problem?

Charles shrugged.

It could be.

Let's go up there and see.

Charles said a few words to the nurse. She climbed up into the bed of the truck and held onto the bar fixed to the back of the cab as they pulled away. A mile or so from Makowe they began to see patients walking in the opposite direction.

The clinic stood in a dusty swale past the villages. It was made of concrete and corrugated iron. On the front wall was a life-size photograph of the tribal leader with the motto *Get Tested* underneath, and next to this a cartoon series of a man lying down looking ill, being administered to by a nurse, then rising from the bed, smiling. When he'd first arrived at Makowe he couldn't believe there were enough people in the area to sustain the place. But they had come: hundreds of them, walking miles, most already testing positive and qualifying for antiretroviral therapy, most having to be screened for tuberculosis as well. He'd gotten used to the routine. The long and difficult drive. Being saluted by the gatekeeper, a young man who sat on a wooden chair in the porch all day, listening to South African rap on his radio and watching people go in and out. He would walk inside and greet the patients, who were already lined up on stone platforms under the awning of the yard.

Sanibonani.

There would be a choral reply. Yebo.

Some mornings the nurses sang hymns to commence the proceedings, while the patients fidgeted and shuffled, and he laid out his equipment on the table – the Oxford handbook, drug formulary, ophthalmoscope, documentation folder, his sandwiches. He would check for the worst cases, call the ambulance if necessary, then fill out the blue government form declaring disease. There was no oxygen, but he could start IV fluids and rifa 4. Then he'd begin with the rest of the patients, asking the translator, how are they today, how long has the fever been, is it a pain like this or like that, screening for coughs, weight loss, neck swellings, checking blood results in the files. He would order ARVs. He would try to drink water regularly.

The clinic had four rooms, one with an examination bed that usually had folders and other detritus dumped on it, where he sometimes photographed patients for his records, a counselling room where the nurses would explain how the virus worked, how to take the pills, that the medicine must always be taken, why prophylaxes had to be taken, and how to ask a husband or another wife to come in. There was a small side room in which he ate his lunch, containing a library – if two shelves stacked with outdated texts, old copies of the Zululand Observer and medical journals, the debris of his predecessors, could be called a library. And there was the storeroom, which was kept locked.

He had learned that his patients would be untruthful or evasive about visiting the Sangoma, that a pause was often needed before starting a course of treatment, to make sure whatever remedy they'd been given was gone from their system. He'd seen babies brought in leaking vivid yellow diarrhoea – the result of unidentifiable toxic enemas. Once he had been performing percussion on the back of an old woman to test her lungs and as he'd tapped she had cried out and leapt up. He'd thought she was in pain. The translator had explained the ancestors were residing in her shoulders. The clinic would run late. Charles would pick him up and say the same thing as he climbed into the truck.

That is the day.

He would be driven back to the doctors' housing complex. Or dropped in town if he needed supplies.

He was used to the routine, the terrible repetition of disease, so many children, the annoying slowness of rural pharmaceutical delivery, and the cultural barriers, but there was always something different, always something new.

When Charles turned off the track and down the slope to the clinic he could see a small crowd had gathered outside the gates. No one was clapping and singing like the picket line back in Mtuba, but he could hear the South African rap station playing from the porch. They were mostly men, eighteen or twenty of them, none he recognized, though some could have been patients, and they were stern-faced. A couple of them had been squatting, as if simply loitering, but they stood as the truck pulled up. The translator and another nurse were standing to the side. Sitting beside them was a woman with a bundle held in her arms. The music was thumping away. The gatekeeper obviously had not taken the padlock off the gate, but it was business as usual with the radio. Charles parked and put the brake on. The engine of the truck whined as it died.

You want to try? Charles asked.

He didn't want to seem hesitant or intimidated, so he opened the door, stepped out, and reached back to get his bag.

I can come in.

Is it going to be necessary?

Ya. I think so.

Charles opened the driver's door and got out. He was a big man, tall, and thick-waisted. He had been employed by the Centre for almost ten years. His daughter and his wife worked in the doctors' housing complex. They approached the crowd together. He tried to meet their eyes, one by one, but could not hold anyone's gaze.

Sawubona. Sawubona.

No one replied. Thiliwe had climbed down out of the back of the truck and was walking behind them. Without pausing, Charles stepped between men and pointed through the bars to the gatekeeper.

Menzies. Open it. The doctor is here now.

The gatekeeper stood from his stool but did not move forward.

They are not coming today, he said. We've got to stay closed.

One of the men in the crowd, no more than twenty-five years old probably and wearing a yellow Vodafone T-shirt, put a hand on the gate and held it. Charles turned to him. Sharp words passed between them in Zulu. Charles called to Menzies again, his tone firmer, and this time Menzies came forward. The man holding the gate rattled it and the structure clanked against its hinges.

He could feel the eyes of the others in the group sliding over and off him. He felt stupid, standing there with his bag in his hand, without the language to help defuse the situation. The altercation between Charles and the protester continued, with Charles pointing at the lock as he spoke and the man slicing the air with his free hand. It was controlled, but there was a crackle, of antagonism, of ill intent. Neither one seemed to be giving ground. Menzies was inching towards his stool again. The radio was still playing.

Thiliwe joined the other nurse and the translator and

they spoke quietly to each other. The sitting woman was looking up at him, staring at him. The other patients had clearly been sent away, or had not thought the clinic would run, but she'd remained. He went to her, put his bag down, and knelt beside her. She passed him the baby. It was wrapped in a cotton blanket. He moved the binding gently. It was malnurished and small and barely moving. Its eyelids were half open, and it was gasping, but it was not really conscious. The nose and mouth were crusted and there was a sour smell of faeces. He looked at her. She knew it already. She had simply been waiting for an official. He could hear Charles' voice, starting to sound frustrated. He could hear feet scuffing on the ground. He stood, picked up his bag and walked through the crowd, holding the baby against his chest. He approached the gate. The group moved to let him pass. He knew they weren't afraid of him, his status as a Western doctor was at best unclear, but also he thought they would be unlikely to challenge him. The mother was following, and the nurses. Charles glanced at him and nodded.

Could you open the gate please, he said to Menzies. I have to look at this child inside.

Menzies was sitting on the stool nodding his head in time to the bass and looking nervously at the man holding the gate. The man patted his hip with his other hand as a threat. He waited for something to happen. He held the baby. Nothing. The stand-off continued. The rap music banged on. Charles sighed and took a step back away from the gate. He felt a trickle of sweat run down his lower back inside his shirt. Suddenly his anger started flurrying, blood rushed into the walls of his throat. Double the rate of inflation. Life was so cheap. Don't be so stupid, he wanted to say. This country is fucked. I'm holding a dying baby and there are going to be two million more. But it wasn't his place, he knew. He was little more than a tourist, and his wages, though they were paid into a South African bank account, were commensurate to a British salary. Instead he looked Menzies in the eye and said,

This child is very sick. Very sick.

The gatekeeper stood from the stool and took the key out of his pocket.

Sure, sure, he said.

He passed the key through the bars of the gate to Charles and sat back down and did not look at the man in the yellow T-shirt. Charles undid the padlock and slid it off the bars. The protester took his hand away and Charles opened the gate. He walked inside, through the yard and into the examination room. He laid the baby on the table.

After they were sure the situation was under control, Charles left the clinic. He set up his station. He examined the baby properly. Its oesophegus was white with candida and there were lesions on the palate. It would not live long, hours probably. He told the nurse and the nurse spoke to the tranlator. The mother spoke to the translator and she left carrying the baby. There were very few patients for the rest of the morning. A couple came into the clinic and he saw to them, some came up to the gate and then left, even though he went outside and called out. The protesters lingered, left, and returned at intervals. The man in the yellow T-shirt disappeared and it was this that made him most nervous. He had patted his hip. Maybe he had been armed. Maybe he would go away and come back with a gun, they weren't hard to find. Though surely this was paranoia. From time to time he went out to check that Menzies had not locked up again, that that everything was all right. He sent Thiliwe home and thanked her for coming in.

Tomorrow I won't, she said. Not while it's like this.

OK, that's your choice. Call the Centre and let them know. Dr Sengupta will be here tomorrow.

I don't think he will be, she said.

At lunchtime he walked a short distance from the building, up a small hill, to get a phone signal. A few of the white butterflies from further down the track were airborne and flitting past. He called one of the other KwaZulu Centre doctors and asked what the situation was elsewhere. The circumcision clinic was shut, and so was the hospital in Mtuba. In other parts of the region the Army had been sent in to keep emergency medical centres running. In Durban, police had fired rubber bullets at protesters. One person had been killed. The strikes were not expected to end for some time. He tried calling his girlfriend in the UK but couldn't get through. Around him the heat was prodigious. The horizon strobed with thermals. He would have to change his shirt.

He ate his sandwiches in the restroom and talked with the other nurse for a while. They were running low on multivitamins again, she said. He finished reading the sanctuary site research paper he had been sent and turned his iPod off to save the battery. When it became apparent that the patients were not coming, the translator and the nurse left. He sent a text to Charles. He took the novel out of his bag, but he didn't want to read it, it seemed irrelevant, and he felt restless. Instead he began to tidy the room and look through the library shelves. There were old copies of journals and sheaves of paper in the racks, folders with decades worth of notes. The clinic had not always specialized in tropical disease, but in the last few years and with the new Government campaign, that had become its primary focus.

There were old rotas. The names changed every twelve months or so. American and European physicians had parachuted in for a stint, had run the clinics, undertaken research and archived it, then left for home. He would too. There was documentation going back years, tables of US FDA licensed drugs dating back to the late eighties, and World Health Organization statistics. He flipped through a thick ring-binder file of collated information, belonging to a Dr. Dickinson, and put it back on the shelf. Then he pulled a copy of *The Lancet* from the bottom of a stack. December 12, 1981. He began to read the first of the Letters to the Editor.

GAY COMPROMISE SYNDROME
SIR,-A remarkable outbreak of opportunistic lung infections
and/or Kaposi's sarcoma in homosexual men has been
reported this year in the United States. i'4 The first report
concerned five men with Pneumocystis carinii pneumonia.

He read the letter and put the journal back in the pile. 1981.
The year of the Maze hunger strikes and the royal wedding.
The year Israel had bombed Baghdad's nuclear reactor. Before
apartheid had ended. Before he, or the new South Africa, had
been born. It was incredible. The disease had advanced
relentlessly. In only his lifetime the infection map had
changed dramatically, filling so densely the lower section of
this continent. The Sub-Saharan figures were shocking to
read, even now, even after the months he had spent seeing the
evidence for himself.

He still felt edgy and nervous. He wanted something
practical to do. He wanted to stretch his legs. Charles would
probably arrive in the next twenty minutes or so. He would
let Menzies lock the gate and go home and he would go for
a walk while he waited. He packed up his equipment and
slung his bag over his shoulder. He shut the door of the clinic
and walked across the yard. The radio was playing. Menzies
was sitting on his stool, leaning back against the wall of the
concrete porch. He got up when he saw the doctor
approaching and turned off the radio. They went through the
gates and secured the complex. Menzies saluted him and
walked away.

There was a car parked at the top of the slope above the
clinic, an old VW Golf. The paintwork was so patchy he
couldn't make out the original colour. The engine was
running and the exhaust fume was dark and greasy looking.
In the passenger seat was the man in a yellow T-shirt. Menzies
walked past the car and nodded his head to the occupants.
But the man was looking down the slope towards him.

His expression was too far away and too vague to see. He stood tensely and returned the stare. He stood very still and kept his head up. The man put his hand out of the window and lay it flat on the roof of the car. Then the car reversed round and drove away up the track, its engine congested and misfiring. He released his breath, released his grip on the strap of his bag. What was that, he thought. He turned and walked out into the scrubland, a few hundred yards.

The heat had lifted a little and the shadows of the bushes and anthills were elongated. There were more white butterflies. They were landing on branches and on the mounds of red earth, swarming past him in the air. They were landing on his dark trousers, clasping and unclasping their wings. He walked a little further until Makowe couldn't be seen, and then turned round and made his way back to the clinic. About a quarter of a mile down the road he could see a cloud of red dust. The white pickup truck slowly emerged from it. He watched it approach and turn down the slope. The wiper-blades were going backwards and forwards. The windscreen was heavily smeared. Charles pulled up next to him. Under the black rubber strips were the crushed remains of the insects. One or two were stuck and fluttering on the bonnet. Charles leaned from the window.

Look at these things, he said. Why don't they get out of the way?

Afterword:

1981-present: The Discovery and Treatment of AIDS

James Higgerson

With the discovery of a new illness, it is the role of health researchers to work backwards and establish the origins of the disease as well as work towards a cure where possible. At present, there is no certainty as to when AIDS was first transmitted to humans, but the earliest current data relates to the Congo in 1959. It is believed that human transmission dates back to the late nineteenth or early twentieth century, but much of the history of the virus remains elusive.

Eight months before *The Lancet* published the letter that the doctor reads in the closing paragraphs of 'That Is The Day,' Sandra Ford, a drug technician working for the Centers for Disease Control (CDC) in Atlanta, noticed an increase in demand for the drug pentamine, used to treat pneumocystis carinii pneumonia (PCP). This is widely known as the eureka moment for the discovery of Acquired Immune Deficiency Syndrome (AIDS), for it prompted further investigation by the CDC into reports of clusters of gay men in Los Angeles and New York who were suffering from opportunistic infections often observed in older patients. These reports led to the letter published in *The Lancet* in December 1981, drawing attention to this unusual occurrence in gay and bisexual men in America, and linking it to a compromised immune system. At the time it was known as gay compromise syndrome, but it was soon discovered that the disease was not limited to men who sleep with men (MSM).

As will have been seen in some of the other eureka moments fictionalised in this anthology, many of science's biggest breakthroughs have emerged from a hunch, or an observation of something unusual. The painstaking rigour of research often follows something that occurs naturally or unexpectedly. Had Sandra Ford not noted an unusual demand for a drug, and had this finding not been taken by others and investigated, it is hard to say where we would be now. The virus was arguably waiting to be discovered, but it was the initial observation of one individual which spearheaded a line of enquiry with the magnitude seen over the past three decades.

In fiction, the 1980s are often reflected upon by protagonists as an era when people became scared of sex, when the fear of AIDS caused everyone to reflect on their own sexual practices. Humorous passages detail the hysteria of parents and the general paranoia associated with the epidemic. That fiction can look back on this from more temperate times shows how things have progressed. In the UK we are lucky to be in a position where we can identify and focus on high-risk sub-groups, rather than the whole population. We can look at the risk of co-morbidity with hepatitis C and the different strands of the virus. Sexual health, as a result of the epidemic, has become a fundamental human concern, whereby the individual has the power to protect their own health, and health professionals can advise, encourage and support people in looking after themselves.

From Sandra Ford's early discovery and the ensuing attempts to explain these clusters of disease, many advances have been made in identifying pathways for transmission, means of prevention and treatment, as well as trying to discover that still elusive vaccine. By 1983, scientists had identified a novel retrovirus that was present in AIDS patients and from here the leaps in knowledge continued.

So whilst the cure is yet to be found, what we do have in 2011 is knowledge of the major routes of transmission, and the power to deliver the prevention message. Since the discovery of AIDS, screening of blood for transfusions has become a legal reality in most developed countries, with more low and middle-income countries following suit over time. The safe sex message is firmly ingrained in the public consciousness here in the UK, as with most other high-income countries. A side-effect of the epidemic is an increased concern for all types of sexually transmitted infection, so if a plus is to be found, it is in wider awareness. The impact here and in similar countries has led to the use of condoms for protection becoming an essential norm, rather than something for those who wished to avoid unplanned pregnancy. Prevention work with injecting drug users is also commonplace, with the increasing acceptance of needle exchanges as a means of harm reduction.

In the 30 years since the discovery of AIDS, the subject has become a major public health concern globally. Awareness of AIDS has increased, and each year the world recognises the impact of the disease, as well as the need for further prevention and awareness activities through World AIDS Day. Less and less it seems necessary to mention the stigma of HIV/AIDS, or to dispel the belief that it is a virus that predominantly affects gay men.

In developed countries, we now have all of the tools for prevention; widespread contraception, a strong public health message and the ability to screen all of those who fear they might be at risk. Short of the cure itself, prevention is the strongest strategy to curbing the spread of HIV/AIDS, and certainly the epidemic has been largely controlled in many areas of the world. Approximately 70,000 new cases were reported in North America in 2009, with another 31,000 in Western and Central Europe. We are able to monitor new infections, and look at the subgroups in which infection is increasing. For example, a rise in HIV infection in the Eastern European region has been noted in recent years, and has been attributed to injecting drug users in this area. This sort of knowledge allows for responses from local, national and international governments in dealing with unwelcome changes in disease incidence.

That Sarah's story is set in Sub-Saharan Africa (SSA) is fitting. More than two thirds of the estimated 33 million people living with HIV globally are from SSA, including 2.3 million children. Of these, 1.8 million people were estimated to have become infected in 2009 alone. 1.3 million adults and children died from AIDS during the same period. Africa is also the only region of the world where more women than men are infected with HIV/AIDS.

Worldwide, unsafe sex is the second highest risk factor for poor health, measured through premature mortality and disability. In 2004, life expectancy in the African region was 49 years. Without AIDS, this would rise to 53 years. Nearly three quarters of premature mortality and disability associated with unsafe sex relates to the SSA region.

The good news is that awareness of safe sexual practices has led to a decrease in the incidence of HIV infection in the SSA region. Monitoring of the disease means that the areas where the epidemic is at a peak can be identified, and the reasons for the disparities between SSA and the rest of the world can be considered and challenged. The goal now is to continue this work, making sexual health a right of everyone, and reducing the health inequalities between SSA and the rest of the world.

It's a well used cliché that prevention is the best cure, but one that applies to much of public health, epitomised by the 30 year story of HIV/AIDS. In another 30 years, will people be reading Sarah's story and shaking their heads in disbelief that there was a time when patients couldn't be cured from the virus? Will the doctors in the Sub-Saharan Africa of the future be thinking back to the archaic times when a woman brought her dangerously sick child for medical treatment with death being the only likely outcome?

The HIV/AIDS story is ongoing, both forwards towards a vaccine, and backwards to establishing how humans first came to be infected. To conclude, a little word from nature. Evidence from South Africa suggests that a sub-group of

HIV+ women have been living with the disease without receiving treatment for over 10 years. The difference between these women and other HIV patients is believed to be the presence of a type of human leukocyte antigen (HLA) which slows down the disease progression. On the basis that these women are likely to survive longer, and pass down this genetic advantage, this sub-group is slowly becoming a larger and larger proportion of the infected population. It seems that evolution is finally having a say in the decades old battle against the virus. Additionally, investigation into the differences between these women and others without this immunity may lead to the *real* eureka moment – and the happy ending – that everyone is praying for.

The Authors

Kate Clanchy is the author of three collections of poetry, *Slattern, Samarkand* and *Newborn*. In 2009, her short story, 'The Not-Dead and the Saved' won the BBC National Short Story Award. She has also written a children's book (*Our Cat Henry Comes to the Swings*) and a memoir of her friendship with a Kosovan Albanian asylum seeker, *What Is She Doing Here?: A Refugee's Story*.

Annie Clarkson is a poet and short fiction writer living in Manchester. Her short fiction has been published by Comma Press (in *Brace*), Flax Books and in various literary magazines.

Frank Cottrell Boyce is an award-winning screenwriter and children's novelist. His film credits include *Welcome to Sarajevo, Hilary and Jackie, Code 46, 24 Hour Party People* and *A Cock and Bull Story*. In 2004, his debut novel *Millions* won the Carnegie Medal and was shortlisted for *The Guardian* Children's Fiction Award. His second novel, *Framed*, was published by Macmillan in 2005, and later adapted into a film by the BBC. His third, *The Unforgotten Coat*, was published this year. Frank also writes for the theatre and was the author of the highly acclaimed BBC film *God on Trial*. He has previously contributed stories to Comma's anthologies *Phobic, The Book of Liverpool, The New Uncanny*, and *When It Changed*.

Stella Duffy is a prolific writer of crime, literary fiction and radio drama. Her novels include *Singling Out the Couples, The Room of Lost Things, Parallel Lies*, and *Theodora: Actress, Empress,*

Whore. In 2002 her story 'Martha Grace' won the CWA Short Story Dagger. Her solo show *Breaststrokes* was *Time Out* and *Guardian* Critic's Choice. Most recently *The Room of Lost Things* was longlisted for the 2008 Orange Prize and won her the Stonewall Writer of the Year award.

Sarah Hall is the author of four novels: *Haweswater*, which won the 2003 Commonwealth Writers Prize for Best First Novel and a Society of Authors Betty Trask Award; *The Electric Michelangelo,* which was shortlisted for the 2004 Man Booker Prize; *The Carhullan Army*, which won the 06/07 John Llewellyn Rhys Prize and the James Tiptree Jr. Award, and was shortlisted for the Arthur C. Clarke Award; and *How To Paint a Dead Man,* which was longlisted for the 2009 Man Booker prize. Her story 'Butcher's Perfume' was shortlisted for the 2010 BBC National Short Story Prize and her first collection of shorts, *The Beautiful Indifference*, is due out from Faber and Faber later this year.

Tania Hershman worked for 13 years as a science journalist for publications such as *WIRED* and *New Scientist*, before turning her hand to fiction. Her first collection of stories, *The White Road and Other Stories* was published in 2009. She is currently writer in residence at the Science Faculty at Bristol University. She is also the founder and editor of The Short Review, a website dedicated to short fiction.

Trevor Hoyle worked as an actor, an advertising copywriter and a lecturer in creative writing before becoming a full-time writer. His environmental novel *The Last Gasp* is currently under option in Hollywood, and his latest novel, *Down the Figure* 7, is set in Lancashire just after the war. Hoyle also writes drama for TV and Radio 4. His play *GIGO* won the Radio Times Drama Award and his *Blakes* 7 episode 'Ultraworld' inspired the album, *The Orb's Adventures Beyond the Ultraworld.*

Maggie Gee is the author of eleven novels, including *The White Family* (2002) which was shortlisted for the Orange Prize for Fiction and the International IMPAC Dublin Literary Award, and most recently *My Driver* (2009), as well as a memoir, *My Animal Life*, and a collection of short stories, *The Blue* (2005). In 1982 she was selected by Granta as one of the original 20 'Best of Young British Novelists', and in 2004 became the first female Chair of the Council of the Royal Society of Literature.

Michael Jecks has written over 30 historical fiction novels, most recently *The Oath*, set against the invasion of Queen Isabella and the decline of Edward II. His short stories have appeared in *I.D.* (Comma), *The Best of British Mysteries 2005* and *The Mammoth Book of Jacobean Whodunits*.

Zoe Lambert's first collection, *The War Tour* is published later this year by Comma. A graduate of the UAE Creative Writing MA, she is currently a lecturer in Creative Writing at the University of Bolton, and has previously published stories in *Bracket* and *Ellipsis 2* (both Comma).

Alison MacLeod has published two novels, *The Changeling* (1996) and *The Wave Theory of Angels* (2005), as well as the short story collection *Fifteen Modern Tales of Attraction* (2007). In 2008, she was the recipient of the Society of Authors' Olive Cook Award for Short Fiction, and her short stories have been published in *Prospect*, *London Magazine*, *The Asham Award collection* and Comma's *The New Uncanny*. She was born in Montreal and is currently Professor of Contemporary Fiction at the University of Chichester. Her third novel is due out later this year.

Sara Maitland's first novel, *Daughter of Jerusalem*, was published in 1978 and won the Somerset Maugham Award.

Novels since have included *Three Times Table* (1990), *Home Truths* (1993) and *Brittle Joys* (1999), and one co-written with Michelene Wandor – *Arky Types* (1987). Her short story collections include *Telling Tales* (1983), *A Book of Spells* (1987) and most recently, *On Becoming a Fairy Godmother* (2003). She has contributed stories to *The New Uncanny* and *When It Changed* and is currently writing a full collection of science-inspired short stories for Comma.

Adam Marek's debut collection of short stories, *Instruction Manual for Swallowing* (Comma) was long-listed for the 2008 Frank O'Connor prize. Since then his stories have appeared in numerous anthologies – *New Writing 15*, *Prospect*, *The New Uncanny* and *When It Changed* (both Comma). In 2010 Adam was shortlisted for the inaugural Sunday Times EFG Private Bank Prize, and in 2011 he was awarded the Arts Foundation Fellowship in Short Story Writing. He lives in Bedford and is currently working on a second collection of stories.

Sean O'Brien has published seven collections of verse: *The Indoor Park* (1983), winner of a Somerset Maugham Award; *The Frighteners* (1987); *HMS Glasshouse* (1991); *Ghost Train* (1995); *Downriver* (2001); *Inferno* (2006), his verse version of *Dante's Inferno*; *The Drowned Book* (2007) and most recently *November*. The latter won the 2007 T. S. Eliot Prize. *Ghost Train*, *Downriver* and *The Drowned Book* have all won the Forward Poetry Prize (Best Poetry Collection of the Year), making Sean O'Brien the only poet to have won this prize more than once. He is also a writer of plays, essays and one novel, *Afterlife* (2009). His first foray into fiction, a collection of short stories titled *The Silence Room* was published by Comma in 2008.

Before turning to crime **Christine Poulson** had a career as an art historian working as a curator for Birmingham Museum and the William Morris Society in Hammersmith.

She has since written three novels set in Cambridge, featuring academic turned amateur detective, Cassandra James, the most recent being *Footfall*. She has also written widely on nineteenth century art and literature and is a research fellow in the Department of Nineteenth Century Studies at the University of Sheffield. Her most recent work of non-fiction, a book on Arthurian legend in British Art,1840-1920, was short listed for the Mythopeoic Award in the USA in 2002.

Jane Rogers was born in London in 1952 and lived in Birmingham, New York State (Grand Island) and Oxford, before doing an English degree at Cambridge University. She taught English for 6 years before the publication of her first novel, *Separate Tracks*. Since then she has written eight novels including *Mr Wroe's Virgins, Island, The Voyage Home* and most recently *The Testament of Jessie Lamb* (Sandstone Press), as well as original and adapted work for television and radio drama. In 1994 she was made a Fellow of the Royal Society of Literature, and in 2009 her story 'Hitting Trees With Sticks' was shortlisted for the BBC National Short Story Prize. She is currently Professor of Writing on the MA course at Sheffield Hallam University. She lives near Manchester with her partner and two children.

Emma Jane Unsworth is a journalist, short story writer and novelist based in Manchester. Her first novel, *Hungry, The Stars and Everything* is published by Hidden Gem later this year.

The Scientists & Historians

Jim Al-Khalili OBE is Professor of Theoretical Physics and Chair in the Public Engagement in Science at the University of Surrey. He is a Trustee and Vice-President of the British Science Association and currently holds an EPSRC Senior Media Fellowship. His research at Surrey, since 1994, has established him as a leading expert on mathematical models of exotic atomic nuclei. He has been a Fellow of the Institute of Physics since 2000 when he also received the Institute's Public Awareness of Physics Award. His television shows include *The Riddle of Einstein's Brain* (Channel 4), *Atom* (BBC4), *The Big Bang* (BBC Horizon), *Science and Islam* (BBC4), *The Secret Life of Chaos* (BBC4), and most recently *Everything and Nothing* (BBC4).

Dr Martyn Amos leads the Novel Computation Group at Manchester Metropolitan University. His research interests lie at the intersection of computer science and the life sciences, and include synthetic biology, nature-inspired algorithms and crowd dynamics.

Dr Robert Appleby is a lecturer in the High Energy Particle Physics Group of the University of Manchester and an academic staff member at the Cockcroft Institute of Accelerator Science. He is also an associate of the beams division at CERN (APB) and a member of the LHCb experiment. His primary research is into the physics of particle accelerators. He is also involved in the International Linear Collider, Large Hadron Collider, LHeC and LHCb experiments.

John Clayson is Keeper of Science and Industry with Tyne & Wear Archives & Museums, based at the Discovery Museum in Newcastle.

Matthew Cobb is Professor of Zoology at the University of Manchester. He studies the genetic basis of behaviour, in particular how animals detect chemical signals – smells, tastes and pheromones. For seven years he studied the behaviour of ants, and he teaches Hamilton's Rule to first, second and third year undergraduates. He is also interested in the history of science and is the author of *The Egg & Sperm Race: The Seventeenth Century Scientists Who Unravelled the Truth about Sex, Life and Growth.*

Sarah Fox is a PhD researcher studying the neural basis of memory at the University of Manchester. Specifically, her work focuses on how naturally occurring changes in network activity, within the hippocampus, influence the way cells in this area form memories.

Kathryn Harris is a PhD student at the University of Central Lancashire specialising in quasar environments in the context of large scale structure (LSS). She is also the Outreach Officer for UCLan's Jeremiah Horrocks Institute for Astrophysics and Supercomputing.

James Higgerson is a PhD student from the Manchester Urban Collaboration on Health at the University of Manchester. His research is looking at alcohol policy and health consequences in urban Europe, forming part of the European Union funded EURO-URHIS 2 project.

Nick R. Love is in the final year of his PhD at the University of Manchester, researching gene expression during the regeneration and wound healing of Xenopus tadpoles.

Denis Noble CBE FRS FRCP developed the first viable mathematical model of the heart cell in 1960 and is a pioneer of 'Systems Biology'. His research focuses on using computer models of biological organs and organ systems to interpret function from the molecular level to the whole organism. Together with international collaborators, his team has used supercomputers to create the first virtual organ, the virtual heart. He held the Burdon Sanderson Chair of Cardiovascular Physiology at Oxford University from 1984 to 2004 and is currently Professor Emeritus and co-Director of Computational Physiology. As Secretary General of the International Union of Physiological Sciences 1993-2001, he played a major role in launching the Physiome Project, an international project to use computer simulations to create the quantitative physiological models necessary to interpret the genome, and he was elected President of the IUPS at its world congress in Kyoto in 2009.

Dr. Tim O'Brien is a Reader in Astrophysics and Outreach Officer at Jodrell Bank. His research concentrates on the study of exploding stars using telescopes around the world and in space, working across the spectrum from radio waves to X-rays.

Giacomo Rizzolatti was the senior scientist in charge of the research team that discovered 'mirror neurons' in the frontal and parietal cortex of the macaque monkey. He is Professor of Human Physiology and Director of the Department of Neuroscience at the University of Padua and former president of the European Brain and Behaviour Society. His awards include the Golgi Prize for Physiology, the Cognitive Neuroscience Society's George Miller Award, the Feltrinelli Prize for Medicine and the Herlitzka Prize for Physiology. In 2007 he was co-recipient, with Leonardo Fogassi and Vittorio Gallese, of the University of Louisville Grawemeyer Award for Psychology.

Zoe Schnepp is an independent researcher at the National Institute for Materials Science (Tokyo, Japan). She was previously a postdoctoral fellow at the Max Planck Institute of Colloids and Interfaces (Potsdam, Germany). In 2009 she was a finalist in the British Council's Famelab, and received a Joseph Breen Memorial Fellowship in 2007. As a final year student at the University of Bristol in 2005, she won the Royal Society of Chemistry Award for the Best Chemistry Student of the Year.

James Sumner is Lecturer in the History of Technology at the University of Manchester. He has a PhD from the University of Leeds on the history of scientific concepts in the brewing industry. Most of his work looks at how scientific and technological ideas have been communicated between different groups of experts and non-experts – usually in situations involving computers or beer.

Dr Angharad Watson read Biochemistry at Oxford. Her studies led to a PhD position at the University of Manchester, where she now works as a postdoctoral research associate, researching complex sugars in the disease Mucopolysaccharidosis.

John Wearden is Professor of Psychology at Keele University. He has also taught at the University of Manchester, as well in the US and Belgium. His early research was on conditioning in animals and humans, but for the last 20 years he has been mostly involved in studies of time perception.

Special Thanks

Although these stories are works of fiction, the authors gratefully acknowledge the following biographies as sources of invaluable information on the scientists in question:

> Andrew Hodges, *Alan Turing: The Enigma* (Vintage, 1992)
> Kary Mullis, *Dancing Naked in the Mind Field* (Vintage, 1998)
> Ruth Sime, *Lise Meitner: A Life in Physics* (University of California, 1997)

A number of additional scientists helped on early stages of this book, and without their enthusiasm for the project it would never have got off the ground. These include Dr David Kirby, Dr Felicity Mellor, Andreas Doering, Dr Tara Shears, Dr Marieke Navin, Dr Vinod Dhanak, Professor Gregory Radick, Baroness Susan Greenfield, Dr Felicity Mitchell, Dr Melissa Baxter, Justyna Sutula, Dr Chris Knight, Ceri Harrop, Dr Penny Lewis, Dr James Baldini, David Gelsthorpe, Oliver Jones and especially Sohail Siadatnejad who acted as initial consultant on the Pavlov and Rizzolatti stories.

The publisher would also like to thank the following: Nancy and Kary Mullis; Suzanne Spicer, Emma Gillaspy, and Erinma Ochu of the Manchester Area Beacon for public engagement; Natalie Ireland and Emily Wiles at the Manchester Science Festival; Catlin Watson and Dayna Mason at the Institute of Physics; Poppy Bowers and Rosie Tooby at the Wellcome Trust; and Dave Mee, Hwa Young Jung, Lia Baron and Natalie Whittaker at MaDLab. Plus Kay Easson, Andy Darby, Will Carr, Trudi Shaw, and Licia Arcidiacono – for her translation help.

Sarah Hall would like to thank Dr James Garvey and the Africa Centre for Health and Population Studies in KwaZulu Natal for their support in writing her story.